She looked at the high hedges that shielded them from the house, at the deepening gloom, then up at Dale. Her lips curved in a new smile, and her voice was ragged from her quickened breathing.

"I'm sick of fancy talk and pretty manners, too. Ah, Dale—I wish to be beaten—and hurt—and ripped—and torn—"

She was still talking when he seized her. She kept on talking for some time, though her words would have made sense to nobody but Dale, and they ended, finally, in gasping, choking, hysterical sobbing.

CHESAPEAKE CAVALIER

DON TRACY

 BARONET PUBLISHING COMPANY, New York

CHESAPEAKE CAVALIER

Baronet Publishing Company, New York, NY 10022

International Standard Book Number: 0-89437-060-X

Printed in the United States

First Baronet printing, May 1979

For Freda and George

CHESAPEAKE CAVALIER

CHAPTER ONE, 1628

THE RESTLESS BREEZE THAT HAD STIRRED FITFULLY since just past noon came from the northwest. It carried a half-promise of the marshaling of thunderheads and rain before sundown, but other winds had made like promises that week and heat still gripped the James River Valley in an acrid, enervating grasp. Dale Morley brought his wrist across his forehead and looked down at his forearm, noting dully how the hairs were plastered to the bronzed skin by his perspiration.

"I've sweated enough," he said aloud, "to soak down every damned corn row in the Colony. Yes, and every tobacco field from here to Henrico. And a lot of good that's done me. Or will do me."

He arched his shoulders to relieve the ache that nagged at his back. As an indentured servant he had thought, somehow, that he would be tireless, able to hoe or chop, carry and haul, from sunup to dark without a muscle twinging, once he got his own land. He had nursed the idea that being a freedman would give him some new strength that would make every piece of work a thing to be tackled eagerly, almost joyously. Ha!

He dragged his wide-brimmed hat down over his eyes, shutting out some of the sun's glare. Raising the heavy, awkward hoe, he worked on steadily, trying to ignore the heat and the sweat that trickled down his body under the sodden canvas shirt and breeches he wore. He was a big man, wide of shoulder and narrow in the haunch, and there was a smoothness to his movements even in the swinging of a hoe at the tough, tenacious weeds.

Dale Morley was eighteen years old that blazing summer of 1628 —or close enough to eighteen to accept that age. Aunt Bess, back in

1

London, had told him he had been born in 1610, but the old sow had soaked her brain in wine for too long for her memory to mean much. Aunt Bess had been no kin of his, thank God for that. She was an old hag who took in unwanted brats for a price, fed them after a fashion and housed them even more sketchily until they were old enough to forage for themselves. Then they were thrown into the streets, to beg and steal or starve, and to bring back to Aunt Bess anything of value they laid hands on, under pain of a beating more thorough than usual if the woman found any of her charges holding back on her. And she always seemed to find out. Bitter experience had proved that.

None of the inmates of this ungentle asylum knew the true facts of their parentage nor were they particularly curious about the matter. They were too concerned with their habitual hunger and Aunt Bess's whistling lash to waste much time wondering who their fathers and mothers might have been.

He thought of her vicious, bloated face now and chopped hard at a clump of crab grass. He was no king's son, certainly, or he would not be here, in the Colony of Virginia, a thousand leagues from England, trying to grub the start of a living from the fifty acres that had been his payment for four years of indentured labor.

Come to beautiful Virginia, they had urged him. Come to the new lands where the climate is always gracious, where good food, comfortable shelter and fine clothing are provided in return for an honest day's work, where employers are always kindly and a man's future was anything he would make of it. Why, even the wild animals of the forests were strangely mild in Virginia, the Indians were friendly, corn and tobacco sprouted from the ground everywhere and ripened almost untended. There's gold in Virginia, too, and who knows but what the turn of your spade might make you rich!

Even without the gold, just a few years of indentured service, they had told him, means you'll be given your own land, fifty beautiful acres, on which to start the building of your planter's fortune.

"If you're sixteen, lad," the ship's captain, O'Halley, had told him, "then here's your chance. I'll carry you to Virginia for your head rights only and promise you a good master when we get to Jamestown."

At fourteen, Dale had encountered no trouble in passing for sixteen, and what was there to keep him in England? He had been drunk more than once, had helped in several street robberies and half a dozen burglaries, had a bitter contempt for all women, the result of grunting, greasy fumblings among vile rags covering dirty skin. He was clever at cheating at dice. He had knifed and barely missed killing another boy of his age in a fight over a shilling found in the gutter. He was, in brief, a *cum laude* graduate of a university that taught its students in the alleys and stews, the taverns and hovels of the London of his time.

If not wholly typical, Dale Morley was not a unique type of emigrant to Virginia. The glowing pamphlets of the Virginia Company may have sounded enticing, but for every man of property willing to leave the comforts of England for Virginia, there were a score, a hundred who signed up for the same reasons that Dale had considered in yielding to Captain O'Halley's urging: to leave an animal existence in London in the hope that Virginia offered something better and the certainty that it could offer nothing much worse.

Come to beautiful Virginia, named to honor the virginity of Elizabeth, and stretching from New England to the Spanish forts of Florida. Come to Virginia, where there are parching droughts and bitter cold, where famines lurk because the planters are too greedy for tobacco profits to plant corn, where whole families are wiped out for lack of clean water, where the friendly Indians forget their gentle manners at times to murder and burn and destroy.

He swung his hoe at the moment a drop of sweat trickled into one eye with a fiery smarting. The hoe blade hit the stalk of a strong, tall plant with a sullen thud. Dale winced and jerked at the rough wooden handle but the damage had been done. He stood, paralyzed,

3

as the plant sagged and toppled on its half-severed stalk. Automatically, he noticed it was a fine plant, bearing more than a dozen young ears.

Dale flung the hoe to the dust-dry ground.

"Now, by God!" he grated. "Damn this hoe to hell and the fool who cuts down the one plant that might have stood a chance of coming through the drought!"

"And that," said a voice behind him, "would mean a bodkin stuck through your tongue if a warden overheard you, Dale Morley."

He turned, brushing his wrist across his forehead, his dark face thunderous. Tiny flecks of light glowed briefly in his deep-set eyes and his wide mouth was a thin line, one corner quirked so that a dimple showed in the cheek on that side. It was a strange expression; almost a smile and still something no man would mistake for the beginning of a grin. Aunt Bess had seen that quirked mouth often and it always had made her grip the handle of her whip a bit tighter.

"The little bastard—big bastard now, though—'ll murder somebody someday when he twists his ugly mouth up at the side like that," she had once told a drinking companion.

He didn't frighten the girl who looked up at him now, standing close to him, between the whispering cornstalks. She was small and sturdy, clad in a white cotton dress below the hem of which showed white wool stockings and square-toed shoes with bright brass buckles. No one not deeply in love with her could have called her beautiful, but there was a comeliness to her round open face that some might say was rare beauty's more lasting counterpart. Everything about the girl spelled neatness: the spotless dress, the tidy blonde hair that showed under the light cap she wore. Even the girl's work-roughened hands were tipped with nails which showed she had used a splinter to dig out the dirt that even the great ladies of England took for granted.

Her eyes were calm as she looked up at Dale, seemingly oblivious of his anger. He could have been the child and she the mother, although he towered over her by more than a head.

4

"Go get your churchwarden," Dale said heavily, "and I'll tell him the same thing, and more. I'll tell him—"

"That tongue of yours will be as full of holes as a bit of lace," the girl interrupted, "unless you learn when to keep it still." She put a hand on his sweaty, dust-stained arm as his scowl deepened. "But I didn't come to scold. You're hot and tempers grow in this drought if nothing else seems to. Come over to the shade by the tree there and rest awhile. See, I've brought you a bannock, cooked the way you like them, with caraway."

Dale's mouth slowly lost its twist. The flame flecks left his eyes. He looked down at her and she calmly accepted the boldness of his searching eyes. There had been a time when she had flinched and reddened under the frank appraisal of his stare, but that had been before she had given him the right to look at her in that way. There had been no attempts at skittish shyness, no protestations, no tears, no recriminations, no blame laid to him, after the first wild incident. Now, what was done was done and done again and the re-doing only served to deepen her love for him and bring the future's security with him that much nearer, that much more certain. So let him look at her and pray God he always would find something in what he saw to start the quiet, lazy smile that was beginning to curve his lips now.

His eyes traveled their familiar journey, inquiring into the V of her dress neckline, with no shawl or kerchief to hide the whiteness of her throat, slipping across her shoulders and down over her bosom, the full, rounded breasts.

It came time to say something, to break the spell of silence before it moved along to something else she did not want to happen now.

"This cake," she said briskly. "Caraway seeds in it, Dale. I've just finished cooking it."

His foot nudged the discarded hoe to one side. His hands touched her arms, just below the the short sleeves, and his fingers moved gently over her cool, moist skin.

"You're good to me, Susan," he said in a low voice. "Cooking bannocks for me on a hot day like this."

5

"A man must have his food," she said lightly, "and I've tasted the pone you cook for yourself. My fear is that you'll die from something out of your cookpot before I get the chance to feed you properly."

He said nothing, but the beginnings of a frown started behind his eyes. Come to Virginia, he told himself, where all the maids are willing to do anything to get themselves a husband.

He shook his head against his own thoughts in one of the abrupt changes that marked most of his thinking in these days. No, he wasn't being fair to Susan Willison. She was—not ugly. She was generous and kind and helpful. Of all the girls in the Province, in the scrubby little place called Jamestown and on the plantations up and down the rivers, there wasn't a woman better suited to his needs. Anybody would tell him that. She was clever with the needle and the skillet. Her voice never sharpened into the screech other females used. She knew what he had been and it made no difference. She had even taught him to read and write when he had been her father's servant, and she had been patient about remembering that back in England he had never said five words without garnishing them with a curse and that now he found the losing of the habit hard.

Yes, Susan Willison had been good to him, better than anyone else ever had been. And he had repaid her by using all the black wits he owned to rob her of something which she, at least, held mighty precious.

Well, he would make it up to her. He'd be the kind of husband she wanted, the hardest-working, least-complaining farmer in the whole damned Province. He'd give her a child a year and he'd turn his back on even the meager folderol the Colony had to offer, the cock fights, the dice games, the taverns. He might rebel against that kind of stupid life on occasion but he could put down his own rebellion.

Tenderness enveloped him and his fingers left off their stroking. He dropped his hands, bent and picked up the hoe.

"Let's sit in the shade a minute," he said, almost roughly. "The

6

water bucket's there and you'll get all hot and dusty standing here in your pretty white gown."

He laid a hand on her shoulder and felt the pressure of her as she unconsciously leaned towards him. He dropped his hand quickly, knowing his own probable response to her nearness and knowing, too, that such things were not in her mind. His hand took hers, as it would take a child's, and they walked slowly over the uneven ground between the corn rows, around the charred stumps, toward the scrub pine and its patch of shade.

Dale steadied the girl as she lowered herself to the ground, then dropped beside her. His blunt-tipped fingers went out to pluck a blade of grass. It was dry and yellow, looking more like October's plant than July's. He grunted and crumbled the spear between his thumb and forefinger.

She turned to him and there was a smile on her mouth. Her lips were cool under his, her breath faintly fragrant, and she drew away quickly as his caress became urgent under the drive of his quickening pulse.

"The bannock," she reminded him.

"With caraway," he said, smiling. "Thank you."

He munched at the oatmeal cake, permitting himself a sip of water from the gourd. He had thought that he did not really want the bannock but he ate it to the last crumb. The pone he had swallowed at noon had been a soggy, greasy slab, lacking enough salt. There was always too much or too little of something in everything he cooked. He had been a freedman since early spring and his cooking still made all his meals a weight in his belly and nothing else. It would be good to have Susan for a wife and enjoy his food again.

With Susan as his wife, things would all be better, easier. She was wise, wiser than he would ever be, and she had the learning he needed to make up for all those dark years with Aunt Bess. Her father would help, too.

Thomas Willison was a vestryman, but one of the easiest of them all, forever pleading for forbearance where others yelled for the

7

ear-lopping knife and the tongue-piercing bodkin. Dale had sneered at Thomas Willison but he knew that he could travel far and never meet another man with Willison's human kindness.

He owned a thousand acres and not one speck of earth had been acquired in a way that was not completely right, not only in the letter but also in the spirit of the law. A short, pot-bellied widower, balding under the black wig he wore, Willison was a smiling, trusting man, as eager to be liked as he was ready to believe the best of everyone. Dale realized that if Willison had been different, less of a believer in his fellow man, more suspicious, more the average planter, he would have guarded his only daughter like a chest of gold against his new indentured field hand, the hulking, black-haired boy from London.

But Thomas Willison had been what he was, and how had Dale Morley thanked him for his friendship? By making Willison's daughter fall in love with him while she taught him how to read and write and, finally, taking the full reward of the conquest one bleak March sundown beside a wind-tattered haycock. Dale still remembered the crows, flocking to roost in the trees near the field, rising in brief, noisy circles and settling again as he lay beside Susan Willison wondering where, that once, was the bitter satisfaction of the victory. And that was how Dale Morley had repaid Thomas Willison and Susan for what they had done for him.

Later, as his term of indenture neared its end, he had spoken of marriage to Susan, he did not know just why. There could be no question of his conscience speaking. A conscience was something rich people might be able to afford, but not a boy from the London slums who was even now but one step above a slave, no matter how generous his master. It might have been that Dale could not imagine Susan marrying him or her father permitting it, and intended the proposal as some kind of grimly cynical jest. Whatever the reason, there was no more surprised a man in the Province than Dale Morley when Susan gently accepted him and Thomas Willison gave his consent.

8

Perhaps the fat little man had been troubled by misgivings over his daughter's obvious liking for his wide-shouldered young servant, or perhaps he just could not bring himself to say no to Susan. In any event, he told Dale:

"Get in your crop, prove you mean to make yourself a planter, and Susan can be your wife the following winter. I'll help you get started, Dale, but not more than I'd help another good servant when his contract's up. It'll be for your own good to make your way alone, your first year as a freedman."

Having finished the last of the bannock, Dale brushed the crumbs from his fingers. Susan stirred beside him and he caught a breath of her body's fragrance. He wondered at her ability to smell cool on the hottest day and warm on the coldest. It must, he thought, have something to do with the baths she was forever plunging herself into, as fond of water as an otter.

He looked out over the cornfield and beyond, to where the tobacco grew, then scanned the skies again in search of a cloud. There was one to the west, but it didn't look as though it held rain. He turned back to his survey of his fields.

Make his way alone, eh? Well, he had done that—or he would do it, if the dry spell would only break. The fifty acres Thomas Willison had signed over to him by the terms of the indenture contract were as well along as any in the valley and further than some, and better cared for. He had three hogs and seven shoats, a cow and a heifer—gifts from Susan's father. There was venison in the storehouse, some mutton, minced and close-packed in tried suet; gammons of bacon, plenty of salt fish. There was meal and rice and cheese, even a little butter. He had learned enough about hunting in the four years he had been in Virginia to be able to bring home his share of geese and ducks and turkeys.

His house was nothing more than a hut, but nobody expected a freedman's first-year house to be anything but a shelter from the weather. Time enough to start building a better place when the first crop was in, the tobacco hanging in the warehouse at Jamestown, the corn milled, the sundries like peas and beans, omini and hops, out of the ground and cared for. Most settlers, when they got ready to put up a larger house, simply put a torch to the old place and burned it down for the nails. There was plenty of lumber at hand and always would be, but nails were hard come by and expensive, coming from England as they had to. But Dale had built his first house well. It would serve as a hall or dining room for the bigger place he intended to raise, with brick chimneys at either end and whitewashed plastering on the inner walls.

Nobody could say he had not done as well as the next beginner in Virginia, even though he was just four years off the cobbled streets of London. If only—if only he could learn to like this life, instead of bearing it, as he found himself doing all too often. He had found things here in Virginia that would have been considered unbelievably precious by everyone he had known in England. He had land of his own, a house, more food than he had known existed before he left London, with still more at hand for the shooting or netting. His clothes might be rough but they were clean and without patches. And there was this sweet-smelling woman beside him.

What had it cost, all this? A few callouses, a little sweat, a bit of bowing to the man who had held his contract for four years, a kindly man who would be his father-in-law when snow came, or before. He should be grateful, content.

Neither of them moved. They sat there, watching the heat waves shimmering over the fields. The fitful breeze appeared to have wandered off to raise false hopes elsewhere. The scorched smell of the dry earth came up from the ground between them, mingled with the sharp tang of the scrub pine. A cicada chattered and buzzed, then cut its whine off sharply. High overhead, a fish hawk circled lazily on motionless wings. For once Dale felt relaxed, free from worry. It was good to be with Susan.

He turned to her and his big hands pressed her down to the dry earth quickly, but with a certain tenderness. He could be gentle with

10

a woman, this boy turned man before his rightful time, until he withdrew into the fury of his own urgency and then he could be ruthless and devastating.

She lay back, her blue eyes regarding him with quiet acceptance. She might have known this was going to happen when she started for the field, the bannock in her hand, but if she had thought of the probability it roused neither anticipation nor reluctance within her. She bore a deep love for Dale but it was founded on something apart from this. There had been times when she had wondered whether there might be something wrong with her because she could not give this the importance other girls seemed to. She once had accidentally eavesdropped on a group of married women talking among themselves and later she had been puzzled over whether the thing they had talked about really was as horrible as their words made it, or as wickedly wonderful as their sliding voices had implied.

Even now she was not sure, although she suspected it was neither. It was something that took place because he would have it so and a need that was almost frightening showed in his eyes at times; she would have been less than kind if she had denied him, after that first occasion.

There was a risk, of course, but not so great as the grannies would have it. If there had been a child while he was still a servant, there would have been some shame attached, and sorrow to her father, though not the lash that striped the bare backs of indentured females in a like predicament. Now that Dale was a freedman and her father had told the whole Colony that she could be his wife, there really was no risk at all. People might count their fingers for a firstborn but this was a frontier settlement for all the high-sounding talk of cavalier gentlemen and it would be enough that she and Dale were married before the child was born.

She thought all these things and more until her mind was caught up in the rhythmic pattern of the moment and then, finally, her love went out to Dale in a low cry which he answered. Later, as they lay

11

there, she telling herself she must get back to her house to start supper, he telling himself he must get back to his corn rows, he lifted his head with a jerk.

"Listen!" he said. His voice was taut, strained.

And then it came, a rolling cannonade in the west, a dull jarring that made the ground beneath them tremble. She turned her head to look in the direction of the sound and saw the great blue-black thunderheads piling up above the hills. A wind came rushing down upon them and the leaves of corn flapped a grateful welcome to the storm that was coming.

"Rain, by God!" Dale said in a hushed voice.

His hand had helped her down but it did not help her up. He ignored her as she got to her feet. He seemed to have forgotten she was there, even when she laid a hand on his arm to steady herself. His eyes were bright as he looked at the forked flicker of lightning and his white teeth were bared in a grin as the thunder crashed and echoed in the lightning's wake.

She fastened the ties of her bodice and turned away.

"I've got to get back," she said. "And you'd better get to shelter."

"Not me," he told her. "I'm going to stay here and soak up some of this rain, along with my plants. My blood's been dusty too long to run indoors at a few drops of water."

She waited for some word, some look, that might tell her he thought of her own welfare in the storm. Then she turned away.

"Good-bye, Dale," she said, but her voice was drowned out by the thunder.

Dale was scraping up the last bits of the old pork and pone that was his evening meal, and his fingers were shiny with grease in the light from the candle, when the horseman came.

The rain was still drumming down. There was the steady wash of the eaves and another plinking drip inside that marked a leak in the roof of the little house. He did not mind the noise. It had a cheerful sound and it gave assurance that his crops were sucking

12

up the water they had needed for weeks. In a few minutes, as soon as he splashed some water into the wooden bowl that had held his meat and pone, he would make for his straw mattress in the adjoining lean-to. Darkness had come early with the storm and it would be pleasant to lie there, listening to the rain, until he fell asleep.

The tattoo on the roof drowned out the sound of a horseman's approach. Dale straightened with a jerk when knuckles sounded on the door. Without moving from his bench, he stretched out a long arm to grab up the matchlock that rested against the wall nearby. He looked at the priming and the charge. The rap sounded again.

Gripping the musket, Dale shoved back his bench, rose and moved to the door. It was almost impossible that there were Indians outside. Indians didn't knock and, besides, old Opechancanough was said to be moving his villages further and further west along the James, miles above the Falls.

Still, a night visitor was unusual enough, and for a man to travel in this storm was more than that. The rapping shook the door.

"Who's there?" Dale called.

"Open up!" The voice was muffled by the beat of the rain.

Dale scowled at the rough paneling. The man on the other side of the door used a tone most men threw at their servants, and he was a freedman. That voice reminded him, too, of the nobs of London and their way of speaking, so contemptuous that a person wanted only to clout them across their smirking, girlish mouths, but dared not.

"I asked who'd knocked," Dale rasped. "What's your business?"

"Business of the Province of Virginia," the voice beyond the panels said exasperatedly. "The King's business. Open up, man!"

Now what, Dale asked himself, as he slowly raised the bar. Had some long-nosed churchwarden heard him cursing? Or, worse still, had somebody seen Susan and him together? He opened the door and the candle guttered for a moment in the rush of the cool, rain-swept air. He moved aside as a man stepped over the threshold, banging the door shut behind him.

He was a big man, as wide-shouldered as Dale and nearly as tall,

13

enveloped in a long cloak with a wide, upturned collar. On his head he wore a felt hat with an exaggerated brim, upturned at one side and pinned to the crown with a brooch that gleamed in the light from the candle. He swept the hat from his head now, spattering water unheedingly across the room, and scaled it to the bench where Dale had been sitting. He flung back the cloak and put his hands on his hips as he turned to stare at Morley.

Dale saw a lean face marked by a pointed beard, narrow mustaches, a long, thin nose and a pair of incredibly bright eyes. The stranger wore his hair shoulder length and the luxuriant mass of curls was no wig.

A gentleman, certainly. The jeweled hilt of the sword he wore, the embroidered falling band at the neck, the high boots—doeskin, surely—with their bright spurs, proclaimed that fact, if the man's dress were needed to supplement his manner.

Dale suddenly was conscious of the coarseness of his own canvas shirt and breeches, the fact that he wore no stockings and that his shoes were caked with mud. He had not shaved that day, either, and he had not had time to wipe the grease of his meal from his hands. So he made his mouth thin and thrust out his chin, staring back boldly. The stranger held his gaze steady as he stripped a pair of gauntlets from his hands. There was a silence that seemed longer than it was and the bearded man spoke.

"Freedman Morley?" he asked. His voice was as hard as the set of his mouth. "Dale Morley, lately indentured servant to Thomas Willison?"

"Freedman Dale Morley," Dale replied in tones just as brittle. "Planter."

The bearded man's eyes flickered and his mouth twitched once before he turned away. He slapped the gloves down on the bench beside the hat and reached for the clasp of his cape. He spoke over his shoulder against the resentment Dale felt at this man's arrogance.

"Captain William Claiborne," he said. "And for your love of

Christ, put down that matchlock before you blow another hole in this leaky roof!"

His eyes fixed on Claiborne's back, Dale reached out to place the musket against the wall. Claiborne draped his long cloak over a wall peg and turned to Dale, his back to the dead ashes of the fireplace, his hands behind him, his booted feet apart. Now Morley could make out the richness of the man's suit, of black broadcloth with crimson inserts showing through the slashes on his upper sleeves, fine lace at the cuffs. The sash that held the sword was of watered silk and the sword itself was a blade that would not have been out of place in any European court.

"You have no stable for my horse, I suppose?" the Captain asked. There was a rebuke in that question.

"I've no need for a stable—yet," Dale replied steadily. "There's the cow shed. That might serve Y'r—"

He bit back the "Y'r Lordship" that had mechanically sprung to his tongue. Those days were over!

"It'll do," Claiborne said curtly, "and let's have some fire here. I'm wet to the bone and I don't fancy risking a chill."

"I was about to go to bed, Captain Claiborne," Dale said in an even voice, "and I let the fire die."

"Build it again, man," the visitor said impatiently. "But see to my horse first." The bright eyes watched Dale's face harden and Claiborne seemed almost to smile as he added: "If you will be so kind."

The hand that had unconsciously bunched itself into a fist slowly relaxed at Dale's side. That was more like it. "The tinder is in the box beside the fireplace," he said ungraciously, "and the flint and steel are on the ledge there. The wood is dry."

He turned to walk through the doorway, into the teeming darkness. Let that teach this man Claiborne that he could build his own fire or go without. Chilled, was he? Then let him stay in his fine home, snug and dry, instead of riding miles through a storm to keep an honest man from his bed.

15

He sloshed through the mud to where the Captain's horse stood patiently, its head bent against the rainy wind, the reins looped over a low branch of the young oak Dale had let stand, for shade, when he had cleared the rest of his home site. He led the animal to the cow shed, kicked open the door. He moved the cow and the heifer to the far end of the shed in the darkness; the horse's reins he slipped through a ringbolt as close to the door as possible.

He slammed and latched the cow barn and went through the mud and rain back to the house. At the door, he sniffed a curl of wood smoke and he smiled in the darkness. Captain William Claiborne, then, had dropped his high and mighty airs enough to make his own fire.

The Captain was seated on a bench in front of the fireplace, his long booted legs outthrust to the blaze that was creeping between the chunks he had lighted. As Dale entered, he looked up and then turned back to gaze into the fire, without speaking. Dale scowled at his visitor's back. The least the man could do would be to drop a word of thanks to somebody who had gotten soaked and mud-splattered to care for his horse.

The fire picked up rapidly and sent out a brisk crackling. Because of the erratic wind and the fact that Dale had pitched his chimney too low, the fire also sent out occasional puffs of smoke. Claiborne coughed, but he did not speak. He seemed entirely at ease, sitting in front of a stranger's fire without telling his sullen host why he had ridden through a torrent to call on him.

"You choose a wet night for your visits, Captain Claiborne," Dale said finally.

"My duties," said Claiborne, "can't wait on the weather. I'm just back from England and while I was away my work as Secretary of the Province fell behind—as always. It's impossible to find a clerk who can really do what they all promise to do."

He swung around on the bench so that he faced Dale, the sword ringing sharply against the wood as he moved. His brilliant eyes looked up at the big man near the doorway.

"No," Claiborne continued, "if I'd have anything done the way I want it done, I must do it myself, and that's why I've had to ride out here through the wet tonight, Freedman Morley."

He broke off and looked around the cluttered room.

"I don't suppose," he said, "You'd have any brandy or sack."

"I have some small beer," Dale said grudgingly, "but only a little and not a good brew. There's plenty of milk in the spring house."

The Captain gave a brief shudder.

"No milk, certainly," he said, "and it's no night for beer." He showed his teeth in a brief smile. "Luckily, I came prepared against your having nothing decent to drink. There's a leathern flask in the inner pocket of that cloak there on the peg."

Dale Morley shifted his eyes to the cape and back to the man on the bench.

"Is there?" he asked, and made no move. Damn a man, he thought, who'd give the insult about another's failure to have drink on hand and then expect the person he'd slurred to fetch him his flask like a lackey.

The man with the sword waited for a space of five breaths and then got to his feet slowly, a quizzical expression showing in the light from the candle. The heels of his boots clacked on the plank flooring of the room and his spurs jingled musically as he sauntered across to the cloak. He reached inside the folds of the cape and brought out the leather flask. He looked squarely at Dale, juggled the flask in one hand for a moment and then walked to the table to set the thing on the board.

"You're a touchy young man, Dale Morley," he said mildly. "I had no thought of offending you by asking you to play the host by getting the flask."

"I was afraid I'd muddy your cloak with my hands," Dale replied rudely.

Captain Claiborne raised his eyes toward the ceiling.

17

"Oh, Christ on the Cross," he lamented. "Another new freedman who thinks the greatest thing in his new life is his right to begrudge another a good coat or silver shoe buckles."

He looked around the room again, walked to a shelf and took down two pewter mugs which he carried to the table. He pulled the stopper of the flask and splashed brandy into both mugs. Dale's nostrils quivered at the heady smell of the liquor but he stayed where he was. Claiborne looked across the table at him and waved a hand toward one of the cups.

"I hope you're not too proud to drink with me," he said, and there was a flat tone to his words.

"I've no taste for brandy," Dale muttered.

Captain William Claiborne's voice cracked across the room like the lash of coach whips, the rattle of musketry.

"Then, by God," he snapped, "you'll learn the taste right now! I haven't ridden to this mudhole to sit in this sty and bandy soft words with a footpad turned farmer, hoping he might do me the honor of drinking with me! Now, drink your brandy and stop acting the fool!"

He saw Dale's eyes move to the musket that was propped against the wall near the door and he added:

"And I remind you, Morley, that I'm an officer of this Province holding the commission of His Majesty, Charles the First, engaged in the execution of my duties."

And, in a softer voice:

"Besides which, I could slit your God damned throat with my sword before you touched that musket. Come, sit down, man, and drink your drink."

As long as these two men were to know each other there would be stretches of silence between them, while their eyes clashed and their wills wrestled. There was one now, taut and strained, and it lasted until Dale Morley took a step toward the table and reached out a hand for the mug.

18

He drank until the cup was empty. The brandy was unlike anything he had ever tasted before, smooth and yet forceful, totally different from the gagging draughts he had swallowed in London, richer than the best the Jamestown ordinaries had to offer at prices Dale could not afford.

He tilted his head back to get the last drops, then set the mug on the table, exhaling gustily and wiping the back of his hand across his mouth. As soon as his hand came down, Dale was sorry he'd made that gesture. Across the table from him, Claiborne was touching his lips with one lace-cuffed wrist, not affectedly, not prettily, but with a certain elegance that made Morley wish he had been a little less the rooting hog in that swipe of his hand across the mouth.

Well, hell take this fine Captain if he didn't like Dale's manners! He was rich and Dale Morley was far from rich and there were no dainty cuffs on a canvas shirt. With a broadcloth suit and a sword at his side, doeskin boots and a hat with a silver brooch, Dale could be a gentleman with the nicest of them. The sovereigns in the purse, the rings on the fingers, made the gentleman, not anything he had worked for or could earn.

He met the bearded man's eyes, then looked down at the mug he had just emptied.

"Another?" the bearded man asked, and it could have been his tone was faintly mocking.

Dale shook his head. Claiborne finished his drink in small, leisurely sips while Morley waited. He'd be damned, Dale told himself, if he'd ask this man the reason for his visit. Claiborne had made the first move by coming there, through the storm; let him make the next.

The Captain did not hesitate, once his drink was finished. He walked back to the fire, turned and folded his hands behind him.

"There are a few questions," he said idly, "I'd like to ask you, Freedman Morley. As Secretary of the Province I have charge of certain records. As I said, the people who were to have taken care

19

of my work during my stay in England proved lax, as usual. So I must do these things myself, catch up with my records."

Dale walked to the bench by the table and sat down, his elbows on the board, his hands folded under his chin as he looked at the Captain.

"When I came here in '24," he told Claiborne, "I gave them the answers to enough questions to make a man's head spin. What's the need of more tiffety-taffety talk now? I've been here four years, and more. In that time, I've answered all the questions."

The bearded man's eyes were cold as they met Dale's.

"That's for me to decide, Morley, not you," he said. A gust of wind, heavier than the rest, hurled raindrops like pebbles against the side of the little house. Smoke drifted out of the fireplace and was swept back by a draft from under the door.

"Some men," Claiborne observed, "don't like questions because they have something to hide. Not you, Morley, I'm sure."

"Not me," Dale said.

"Good. Very good. Suppose, then, we go over what's already on the records to make sure they're right. These clerks of mine—"

A sheet of foolscap appeared in the Captain's hand from somewhere and Claiborne held it so as to get the uncertain light of the fire.

"Ah yes. Reached Jamestown May sixth, 1624."

He looked up at Dale.

"Right?"

"'Twas May of that year. I suppose it was the sixth."

"One of forty-three persons brought to the Province under contracts of indenture aboard the bark *Solace*, Michael O'Halley, master."

"And a devil he turned out to be, once the ship was at sea," Dale rumbled. "All smiles and promises he was, at London when he got my mark on his paper, and in Plymouth waiting for the ship to be fitted out. An hour past Gravesend he showed us all the kind of a turd-eating dog he was. Kept us penned below decks like rats and

20

roaches, fed us biscuits that crawled, used the knout on anybody, man or woman, that dared raise a voice for their rights."

"And you," said Claiborne easily, "most certainly were one of those who raised a voice, judging from what I've seen of you."

"Yes," Dale admitted. He felt his blood quicken at the memory of the floggings he had taken, manacled to the foremast during that voyage. He remembered O'Halley's roaring curses as he swung the cat with its lead-tipped thongs. O'Halley, he thought, would be a good man to lay hands on one of these days.

"Yes," he said again. "I got the lash more than once. But it always took three of O'Halley's men or more to tie me so he could whip me."

"So?" Claiborne asked in a rising inflection. "Perhaps you're making a mistake in aiming at a planter's life. There's need for a Hercules like you among my Indian fighters and explorers."

Dale felt the dull flush mount to his cheeks.

"I didn't mean to boast," he said stiffly.

"Nor I to sneer," Claiborne returned equably. "There really is a need for fighters in my little army."

"I'm a planter," Dale said, "no soldier."

Claiborne seemed to study the younger man for a moment. Then he shrugged lightly and returned to the paper he held.

"Let's see," he said. "Landed Jamestown—hmmm—indentured to Thomas Willison. Good man, Willison. Hmmm. When was your indenture up, Morley?"

Dale hesitated.

"By the contract," he said, "it was up in May. Mister Willison gave me my fifty acres before that so I could get at the job of planting my first crop and getting my house built in time."

Claiborne's eyebrows went up in surprise. And well they might, Dale thought. Thomas Willison had done the unusual in freeing him from his contract before it ran out. With labor at a precious premium everywhere in the Province, too many planters sought ways of keeping their servants bound to them after their contracts expired. They accused the indentured men and women of thievery, malingering, running up mysterious debts that had to be paid off in labor. And each time, it seemed, the authorities backed up the planter against the servant, no matter how flimsy the case, how obvious the lie against the indentured defendant.

"So?" Claiborne was saying in a soft voice. "Planter Willison must have thought highly of your work, Morley. Or did he reward you thus for some special deed?"

The flush returned to Dale's cheeks.

"He liked my work," he mumbled, "and there was something else. I'm to marry Mister Willison's daughter, Mistress Susan, when my crop's in, if you must know."

"Ah," said Captain Claiborne thoughtfully. "I see."

He looked down at the paper he held, seeming to study it. A log in the fireplace burned through and sent up a cloud of sparks. The rain still drummed down on the roof but the drip of the eaves and the leak in the roof seemed to have slackened somewhat. The main forces of the storm apparently had spent themselves and the rain was getting ready to move on, down the river and out to sea. "I see," Claiborne said again. He replaced the foolscap in an inner pocket of the rich suit and left his stand before the fireplace. The sword and spurs made a quiet clanking as he moved back to the leather flask on the table at Dale's elbow. He splashed brandy into the two mugs and picked up his. He turned back toward the fire.

"This is awkward," he said without turning. "I didn't know you were to be married, Freedman Morley."

"Awkward?" Dale asked. "What's awkward?"

Claiborne sipped his drink. He still kept his back to Dale and looked into the fire when he spoke.

"The Secretary of the Province of Virginia," he said slowly, "has many duties. One of them is establishing proof that a man is entitled to a grant of land here. He must guard the Province, and the King, against swindle."

Dale swallowed. His throat was suddenly dry and he reached for the mug near him.

"I don't know what you mean," he croaked.

Claiborne turned, his cup cradled in his big hands.

"You spoke harshly of Michael O'Halley, master of the bark *Solace,* awhile ago," he said. "You'll be happy to know that the captain is in trouble, serious trouble."

"I hope he gets the ax," Dale ripped out.

Claiborne allowed himself a brief smile and raised the mug to his lips.

"Hardly that," he said. "The ax is mostly reserved for unpopular royalty, but your friend O'Halley may be hanged, for all I know. It depends, I rather imagine, on whether he can scrape up enough money to pay the Duke of Buckingham for Buck's intercession with His Majesty. And Buckingham's help comes high—higher, I think, than any sea captain can afford."

"I know nothing of royalty or dukes, either," Dale grumbled. "What did that damned O'Halley do?"

"Why, the good captain merely pressed, kidnaped—what you will—a young gentleman who unhappily for O'Halley was a member of a prominent family. I can tell you the young man was the son of a high family. It came out that the young fool was paying off some sort of wager and was in—er—a part of London he didn't usually frequent, in some sort of rag-and-tatter disguise."

He sipped his drink before he continued.

"The young man was lucky enough to get in touch with his family somehow before O'Halley's ship cleared port. The good captain, of course, intended selling the young man's head rights. After those head rights were sold—well, just what O'Halley intended doing with the man he kidnaped isn't clear, although there are suspicions."

Dale nodded. He knew about head rights. O'Halley had brought him to Virginia for his own head rights.

Thomas Willison had told him how the head rights system

23

worked. The law said every person over sixteen coming to the colony was entitled to fifty acres. But the law said further that these fifty-acre grants would not go to indentured servants or slaves but to the person who paid the passage from England to Virginia for the servant or slave.

Willison had explained how the law was all right in its intent. It had been set up to encourage people of substance, wealthy men with many servants, to settle in the new colony with the assurance of plenty of land.

During the years, though, the head rights plan had gotten out of hand. Some planters wanted more land but not more servants. Others wanted the servants but had all the land they could tend. That was how trading in head rights, as open a business as trading in cattle or horses, got its start.

Sea captains like O'Halley found they could do profitably by loading their miserable ships with humans like Dale Morley, taking them to Virginia without spending a farthing more on their food than was absolutely necessary to keep them alive, and selling the head rights, each representing fifty acres of rich land, to the highest bidder at Jamestown. The buyer took only the head rights. He registered the name of the new arrival as his servant, transported by him, and got his grant. Meanwhile, the sea captain sold the indentured man's work contract to a planter who wanted field hands but no more fields at that time.

"There was a terrible mess, of course," Claiborne was saying. "O'Halley was clapped in prison and the young gentleman's high connections demanded that the King's Ministers of Plantation inquire into the whole business of transporting servants to this Province."

He paused and smiled wryly.

"Unfortunately, I happened to be in London at the time all this happened. I found myself right in the middle of it. The Ministers of Plantation summoned me, demanded an immediate answer to the slander that we were settling Virginia with kidnaped persons."

"I wasn't kidnaped, if that's the question you want answered," Dale said, bluntly. "I came here of my own free will."

Captain Claiborne touched his mustaches with the back of a forefinger and regarded Dale with eyes gone grave.

"Eh, yes," he acknowledged. "But there was something else, Morley, that I came across while rooting through the logs and records that a very scared Captain Michael O'Halley furnished me. A question of your indenture contract, Morley."

Dale swallowed again, reached for the mug again.

"What's wrong with my contract?" he demanded. "It was for four years and I served out my time, all but the month or so Mister Willison gave me. And you can go to him and ask him if—"

Claiborne's voice suddenly went hard again as he cut in on Dale's rush of words.

"I don't have to go to Willison, Morley," he said. "O'Halley's books had the address of that dunghill where you lived in London before you signed with him. I'm a thorough man, Morley, when I have a duty to fulfill, especially when the King's ministers are giving me orders. I went to that rathole myself."

There was something almost like a purr in his words as he said:

"You'll be happy to know your Aunt Bess is alive and well. She sends her fondest love and hopes your eyes scale over and your nose rots off from the Italian disease. An ill-tempered woman, your Aunt Bess."

"She's no kin of mine," Dale said fiercely. "You know that, if you talked to her—through you must have made coins clink to get her to open her sewer's mouth."

Claiborne nodded.

"Yes," he said, "she told me the name 'Aunt Bess' was one of—er—endearment. But that's not important. What is important is that she told me your age, Freedman Dale Morley!"

"My age?" Dale asked wonderingly.

"Yes, your age, man! You made your mark on O'Halley's paper as being sixteen years old when you were two years younger. Admit it. Didn't you?"

"But—but what difference does that make?"

Captain Claiborne struck the table a light blow with the flat of his hand.

"You do admit it, then?" he asked.

"Maybe," Dale said carefully. "But—"

"There are no buts, Morley. An indenture contract doesn't mean a thing if the signer is under sixteen! No head rights could be collected for you if you were fourteen. Willison had no right to buy your indenture. If you came to Virginia at all, at fourteen, it would be as an apprenticed boy—and you would serve your full apprenticeship in some trade for a hell of a lot longer than any shortened four-year term. Nor would you be eligible for any grant of land from your employer when you finished your apprenticeship."

Dale licked his lips.

"I—what are you going to do?" he asked.

Claiborne hunched his shoulders in a negligent shrug. "Do? There are several thing I *could* do. I could demand the return of the fifty acres given on your head rights from the planter who bought them. Of course, he would be entitled to some return—in labor —for the money he put out."

Dale Morley clenched his hands on the table in front of him.

"What would that mean?" he asked, his voice hoarse.

Claiborne dealt him half a smile. Another log in the fireplace collapsed with a display of sparks.

"Why I suppose it would mean you'd be bound over to that planter," he drawled. "Or perhaps Thomas Willison might see his way clear to pay the loser in this deal for your freedom."

"No!" Dale said sharply. "I won't have that!"

"Just what do you have to say about what you'll have and what you won't?" Claiborne asked, in a gritty tone. "The courts will decide that. Have you got some nimble-tongued attorney hidden away somewhere about here? Some clever advocate? Or perhaps you have the ear of the King's ministers."

Dale stared at his tormentor, his eyes bright with hate. A few hours ago, he had considered this little farm of his on the banks of the James a burden, something that would keep him chained to an existence he really did not want, deep down. Now, when his property, his freedom, was threatened, he was ready to fight for it. But how, exactly, could he fight?

"You—you have no proof of my age," Dale Morley croaked. "My birth was never written down in anyone's Bible."

Claiborne laughed.

"No proof, Morley?" he asked. "D'you think that after wading through London filth to find your noble residence I'd leave without some kind of paper, attested to by that beldame who brought you up? I told you I was a thorough man, Morley. I got that hag's mark on a paper swearing you were born in 1610 and brought to her when you were a baby, for reasons undisclosed."

"She lied," Dale muttered. There was no conviction in his protest.

"I don't think she did," Claiborne said mildly, "but she might have, seeing that she hates you so. It's possible. But even if she did, what has that to do with our case, Morley?"

Dale passed a hand roughly over his face, feeling the stiff bristles under his palm. He shook his head in an unconscious movement, trying to clear it of the confused, hopeless thoughts that rioted there. Without volition, he reached for the pewter mug in front of him and drained it.

There was the snickling sound of spurs and the sword as Claiborne moved toward him. When Dale looked up he saw the Captain was smiling again, as though he were enjoying this spectacle of a bigger man, a younger man, caught in a gill-net of circumstance that made him helpless. Yet there was something else in Claiborne's smile; an expression that might have shown facets of friendliness, or even compassion.

Dale Morley drew away sharply as the Captain's hand moved out toward him, a ring glistening on one long finger. But the hand touched his shoulder and stayed there and Dale could feel an indescribable something—a warmth, a magnetism, a vital power—that

27

seemed to flow from Claiborne, through the damp cloth of the shirt, to Dale's core.

It was foolish and it was only because he was overwrought, he knew, but Claiborne's touch, be it menacing or reassuring, seemed to carry a warning that henceforth Dale's life would be twisted out of the straight rut that had stretched ahead for him, before this dark man had come through the rain to pound at his door.

Captain Claiborne laughed lightly as he looked down at Dale.

"Oh, come now," he said. "It's not so bad as all that. You look as though you'd seen Beelzebub himself, and even my worst enemies haven't been able to find the actual horns and tail—yet. No, Morley, there's no need to look as woebegone as that."

"But—but you said—"

The Captain touched his mustaches again and shrugged.

"I'm not exactly decided," he said, "but—well, there are many ways for a man to carry out his duties and some of them are ways in which he needn't abuse his trust as a King's officer and yet may throw the dice in favor of a good man who needs help."

His smile widened.

"Give me a little time, Morley," he said, "and I'll find a way out of this fix for you. You're a young man, strong, high-spirited, and the Province—and I—have need for more of your kind and fewer farmers. There are wars to be fought, new lands to be opened up, the enemies of the King and Church to be dealt with and a freedman fights better than a servant or a slave. We need the fighters, Morley, and there'll come a time when we need them more than we do now."

"But I'm a farmer," Dale protested.

Claiborne's long fingers tapped at the hilt of his sword as he looked down at the man at the table.

"That's right, Dale Morley," he said, amiably. "You are, aren't you? But for how long, I wonder? How long?"

Chapter Two, 1628

THE CORN WAS CUT AND SHOCKED. THE POTATOES had been hoed out of the earth and the yellow squash had been cut from their leathery vines. The broad green tobacco leaves had been tied in bunches at their stems and hung in the drying sheds. The hay was in—not enough of it, of course, because no planter would raise hay where precious tobacco might grow, but more than had been put away the previous year. The woodpiles were high. The ducks were winging southward in great flocks.

It had been a good crop year for Virginia, in spite of the early summer drought. The corn had been so plentiful that as early as the first of October some of the bigger planters were penning their hogs and fattening them on roasting ears instead of letting them forage until the first deep snows. The tobacco yield had been good, but the price in England stayed high.

Even the graybeards who had survived the grim winters of 1610 and 1622 forgot to hoard against famine that fall. Jamestown might still be an unprepossessing cluster of weatherbeaten buildings set in the mud of the James River flats but there was an air about the place that breathed a confidence and a sense of security that had been lacking in other years.

And along the rivers, the James, the York and the Appomatox, and in the coves where the plantations swept down to meet the water, there was an abundance of the necessities and of the luxuries, too, unsurpassed in the history of the Province. Every ship that made its way up-river to the plantation docks brought the planters' womenfolk bolts of silk and satin, serge, flannel, wool and calico, yards of lace, fans with sticks and guards of ivory, painted by the same craftsmen who served the Court of France's Louis the Thirteenth, gowns fashioned by London dressmakers and as stylish as those worn by any woman who curtsied before Charles in England.

For the men there were shirts of silk and fine lawn, the latest thing in cuff ruffles and falling bands, coats with enormously puffed sleeves and exaggerated slashes, breeches that were tied just below the knee with flaring bows, silver shoe buckles to replace the steel buckles most of them had always worn, fine Toledo blades, the new snaphance muskets, wigs more elaborate than the Colony had ever seen, plumed beaver hats with sweeping brims, butts of fine sack and Madeira, casks of brandy, bottles of the cordials that were just beginning to put in an appearance on the best tables of England. There were even a few books.

On the more practical side, there were blooded horses, cattle, farm tools, furniture, indentured servants and slaves, iron household utensils, needles, tea, hardware and like goods arriving in quantity at Virginia that fall.

Dale Morley shared in the general prosperity. He bought a roan mare named Bella at a price that represented almost half the value of his tobacco crop. She was a beautiful animal, sleek and spirited, nervous and fidgety, with the eyes of a woman in love.

He knew he had to have the mare the first time he saw her in the small herd that was taken off the vessel *Pollux* at Jamestown in September. He had walked the miles to town in a blazing heat that made chalky dust of the narrow cartway and he was struck suddenly by the thought that he could afford to ride back. He had in his pocket a paper, signed by an official of the Province, crediting him with so many pounds of tobacco stored for curing in the common sheds. It was a small lot, compared with the thousands of pounds the big planters had to their credit, but it would be enough to buy a horse—that horse.

Dale was no horseman. Before he had come to Virginia, his only contact with horses had been scuttling out from under their hoofs as coaches lumbered through the narrow streets of London; that, and using their dung in street battles between gangs. As Thomas Willison's servant he had taken Willison's plug from the barn to the house, but those brief trips had been made at a walk with Dale clutching the sorry nag with hands and knees while he looked down at the ground, which seemed a long, long distance away.

Actually, he had no need for a horse, not even for the plow. His fifty acres had been chopped out of thick woods and burned over. The blackened stumps dotted his fields and would stay there until they rotted away. In all the James River Valley there were not a dozen fields that did not have to be worked by hand because of the stumps. A plow was as rare in the Province as a gold watch, and less useful.

Susan Willison had made it clear that Dale needed no horse. A horse never had been included in the plans she had made for them. Those plans had earmarked the proceeds of Dale's first crop for enlarging Morley's house and buying a few pieces of furniture. With the gains realized from the next year's crop, Dale would buy up the head rights for another fifty acres. The next year, he should be able to buy two more head rights and perhaps a servant's contract. The next year—the plan stretched out into the future far past Dale's ability to reckon.

But no horses had been considered. Cows, yes, and beef cattle, hogs, sheep and hordes of stupid, squawking fowl were all in the picture Susan had painted, but when Dale had mentioned the idea of getting an animal he could ride, the girl had shaken her head.

"Whatever would we need a horse for?" she asked. "Our goods will go down the river by boat; what we need will come up the river by boat. We'll build a skiff to take us where we want to go. And where the skiff won't sail, we'll walk."

"Like the couple of clods we'll be," Dale grumbled. "A man ought to have a horse to ride."

He could see the glance she gave him and the tiny frown that came down over her blue eyes.

"You mean a man like Captain Claiborne?" she asked, her voice

31

sharpening. "Perhaps he's the one who told you that you ought to have a fine horse. Did he mention a silver-mounted bridle, too?"

She took a backward step before the dark face he turned on her.

"Damn it," he grated, "must you always be throwing Captain Claiborne up to me, as though he was making a fool of me? Let the man stop by my place, let him say a word to me or share a glass, and you're down on me as fast as your skirts will let you run, rattling your tongue with your questions of why Captain Claiborne should interest himself in me. I'm sick of it!"

Her chin came up and she faced his anger.

"Why does he, then?" she asked, shrillness in her words. "Why does he interest himself in you, Dale Morley? Hardly a day passes but what he finds some excuse to come here and interrupt your work, take you from your fields, make you drop whatever you're doing to play the host. Why should the Secretary of the Province, the high and mighty Captain Claiborne, so put himself out to give you such close regard?"

"I've told you why!" Dale blared. "I've told you a hundred times that the Captain has the handling of my indenture contract. He's trying to clear up the matter so that I'll not be the loser. There are questions he has to ask me, things he has to know, and those matters bring him here. He could drag me to Jamestown, but he has the kindness to ride here instead. And for this kindness you return this woman's suspicion."

She walked up to him, past the glare with which he had fixed her and close enough to put her arms around his middle as she rested her head on his chest. She held him tightly for a moment, not speaking, and Dale somehow knew that it was not that she was looking for comfort in his arms but, rather, that she sought to protect *him*, hold him with her love. And from what could she protect him?

"Oh, Dale," she murmured. Her lips moved on his skin where his half-buttoned shirt lay open. "Perhaps I'm wrong—I hope I'm wrong—but I'm afraid of this man Claiborne. I wish you'd never seen him."

32

His anger ebbed as abruptly as it had surged. He clasped her close and bent his head to put his cheek against her soft, fragrant hair. She was warm and yielding in his arms and presently, when it came time for kisses, her knees would tremble and her mouth would open, despite herself, and he could make his gallop atop a sweeter mount than any damned horse such as had started this talk.

"Afraid, Susan?" he asked. "You've no cause to be. Captain Claiborne is my friend—our friend. He has an interest in me."

"Yes," she acknowledged, "and that's what puzzles and frightens me. He has an interest in you and it's never been because of your indenture contract."

He pushed her away gently and held her shoulders, looking down at her. Her mouth was firm, her eyes steady, as she bore his searching scrutiny.

"What d'you mean?" Dale asked. "Why else would Captain Claiborne seek me out, of all the people in this Province?"

"I don't know his reason," Susan said stoutly, "but there is one. His story about Captain O'Halley and the rest is a lie, on the face of it."

"A lie?"

"Yes, a lie and a lie with a dark purpose. Think back to what he told you and what you told me. He happened to be in London when this Captain O'Halley got in trouble. The Ministers of Plantation ordered him to investigate. Why him? Why not the King's officers?"

"But it had to do with Virginia and the people O'Halley brought here. I've told you that."

She tossed her head impatiently.

"I'll not believe Captain Claiborne was appointed to investigate," she said, "but even if he was, why would he dig so deeply into your case and no other? Have you heard of anybody else in the Province, any of the others who came over on the same ship with you, being checked? No. But this brave Captain is so taken by one name among the scores O'Halley must have furnished him—if O'Halley really *did* get in trouble and if he *did* give Captain Claiborne those records

33

—that he personally searched the City of London until he found where you lived and talked to—to the woman who knew you."

She looked up at him in earnest appeal.

"Can't you see, that none of it's right? Suppose O'Halley did give him an address supposed to be on his records—and you can't recall giving any address. The street, the section, would tell Captain Claiborne that you were no young nobleman kidnaped by the sea captain, such as the man who started this investigation was supposed to be. He must have seen at a glance that you were a—a nobody. Oh, Dale, I love you, but that's what you were on those records, a nobody. Then why did Captain Claiborne concern himself with you?"

Dale slowly dropped his hands from Susan's shoulders. There were too many questions here, and some of them were questions that had nudged his own mind at times since that stormy night when William Claiborne had appeared at his door. Claiborne's story had been convincing enough that night but it was the Captain himself who had made it so. Later, there had been certain doubts but he had refused to give them serious thought. He was nobody to question the workings of authority. He could read and write a little, thanks to Susan, but Captain Claiborne was a learned man, an official of the Province, a person of wealth and power. There could be no other reason for his interest than the indenture contract.

"He—he must have done what he said he did," he faltered. "He spoke of the old bitch who called herself Aunt Bess. And he knew my birth year."

He passed a hand over his forehead, rubbing at the confusion that churned within his brain. He was no thinker, nor would he ever be. He had muscles and a strong back, he could use his hands and his shoulders and his legs with the best of them, but he was not made to untangle puzzles nor mull over any problems beyond the simple numbers Susan had taught him.

"It must be the way Captain Claiborne told me," he said. "It has to be."

That had been his final word, that time. because he had gone on
34

to something else, to a more pleasant pursuit, but even that interval had left him vaguely unsatisfied. He wondered whether it was because some flavor of the thing must be lost with each repetition or because Susan had paid more attention, that day, to the questions in her head than to the final mild excitement that was all she seemed capable of feeling.

Well, the passage had served one purpose, anyway. The talk had not gotten back to the question of whether Captain Claiborne really had put the idea of a horse in Dale's mind. Because he had, in a brief, indirect word.

"A young man can't learn things, better himself, without getting around, seeing things beyond his own fields. In this country a horse is as valuable to a man, especially a young man, as a library."

Now, as he looked at the line of tethered horses, still frightened and weak from their sea voyage, Captain Claiborne's words came back to him, together with the realization that he carried a letter of credit for enough to buy that roan mare, the third from the far end of the line, and ride those dusty miles back to his place.

He moved closer to the mare, elbowing his way through the small crowd that had gathered. It was high noon and the big planters, the men of wealth, were not abroad. They would come down-river or across from the southern hundreds later in the day, when the sun had lost some of its ferocity. Those who were in town for reasons of business or politics were gathered in the taverns and ordinaries for the mid-day meal that would last for hours, dragged out by talk and tobacco smoke and heady port. The men who clustered around the horse trader and his string now were the wishful, the curious, the idlers, with here and there a small planter hopeful of finding a spavined nag he could afford.

"Here they are, gentlemen," bawled a squat, bow-legged man with a thatch of violently red hair. "No finer pieces of horseflesh were ever landed on the shores of Virginia, I'll swear by the Book. From the stables of an English gentleman who met reverses at the gamin' tables and must pay his creditors, else they'd not be offered for sale."

He wiped his face with a dirty kerchief and swelled his thick neck to roar again.

"And cheap, gentlemen, cheap! I'll be ashamed to face the gentleman who gave me the commission to sell 'em when I get back to England. Aye, I'm tempted to stay here and send the few pennies back by messenger. I'll let another take the hidin' that'll be comin' when His Lordship finds out the prices I'm sellin' fer."

The roan jerked back on her halter as Dale walked up and extended a hand. The mare's yellow teeth were bared and her eyes walled frantically. Her front hoofs began a nervous tattoo on the ground and she switched her rump from one side to the other, bumping the animals tethered on each side of her.

"Steady," Dale said softly. "Steady, little mistress. Steady, lady."

The horse dealer glanced down the line to find the cause of the commotion, then moved toward Dale quickly on his bandy legs.

"Aye, sir," he bellowed, "ye know yer horseflesh, I see! The finest mare of the lot, three years old and sound as a sovereign. She's never foaled, that one, but her get will be the finest, mark that."

He reached up to grasp the halter, then twitched his hand back as the roan slashed at him with her teeth.

"Ah, ah, ah!" the red-haired man chided. "That's naughty, Bella!" He turned to Dale apologetically. "A bit feisty now, sir, but it's the voyage, you understand. Bella's as gentle as a newborn lamb, sir, you have my word to that. Why, His Lordship, the gentleman who's selling these horses, used to put his baby daughter up on Bella with never a fear."

Dale stared at the mare, fascinated by the spirit shown by the animal. The bow-legged man was rattling on, exclaiming over the mare's good points, promising great things in speed, durability and progeny.

"How much?" Dale asked bluntly. The red-faced man's little eyes flicked a searching look at him and then shifted away.

"Twenty-five pounds," he said, and added firmly: "Sterling."

Dale winced. Even with the advance of tobacco prices, twenty-five pounds sterling was more than he had any right to think of spending, even if Susan had never told him he couldn't buy a horse.

Susan had told him he couldn't buy a horse! Well, Christ on the Cross, what business had she to tell him what he could buy and couldn't buy with the money he had earned by his sweat and aching muscles and sore back? Susan was a woman, and he'd be a man unworthy of the name if he let her bully him now, even before she had a wife's rights. Her father might be able to say this and that; he owed something to Thomas Willison for helping him the way he had, but he owed Susan nothing more than a pat on the flank when the morris dance was finished.

He reached for the credit letter in his pocket.

"I'll take the mare," he said, and he was unconscious of the fact that he spoke through clenched teeth. "Here's a statement of the tobacco I've got stored and it's more than enough to cover twenty-five pounds sterling."

The bandy-legged man gaped openly at Dale. In all his days as a trader, most probably, he never had sold a horse without prolonged bargaining, and suspicion followed hard on his amazement.

"Well, now," he hedged, "I know nothin' about this tobacco tradin'. My price was twenty-five pounds sterling, not tobacco."

Dale pointed a long arm past the squat man's red head.

"There's the public warehouse," he said. "Go there with me and they'll sign the right amount of tobacco to you from my lot, then buy the tobacco from you for pounds sterling. You won't have to touch a leaf. And if you're going to do much business here, my friend, you'd do well to learn something about tobacco trading as well as horse trading."

"How's that, sir?" asked the dealer.

"Well, if I had your position, I'd take payment for my horses in tobacco. I'd wait in Virginia till the price went up. Then I'd pocket the difference between what I got the tobacco for and what I sold it for, and your fine nobleman in England would never know the difference."

Cupidity was the keynote of the bow-legged man's smile.

"Now truly, sir," he said, "you've an idea there. And I'd never have to handle the stuff, eh? Just take it for my horses and sell it at a fat profit, eh, and make a tidy bit besides my commission on the sales. Hah, that's for Jack Bagshaw!"

He was struck by a sudden thought and the smile faded.

"But what if tobacco prices go down?" he asked. "What then?"

"They won't," Dale promised recklessly.

"Any guarantee they won't?" Bagshaw asked cautiously.

"No, man! Of course not."

The red-haired horse dealer heaved a deep sigh.

"There's always a catch, ain't there?" he asked. "No way for a man to make an honest shilling without a risk of havin' his ears cut off, or worse. No, I'll take the gold and leave the gatherin' of fortunes to them that don't have to make an accountin' to the most shrivel-souled bastard in all England. Let's get to this warehouse you spoke of and complete the deal."

So it was that Dale headed back from Jamestown on horseback instead of afoot, as he had come. He was late getting started. There had been the matter of a saddle and bridle (five pounds more to Jack Bagshaw for a piece of worn and battered gear) and there had been the involved business of getting the mare, Bella, to let him mount.

Dale knew there was more to getting into the saddle than a rider like Captain William Claiborne made it seem; his experiments with Thomas Willison's plug had proved that. He was determined that none of the people around the horse sale in Jamestown should see his first attempts to mount the roan. His Lordship's baby daughter might be able to control the horse but Dale suspected that things would be different when he tried to get into the saddle. Muttering something about leading his horse until her excitement wore off and she was out of the crowd, he walked at the mare's head, holding the bridle, one hand stroking the roan's sweaty coat, his voice trying to tell the nervous animal that he was her friend, that the things that had frightened her were gone for all time.

A mile or so out of town, the mare seemed easier. Dale led her to a shaded grassy patch beside the cart road and let her graze. He held the reins loosely while Bella fed and then rolled in the coolness of the glade. When she got to her feet, Dale took the roan to a branch that trickled nearby and let her drink. As the mare raised her dripping muzzle, Morley was able to stroke his horse with no more than an occasional toss of Bella's head. He stayed there beside the brook for some time, petting the mare, fondling her ears, talking to her in a low, intimate voice, and then led her back to the road.

"Now, Bella," he said. "Now, lady."

He got one foot in the stirrup, lurched up into the saddle, and fumbled for the other stirrup. The mare stood quiet under him, shivering for a moment and then at ease. Dale gathered up the reins and clucked his tongue. Bella's ears went forward and the mare backed a few steps. He tightened the reins more and the horse backed further, into a bush. Dale relaxed his hard grip on the worn leather lines and the mare stopped her backing. He clucked his tongue again and Bella began to move forward at a walk.

A walk, however slow, was good enough for Dale. He leaned forward in the saddle and patted the roan's neck. Riding this animal, his own horse, gave him a feeling he never before had experienced. This was being a man, a real man, a man who could meet the richest planter in the Province at eye level when he was in the saddle. He had looked up to others, in fact and in mind, too long. It was time he began some looking down and Bella would provide the means.

Unbidden, the mare broke into a trot and Dale found himself jolting, clutching at the reins again, sliding first one way and then another in the saddle. He knew he was doing everything wrong and he had no idea of how to do it right, to make his body join the horse's motion instead of fighting it. Bella might be an easy-paced mare (as indeed she was) but Dale found his teeth clacking, his head snapping, his spine jarring from buttock to nape before the roan had covered half a mile.

"H-h-hold up, Bella," he chattered. "Sus-steady, little m-m-mistress."

The mare kept on, unchecked. It was cooler now, as the sun began dipping behind the hills to the west, and the cart road lay in shadow for long stretches. Bella had grazed, drunk and rolled. Now she wanted to stretch her legs to clear her mind of all memory of that pitching, tossing hell in which she had been imprisoned for endless days.

As horses will, she sensed the uncertainty of the man on her back and it aroused a perverse streak in her that sent her surging forward in a canter. That was too much for Dale. He clung to the pommel of his saddle for a while, clutched wildly at the mare's mane, missed and went sliding over the side, onto the dusty road. Bella kept on her way, galloping free.

Dale sat in the dust, his legs spread wide apart, leaning back on his hands. The fall had jolted him but he was not hurt, physically. His eyes were hot with anger and humiliation as they followed the roan, in full gallop now, heading down the cart road, the dust puffing white and thick beneath her hoofs. God damn the mare, the red-headed horse trader, His Gambling Lordship and His Lordship's tiny daughter!

He yelled once, a hoarse command to whoa, but his voice seemed only to dig spurs into the mare's flanks. Bella rounded a curve in the lane and went out of sight.

Dale climbed slowly to his feet. As he brushed absently at the sandy powder that soiled his breeches he told himself grimly that the mare was running in the right direction, at least. Unless the Indians got her—and Opechancanough's savages had not been seen below the Falls for months—Bella would be safe enough. Horses were not so common in the Province that he couldn't track her down and reclaim her from whoever found her.

But the story, certainly, would be spread up and down the valley; about Morley, the erstwhile indentured servant who tried to turn gentleman as soon as his first crop was in; the man who bought a saddle horse at the cost of half his tobacco profits; the man who gave himself airs above his real station. And wound up sprawled in the road, watching his new horse run away.

40

He began trudging up the cart road, feeling the biting ache of thigh muscles so recently put to new use. And as he walked, his mind was busy dredging up uncommon curses to hurl after the departed Bella. She had made a fool of him, as surely and as deliberately as though she were a woman who had known from the start that he had been masquerading as a member of quality, a rich planter, instead of admitting he was the nameless newly-freed servant he really was.

What was it, he asked himself, that made him do things like buying the mare? Why didn't he swallow the fact that he was a fifty-acre farmer who some day might get a hundred acres, five hundred, even a thousand, if he worked hard and bussed the right buttocks? Where had he gotten this idea that he was any different from the others who had journeyed to Virginia as servants, looking forward to the time when they would be their own masters?

He was free now, his own man, and he had thought that would be enough. But it wasn't, not by half. It had not been long ago when he had thought that a full meal, a soft bed, a roof over him and a woman under him were all he would ever need. Now he wanted clothes of velvet and broadcloth instead of canvas. He wanted doeskin boots instead of the crude, ugly shoes that pounded under him now as he walked along the lane. He wanted a sword at his side, hung from a silk sash. He wanted lace at his cuffs, a falling band rich with bright embroidery, a wide-brimmed hat with a plume, rings on his hands, a blooded horse to ride, plate on his table, silver spurs on his heels.

Yes, he wanted everything Captain William Claiborne had; his way of life, his easy confidence, his manner of accepting everything he had—wealth, power, charm—as nothing more than his rightful due. He wanted to be able to swing himself into a saddle with Claiborne's smooth grace, sweep off his hat to a lady with the captain's courtly polish, wear the enigmatic smile that the dark-browed Claiborne sometimes wore.

He plodded on, head bent against the flies and the heat of the

41

waning day. He was walking forward, his mouth cast in that curious quirk, when he heard the sound of horses, ahead of him and coming closer.

It was Captain William Claiborne, sitting his black stallion easily, as though he were a part of the animal, riding as Dale Morley had thought of himself as riding. He was wearing a suit of light blue, almost gray cloth and the plume of the rakish hat was of blue-dyed ostrich. He had on high boots and gauntlets, and in spite of the heat he looked as immaculate as though he had just left the hands of his dressing servant.

He rode with his left hand holding the black's lines high. In his right hand he grasped the reins of Bella's bridle. The roan was placid, totally unlike a horse that could unseat her rider and play him for a fool.

Claiborne reined in when he saw the man in the road. The black danced in a sidestep for a moment, cavorting as though to show the mare what a fine animal he could be if it were not for this human on his back, then quieted under a brief command from the Captain. Claiborne leaned down over his horse's neck and smiled, with the glint of white teeth.

"Well, well, well," he said softly. "Dale Morley, or I'm a Jesuit."

Bella, the roan mare, pricked up her ears and peered at Dale past the black's flank. She nickered softly, as though laughing. Claiborne caught the direction of Dale's glance and turned in his saddle.

"Caught her up the road, about a mile," he explained. "Nice mare. Don't recognize her, though. She's run away from somebody. You didn't chance to see a footweary horseman along this way, did you? I think this is one of young Tindall's. He's always buying horses and never learning how to ride them. It would be like him to be thrown by this little mare. He probably passed a pretty maid, unlaced her bodice and threw up her skirts in his thoughts and put the spur to his horse in the doing. I mind the time—"

"The mare is mine," Dale interrupted bluntly.

Claiborne's eyes widened in frank amazement.

42

"Yours? You mean you own this mare?"

Dale nodded. Damn the man, he thought, for always being where he should be for his own advantage. There were a thousand men in the Province who could have caught Bella, yet it had to be Captain Claiborne with his sneering grin who had come across the runaway. This man, intentionally or not, had led him into the folly of buying a horse and now was here, on the spot, to laugh at the results.

"I bought the mare in Jamestown this morning," Dale said.

He was glad that he had managed to keep his voice even. He walked up to the roan, past Claiborne, and put his hand on the old bridle.

"You bought her? Then why—oh, you've been unhorsed. What happened?"

"I'm not the rider you are, Captain Claiborne," Dale said, in the same level tone. "She threw me."

Let him laugh at me, damn him! Let him laugh at me and I'll drag him out of that saddle and choke the life out of him!

William Claiborne looked at Dale and then back at the gentle roan. A chuckle started in his throat, forced its way into his mouth and emerged as a bellow. The black stallion danced again under the jarring motion of the man in the saddle. Claiborne leaned back his head until his beard pointed at the horizon.

"Christ on the Cross," he gasped, after the first paroxysm of laughter passed. "My Dale Morley thinks he can be a gentleman by getting himself a horse, and the mare wastes no time in showing him there's more to riding than putting a saddle under a man's hunkers."

He threw the roan's lines toward Dale and used his free hand to clutch his middle.

"Ah," he gurgled, "I'd have given a hundred pounds to have seen it! It must have been good! I can imagine you, thinking yourself the lord of—"

His hand blurred. The blade at his s le whipped out of its socket, flashed in the dying sunlight and described a neat cross in front of

Morley's face as Dale lurched at his tormentor. The black danced and the roan snorted and sidled, dragging at the reins Morley still held, but the sword never seemed more than an inch away from Dale's eyes.

"Hold, you fool!" Claiborne barked. Then he added, gently: "I can blind you before you peep and I can slit your gullet with one slash. So hold, Dale Morley, lest I have to kill you before I can ask your pardon for my witless words."

Dale backed, the swordpoint bright and sharp before his eyes.

"I was wrong," Captain Claiborne said, "to laugh at your bad luck in being thrown. I've been unhorsed a hundred times, myself, and I know how you feel. It's not the bruised buttocks but the bruised pride that hurts. And I was wrong in what I said about your buying the mare. She's a fine mount, and a man who wouldn't try to better his station deserves the slave's yoke he wears."

He watched Dale carefully as he replaced the sword in its steel ring on the sash.

"I've been at your place, expecting to find you there," he said. "I dropped off a suit of clothes that some idiot tailor in London made to wrong measurements. The suit's too big for me, but it should fit you."

He held up a hand to check Dale's rush of words.

"Now, wait," he counseled. "I'm not giving you the suit, you young spitfire. I wouldn't do that—to a friend. If it fits, you can buy it from me. If it doesn't I'll offer it to Tindall or Talbot Bristoll or another of my friends. I thought of you because of your size, Morley."

"It—it probably costs more than I can pay," Dale said hoarsely.

"We'll see if it fits, first," Claiborne said negligently. "And if it does, why you can wear it to supper at my place tonight."

"Supper—at your place?"

"Why, yes. You know where I live, I think. I'll expect you in about three hours. There'll be company for you there, ladies and gentlemen who can make you forget my crudities of a few minutes ago, I'll swear."

44

"I'm not coming," Dale said harshly.

Claiborne leaned in his saddle to put a gloved hand on his shoulder.

"Yes, you are," he said softly.

He smiled again and then prodded the black with his spurs, sending the big stallion at a trot down the road toward Jamestown. Dale's bitter eyes followed man and horse out of sight and then he turned back to the mare.

He wasn't going to supper at Claiborne's, even if the suit fit. He wouldn't go. He wouldn't wear Claiborne's cast-offs, no matter if the suit was of velvet with lace cuffs down to his fingertips. The Captain was wrong if he thought Dale would come to his place to be exhibited, for reasons of Claiborne's own, as some human dancing bear, an oddity for the amusement of the other guests.

No, he wasn't going!

But he knew he was, really. He had to, because this was his first chance really to see the world he wanted to live in. The world he was going to live in.

He had no stable for the mare, so he turned the cow and the heifer out to pasture to make room for the horse. He told himself he would start work on a stable the first thing next morning.

He was leading the mare into the cow shed, burning to get to the house to see the suit Captain Claiborne had left him, when Susan came over the rise that lay behind the little barn. She picked her way carefully, her skirts held up at one side. She was wearing no frown, but there was a set to her lips.

"I see you had to have yourself a horse, after all," she said, in a tight voice.

He lifted a hand to Bella's neck and smoothed the roan's mane. Let Susan do the talking. If she expected him to drop to his knees, beg her pardon for buying the mare, she was wrong.

"With all the things we need," she murmured unsteadily. "The new rooms on the house, the furniture—"

45

Her voice trailed off. She stepped closer to the roan and stroked the horse's rump.

"She's beautiful," Susan said. "But we can't keep her."

Dale's teeth clamped shut with a click. This was his chance to let the girl know there was no "we" connected with this horse, nor with his whole future. She might have seemed desirable once but now she was a pasty-faced woman who thought she could tell him what to do and what not to do, pursing her prissy mouth to let him know she was displeased, wanting him to be a farmer who didn't look for anything beyond his own acres.

"I'm going to keep her," he said roughly. "And if you're worrying about the money I spent, think what this mare's colts will bring. The man who sold her to me said she was of good stock. Her foals will bring me enough to pay off your father what I owe him. Her colts will bring me enough—"

He meant to tell her that Bella's get would bring him real independence, freedom from Thomas Willison's obligation and the hold of Thomas Willison's daughter. But the quiet smile on her mouth, as she stroked the flank of the mare, stopped him.

"Will the colts bring you enough to buy a cradle, Dale?" she asked. "We'll need one—before another seven months are up."

The black man came out of the shadows on silent feet to take Bella's bridle. He was a giant in livery and his eyeballs were startlingly white in the darkness.

"Yago, Sarrh," he said, in a soft, slurring accent. "I tek'the horse, Sarrh."

He was a Bantu, from the blackness of his skin, and probably one of the big, lithe-muscled men set ashore at Jamestown by the Dutch slave ships plying between Guinea and the Colony. Slaves were becoming more and more important in the Province, and more profitable to those who could afford them. An indentured servant like Dale had to be given his parcel of land and six months' sub-

46

sistence when his contract was up, but a slave could be worked until he was worn out. Better still, he could beget more servants if he was given a mate, or two, or three. A prime male "Niger," Dale had heard, was worth a dozen indentured white men and the big planters who didn't need the head rights the indentured servants brought with them, were buying up the black men as soon as they were landed at Jamestown. Some of the planters up near Henrico were using the female blacks as house servants and finding them capable, even though they had to be taught not to grease their bodies with pork rinds and instructed in covering themselves decently.

Dale slid down from the saddle, trying not to look too awkward in front of this Yago; the ride to Claiborne's place had been very trying.

He stretched as the Negro led Bella away. He felt stiff and cold. The stiffness was not all because of his ride and the night was warm for an October evening. What Susan had told him had chilled him and the cold still lingered in his marrow. She was with child and that meant he would have to marry her and rear a succession of brats on the little plantation beside the James River. He'd never have a Yago to take the bridle of a guest's horse or wear doeskin boots or a cape with a silver clasp.

He looked up at Captain Claiborne's house. It was of brick and a full two stories high. The place had a look of permanence and Dale guessed that Claiborne had imported the bricks from England before the kiln south of Jamestown was started. Wide, flat chimneys reared themselves at each end of the main building, bisecting the angles of the gables and keeping their tops shrouded in darkness, out of reach of the light from the lanterns that hung on the porch. Lighted windows showed that Claiborne had built a one-story wing on the left side of the main building. Other lights, showing through the misty darkness, pointed out the scattered outbuildings.

The front door of the house stood open and from inside came the sound of cross-current talk, the tinkle of a clavichord, a shrill snort of laughter. Dale mounted the porch and walked into the narrow

47

hallway, his nostrils widening at the scent of women and tobacco, wine and wealth.

At the further end of the hallway, where it entered the main room of the house, a woman with a glass in her hand stood talking to a man who wore a luxuriant reddish wig. The man used effeminate gestures as he flourished his lace handkerchief and dabbed at the girl with a long forefinger on which was a ring with a heavy stone.

The woman's face was delicately chiseled, with a high-bridged nose and flat, clean planes of smooth skin stretching from her prominent cheekbones to the crisp line of her jaw. Her mouth, though, was wide and incongruously soft, the lips set in a curving pout, the corners down-drooping.

She turned toward Dale as he approached, her thin eyebrows arching and her deep brown eyes quickening with interest as she surveyed the span of his shoulders and the swing of his long legs. She was wearing yellow, with green trimmings, and the combination suited her as it seldom suited any woman.

She sipped her drink and looked at Dale, frankly appraising. Well, he thought, let her look. The suit he wore, the one Claiborne had left at his place, was as good as any she'd see that night and it fit as though it had been made to his measurements. It had been a stroke of luck for him that the London tailor had made his mistakes in the right places. From what he had been able to see in the bit of glass he used for shaving, he was as much a beau in this suit as if he'd spent his whole life in drawing rooms. His manners, though, might give him away, unless he watched carefully and did what the others did.

The man to whom the girl had been talking noticed her disinterest in what he was saying and turned toward Dale with a haughty, sleepy-eyed face gone hostile. Dale recognized him, although the woman was a stranger to him.

The foppish young man was Talbot Bristoll, son of one of the biggest planters on the Appomatox River and owner of a spectacular reputation. At twenty, Bristoll was supposed to have been sent

48

down from Oxford for killing a fellow student in a duel that had peculiar sidelights. He was said to have made a fortune bigger than his father's in one night's gaming at a London chocolate house—and lost it back, and more, the following night. There was talk that he had finally been advised to leave England and return to Virginia, permanently, after he had become involved in an affair with a lady of title; an affair that brought him into a clash with none other than George Villiers, Duke of Buckingham.

For all his effeminacy, his simpering voice and his mincing walk Talbot Bristoll was admittedly a deadly swordsman, a brilliant horseman, a reckless gambler, a tireless man-hunter in the excursions sent out against the Indians three times each year to keep the savages reminded that the Peace of Powhatan had long since been broken by both sides.

"He's a devil, when he's killing," Captain Claiborne had told Dale on one occasion. "I'm no more squeamish than the next man when it comes to fighting the Indians, but I've seen him do things that have made my blood curdle, and do them with a smile."

Clairborne had looked at Dale thoughtfully that time, and had added:

"I'll have to arrange for you to meet him. He's damned interesting, for all the fact that he sets a man's teeth on edge with that voice of his, at times. But when you meet him, don't be fooled by the way he walks and talks, Morley. Too many people have and have wound up with Bristoll's blade in their guts. Which reminds me, you ought to learn how to use a sword—but of course you'll never need to know that, will you?"

Now Dale watched Bristoll's eyes travel slowly, disdainfully, from his feet to his face and he felt a flush start at the other man's barely disguised sneer. He told himself he shouldn't have come here. His clothes might be right, but there was something else that he lacked and which men like Bristoll could pick out at once and smirk at.

For a moment, he was tempted to turn and make his escape from

49

the double scrutiny he found himself undergoing, the girl's speculative, the man's insulting, and then he set his jaw and met young Bristoll's gaze squarely. The man half-blocked the doorway to the room beyond and Bristoll showed no inclination to move aside to let Dale pass. For half a breath, Dale hesitated and then kept on his way. As he came up to Bristoll and the full-mouthed girl he made a brief bow, knowing it was awkward.

"Your pardon," he said. "I'm looking for Captain Claiborne. Could you direct me?"

Talbot Bristoll's mouth curled as he returned Dale's bow with a practiced sweep. Straightening, he whisked the handkerchief across the upturned tip of his nose, as though inhaling perfume to rid his nostrils of a barnyard odor. Dale felt the muscle at one corner of his mouth jump sharply as a surge of black anger rushed up within him.

"The Captain is about, somewhere," Bristoll said in a languid, girlish voice. "But as you can see, he's entertaining. I doubt that he wishes to be bothered."

There it was, the direct insult. Dale could take exception to it and thereby take his own life as certainly as if he were to stab himself through the heart. By making a move that would give Bristoll a chance to claim cause for a duel—and the man obviously was looking for just that—Dale could offer himself up to this young killer's sword like a man kneeling to put his head on the block.

Or he could accept the insult and live—until he learned how to use a sword himself; not so perfectly as Bristoll, perhaps, but well enough to kill this pretty boy.

The blood was pounding behind his eyes with aching fury, there was a roaring in his ears, but the mechanism of Dale's brain amazed him by clicking dispassionately as it held his temper in check.

He essayed another bow.

"My name is Morley, Dale Morley," he explained. "Captain Claiborne invited me to supper tonight. If I could find him—"

"Ah, yes," Bristoll murmured. "Well, doubtless one of the servants can direct you. Now, as I was saying, Jenny—"

50

He turned his back on Dale in a smooth pivot that placed him between Morley and the girl. He was flirting the lace handkerchief again, in the manner of a man brushing away a bothersome fly.

"And there you are," called a voice from over Dale's shoulder. He turned to see Captain Claiborne. The blue suit the Captain had worn earlier that evening had been exchanged for an outfit of black silk that caught the gleam of the candles and sconces and sent the brilliance back in a thousand shifting highlights. Another sword, more delicate and more finely chased than the weapon he had drawn on Dale a few hours before, hung from a sash of deep maroon. In place of a falling band, Claiborne wore a wide, high ruff that was blindingly white against his black suit and dark beard.

His bright eyes moved from Dale to Talbot Bristoll. If he had caught any of the by-play that had preceded his arrival, he gave no sign. His bow to Morley was as courtly as though he had not held his blade an inch from Dale's face just a short while ago.

"Welcome, Dale Morley," he said, and seemed to mean it. Dale essayed an answering bow that was a slight improvement over the awkward bob he had made to Bristoll and that young fop's lady. Learning how to bow correctly, finding out how and when to say the gracious things that appeared to be expected, would take time. Well, he had plenty of time and—damn all, he was forgetting Susan again.

"Have you met Mistress Loman?" Claiborne went on. "Talbot, did you do the honors in my absence?"

Mistress Loman, then, was the girl in the yellow and green gown, the one Bristoll had called Jenny. He turned and found the dark-eyed girl's eyes on him again. He noticed that this Mistress Loman wore her kerchief opened wide at the throat and tucked into the low bodice of her dress in such a way that there was no missing the fact that she was possessor of a pair of breasts that rose proudly to meet his gaze.

Unconsciously, he ran his tongue over his lips. By God, there were

51

two melons that seemed to be asking for plucking! But he had to stop thinking things like that. He was with the gentry now, not in a London alley or a field beside a haystack. Women such as this Loman girl were no randy flop-to-the-floor sluts or—and he had the grace to wince inwardly at the thought—unknowing farm girls, either. These women demanded careful, delicate handling, with graceful words and even poetry. They had to be told in whispers that they were the most beautiful, the sweetest morsels in all Christendom. To win the rewards they had to offer, a man would have to know just when the gentle pressure of a handclasp was proper and when a kiss might be shared behind a fan. A man would have to think up new, clever ways to say the things he meant; he would have to take a role in a lengthy, involved bit of play-acting that would require talents a Dale Morley didn't own; talents he would have to cultivate.

"I saw you in the hallway," Talbot Bristoll was saying, "and hesitated to steal that privilege from my host with him so close at hand."

That was what he would have to learn, Dale thought; that nimbleness of wit that could carry him through any situation with such natural ease. If he had been in Bristoll's place, he would have stuttered and stumbled, letting Caliborne know he had been rude to one of the Captain's guests. But Talbot Bristoll was as casually self-assured as though it had all happened just as he told it.

"And it is a great privilege, indeed," the Captain said. "Mistress Loman, may I present my friend, one of the new planters of the James Valley, Dale Morley?"

The girl's curtsey was low and Dale stared down at the shadow that marked the division of that arrogant bosom. He almost sucked in his breath at the sight of all that beauty revealed, but he stopped himself in time, and just in time.

"And Mister Talbot Bristoll," Captain Claiborne said. "One of my lustiest lieutenants when there's Indian fighting to be done, eh, Talbot?"

52

Bristoll flaunted his lace handkerchief at the Captain in a gesture that was purely feminine.

"Your kindness smacks of flattery, Captain," he said in his girlish voice. "The whole Province knows there's but one truly lusty Indian fighter in Virginia and his name, I fear, is Claiborne, not Bristoll."

He emitted a high-pitched laugh, showing his strong, yellow teeth.

"Although," he added, "I've had the luck to test the story that Indian squaws never cry out, no matter where they're given a taste of the sword—and found it false."

He was a dauncey darling, this Talbot Bristoll with his limp wrist and his dangling kerchief. There was something else, too, that fed Dale's loathing; the curl to Bristoll's fleshy lips, the quicksilver light in those tired eyes when he spoke of his experiments with Indian squaws. Claiborne had said that Bristoll's warpath tactics were often grisly and Dale could believe it now. To boast about torturing a woman, even an Indian squaw—he shook his head openly, despite himself.

Talbot Bristoll's eyes quickened again as they took in Dale's gesture.

"You doubt I disproved the story, Mister Morley?" he purred.

"Oh no," Dale said. "It was just—I was thinking of something else."

"And who could keep his mind on Indian fighting with all this loveliness about?" Captain Claiborne broke in. He put his hand to Dale's elbow and turned him toward the girl. "Dear Genevieve," he said. "Be a treasure, as always, and show my friend about the house, have him meet some people and see that he gets some food and drink. Captain Martiau is here with some tiresome business that must be cared for now. He sails up the Chesapeake tomorrow and this can't wait. You can be my hostess."

"But hostess for this supper only, mind," Talbot Bristoll warned, with a whinny of laughter. "Don't carry your pleasant duties too far, Jenny."

53

The girl smiled as Dale stared. He had thought that she would flush or show anger at the leering remark, but evidently ladies of quality could laugh at that kind of comment, probably because they knew themselves to be inviolate, so undeserving of the taunt that they need take no offense.

Genevieve Loman's hand was light on his arm and he could smell the warm spice of her perfume as she moved to his side. She still held the glass she had been sipping from when she first saw him and now she raised it to her full lips and drained its contents before she spoke.

"Our first port of call," she said, "will be the wine table, I think, Captain. Your Mister Morley looks parched and as for me, I'll confess that every sip I take of that wonderful sack makes me want two more. I'll be quite undone before the night's over, I know, but if I am, I'll shamelessly admit that my undoing was all my own doing."

There was another high-pitched laugh from Bristoll as Genevieve Loman moved toward the main room whence flowed the steady torrent of sound that testified to the success of Captain Claiborne's supper party. The clavichord was jangling tinnily and a man's voice, soaring above the hubbub, was roaring out a song. Dale caught a fragment of the roundelay.

> . . . *wine makes the thoughts aspire,*
> *And fills the heart with heat,*
> *And not only the heart; another part,*
> *Is warmed and made complete.*

A set of dancers were pacing through their steps at the far end of the room, trying to keep to the uncertain beat of the clavichord. The dancers were flushed and perspiring; now and then one would lurch in a half-stagger before going on with the measure. The girl who was playing swayed on the bench. She was an extraordinarily homely woman with a thatch of coarse red hair that hung down over her freckled cheeks in lank strands. A man in sober brown broadcloth, hanging over the end of the keyboard, said something

54

to the red-haired woman as Dale watched and the girl put back her head to whoop with shrill laughter that ended in a fit of coughing and disrupted the music altogether.

At the end of the room opposite the place where the dancers went through their gyrations, a group of men and women contributed their babble to the general uproar. Genevieve Loman guided Dale in that direction.

"There's the wine table and the collation," she said, "and I, for one, am both hungry and thirsty. You shall feed me and pour me a glass, Dale Morley, and then there will be time to meet the people who interest you."

She gave him a sidelong glance from under the thick fringe of dark lashes that outlined her eyes.

"Strange I haven't met you before this," she murmured. "I'd thought I'd met all of Captain Claiborne's friends in the Colony; all but those great bearish creatures with deerhide coats such as work his trade routes for him, that is. Is that where you've been, Friend Morley; in the wilderness making your fortune trading with the Indians?"

"No," Dale replied. He tried valiantly to keep his eyes from returning to that valley between the girl's breasts. "I'm no trader, or Indian fighter either, like Bristoll. I'm—uh—I'm just an ordinary planter."

"Of course," the girl said lightly. "Captain Claiborne said you were a planter, didn't he? A newcomer to the James Valley, did he say?"

"Eh—yes."

Well, he was a newly-created freedman, at any rate, and if it suited the Captain to skip the four years he had been in Virginia as an indentured servant, Dale didn't intend to raise the issue, certainly.

"Welcome, then, to these parts, Friend Morley," Genevieve said, "and—ah, here's the wine table. I'll have the sack and naught else, please."

Behind the table, laden with decanters, jugs, demijohns and bottles, stood a black man in demi-livery. Whereas the slave who had taken Dale's horse had been a giant, this Negro was so small as almost to be a dwarf. Dale had only to look on for a moment to see that what the little man lacked in size he made up in dexterity. No matter how fast and how many were the orders hurled at him in that pandemonium, the black kept pace with the demands, his hands flashing among the vari-sized containers, grabbing up this one and returning that one to its place, keeping the glasses brimming and never slopping a drop of wine or liquor onto the spotless sanded board.

A few feet from the wine table was the sideboard where rested the hams and cold fowl, the sausages and cheeses, the pickled eggs and the minced mutton, the roast of beef all blood-red in its center and charred at its edges, the herrings in their vinegar and spices, the great smoked salmon with flesh as red as the beef and the smoked cod tongues that had been brought down from the north.

Tending the sideboard was another slave, a tall, slender man with sharp features that went oddly with his dark skin. A Haitian or a Barbadoes man by the looks of him, Dale thought, one of the blacks most highly regarded as house servants, butlers and such but too much of a luxury for most slave-owners because of their inability—or unwillingness—to do a decent day's work in the fields. The sideboard attendant wielded a long, gleaming knife as he worked on the hams and the roasts, the salmon and the fowl, the steel slipping purposefully through the meat, with a skill that matched the tiny Negro's talent with the bottles and glasses.

Dale edged closer to the wine table, his eyes busy. These might be cavaliers and their ladies, but they ate like ordinary human beings, anyway. They reached for slices of beef as they fell from the up-standing ribs and crammed the meat into their champing mouths; they grabbed up capon drumsticks and chunks of cheese, they dipped the spiced herrings out of their brine and added them to the bulging cuds they already were working on. Men and women alike ate with

56

sauces and juices dribbling down their chins, to be wiped away by a lace cuff, a kerchief or, on occasion, the back of a hand. When a man or woman came too close to choking there was always a long draught of wine at hand to sluice the gullet, clear the way for more tremendous mouthfuls. And while they ate, steadily, ravenously, somehow they found the time and a way to talk, over and around and through their food.

"—and she took the wager, hoisted her skirts and rode the horse like a man. Damnedest thing I ever saw. Lucky it was a moonlight night or she'd have broken her neck. She won the wager, too; covered the distance with minutes to spare. Harry, though, said later he'd won a wager bigger than what he had to pay her, betting he'd have her lifting her skirts before midnight. Eyah-haw-haw!"

Which woman was that, Dale asked himself, who had done such a thing? Which of these girls would ride a horse man-fashion and probably show everything she owned to all who would look? Or which one wouldn't?

"—have it straight that the Devil's spawn intends to petition His Majesty for a grant here in Virginia. Not that we'll ever have him or any of his kind, but there'll be trouble yet with Baltimore and his tribe. Man I know in London writes—"

"—and a beautiful gown it was too, love. *She* said her brother sent it to her from London and I nearly laughed in her face when she told me that. Everybody in the Province knows who measured her for that cloth, love."

The talk billowed about Dale, rising in crescendo, making his ears buzz with confusion as he tried to capture every word that flew past him. If he felt any disappointment in the fact that these people acted like this, talked like this, swilled and guzzled like this, so ordinary when he had thought them so untouchable, Dale did not admit it to himself. Indeed, by their hoggish eating, their frantic, sniggering talk, their rising drunkenness, their constant interchange of aphrodisiac half-approaches and half-acceptances, these men and their ladies brought themselves closer to Dale, down from the Olympus

57

where his mind had placed them. They had learning he did not possess and money he did not own, but to these men, as to him, a woman was no more than a soft body that contained ineffable delight when suitably employed. And to these women, as to other women Dale had known, a set of broad shoulders, a lean middle and a pair of big hands that could stroke or bruise meant more, sometimes, than a title or even a fat purse.

He wrenched his mind away from these thoughts to take care of his errand at the wine table. The little Negro deftly filled two beakers with the limpid sack and he began to make his way back to Jenny Loman. She took the glass he offered and rapped the knuckles of his hand gently with her fan.

"That's for nearly forgetting me," she said. "I thought I'd perish of thirst before you came back. What happened? Did you meet some beautiful lady who bewitched you? That Bett Spears, perhaps? She's supposed to be the most beautiful woman in the Colony, you know."

"I don't know who Mistress Spears is," Dale replied, "but—uh— I have the most beautiful woman in the Colony right here with me."

It was his first attempt at a speech like that and he thought it was not too bad. That blurped hiccough with which he had launched the compliment would never have come from a gentleman like Talbot Bristoll, perhaps, but the girl didn't seem to notice it.

Genevieve Loman sipped at her glass, her restless eyes roving over the crowded room. When she brought down her hand a drop of wine trembled on her lower lip and Dale saw her pointed tongue dart out to wipe it away.

She laid a hand briefly on his arm.

"You'll have to watch out for me, Friend Dale," she said softly. "I'm apt to do silly things, once the wine has captured my head, and I might need a—a protector."

Ah, so? A protector, is it, that you think you'll need, really? Or— but he had resolved to be cautious. He made his reply with a deep bow, the neatest yet. Aye, he was learning.

"Honored," he said, because that was a word that could scarcely

58

do him any harm and the girl could make of it anything it pleased her wine-tilted mind to do. The short words were the best, the safest.

The man who had been bawling out the roundelay abandoned it abruptly and lurched through the crowd up to Genevieve Loman and Dale. His wig was awry, his falling band spotted with wine and food; his round, pug-nosed face was bright red and dripping with perspiration.

"Ah, Jenny," he said, "we were to have a duet, remember, and then you deserted me. I had to raise my sweet voice alone, with Chrissy Gauer hitting all the wrong notes with her thumbs, God bless her! You're cruel, Jenny, both to me and the ears of my audience."

He grinned at Dale, his small blue eyes friendly. He had the face and roly-poly figure of an overgrown baby and Dale liked the man immediately. His grin was the first honest, open greeting Morley had received in this place and it was refreshing to meet a person who did not seem to be maneuvering at the start for either a duel or a bed.

"Don't think I know y'r friend, Jenny," the chubby man said. "Take care of the honors, pol, do."

"Mister Thomas Tindall, Mister Dale Morley," Genevieve Loman said, her tone indulgent. "You two gentlemen are neighbors, I think."

No bow this time, although Dale had begun shifting his balance to get that left foot back as nicely as he had the previous time. Instead of bending at the middle, and possibly because he was afraid of his uncertain equilibrium, Thomas Tindall thrust out his hand to be shaken.

Dale hesitated for a split second and then joined the handclasp. It was the first time he ever had shaken hands. He liked the feeling. Beside it, a bow was a graceful thing, but as empty as a court fool's bladder, meaning nothing. In this gesture, the most practiced courtier could do no more than the least-graced peasant and, to Dale,

59

there was something good about that. He hoped the custom would catch on, even though he meant some day to be as clever with a bow as Talbot Bristoll.

"Certainly, certainly," Thomas Tindall was chortling. "I've heard Captain Claiborne speak your name often, sir. Wonderful man, the Captain. He beats me bankrupt in every game I play against him and still I love him. Honored to meet you. Jenny, you're more dazzling than ever, truly. They're makin' up a new dance set. Join us? No? Well, later on, perhaps. Night's just begun, eh? Ah, Mistress Caroline, join me, do, in a . . ."

He bumbled away, smiling, sweaty, happy with an exuberance that could not all have been due to the wine. So that was the Thomas Tindall Claiborne had so often spoken of; the enormously wealthy young man who, though he couldn't keep count of the cards in his head or put a winning cock in a main, was a member of the Virginia Assembly and a worthy man in a debate and at drafting a new law, too.

"Dear Tommy," Genevieve Loman was saying. "He has the voice of a jackdaw but he will sing. He treads a step like a coach horse, but he must dance. He would be the greatest beau in the Province, but he is forever calling the lady he would win by her most hated rival's name, just at the wrong time. And everybody loves him, in spite of all that. But let's at some more wine—brandy for you, Friend Dale—and some food. These gluttons will empty even Captain Claiborne's larder before we get a bite, unless we hurry."

She ate, he was glad to see, a great deal more daintily than most of the other women. She used her fingers, as did the rest, but she took small bites with her white, sharp teeth and she was careful of her chin. Dale ate little; not because the outlay of food did not make his mouth flood, but because the less he ate, the slimmer the chance that he might drop some huge gobbet of food down his front or gum the corners of his mouth with sauce or swallow something the wrong way and, like as not, suffer an appalling eruption that would
60

make him an outcast forever. The others around the sideboard did not seem to care how much they dripped and drizzled, but they were established, they were quality, they could belch and cough, hiccough and choke, with utter unconcern at what the blacks attending the tables might think.

The slaves (he had learned by this time that the little one was called Benji and the tall meat-carver, Toss) bothered him. He knew they were only pieces of property, worth so many pounds of tobacco, dockside, but he still tried to keep his scarred, calloused hands with their broken nails away from the glances of the two blacks. And that, he reasoned, was foolish, because he always had been better than those two.

And yet . . . if Negroes hated, their eyes did not show it. If they complained, they kept their complaints out of a white man's hearing. They were as quick to laugh as they were to weep, they worked until told to stop, ate, slept, begot. Certainly there was no dignity to their lives as slaves and yet Dale had seen the tall man, Toss, look out over the tumbled, noisy throng with the air of a high-bred person overlooking a rabble, not liking what he saw but capable of understanding that these people were not to be blamed too harshly because they knew no better.

Now, by God, there was a thought! The mixture of sack and brandy had been too potent, that was all.

He took the girl's glass and made his way through the crowd to the wine table; thrust the glasses at Benji.

"A sack and a brandy," he growled, to show this black man that he, Dale Morley, was a white and a freedman. "And hurry it, you hear?"

The slave showed white teeth in a grin, splashed the drinks into the glasses with his miraculous skill and handed them back.

"Sack and brandy, sir," Benji said in his liquid voice, and turned to fill another order.

61

After that, there were more drinks and more food. The crowded room grew hotter, the talk louder, the breast-crease that showed over Genevieve Loman's gown, longer and deeper. He met other gentlemen and ladies, made his bows, exchanged words with the others, laughed at their witticisms and heard them laugh at—was that Dale Morley who had turned a phrase so neatly?

Genevieve disappeared and he found himself talking to the red-haired girl with the leathery skin who had played the clavichord. She was almost completely drunk now, her mouth sliding loosely from side to side as she clutched his arm and swayed against him.

"Chrissy Gauer's m'name," she burbled. "I play for the dancin'. Only reason 'm asked any place, I'll be bound, and I know it but I go anyway. Go anywhere, anytime, where there's good wine and good food and no snoopin' churchwarden to tell me nay."

She peered up at him from out of red-rimmed eyes.

"You a churchwarden?" she demanded.

"God, no!" Dale laughed. "Do I look like one?"

She swayed as she leaned back to look up at him again.

"Well, no," she said, after a moment, "but I don' know you, y'see. Y'might be one or y'might be Sir Thomas Gates as a boy, f'r all I know."

She tittered, clung to his arm, thrust herself against him. Her breath was as unpleasant as her gnarled, stained teeth as she grinned crookedly at him. Before he could reply, he felt a hand on his shoulder and heard Captain Claiborne's quiet voice in his ear.

"I hope you're enjoying yourself," the Captain said. "I'm a poor host, surely, to leave my little supper party before it has fairly begun, but Captain Martiau's business would bear no putting-off."

He noted Dale's uneven stare and tightened his grip unobtrusively to steady him against his sway as they moved aside.

"You'd best plan to stay the night," Claiborne said. "It's growing late and you've a long ride, a new horse."

"B-by your leave," Dale managed, "I'll ride me back to—to *my plantation.*"

Captain Claiborne smiled imperturbably as Dale scowled, trying to remember just how he had been so clever in emphasizing those last two words.

"Oh, that," the Captain said lightly. "Well, you do plant things, don't you? What would you—that I give Mistress Genevieve a full accounting, starting with Aunt Bess?"

He clapped a hand lightly to Dale's shoulder.

"Show a smile, Dale," he said. "Here in Virginia, if I say you have a plantation, you have one, even if a person could spit from one side of it to the other. Ah, I'm not boasting. A thing fitted here and another there and I watched my chance to be in the right place at the right time and finally I got my unjust reward, by being commissioned Secretary of the Province. Anyone could have done the same thing. You can do the same thing, I swear, or more."

He paused and touched his mustaches with the tip of a long forefinger.

"If you'll let me help you," he added. "If you'll not fight me at every turn—question my every motive."

Groping into the fumes of the wine and brandy, Dale clutched the thought that this was his chance to ask the question Susan had raised. He tried to steady himself, hold himself erect, throw off his drunkenness.

"But why," he asked, "why do you duh-do these things for me? Wh-why do you help me?"

Claiborne's eyes were two live coals, set in the peep-holes of a blank mask. Or perhaps it was the drink that made him seem like that. Then the mask broke into the component parts of the Captain's pointed face.

"That would take more telling than I could give you here," he said. "I'll talk to you later, in a quieter place."

Dale hesitated, uncertain, wavering. Claiborne's hand came out again and touched him gently.

"Do this for me," he urged. "I'm not much in the habit of asking favors of this kind but I do, this once. Go to the office—it's just off that hall there—and wait for me. I'll bring a demijohn of brandy that we can finish between us. There's much I'd talk over with you, if your head's clear enough to listen."

Claiborne's hand steered the big, black-haired youth in the right direction and Dale found himself treading an uncertain course toward the hall the Captain had indicated. The brandy churned in his stomach, warring with the spiced foods, and for a moment he thought he was going to be sick. Then the wave of nausea passed and his head cleared long enough for him to make his way to the office that opened off the hall. He tumbled inside the small room and banged the door closed behind him. Suddenly, he wanted to be rid of that hammering cacophony that flooded the main room, the jangle of the clavichord played by somebody not even as gifted as the drunken Chrissy Gauer, the whooping shouts of the men and the squealed laughter of the women. Here in the office the air held little of the wine and perfume smells that had made the main hall reek. He dropped into a chair and let his eyes rove around the room.

The walls were covered with maps, some old and yellowed, others fresh and crisply drawn. He focused his eyes on the nearest chart and, after an interval, deciphered its tracings. He took one of the candles from the desk and held it close to the map.

He was walking over to another chart when the door opened and the Captain entered, carrying a decanter and two silver mugs. He shot a glance at Dale, by the wall, and then moved to the desk to put down his burden.

"Looking at my maps, eh?" he asked. "I pride myself that it's the most complete set of charts in these parts. And true charts, too."

Dale walked to the desk to replace the candlestick and pick up the mug Claiborne had filled.

The brandy was good; better than the liquor Benji was handing out in the main room. Dale sipped it again and thought it cleared his head still more. Claiborne moved to the chair in front of the desk and sat down, waving his mug at Dale in an invitation for his guest to take the other chair.

64

The amenities disposed of, Claiborne studied him gravely. At length he broke the silence.

"I told you once, I think," the Captain began, "that my secretaries and clerks were a pack of brainless ink-spillers. I know that some of those I've had have spied on me for my enemies. I need a man I can trust; a man I can teach to do things the way I want them jone. You know how to read and write—not much, perhaps, but enough for a start, and I'll provide for more teaching. Be my clerk, my lieutenant. Travel with me and keep my journal and my accounts. Sit beside me in the Assembly. Live here at this place while I'm in Jamestown. Go with me to London. By God, I'll show you women there!

"I'll show you more than that. I'll show you a place on the Potomac River where the water comes roaring down a mile or more of steep falls. I'll show you the island at the top of the Chesapeake where the Susquehannocks live. You'll see the villages of the Pascataways,where they hold a ceremony, a dance, once a year and God must join hands with the Devil there that day because the dance is as holy as a communion and as randy as a bawd's ball, at one and the same time."

The light from the candles on the desk struck sharp shadows into Claiborne's lean face as he bent toward Dale. His voice was low and intense.

"What more can you want?" he asked. "I see you hesitate. Is it because you can't bear to leave those scrubby acres of yours? Or is it that you think I'll be a harsh master?"

"No," Dale said. "No, it's none of that."

"Then what ties your tongue? What keeps you from saying yes?"

The last drinks of brandy had cleared Dale's head, or at least had revived his memory. While the Captain had been outlining the delights he had to offer there had been a shape steadily emerging from the mists that had clouded his brain. The figure was short, solid, inexorable. As Claiborne spoke of London, the falls of the Potomac, the rites of the Pascataways, the face of the woman emerging from the fog defined itself now and she seemed to be smiling up at him again and asking him if Bella's colts would bring him enough to pay for a cradle.

"It's not the farm—the plantation," Dale said heavily. "I'm to marry Susan Willison."

Claiborne waved a hand, the lace at his cuff swinging with the movement.

"That!" he scoffed. "Give Thomas Willison back his fifty acres —I'll find you fifty times fifty—and you'll be clear of all that. You're not going to tie yourself to a wife, a planter's lass, at your age, are you? And miss all of this I offer?"

He reached forward to tap Dale's knee.

"Look you, Dale," he said. "Come with me for a year. Just that. There'll be no contract, no papers signed. If, at the end of the year you want to go back to your farm and your peasant girl, you'll go with my blessing and a fat purse to make up for the time you spent with me. What more would you?"

Dale drained his cup and placed it carefully on the desk beside Captain Claiborne's. He stood up, rubbing his broad palms down the side of his legs, unmindful of the grease stains they might make on the rich cloth.

"I thank ye," he said, reaching cautiously for the right words, "but I'm to marry Mistress Willison. It—it has to be soon, Captain Claiborne."

There was a silence in the small office, with the noise from outside muted momentarily in one of those inexplicable pauses that settle over all gatherings of its kind, at times. In the quiet, Dale saw Claiborne grip his mug until the knuckles whitened. The Captain's teeth were together as he ground out the words:

"So she caught you, eh? And she doesn't know the kind of rabbit she's snared, I'll vow!"

He recovered himself immediately. The blood flowed back into his knuckles and the hard lines that had sprung to his face disappeared, as though a painter had wiped a cloth over wet work that
66

had displeased him. He reached for the decanter again as Dale watched him; splashed more brandy into the mugs.

"Sit down, Morley," he said. "There's reason to drink now—to your happiness. A husband and a father, at one and the same time, eh? Oh, don't push your lip at me, man! There's nothing strange in that. While men are as they are and women are women it will happen, and nobody the worse for it. Drink your drink."

He took his own and regarded Dale over the rim of his cup as Morley slowly lowered himself to his chair again. The music, the shouting, the turmoil of talk started up again, louder than ever, in the main room.

"There's no reason why you still can't be my clerk, though," Claiborne said. "Your marriage doesn't have to change that. I'll give you and the new Dame Morley a better living than you could scrape out of that cockleburr patch in a century. It might even be better this way. The lady taught you your letters and your numbers, you've told me, and she could help you with the accounts you'd keep. I'll have a house built in Jamestown for you and while you're away with me, she can take a hand with the copying, if she's so minded."

"I—I don't think—"

"You think she'd refuse to move to Jamestown, eh?" the Captain broke in. "Or don't you think she'd help you with your new work?"

"It's not that," Dale said haltingly. "She—uh—she's partial to farm life and—and she"—he swallowed and blurted out the next—"she is mistrustful of your purposes in helping me, Captain."

Claiborne seemed to take Dale's statement without surprise. One of the candles on the desk began to smoke and he leaned over to snip the wick with a pair of brass shears. The flame bobbled and then rose again, strong and clear, as the dead wick fell.

"Oh, yes," the Captain said. "It was to be expected, maybe. Her father, Thomas Willison, and I have had our outs in certain dealings, though we're friendly enough now, and who could be less than friendly with that round litle man, eh? But he may have told his daughter I was Satan in a silk suit, at one time or another, for all I know."

67

He leaned back in his chair, one hand touching the slashes of the other arm's puffed doublet sleeves, the long prehensile fingers plucking at the cloth.

"But she'll change her mind, Dale, once I've spoken with her," he said. "I take some pride in being able to guess what the ladies want to hear and in putting it as neatly as any man who spends half his time in the wilderness can. Once I talk with her and give her a glimpse of her chance to wear fine dresses and meet great people she'll be hot to go with you to Jamestown. Not a woman alive but'll forgive almost anything for a chance to dance a *pavane* or step the measures of a *courante,* my boy."

Dale frowned dubiously. He could not paint the picture of Susan Willison showing any interest in a dance or fine clothes or anything, in fact, besides the damned chickens and sheep and cows and corn she had her stubborn mind set on. By God, Susan would rather stay up all night attending the dropping of a calf than spend the hours in a gathering like this. As for fine dresses, he could not imagine her comfortable in the stiff satin or whispering silk these women wore. As for her carrying on a conversation with these people who gave two meanings to nearly everything they said—he shook his head.

"I—I don't know," he told Captain Claiborne.

Claiborne had been leaning back in the heavy oak armchair and now he brought its front feet down with a jarring thud.

"Then, by the forgotten saints," he barked, "it's time you found out! 'I don't know,' 'I don't know'—what kind of mewling talk is that? You're to marry this—this lady, aren't you? You'll be her husband, won't you—or is she going to be yours? Will you have the say, or will she? What kind of petticoat ties will you let her put through your nose, Dale Morley?"

He left his chair and began pacing up and down the small office, his shadow on the far wall a grotesque, misshapen thing.

"I offer you a chance to better your position and your purse," he declaimed. "I promise you adventure and gold and women—ah, you'll be like any other married man and want a change from cold mutton, in time, Morley! It's an opportunity any other man in the Province would leap at, like a salmon to a smelt, and what do you do? You sit in your chair, squeezing your knees together like a maiden about to dampen her skirts, and say you don't know."

He threw out a hand. The shadow made the gesture an enormous sweep by some giant's club.

"Forget all this, then," Claiborne rapped out. "Forget I ever thought you could make anything of your life besides a bent-backed existence on a James River farm. Run to your Mistress Willison, Dale Morley, and tell her the wicked William Claiborne tempted you but you resisted, by God, and you're still pure and ready to do her bidding. I was mistaken, I see. I thought you were a man who wanted to taste life, not gnaw on the bones the others leave you. You're willing to glower and mutter and make faces, as though there were no more dangerous a man in all Virginia to cross, but when the dice are handed you to make your throw you drop the cup, lest your lady might not like your toss."

He walked to the desk, picked up his mug and drained it.

"Pfa!" he said, the word loaded with contempt. "I'll have Talbot Bristoll as my lieutenant, instead of you!"

"Not that man!" Dale said impulsively.

"And why not?" Claiborne demanded. "Certainly, he talks like a maid and walks like one, too, but he can read and write, after a fashion, and somebody else can do the accounting. His scribble might look like two wild doves chasing each other across paper with inked feet, but he doesn't wait on any woman's whimsey."

"He boasts of cutting Indian squaws," Dale muttered.

"So that riles you, too, eh?" Claiborne sneered. "God, I've got a faint-hearted thing here! Where I'd take you, if you didn't have to run for the shelter of a woman's skirts, you might see things that'd make you think Bristoll didn't do enough. There are no prissy-mouthed, sister-loving things out there in the wilderness, Morley. My men are no Captain John Smiths who can have an Indian wench save them from torture. The men I've lost—the ones I've found

69

again, too late—couldn't have wished for any Pocahontas. All they wished for was death, and that as soon as it could come to them."

He glanced up at Dale and then turned his eyes to the decanter. "You'd have no stomach for that, I know," he said.

Dale felt the muscles tightening and flexing beneath his skin. His inner self crawled with the need to get out of this shell, this man who sat in a suit of clothes that had been lent him, this big body that was tied to a fork and a rake and a hoe and a squatty girl who'd have a big belly in another month or so; this Dale Morley who'd spend the rest of his life with cow-droppings on his shoes and the senseless cackle of chickens in his ears.

"I could find out," he said carefully. "I could find out whether or not I had the stomach for it."

There was a pause as Captain Claiborne kept his eyes fixed on Morley. Then the Captain reached for his cup.

"Well, now," he said thoughtfully, "you surprise me, I confess. I put the goad to you to make you boast and you hold your tongue. Would the lad I met at your place on that rainy night have done that, I wonder? I have my doubts of that, and that would mean that you're learning something of what I'm like."

He seemed to be musing as he looked down into his cup.

"Would you could come with me, Morley," he said in an absent voice. "Oh, you'd find me a strange man to work with, at times. My enemies call me undependable, saddled with a Devil's temper. I'll admit my patience, my forbearance, are not my strongest virtues. My tongue's too quick to move and I've done injury to those who might not have deserved it, when I've been in a rage."

His dark eyes swung up to meet Dale's.

"You'd have to learn to watch my moods, Dale," he continued, "and shun me like the plague when I'm hag-ridden by a dark spell. Yes, you'd have cause to hate me at times, I'll warrant, but you'd have reason to—love me, too. You'd be rewarded and well rewarded, for your loyalty to me."

He leaned back in the heavy oak chair again.

70

"And you'd pay for any disloyalty in like measure," he said. "Others who have tried treachery with me have found that out. I'm not a gentle man, Morley, but I'm appreciative of a man's faithfulness, his sword beside mine in a fight, and I would strip my house, my purse and my body for him if 'twould help him."

His hand went to the cup.

"Mistress Willison is distrustful of my motives, eh?" he asked. "There's a woman for you, boy. If the gates of Heav'n were flung wide for any one of them, she'd look beyond the threshold carefully, by God, to make certain the Guardian Angel was not tricking her. Christ's thorns, do I have to fill a ledger with an account of why I like a man and want to help him?"

"She—she doesn't understand," Dale offered. "And, as I've told you, she has her heart set on my becoming a planter."

Captain Claiborne slowly shook his head, emitted a long sigh. His hand went out for the nearly empty decanter as he spoke.

"Well, that's your word and that's an end to it, I suppose. This won't ruin our friendship, though—or, at least, I'll be as good a friend to you as your wife permits. Come, there's enough here for another dram. We'll drink to your great success—as a planter. All fine crops and never another frost or drought."

"A minute, Captain," Dale said. "You—you misunderstand. I— if you'll have me, I want to go with you. No matter what Su—what anyone says, I want to be your lieutenant, if the offer holds."

"It holds," William Claiborne said. "And pray God you never have cause to be sorry it does. Your cup, Dale, for the most important drink you've ever poured down your gullet."

The fumes of the rich brandy were sweet in Dale's nostrils as he raised the beaker. From now on, everything would be like this; fine drink and heavy silver, handsome clothes and rare foods, a slave at Bella's bridle when he dismounted, women with smooth, unfreckled skin.

It would be good. All of it.

71

Susan Willison and Dale Morley were married in the church at Jamestown on a raw November day in 1628, with gray clouds in the northeast carrying a threat of snow.

Captain William Claiborne had almost complete charge of the whole affair. He might disapprove of Dale's marrying Susan except as an event made necessary by a biological accident but it was he who made the arrangements, he who drew up the lists of guests, he who had charge of the dinner party that followed the ceremony, he who even presented the bride with the bolt of russet satin from which Susan and her friends fashioned one of the loveliest wedding gowns ever seen in the Province.

Poor Thomas Willison, the bride's father, was shunted to an onlooker's bench during the preliminaries. The round-faced, dumpy little man may have set up some feeble protests at the start, claiming it was his duty to take care of the wedding details, but Willison had a respect for Claiborne that amounted almost to awe and the Captain had no trouble in easily, smoothly usurping the father's place in all but the ceremony itself.

"I'll take care of this," he was forever saying, "and it so happens I'm in a position to deal with that, Mister Willison, with no trouble at all, I assure you. As for this other thing, I've already given word for somebody to see to that."

Only once did Thomas Willison make a protest stand. That was when he discovered that Captain Claiborne had made plans for the wedding to be held at the new St. Luke's Brick Church, in the Isle of Wight Hundred.

"My daughter will be married in the church where I'm a vestryman," the little man said stoutly, "and in no other place."

As for Susan, she had been almost listless about the impending wedding.

"Whatever *your friend* decides," she had told Dale more than once, "will suit me. It'll have to suit me, I'll warrant; whatever *he* says."

He, of course, was Captain Claiborne and Susan Willison hated him as much as it lay within her ability to hate anyone, and that talent had developed in recent weeks, despite herself. Hating someone was a new thing for Susan and her acceptance of the black emotion surprised her at times. She always had thought that hatred was born of some great injustice and even then survived only by dint of careful nurturing. But this thing she felt toward Captain Claiborne had had no definite hurt to sire it and had thrived, unbidden and untended, in the secret recesses of her mind.

She had always been a simple girl, a plain girl, and her life, till then, had been an uninvolved process, no less happy because it was made up of the small things, the things that were as natural as eating and sleeping, warming oneself at a fire in cold weather and drinking deeply of cold well water in hot weather. Her love for Dale Morley had interrupted the placid span of her years; his blunt passion had stung and unnerved her when she first had encountered it. But even that unaccustomed frenzy, touched now and then with real ecstasy, had not changed her as much as her resentment against Captain William Claiborne was changing her, had changed her in the time between the night that Claiborne had come riding out of a summer storm and this, her wedding day.

She was marrying a man, the father of the child she carried within her ripening body, the only man she had let touch the hidden places of her body and her brain. Yet she had lost him before she could bear his name or his child and for that she blamed Claiborne more than she blamed Dale, or even herself.

Claiborne had given Dale things she could not match. She caught the shine of Dale's eyes when he had told her of the position that had been offered him as the Captain's clerk, about how the plate at Claiborne's supper party had been thick enough and heavy enough for the King's table itself.

"I can give your father back his fifty acres," he had told her. "Captain Claiborne will build us a house. It's like an old marm's fairy story, all of it, but it's true!"

"Why?" she had asked, flatly. "Why does he do all this? I keep asking that question but I never get an answer. Why?"

"Because—because he likes me," Dale had flung back at her.

"Christ's thorns, does he have to publish a tract with his reasons why he likes a man and wants to help him?"

Claiborne's words, not Dale's, Susan had known; but there could never be any proving that or her feeling that there must be something evil in a man of William Claiborne's power and position going to such lengths to change the life of a newly-freed indentured servant like Dale Morley.

It was an old conflict by the time of the wedding day and Susan Willison knew she had lost it, weeks before, after the day Dale had told her he was bound to be Claiborne's clerk with some sort of fabulous future, Indians to be fought, riches to be gained, ships to be sailed, lands to be explored, thick furs and corn and meat to be traded for gewgaws. How could a simple girl, beginning to swell with her man's ill-timed child, compete with that kind of picture?

So, eventually, she had acknowledged the inevitable. Silently, except for a bitter word dropped here and there, she accepted William Claiborne's invasion of her life and hopes. Her face grew thinner and her eyes took on a shadow but she never reproached Dale with more than an oblique word after that brief, wild flare-up that had followed his announcement that he intended to leave the farm and serve as Captain Claiborne's lieutenant.

She accepted the Captain's urbane interference in the wedding plans; she accepted her father's near groveling at all that Claiborne proposed; she accepted the bolt of russet satin; she even accepted Dale's asp-and-sparrow attitude, toward the last. She had a child who needed a church-recorded father and the thing stirring beneath her kirtle was more important than any of the wounds she might think she suffered. Maybe later—but she would be a fool indeed to think that a few words from the Book of Prayer would change anything. No, she had lost Dale to a man with a sharp black beard and a pair of bright black eyes; the man who everybody said would someday be Governor of Virginia.

The priest was a man just arrived from some foreign place to the north: the Reverend Richard James. From the looks of him, he was a man who put more thought on Hell than he did on Heaven and that probably was right because she must be doomed to Hell. The Reverend Richard James had only to look at her to tell she had sinned, by her fornication and by this hate she had for Claiborne. Perhaps he would even refuse to read the service over a woman as ungodly as she.

But when the time came, she left the pew with firm steps and lowered herself to kneel beside Dale in front of the small altar and the tall, spare priest. She made her responses and she was dimly conscious of Dale's deep voice echoing hers. Her hand was cold in Dale's as he slipped over her finger the ring Captain Claiborne had provided.

So this was the moment, then. This was the time that was to have been her happiest, except now it was all different from what she had imagined it and her thoughts were as gray as the skies in the northeast. It was a splendid wedding, she supposed dully, with the men on their side of the church wonderfully fine in their rich clothes and the women on their side as colorful a collection as ever had assembled in that church. There were a few gowns of cotton and flannel, a few suits of coarse worsted sprinkled through the crowd and these clothes marked the men and women who had been her friends and Dale's in the time when she had been so calmly certain that the man she loved loved her and would find an easement from his troubled mind in her love for him. The others, the gentlemen and the ladies, were mostly Claiborne's friends and, just recently, acquaintances of Dale's.

No use to ask why all this had happened to Dale and her. She was done with asking why. Her child had a name now and that was what mattered.

She held her smile during the supper party at Claiborne's home, responding to the toasts, eating the food, watching the dancing, listening to the compliments, seeing her father bob and grin and find the happiness in this occasion that she had missed, watching Dale fitting himself among these people in a way that belied the fact that

75

a few months before he had worn canvas and had scrabbled in the dirt for a livelihood.

Throughout the affair, Captain Claiborne attended her with a charm she could not deny, though she might hate him. His was the finger that brought a slave to her side with food and wine. His was the voice that kept alive a conversation that dealt with things and people she knew and could talk about. It was Captain Claiborne who led Susan through the measures of a simple dance set and it was Captain Claiborne who rescued her from one guest, far gone in wine and coarse-tongued on the subject of marriage beds, with a brief, smiling word that smoothed everything over without any pother or fuss.

It was close to the end of the party when Claiborne spoke of what was on his mind.

"Your husband, Dame Morley, has said you mistrusted me," he said in a quiet voice. "I hope he was wrong, or that you've changed your view."

Susan bit her lip and looked at the fan in her lap. A fan was a silly thing to be carrying, she thought, when the weather outside this place was almost bitter, but it was a beautiful thing, with a scene showing ladies and gentlemen and a fountain painted on it. A gift from Captain Claiborne, of course.

"There were—certain doubts," she murmured uncomfortably. "It was hard for me to see—"

Her voice trailed off uncertainly. Then her chin came up and she swung her head to look directly at the man beside her.

"I mistrusted you, yes," she said firmly. "If I still do it's—it's because I don't want to see Dale hurt. And I have a dread, Captain Claiborne, that he'll be hurt—through you."

The black eyes flickered for an instant, but Claiborne's smile held steady.

"Believe me, Dame Morley," he said, his voice spiked with earnestness, "I think a great deal of Dale. I think more highly of him than some might understand. I think of him like a—a—"

76

"Son?" Susan asked squarely. "Dale never knew his father, you know."

Claiborne's eyes were mocking now as he met the girl's gaze.

"I know that," he said, nodding, "but I can't lay claim to being Dale's father, truly. No, my admiration and affection for your husband can't be laid to any blood ties, much as I'd welcome that."

He left his chair and stood before her, resplendent in a suit of plum-colored silk, his lean hand held out toward her.

"The hour's growing late," he said gently, "and I know you're tired. I'm a thoughtless man to keep a couple from their bridal chamber with my blathering. The skiff's been ready for an hour. One of my men will sail you up-river. It's a chill night but there will be plenty of coverings. If it were any occasion but this, I'd insist that you two spend the night here."

"Oh, no!" Susan said sharply. "I—we—must go home!"

He nodded, his eyes somber.

"Of course," he said. "And I wish you every happiness, Dame Morley, even though you'll not be my friend. Perhaps, in time—but here I am holding up the joyful excursion again with my talk. I'll find your cloak—and your husband—and see you on your way."

Later, as the skiff moved through the darkness, up the James, the great Negro, Yago, in the sternsheets, Susan slipped her hand into the crook of Dale's elbow as they half-sat, half-lay close together, just forward of the mast. The girl, the bride, hugged herself to her husband's arm in a quick, convulsive movement that brought an answering stir from Dale.

"Are you warm enough?" he asked. "Here, I'll put my cloak over both of us and hold you next to me—so."

It was the first time in—how long?—that he had been even brusquely tender and her gratitude at his move that brought her close to him welled up within her in a choking surge. *Ah, love me, love me,* she thought. *I will be so good to you, and good for you! I can learn to be wanton, if you'd have me thus, and I can be your sister, your playmate such as you never had when you were a little*

77

boy, when you'd have me so. Aye, I've been bitter and with a mean tongue, but I'll change. I'll be all laughter and gaiety and if you will it so, I'll learn to fix myself up like the ladies who came to my wedding. Yes, I'll make you proud of me, Dale, after I've had my child and get my figure back. But now, Dale, love me. Love me, in spite of what I'm going to look like in a few weeks, in spite of Captain Claiborne and his pretty sneers. Love me, Dale, lest I die.

"Are you warm enough?" Dale asked again, drowsily. "We're almost there. See, there's the light that marks your father's dock."

His arm over her shoulders tightened.

"We'll be alone in the place," he reminded her, "except for the servants. Your father's staying with Captain Claiborne for the night."

"Yes," she said, and the eagerness in her own voice surprised her. It had been so long, it seemed, since she had been eager about anything, even love. "Yes, Dale, we'll be alone."

"With no one," he murmured, almost growled, "to come interferin', nor a damn for us to give to anybody who might come snooping. We're man and wife now."

She saw the white blur of his face as he looked down at her. The skiff listed a bit as Yago came about for the run toward the lantern on the Willison dock.

"My wife," Dale said slowly. It was as though he were experimenting with the words. "Aye, my wife, my woman, my Susan, and you've given no complaint beyond a tear or so when you thought nobody was looking. I've cursed you—I've almost beat you—and all the time, I wasn't fit to touch your shoe buckle."

He brought her to him until they lay together, their bodies touching from breast to knee. Her eyes shone up at Dale's, luminous in the darkness, and her fingers reached up to touch Dale's cheek, lightly, as a mother might touch the face of a child who had been away and now had come back.

"Dale," she half-whispered. "You do love me, don't you? It's not only because—because of the child?"

78

"No!" he said fiercely. "It's not the child. I love you for yourself, Susan. And I'll be good to you! You'll see! I'll be good to you, my —my beautiful Susan!"

His head fell to the curve of her neck and she looked up at the dark sky triumphantly.

This hold Captain William Claiborne had fastened on Dale, she thought—did the Captain think it could possibly be nearly as strong as the hold a woman's love for a man, her husband, could be?

The more fool he, if he did.

Chapter Three, 1629

"MY ACCOUNTS HEREIN SET FORTH AND TOTALED, show there has been a good period of trade since my last accounting, although the winter was severe and the Indians in most localities were hard put to do any trapping because of the frost and snow. Our Company can call itself more fortunate than any other Company in these parts in the taking of furs and I may pride myself that this is so because I have been able to know these savages better than any other man in this Province and hold their trust. It is with esteem—you can finish up the rest of it in the usual way, Dale."

Captain Claiborne scaled the sheet of foolscap he had been holding onto a pile of papers at one side of his desk and leaned back in his chair, rubbing his eyes and yawning. Dale, at a smaller desk across the room, raised his head and peered across at the Captain, his eyes squinted against the glow of the candle at his elbow.

"This is to go to Cloberry and Company?" he asked. Claiborne left off massaging his eyes and scowled over at Morley.

"Now, by God!" he rasped. "There's a question! Who else would a letter dealing with accounts of fur trading go to? To the King, perhaps?"

Dale's square-jawed face flushed as he rapped out his reply.

"To the Devil, for all I care!" he flared. "It was no more than a week ago that you told me never to take a letter's address for granted! That was when I thought because a letter was written to a certain man it was to go to him, not to a third party who'd get it to another person who'd—ah, the whole thing's too topsy-turvy for my liking!"

Claiborne laughed lightly as Dale returned to his writing. The tip of Dale's tongue showed at the corner of his mouth and his eyes were wary as they watched the progress of the quill. He had improved as a scribe but his skill still was not such that he could trust his quill far. It had to be watched constantly, lest it make off on a letter that wasn't intended or shake loose a damning blot.

He finished the task and sanded the writing carefully, then leaned back in his chair to look across the room at the Captain's desk. How many more letters had to be copied that night before he was released from the torture of quill and inkpot, ledger and cash box? His eyes veered hopefully to the decanter close at Claiborne's side and he wet his lips with his tongue. Not much hope, though. Experience had long since proved that the Captain wouldn't lift the stopper of that decanter until the day's last bit of business was finished.

Dale had learned other things about the Captain. He had learned that Claiborne was a tireless worker, in the field, in his office, in his home. He might play the bountiful host, the tavern blade, the beau of the ladies, but actually he always was Secretary of the Province of Virginia and factor for William Cloberry and Company, traders, of London.

This evening had been chiefly spent in transacting Cloberry business and Dale had been yawning since soon after the candles were lit. Provincial matters were more interesting to him, and letters that dealt with Indians and adventure the best of all. But long accountings of pounds, shillings and pence, interest and commissions, that was better work for Susan than for him. But Susan was a grotesquely swollen creature and she kept to her room, barely stirring out of the new house the Captain had built for them, and he had the task all to himself, and hated it.

He looked again at the decanter and the Captain caught his eye and laughed.

"Are you parched, Dale?" he asked "I am, too. Let's say we've done the lot, though we've not, and get at the rest of these affairs in the morning, eh?"

81

"A fine thought," Dale said jubilantly.

He flipped shut the lid of the inkpot, wiped the quill clean and stacked the uneven sheets of foolscap in a pile. The ledgers and the cash box went into the big strongbox in the corner of the office and Dale forced shut its cumbersome lock, and gave the key to Claiborne.

"And how is Dame Morley, Dale?" the Captain asked.

Dale shrugged his shoulders.

"I see no difference," he said, "though old Granny Gillespie, the midwife you got for Susan, clucks and squawks around the place like a brooding hen. She's well enough, I suppose. I know little about these things."

He moved to the decanter to fill a pair of glasses. When he handed Claiborne his drink, he said:

"She—she thanks you for the things you sent her and bids me remind you that we're already so far in your debt that—"

"Nonsense," Claiborne broke in. "You'll earn everything I may have given you till now before you're through. Soon's the baby's born, you'll begin to sweat, Dale Morley, and start calling me a hard taskmaster. I couldn't send a new husband and father-to-be into the wilderness, could I, and be forced to meet your wife's reproachful looks every day? You had your work to learn here, besides, so I took young Bristoll up the Chesapeake with me, in spite of your long face at the time."

He looked at Dale over the rim of his glass and added:

"He did right well, too, Dale. I'll confess I had my doubts about his stomach for the wilderness, in spite of those Indian expeditions I took him on, but he seems to fit into the forests, for all his pretty manners, on a trading mission as well as a war party."

"A puny clerk," Dale had grumbled. "A hump-backed, squint-eyed scribbler you'll have me, Captain Claiborne. I joined you to see some life, something to make the blood run fast, Captain, and all I've done since is get my fingers messed with ink and wear my brain out with these damned additions and divisions. Even the farm was more manly than this."

"Then get back to your farm, if you would!" Claiborne's voice had crackled, ripping out of his calm like jagged lightning forking down from a cloudless sky. "Get back to your cow dung and corn stalks! I'll not hold any man to my service who wants to go!"

There had been another of those frequent silences between the two men, when their separate wills had come to grips in a struggle that almost shrieked its intensity. And, as in the past, it had been Dale's eyes that had fallen first.

"Or stay," the Captain said swiftly, in a softer voice. "I need you here, Dale. Your services, and your wife's, will be worth more to me here in Jamestown this winter than a half-dozen lieutenants with me on the Chesapeake. Stay, boy; you'll not regret it."

He had that knack, the Captain, of beating a man down with his voice and then, when the other realized he was beaten, of being quick to let the other keep his self-respect, or some semblance of it, by a word, a gesture, that seemed to put Claiborne on the defensive, place the loser of the joust at an advantage. Here, he had saved Dale from the need either of storming out of the place and back to the fifty acres beside the James or humbling himself by begging to be kept on Claiborne's staff. Yes, the Captain's touch was a soft and clever one, right enough; like a painter's or that of a man who shaped faces and whole bodies out of clay and stone, a sculptor.

And now the Captain was back and the prime furs and the miscellany, such as agate and garnets, a handful of raw amethysts, some Indian beadwork as curios, bundles of deer antlers and the sawn lumber, were aboard the Cloberry ships and ready to sail.

"Another cup?" Captain Claiborne asked, "or are you in a hurry to get back to your wife?"

"I'll have another," Dale said. "Granny Gillespie is with Susan and I'm only in the way, these days." He sighed. "If it's this bad now, before the child is born, what'll it be with the brat whoopin' and howlin' around the house? I've never before felt so worthless, with Granny looking at me as though I was dirt. I'll be glad when this is over and Susan up and around again, so's I can have a decent meal and get that old crone out of the place."

83

The wine babbled from the mouth of the decanter into the mugs as Claiborne poured.

"She's not well, Dame Morley?" he asked, his eyebrows rising. "I thought she looked like a fine, strong woman, fairly made for having children."

The crease of a frown stretched across Dale's forehead, just above the eyes. He looked down at his feet as he answered, his voice slow and troubled.

"I thought the same," he said, "but Granny is all a-pother about something, certainly. She won't tell me what; says it's nothin' a man should know or would understand if he was told. Anyway, she's packed Susan off to bed like a person with the plague and she's keeping her there, till the babe is born."

"Which will be when?" Claiborne asked carefully. Dale shrugged.

"God knows," he said. "I've lost all count, but it should not be long, according to Granny. You—are you sure she's a good midwife, Captain?"

"The best that can be had in these parts," Claiborne nodded. "Oh, I know there are some who would say she is too old. But I got her for Dame Morley, Dale, because I know she's better than anyone else in the Province at these things. Why did you ask me what you did?"

The younger man hunched his shoulders again.

"Oh, some woman has gotten at Susan with a fancy story, I'll warrant," he said carelessly. "The girl has been strange lately—almost as though she feared something or somebody. I've seen her eyes follow Granny Gillespie about the room as though she was afraid the old crone would turn into a witch at the next minute and fly out the window. And today she told me she wished there was another woman attending her. I put it down to a woman's vapors—they're supposed to have 'em at times like this, I hear—but I thought I'd ask you about Granny, to make sure."

Claiborne walked across the room to lay a hand on Dale's shoulder.

84

"Come, man!" he cried. "You're just a new father-to-be, sufferin' the first pangs. There's nothing wrong with you that can't be cured by a decent meal, a few glasses and some good companions at the table. Stay with me this night and we'll sweep the gloom out of your head, I'll promise. There'll be Tindall and Finch and some others in. I'll warrant you haven't had a good meal for a week, nor a glass too many to make you forget your troubles."

"That I haven't," Dale admitted, "and I feel the need of both. But there's Susan and—"

"You said yourself you were but in the way," Claiborne pointed out. "I'll send a man past your place with a note to Dame Morley to let her know you're in safe hands, eh? She'll surely be glad to be rid of you this one night, I know."

Dale's hesitation was so brief it could hardly be called that. He supposed he should be with Susan in her sickness but of late she had become as querulous as a hungry cat and sharp-tongued, too, in her misery, being pleased by none of the things he tried to do for her. It would be good to get away from the house and a cadaverous Granny Gillespie, the swollen, whining, unbeautiful Susan, the miserable meals and the hushed air of the place. There was a lightness in his heart that had been too long absent as he smiled at Claiborne and said:

"You have yourself a guest, Captain Claiborne, and I thank you."

The Captain sprang into delighted action.

"Yago!" he bawled. "Toss! Hurry, you two!" And when the blacks arrived, breathless: "Yago, you ride to Mister Tindall's place and Mister Finch's. Toss, you go to Mister Peregrine's and Mister Bristoll's—ah, yes, we'll have Talbot, too; I want you two to get to like each other. Now, Toss, Yago, give the gentlemen my compliments and say they're invited to supper and the evening here. Ride, now, and if I catch either one of you dawdling amongst the wenches I'll have your skin in ribbons."

He turned back to Dale, rubbing his hands, as the slaves left.

"Fine, fine!" he said. "We'll have a real riot tonight. It's been so long since I've dropped the damned worries of the Province

85

and Cloberry that I'll feel like a young buck at his first rutting tonight, I'll warrant. Here, Dale, amuse yourself with this decanter while I see to our dinner. I'll join you soon."

The time stretched as Dale busied himself at the decanter. His head was buzzing cheerily when Claiborne returned to the office and it was close to swimming when the others arrived. It was an uproariously gay gathering from the start. The others, except Tindall, were all good friends of Dale and even the mincing Talbot Bristoll seemed less superciliously acid this evening. He greeted Dale with a brief nod and thereafter confined his conversation to the others; but at least he did not cast any asides in Dale's direction or deal him any of the haughty-eyed glances that had, in the past, so infuriated the young clerk.

The food was varied and delicious, the drinks plentiful and potent, the talk more lively and louder by the minute. This, then, was Captain William Claiborne with the reins loosened; this was Claiborne with his guard down, his armor off, and twice as gifted a dinner companion as any other man Dale ever had met. As the wine took hold, Claiborne sang bits of songs, recited fragments of poetry, dropped into the conversation a story that concerned a *bal masque* and the cuckolding of a pompous Duke, kept the others doubled in purple-faced laughter. Even the sleepy-eyed Talbot Bristoll forgot his stand-offishness enough to join the laughter and, awhile later, to take part in the chorus of a bawdy song that Claiborne trolled out.

Someone produced a set of dice and Dale watched avidly as the others cast the bone cubes onto the wide oak table set in one corner of the room. Dale did not play, nor did the others seem to expect him to play, for nobody offered him an invitation. Some time before, Captain Claiborne had made Dale's position clear to him, as far as all gaming was concerned, and the others apparently knew of it.

"You'll drink with me and eat with me and sleep with me and

ride with me and fight with me," Claiborne had said, "but you'll never gamble with me, so long as you're my secretary and my lieutenant."

So Dale watched and drank more and watched again as the sovereigns went from one winner to the next and Thomas Tindall grew scarlet-necked and sweaty, while Talbot Bristoll won and won, from all but Claiborne, and grew more and more distant and disdainful. Samuel Finch was a short, bulky, dark-skinned man with a quick, curling smile which did not falter, even when he borrowed quill and ink to scribble a sheaf of debtor's slips. Peregrine was a thin young man with protruding teeth and a pair of bulging eyes. His father had been one of the first settlers at Jamestown, had survived the famines and the massacres to make a sizeable fortune in tobacco, then die of lung fever to leave his money for his son to enjoy. John Peregrine was enjoying the spending of the fortune, after his fashion, but his every pleasure was tempered by the realization that each penny spent brought the day closer when he would have to go to work.

Dale's head was cloudy and nodding when the dice game finally broke up. Somebody—was it Tindall or Bristoll?—was saying something about petticoats and somebody else—Peregrine, probably—was protesting that it was too long a ride at that time of night. Whoever it was that protested, his arguments were soon hooted down and Dale found himself in the saddle, astride Bella, and following the others as they walked their horses out of the yard. Claiborne was in the lead and beside him rode a black, Yago, holding a huge blazing pine knot aloft to light the narrow lane into which they turned. At a word from Claiborne, Yago dug his heels into his mount's ribs and the cavalcade picked up speed.

Dale had learned to be a better horseman in the months that had passed since he had bought Bella at Jamestown, but he still could not be called accomplished by any but the most generous. He clung to the little column now, though, and he was not far

87

behind when the group drew up in front of a small house, surrounded by tall willows, back from a lane Dale never had ridden over before.

"Whose place is this?" he asked Tindall as he came out of the saddle in a lurching tumble. "Never been here before."

" 'S great place," Tindall said happily. "Come out here every once in a while. Beautiful ladies, every one of them, and friendly, too. Just have a good time, Dale, and don't mind how ye do it."

Inside the place, Dale had jumbled impressions of a crowd of young women in considerable disarray, laughing and squealing at the invasion that Claiborne and Bristoll led. In the darkness that preceded the lighting of candles in the main room off the hall, Dale collided with something soft and reached out to clutch. His groping hands encountered linen and bare skin, closed over the warm, smooth globe of a woman's breast.

"Christ, man!" a girl's voice panted and he felt her breath on his cheek. "Can't you wait for a more seemly place than the hallway here?"

"Wait for you? Never!" Dale grunted and swung the girl in toward him, bent over her as she grasped him, straining herself up toward his body. He found her mouth and grunted again as he felt her lips open under his and her tongue begin its play. Then there was a scream of cheering and he looked up to find the tapers lit and the others yelping their ribald chorus at him and the girl he held. He looked down at the prize he had captured in the darkness of the hallway.

Well, she was not the most beautiful girl he'd ever seen, nor yet the ugliest, and her skin was milk white, her eyes were brown and set in smudged sockets and under the shift her belly, by God, was flat and that was what counted now.

He frowned stupidly at the others and turned to the girl.

"Where?" he asked thickly, while Thomas Tindall and the others laughed.

"In there," she said, and half-led him, was half-dragged by him, into the small, dark room to the left.

The door kept swinging open an inch or so but that made no difference. The bed was lumpy and smelled sour but that made no difference, either. What counted was that this girl was thin, was thin, by Christ, was thin and she helped him and didn't keep herself apart from him and was with him and around him and squirming and wriggling and bouncing and there was the sharp scent of perfume and ah God it was wonderful wonderful and he had missed this and this and this and this until she whispered and he whispered back, though they both might have roared for all he knew and the world fell away and he went with it.

It was light when he opened his eyes and the room was an unlovely place, the girl beside him an unlovely creature. She lay sprawled every which way, repulsive in her sleep, her mouth agape and snores rattling in her throat. Her hair was a tangle and her skin received no kindnesses from the morning sun.

Dale looked at her, swallowed back the bile that rose in his throat and swung his feet over the side of the bed to the floor. His head was caught between the hammer and anvil of pain and the jarring, pulsing ache that spiked his brain made him press his fingers to his eyes a moment, before he bent to pull on his shoes.

The girl, whoever she was, snored on as Dale tried to straighten his disheveled clothes and brush back with uncertain hands the lank strands of hair that fell in front of his red-rimmed eyes. He needed water for his throbbing head and his coated mouth and throat, needed water and some air that was not fogged with the stink of stale wine and foul breath. He stumbled toward the door, kicking aside the wadded scrap of linen that had been the girl's shift.

What was her name, he asked himself, and what did her name matter? She had been just a woman, any woman, at the time. He looked back at the girl on the bed and his mouth went uneven with disgust—at himself more than at the slut who lay there. After a drink and a douse for his head, he needed a bath and a rough cloth to rub himself clean.

He had to get back to Susan, too. Even though Claiborne had

89

sent word to her, she would be lonely, left in the house with nobody but the old woman she seemed to fear. He had no idea of the time, but the sun's rays slanted almost vertically through the window beyond the bed and that meant the morning must be well spent.

He left the fetid little room and walked down the hallway to the main room. Just inside the door, Thomas Tindall lay snoring on a bench, his round face as peaceful as a child's, a faint smile on the pouting rosebud mouth. He wore one shoe. The other foot had neither stocking nor shoe and somebody had drawn black rings around his chubby leg, using soot from the fireplace.

Beyond Tindall, with her head pillowed on her arms at a table, sat a woman in a rumpled gown, its skirt pulled up to reveal bony knees and wrinkled stockings. Her face, turned toward the door, was flushed and swollen and a rivulet of saliva dribbled from the lower corner of her mouth.

Faugh! Where could he find water?

He went through the disordered room, circling an overturned bench, the fragments of a shattered clay pitcher, a wrinkled bit of ribbon that apparently had been a garter. A skinny, black dog that had been sleeping in a corner of the cluttered room got up and scuttled out a door at the rear of the room. Dale followed.

This was the kitchen, in a fine state of disorder, with scraps of food littering the place, the fire dead on the hearth, plates and bowls unwashed on the table, a dog mess on the floor, swill overflowing from a bucket beside the back door. These harlots might perfume their skins but they lived in a sty a black slave wouldn't boast to own.

Outside, the air was clean and crisp, though the sunlight shot needles of pain into his eyes when he first emerged from the house. There, on a bench beside the door, were three buckets of water and Dale bent gratefully to plunge his head into the nearest one. The cold spring water seemed to wash his brain, inside his skull, and when he straightened, the pounding ache was already quieting.

90

Again he bent to splash more of the invigorating stuff into his face, to rinse the gummy stickiness from his eyes.

The water he drank from the second bucket eased the fire in his throat and cut the coating of his tongue and mouth though it churned a bit when it reached his stomach. He drank deeply, then lowered the bucket to the bench and wiped his dripping chin on the sleeve of his wrinkled coat.

Now he could make the ride to his house and Susan's bedside. He'd change clothes before he went to her, get in a bath if he had time before he went up to the room where she lay, mountainous and fretful, plaintive and complaining. He could not tell her what he had done but he would try to make it up to her, some way; by sitting with her past the time when he usually got restless and wished to be off, by relaying to her the small talk she seemed to set so much store by, by making her laugh if he could.

First, he had to find his hat, the new beaver with the flaring brim that Captain Claiborne had ordered from London for him. He remembered taking off the hat when he staggered into that dark hallway, the night before. He hoped the thing hadn't been trampled on in the riot that had followed.

He went back through the noisome kitchen, through the littered main room with its two sleeping figures and out into the hallway. The hat was in a corner, dusty and bearing a heel-print, but not too badly damaged. He set it on his head and made for the front door. Bella should be outside with Yago tending her and the other horses. Claiborne probably was long gone, but he would be sure to leave the slave there with the horses until the last carouser had hoisted himself into the saddle.

Yago was there, and so was Captain Claiborne—and the Negro, Benji. The horses were tethered under a willow tree beside the weed-grown lane and the Captain stood between them and the house, talking with his slaves.

"Yonder he," said Yago softly, as Dale closed the door of the strange house behind him. "Yonder Mas' Morley, sahr."

Claiborne turned and Dale saw that it was as though he had taken to his bed at an early hour the night before, had risen from a deep, satisfying sleep, bathed, shaved and dressed with his usual care. The skin of his face, where it was not covered by the pointed black beard and the mustaches, was a healthy glowing bronze and his eyes were as clear as on any other day, his dress never more faultless. Dale knew the Captain had been deep in drink the previous night, had led the way in the debauch, and still there he was, as unaffected by the excesses of the wild night as though he had never tipped a goblet of wine.

The Captain looked at Dale, held his eyes and walked toward him. There was something in his expression that did more to sober Dale than the cold water from the buckets beside the back door had done. Claiborne's face was grave, bleak, pulled down by the fingers of some concern that Dale knew, instantly, had to do with him.

Then the thought was there, like a shaft of sunlight striking through a dark cloud, like a pine knot kindled suddenly in a black night—*Susan!* Each step the Captain took toward him made that thought clearer, and apprehension gave way to dread, and dread to terror in that short distance Captain Claiborne paced.

He was stiff with panic as the Captain came up to him and placed a hand on his shoulder. Claiborne's lips moved but his words did not penetrate the roaring that filled Dale's ears. The water in his belly turned to molten metal and surged upward again, and he swallowed against it. He forced himself to listen to Claiborne's voice.

" . . . an hour ago, or thereabouts, Dale. They—they tried to reach you but—ah, something went wrong. Benji knew where we had gone when we left my place but Toss didn't and Benji was riding an errand for me when they came for you. I'd give my soul to have sent you home last night, Dale, or to have kept us all at my place where we could have been reached. Believe me, I—"

"Tell me!" Dale burst out, the words wrenched from between his rigid lips. "What happened? What is it?"

Claiborne's other hand came up to grip his shoulder. His eyes were still steady as they stared into Dale's.

"Your wife, Dale," he said. "I tried to put it—easily."

"To hell with your easy words," Dale grated. "What about my wife?"

"She—"

"Is she ill? The child?"

"Steady, man," Claiborne said. It was as though he were holding in the fractious black stallion. "Steady. It was God's will—or Someone's."

Dale's voice was a dry husk, wrapped around black, wormy kernels of sound.

"She's dead," he said flatly. And there it was, and all that could ever be said after that about Susan Willison could mean nothing more than that.

Claiborne said nothing. Beyond him, the blacks, Benji and Yago, turned away from their rolling-eyed staring and looked at the horses. The tree beneath which the mounts were tethered was a willow, its buds new and freshly green. One of the horses stamped and shook its head, bothered by an early-hatched fly.

"I killed her," Morley said dully. "She gave me everything and I gave her nothing I didn't give that whore inside the house, there. She asked me to get rid of that midwife. She was—she was afraid of Granny Gillespie and I laughed at her. I killed her, as surely as if I'd—"

Claiborne's fingers tightened their grip on his shoulders.

"Not you," he said levelly. "The child was—misshapen. Out of its proper position or something like that. It came early. Granny Gillespie, the neighbors, did everything that could be done. You couldn't have helped by being there. Granny's word was that she wanted to send for you when the trouble first started but your wife would have none of it."

"She didn't want me there?" Dale asked dazed. "But she must have!"

The Captain shook his head.

"No, Dale," he said quietly. "A woman makes that journey alone, believe me, and she wants no man to try to walk with her, no matter how she may love him. No, he must wait until she returns, and if she doesn't, then it's better that her good-bye was said before she started, not screamed back at him from some cruel bend in the dark journey."

"Words," Dale sneered. "Pretty words. If I listen to you long enough, you'll have me thinkin' it was right and proper that I was wallowing on a whore's bosom while my wife was dyin'."

He wrenched himself out of Claiborne's grip and took a step away. He put his hands to his face and groaned as he swayed.

"Better her good-bye before she started, eh?" he said in a muffled voice. "God help me, I can't remember whether I bade her good-bye yesterday mornin' or not. I often lacked even that small kindness, because her swollen belly offended me. *Offended me!*"

A sob ripped at his throat and he started toward the place where Bella was tethered. Claiborne touched his arm but Dale thrust the Captain's hand away in a desperate furious fling. He walked as he had walked the night before and when he reached Bella, he fumbled with the reins that Yago handed him. He got into the saddle with the Negro's help and wavered there a moment, waiting for his eyes to clear.

Behind him, he heard the front door of the house he had left slam open. Thomas Tindall's voice split the silence of the moment.

"My shoe!" Tindall bawled. "Find me my shoe and find me some wine before I tear down this place, stick by stick! Captain, were you the artist that daubed my leg with soot, to make me think I had the pox? Ho, Dale, ye're not leavin', are ye? Ye're easy satisfied, I'd say, with but one arrow shot from your bow before ye—"

"Quiet, man!" Captain Claiborne thundered.

"Quiet? It's no mornin' to be quiet, Captain! It's time to sing and wake the ladies, so's we can be to our fun again. It's time to—urgh—"

94

Tindall's voice was choked off to smothered mumbling as Dale touched Bella with his heels and began the ride to the room where Susan lay, past waiting now.

He kneeled beside the bed and touched his forehead to the cover, but nothing would come; no tears, no prayers. There were memories, yes, but they were neither clear nor poignant. Susan Willison had been closer to him than any other being and yet, even now, she seemed a dim figure, tenuous, lacking detail.

She had loved him, wholly, unselfishly, and his mind should be filled with bright portraits of her in her every mood; laughing, tender, flushed with happiness, made pale by some hurt he had dealt her, her small nose reddened by the cold, her round face freckled by the sun. He should be able to envisage her sturdy, compact body in a thousand poses, hear her voice again in all its inflections. He should be able to remember how her hand had felt in his when it was warm and alive, how her bosom had lifted to her breathing, how her lashes had made tiny fans beneath her eyes when she was sleeping. He should be able to recall how she had looked and the sounds she had made during the rare times when she had been transported by her love, joined to his desire.

But he had no portraits; he could not summon up the definite recollections that might have tempered the knowledge that she was now out of reach of his most earnest resolves to give her everything he had withheld from her. He found himself empty-handed because while she had been alive and with him, he had always stepped back from her efforts to make herself part of him; he had been fearful lest she clamp too close a hold on him. He had not shared himself with her, nor let her share herself with him, so now that she had left, no part of her that he might have possessed, his alone, remained to him.

Oh, there were things about her that he remembered: the mole just over her left hip, the front tooth that was a trifle crooked, the

95

sweet smell of her on the most sultry day, her clean fingernails. But the important things, the things about her that would have given him a memory that would have helped him, were gone with her.

Now it was as though there never had been a Susan, for all the days she had spent with him. He should feel himself freed of a burden, instead of weighted down by this emptiness, this sense of lack, this hollow taste of unfulfillment.

He waited there beside the bed and then got up slowly, rustily, and stood for a moment, looking down at the still, covered figure that lay there. Without the bloating of pregnancy, Susan Willison made a tiny lump in the middle of the wide tester bed. He had looked at her face; he would not uncover it again. From her expression, the journey Claiborne had spoken of must have been dark, indeed, and twisted by tortuous bends.

Any man but he could have found some words to say, some gesture to make, to show the only part of Susan he could still reach, that he was bewildered, that all the things he had learned of life could not help him now. Dale could only make an awkward, meaningless move of a hand before he turned away and walked out of the room.

The old midwife, Granny Gillespie, was huddled on the bottom step of the stairs, leaning against the newel post. Dark-skinned, as wrinkled as wadded parchment, all but toothless, she slid her eyes at Dale and then twitched them back again.

"The first one I lost in a hundred bornin's," she mumbled. "Poor little dearie. Poor little sweet. Old Granny tried, but there was no stoppin' it, once it started. Y'can't blame Old Granny, sir. Oh, no, y'can't."

She raised a claw to clutch at his sleeve.

"No more y'could've saved the bairn," she mouthed. "Old Granny tried. Not ready to come, he weren't, but he must try and out, rippin' and tearin' the poor little dearie till—"

"For Christ's sweet sake," Dale snarled, "stop your blathering before I slit your throat!"

He walked on, Granny's mumbling dying out behind him, and went into the main room off the hall. He forced himself to go straight to the chair where Thomas Willison sat, facing the window that looked out onto the cart path that was the uppermost end of Jamestown's muddy main street.

The little man's face was gray and slack, the round cheeks suddenly sagged to make dewlaps, the prim mouth loosely open, the eyes dull and unseeing. He always had been an energetic person, as nimble as a cricket for all his paunch, possessed of a high-pitched laugh that sounded often. Now he sat unmoving, his eyes fixed on nothing in a glazed stare, his pudgy hands limp on the arms of the chair, his feet wide apart and his legs lax, like a puppet with all its strings cut. As Dale came to his side, he turned his head slowly, but there was no light of recognition in his eyes when he looked up.

"I'm sorry," Dale said. "I ought to have been here. I didn't know."

Willison's mouth moved experimentally, without sound, and then his words came haltingly.

"She was a sweet girl," he said, in an empty voice. "All I had. Now I've nothing. Nothing."

"They tried to get me in time," Morley said. "They didn't know where to find me."

"As happy with a rag wrapped about a stick as another child would be with a fine French doll," Thomas Willison went on. "Never a mite of trouble. Clean and good she was since she was a little girl."

"Clean and good," Dale repeated. "Aye, she was that."

"I should have said her nay that once," Willison said. "When she came to me about the marrying, I should have denied her that."

His dull eyes flickered for the first time.

"She was too good for you, Dale Morley," he said. "You weren't fit to touch her hand. But she loved you. She would have you."

97

One of the limp hands slid off the chair arm in a weary gesture.

"And now this is what her love has brought her," he said dully. "I think she knew 'twould end this way. Only a week ago, she asked me to take her home with me. She said she was afraid here."

"She—she said that?" Dale asked. "She wanted to leave me?"

"Not you, so much, as this place and that midwife," Thomas Willison said. He might have been reading an uninteresting pamphlet aloud. "I put it down to a whimsey, as women will have when they're near birthing, and perhaps it was. But now I wish—I wish—"

Slowly, slowly, as though each movement demanded great effort, Thomas Willison got up out of the chair. Standing beside Dale Morley, he became a shriveled pygmy, an insignificant, ineffectual little man whom grief had not dignified but, instead, had made almost ludicrous, with his aimless eyes, the uncertain movements of his hands, his teetering stance.

"You did this, Morley," he said, his voice breaking in a squeak. "She would not tell me, but I knew you hurt her from the first minute she turned away from me to you. You weren't the man for her. If her mother had lived she'd have been able to—to warn her. But her father was an old fool and—and she came to this."

He started on his uneven way toward the door.

"It's not Christian to hate a man, Dale Morley," he quavered, without turning, "but I think I hate you, for what you did to my Susan. You and that damned fine Captain Claiborne of yours. Together, you killed her."

"How can you say that?" Dale cried after him. "I—I loved her, too, as she did me! I wouldn't hurt her! The child—the child was to blame! Ask the women who were here; they'll tell you!"

But Thomas Willison went through the doorway and down the hall and out of the house without answering. The door, closing behind him, sent a hollow reverberation booming through the silent rooms.

The Reverend Richard James droned through the funeral service in a monotone, obliquely asking a stern God to be as generous as possible with the soul of Susan Morley, despite her sins.

Sins, Dale asked himself, what sins was Susan guilty of, save those he had inflicted upon her?

There was not much more than a handful of people in the church and fewer still at the grave that drizzly morning. Dale stood alone, Thomas Willison opposite him across the ugly gash in the green burial ground, and watched the wet clay leave the digger's shovel and fall with a thump onto the rough pine coffin that held his wife and child.

The father's tears ran ceaselessly from his pouched eyes and trickled down his sagged face but the husband's cheeks were dampened only by the rain. He may have winced at that sound of mud falling on the coffin and his face may have been white and strained but he could not weep. He had long since forgotten how.

Dale started on his first trading voyage a fortnight after Susan was buried.

"I'd not intended sending you out so soon," Captain Claiborne said, "but I suppose it would be wise. New lands, new pursuits are what you need now, rather than to stay here in Jamestown."

He tilted his chair back, his hands tented beneath his chin, and asked his question.

"You blame me, Dale, for keeping you from your wife that night, for leading that damned frolic where it went?"

Dale frowned, pondering the question. True, at first he had held the Captain guilty of putting him in a whore's bed when he should have been with Susan during those last few hours, but he had been able to reason since. Now, he could see that the blame was his, if anybody's, and his alone. He had known Susan was close to her time, though nobody, not even the midwife, had suspected that she was that close. Another man, perhaps, would have drunk his

99

glass of wine and ridden home to his wife, to make sure he would be there if he were needed. He had stayed at the Captain's on his own, nobody had persuaded him to stay against his own judgment, nobody had dragged him bodily to the place that housed the squealing women.

"No," he said slowly. "No, I don't blame you, Captain. It was the Devil's doing that I did what I did and was where I was when she died."

"And you don't hold it against me that I brought Granny Gillespie to your wife, instead of a younger woman, perhaps?"

"No," Dale said again. "The women who were with her at the last said there was no stopping the blood, once it had begun. They said Granny did all anyone could do. Susan's fears were just—whimsey, as her father thought."

Claiborne brought his chair down, his long fingers stroking the pointed beard.

"Good, then," he said. "I feared you'd hold it in your heart against me and I'd find it hard to blame you if you did. I know Thomas Willison has been talking wildly about me sending Dame Morley a midwife who terrified the girl. He's made it sound as though I had some evil scheme in mind, poor man."

"Aye, he's been talking, right enough," Dale growled. "He's told his story to half the Province, about how I mistreated Susan and left her to die alone while I was out carousing. It's got so bad I have to look twice to see whether each man I meet is my friend or Willison's."

"In a different instance," Claiborne said thoughtfully, "I'd have his words pinched off, but—well, let's at this voyage you're going to make. By the time you're back, I'll warrant, Thomas Willison will have talked himself out and it'll be forgotten."

He reached for a sheaf of papers on his desk and ran his eyes over them, shuffling them rapidly.

"You'll go aboard the wherry, the *Cockatrice*," he said, "with Captain Martiau in command."

100

"You're not going, then?"

"No, not this time," the Captain said. "There's a great pile of Provincial business to be cared for and that fool Harvey hasn't the will to say nay to a petulant child. God speed the day when we get another Governor as strong as Tom Gates and George Yeardley were. This Sir John Harvey we have now shies like a colt at a shadow. So you see that I must stay here."

The *Cockatrice,* Dale thought, was an unexciting craft to look at for one named after the great, writhing serpents of the deep. It was, actually, a long, narrow barge carrying a hermaphrodite rig. She bore a square-rigged foremast with foresail, topgallant and skysail and a fore-and-aft rigged mizzen. She lay low in the water and she plainly showed the results of hard usage with little rest. She was old but she was clean, far different from the smelly hulk that the *Solace,* Captain O'Halley's ship, had been.

Captain O'Halley; it had been a long time since Dale had even brought the name to mind. Claiborne had not mentioned the subject of Dale's under-age indenture in months and none of the letters, orders, proclamations or petitions that he had gone through in his duties as the Captain's secretary had so much as hinted at the name O'Halley.

It could be that Susan had been right in her doubt that Claiborne had ever been ordered to inquire into O'Halley's affairs, and in her conviction that the Captain had some other reason for interesting himself in Dale.

Well, he asked himself, what did it matter? Enough that he was Claiborne's lieutenant and favored by the biggest man in the Province, as everyone agreed. Enough that he was to sail aboard the *Cockatrice* in the morning, to learn the business of trading with the Indians. Enough that he could leave Jamestown and Thomas Willison's clacking tongue, the sidelong looks he saw, or thought he saw, given him by the men and women who had been Susan's friends.

"So you're making this journey with us, eh?" a heavy voice said, at his shoulder. "You should find pleasure in it, this time o' year and at the friendly places we're going to touch, this trip."

Captain Nicholas Martiau smiled at him through his thick beard, then turned to spit into the scummy water that idly lapped the muddy shore. Some of the wherry's crew were loading a longboat with supplies to be ferried out to the *Cockatrice,* lying at anchor in midstream.

"Glad you're going with us," Martiau continued, "though we won't be able to give you much in the way of excitement on this voyage. Captain Claiborne tells me you're burnin' to sight your musket on an Indian. Well, if 'twere the Susquehannock country we were headin' for, y'might have your wish—there's no bein' certain about that breed, whether they'll trade or fight—but we're callin' on the fishin' tribes this voyage, Pascataways and Wicomesses."

He was a barrel of a man, this Captain Nicholas Martiau, with a voice that rumbled when he whispered, and deafened when he shouted. The eyes that turned back to Dale after brief scrutiny of the working party at the longboat were pale blue, surrounded by a network of wrinkles etched by wind and sun. His beard was full and blonde, with streaks of gray, and his hair was worn long and, at times, caught back in a pigtail such as common sailors affected. He wore a breastplate more often than not, and a heavy cutlass usually hung at his side. The boots he invariably stumped about in were of heavy leather and between the clank of his armor and weapon, the thump of his boots and his roaring voice, Captain Martiau, Dale thought, certainly must be the noisiest man in the whole Colony.

"The fishing tribes?" Dale asked. "You mean these Indians we'll see aren't warlike?"

Captain Martiau hunched his thick shoulders and spat again at the water.

"All Indians," he said, "are warlike when the liking seizes them, but the fishin' tribes, as we call 'em—the Wicomesses and the
102

Pascataways and the Yaocomicoes—have to be almighty hard put to get the liking. They've always been friendly with us, with a couple of exceptions, and the times they did rise up against us was usually more our fault than theirs, or so Captain Claiborne says. The Captain, though, is fairer to the Indians than most big traders. You take that Captain Yonge, for instance—but don't let me get started talkin' about that hound of hell!"

"Yonge?" Dale asked. "I think I've heard the name."

"Aye, you have if you've been with Claiborne long, I'll warrant," Martiau said grimly. "He's a trader—of sorts, though he seems to spend more time makin' trouble for Claiborne than he does in gettin' his furs. For some reason, he hates our commander, this Yonge, and nothin' would please him better than to see Claiborne banished from Virginia or, better yet, slain by the Susquehannocks. And for my part, I'd like to see Yonge with his head on a Susquehannock block, myself."

He paused to bawl an order to move lively, directed at the loading party. He watched them for a moment, grunted in satisfaction and turned back to Dale.

"We sail at the full tide tomorrow mornin', Mister Morley," he said. "That'll be soon after dawn and I don't abide tardiness in my crew or my passengers, so you'll please be on time. As you know, Mister Bristoll will be with us and—"

"Bristoll?" Dale asked, his voice reflecting his surprise. "Is that—is *he* going to be aboard?"

The bearded Captain glanced at him, his eyes lighted by a twinkle of amusement.

"Oh, yes," he said easily. " 'Tis Captain Claiborne's orders that he go along with us, to add to the learnin' he got on his trip this winter, and to help you along, so to speak, on your first voyage."

"I want no help from him!" Dale said hotly.

"And one thing more, Mister Morley," Captain Martiau said, his voice suddenly taking on a bite. "My orders from Captain Claiborne were that you two young men will forget your personal differences

103

durin' this voyage and learn to work together in the Captain's interests. He made that very plain to me, Mister Morley."

Dale subsided, though the chagrin of knowing Talbot Bristoll would make the trip with him kept its keen edge. This first trading trip, he told himself, was turning out to be something far different from what he had looked forward to. He had thought William Claiborne would sail with him, but the Captain had relegated the command to an aide, instead, and now came word that Bristoll, with his damned superiority, his sneer and his way of looking down his long nose at Dale as though Morley were a queer sort of obnoxious insect, was going to be along, too—the trip was apt to be far less pleasant than he had thought it would be.

"You two will share a cabin," Captain Martiau went on, "so it would be easier on you, Mister Morley, if you resolved yourself to get along with Mister Bristoll."

"I will," said Dale stiffly. "If there's trouble, it'll be of Bristoll's making, not mine."

The *Cockatrice* stood down the river from Jamestown a half hour past dawn the next day, aided by a westerly wind that put a bone in the wherry's teeth when she was a scant hundred feet from her mooring. Leaning against the aft rail near the wheel, where Captain Martiau stood beside the helmsman, Dale peered uneasily at the steep list of the wherry's deck as the ship bellied her canvas and fled downstream.

He did not like boats; he never would like boats, he knew. There was something frightening about the independent surge of this vessel. The shore slid past at an astonishing pace and yet there was none of the healthy jar of feet or hoofs beneath him, only the slick swish and gurgle of the water, so dangerously close to the deck.

He gripped the taffrail tightly enough to make his knuckles whiten as he clung there, oblivious of the gloriously fresh wind that brought the smell of the open sea to him, the beauty of the shoreline that glided past on port and starboard. He would stay there, where he was, until the deck became level again. To try to cross it now to
104

the companionway that led to his cabin below would surely mean that he would slip and go sprawling, perhaps to roll over the side into that green, foam-streaked water.

He looked aloft, to break the fascination the rushing water seemed to hold for his eyes. The wherry's crew were shaking out the skysails and Dale wondered how any man could brave the upper reaches of that towering foremast, to dance along a single rope while they unfurled the stained canvas, a mile, it seemed, above the deck and the churning water. Never would he so much as put a foot on the rope ladders that Captain Martiau had pointed out to him as rat-lines. If his position with Captain Claiborne meant he would be called upon, at any time, to go aloft, the Captain would have to find himself another man. Better the hot little farm beside the James. . . .

Dale went to the bow and watched the low-lying James River shoreline go past, more slowly now as the wind died while the sun climbed the sky. He saw Fort Comfort, a parapet with the snouts of three six-thousand-pound cannon, three sakers, two culverins and a falcon, protruding from their embrasures. A strong enough place, Dale thought, to turn back even the whole Spanish fleet, and surely forbidding enough to discourage the New Englanders or Lord Baltimore, should either of them try to force their way into the river. Perhaps Claiborne worried needlessly about the threat of an invasion of Virginia. Still, it was always to be remembered that a king's signature on a scrap of parchment could render those guns as useless as though they never had been mounted there.

Once past the fort, Captain Martiau turned his helm to point the wherry's bowsprit northward, up into the broad reaches of the bay the Indians had named *Tchiss-a-big*—wide water tapering at one end —and which the white men had made fit their tongues better as Chesapeake. Now the *Cockatrice* lurched and rolled under the cross-rip swells that marked the joining of the bay and ocean currents and Dale's stomach joined in the motion. He staggered away from the rail and found a place to sit near the fife rail near the foremast and there he sat, pale and wan, until the wherry made her way through the brief turbulence. Talbot Bristoll, he noted bitterly, was totally unaffected by the roll of the ship and Dale's gorge rose when he saw the man he despised gnawing hungrily on a cold chop while the ship was pitching its worst.

Once through the rip, though, Dale could appreciate the beauty of the scene. To his left was a shore of thick forests, interspersed with tidy clearings that marked the oūter fringe plantations of the James-town Colony. To his right spread a vast expanse of sun-brightened water, incredibly blue and dotted by jaunty little whitecaps that were more merry than menacing. The eastern shoreline showed low on the horizon and between the wherry and that shore there showed no sail nor any other mark of encroaching civilization. The time would come, and Dale would live to see it, when that bay would be a great waterway; but now the *Cockatrice* was alone on that grand spread of waves; she might have been the first prow to split that deep since the Creation.

On each side of the wherry as she ploughed northward were fre-quent upheavals that churned the water into foam in patches of an acre or more. Now and then Dale could see a large, striped fish leap free of the water to crash down again with a resounding smack of its broad tail.

"I dunno their true name," a sailor said in passing, answering Dale's question, "but we call 'em rockfish, though how they come by that name I don't know, neither."

Pursued by the rockfish were wide carpets of tiny fish that went by the name of alewives, another mystery. And over the alewives and the voracious rockfish wheeled flocks of gulls, screaming and diving as they gorged on the remnants of the rockfish's feast.

The wherry's passing sent up flocks of ducks and geese, number-ing thousands upon thousands. White swans streaked past, their long necks outstretched, leading their gray cygnets out of the path of the *Cockatrice*. Once Dale spied a huge sea turtle basking on the surface, possibly asleep. The wherry veered in the turtle's direction —sea turtle was a delicacy not too common even in that piscatorial

106

paradise—but some warning disturbed the great shelled creature and it dived with a churning of its broad flippers and disappeared.

He was taking in all these sights, as much agog as a country clod at a fair, when there was a step beside him on the deck and he turned to find Talbot Bristoll lounging into a place beside him at the rail.

"Know you where we're bound?" Bristoll asked. "Did Captain Claiborne tell you more than he told me?"

"Perhaps," Dale said importantly. "I know we're touching at the mouth of the Potomac and later sailing to the east, to some island further up the bay."

"Kent Island," Bristoll nodded. "We touched there on the winter trip, when I was alone with Claiborne. A nice spot, as such places go, and the Captain seems enamored of it."

"The Indians are friendly there, too?" Dale asked.

"Friendly enough," Bristoll replied. "They're Wicomesses or some such heathen name and their men are not much. Their women, though, are comely and lively, when the rum's in 'em."

He glanced toward the stern where Captain Martiau still stood beside the helmsman.

"But don't let Claiborne or Martiau know you feed 'em rum," he cautioned. "They're both dead against that, though they don't mind a bit of dalliance now and then if the chiefs have no objections—and they seldom do."

Dale remembered the Indians he had seen at Jamestown and his nose wrinkled.

"I'd hardly choose a squaw for a bedmate," he said virtuously. "Besides their smell, I'd be afraid of the pox."

"Oh, they're clean enough," Bristoll said easily. "They're forever bathing, no matter what the weather, and there's no pox amongst them. I'll warrant they smell as sweet as those Jamestown beauties who entertained us not so long ago."

So there it was, a reminder of an occasion Dale would best have forgotten, with an inflection that told him clearly that he could never criticize another's taste in bedfellows after having floundered in a harlot's bed while his wife lay dying, alone except for an ancient midwife until the neighbors came. Dale's hands gripped the rail for a moment and then grudgingly relaxed. If this man, Bristoll, sought to provoke him to a flare-up that Martiau would mark as his fault, he would need to say something more than that. All that was past and the bitterness of the memory couldn't be eased by any clash that would endanger his future with Claiborne. There would come a better occasion than this to throw Bristoll's words back in his teeth, stuff them down his throat, and he could wait.

The *Cockatrice* fell off a point or two of the compass and began beating up against a quartering wind, heading northwest by west. At a roared command from Captain Martiau, the crewmen scampered aloft again, to reef in the skysails, topgallants and foresail, to allow the wherry to tack along on its jib. The speed of the ship slacked off until the wherry idled at a leisurely pace, moving in closer to the bay's western shore. The lurch and roll of the vessel decreased as she slowed and Dale's uneasy stomach settled enough to let him eat the midday meal dished out in pannikins by the *Cockatrice's* cook.

It was mid-afternoon when the wherry edged into the broad mouth of the Potomac and the sun was beating down with mid-summer intensity. Now Dale could see a fleet of long canoes drawn up on a sandy shore some two or three miles inland from the river's mouth and, beyond the beach, a cluster of rude shacks that, at a distance, appeared to have been built of mud. Along the shore were grouped knots of unclad people, their shiny skin reflecting the sun's rays with a peculiar brilliance.

"There are your Indians," Bristoll said. "Heed my advice for what it's worth and never go into one of their huts unless you must. The creatures themselves are clean enough but their hovels stink to heav'n and the smoke's enough to make a chimney cough. How they stand it, I don't know. A couple of minutes inside one, on my last trip, and I was sneezing and crouping for an hour."

The wherry followed a slow, zig-zag course into the river, a man at the bow constantly sounding the channel with his lead and bawl-
108

ing back his findings to the Captain standing beside the helmsman. As the *Cockatrice* drew closer to the beach, Dale could see that all the Indians, men and women, were clad only in a skirt fashioned of deerskin, caught about the waist. The men stood apart from the women, impassively watching the wherry's approach, their arms folded across their chests, their eyes fixed unmoving on the ship. Dale saw the reason for their glistening bodies and faces was the oil with which they had coated themselves. Later, Captain Martiau explained that the oil was daubed on to protect the savages from the ravenous mosquitoes of the adjacent marshlands. The braves, Dale saw, wore stripes of red paint running from their cheekbones to their jaws and some had crude designs daubed in red paint on their hairless chests. Most of the men wore one or two eagle feathers fastened to their heads by beaded bands. Closer inspection showed each band had the design of a fish at its front, over the forehead.

The women were as oil-coated as the men but wore no paint. They were, as Bristoll had said, comely figures, with high-arching breasts and spines that were ramrod straight. Certainly they were a far more impressive group than the stragglers from the Rappahannock tribes that Dale had seen at Jamestown.

Behind the women, who stood apart and further from the water than the braves, were the children, all stark naked and ranging in age from toddlers to boys and girls just entering puberty. Indeed, Dale's eye picked out two or three girls whose mammary and pubic development made his eyes slide away and return again, despite himself. He cursed himself for looking upon children with a lecherous eye and forced himself to hold his gaze to the braves.

Not so Bristoll, at the rail beside him. He was as voluble in pointing out to Morley the half-developed charms of the younger, unclothed girls as he was in commenting on the primitive beauty of the older women.

"There, now," he said, in Dale's ear. "Mark that squaw standing near that clump of bush to the right. There's not a woman in Virginia but wouldn't hesitate to match bosoms with that one. And the

109

one just bending to fix her footgear. Saw you ever a breast to equal hers, Morley, in all Jamestown?''

Though he guessed the Indians understood nothing of what Bristoll said, Dale felt his face flush with embarrassment for these women. Savages they might be, but still Dale could not find it right for Talbot Bristoll to enumerate the women's charms aloud, as one would point out the good parts of a hound bitch or a mare. He left the rail and Bristoll's side and went aft to where Captain Martiau was giving the orders that warped the wherry into a small cove, close to the beach.

"Let 'er go!" Martiau roared as Dale came alongside him and the anchor went over the side with a splash. The wherry swung around into the wind and the jib slatted for a moment, before the men handling the lines let the canvas drop.

The bearded captain turned to Dale and his teeth showed briefly in a smile.

"And so here ye are, Mister Morley," he said, "ready to do your first trading with the Indians. There's a few things ye'd best remember. Never take a personal liking to an Indian, squaw or brave. Think always that each one is out to diddle you if he can and kill you if 'twould serve his purpose. Never let an Indian, no matter how peaceful, get behind ye, and leave the Chief's wives alone. Above all, don't spoil 'em with too many presents and, when ye learn their lingo, never let 'em know a special fur is worth a tinker's dam. There are more rules, but you'll be learnin' 'em, I'll warrant, as ye go along. If ye *do* go along, that is. There's been many that've dropped the business of Indian trading early in their career, for one reason or other—mostly violent.''

Dale was in the first longboat, with Captain Martiau and Talbot Bristoll, that reached the sandy shore where the Indians waited. The boat carried no trade goods but there were presents for the Chief, Werowance, and the ranking Pascataway braves.

110

Werowance stepped forward from the other men as Captain Martiau left the longboat and walked up the shore, Morley and Bristoll behind him. The two commanders, red man and white, halted several paces from each other and Martiau burst sonorously into a series of guttural exclamations. When he had finished, Werowance replied with a similar outburst, turned and beckoned to the nearest brave behind him. That man, an older Pascataway liberally daubed with red streaks, came forward holding a three-foot arrow tipped with stag horn. He handed the arrow to the Chief; Werowance bent to lay it on the sand, its tip pointed toward himself and the other Indians, away from Martiau. Then he straightened and spoke a few more words. Martiau replied.

"Know you their talk?" Dale asked Bristoll in a low voice. The other shook his head.

"A few words," he said, "but none of what's said here. I know the ceremony, though. The chief is pointing the arrow at himself to show Martiau he's peacefully inclined. Were he unfriendly, he'd point the arrow at Martiau and we'd have to chop our way back to our boat with our blades, most likely."

"We took a risk, then, landing before he showed the arrow?"

"Not much of a risk," Bristoll replied easily. "They have their women and children here and if they were for war, the squaws and brats would not be along—though I've heard the Susquehannocks once lured a party ashore by showing their women and then brained the traders the moment they set foot on land. But these are Pascataways, not Susquehannocks, and, by reputation, they're not given to such tricks."

The welcoming ceremonies completed, Captain Martiau began distributing the gifts he had brought Werowance and his sub-chiefs. Mostly, the presents were trifling gewgaws, more fit for children than for these grave men, but there were among the gifts a few valuable articles: a butcher's cleaver for Werowance, a pair of nankeen breeches, a pewter buckle, a cloth cap. The men's presents distributed, Werowance grunted a few sounds and three women, older than most of the other squaws, came forward timidly. To each of these, Werowance's wives, Captain Martiau gave a cheap bangle that was accepted without a change in the women's impassive expressions.

"Now, Mister Morley," Captain Martiau called, and Dale stepped forward. Martiau handed him a linen shirt. "Give this to Werowance," he said, "and make a nod with your head when you do. I'll explain."

Dale thrust the shirt at the Pascataway chief while Martiau grumbled a sentence. The Chief's black eyes moved from the shirt to Martiau and then to Dale, who bobbed his head in a brief bow. Werowance took the garment, grumbled a few more words and put it beside him on the sand, with the rest of his presents.

"I told him you might come alone, next time," Martiau explained. "It's best to be ready for any unexpectedness that might bring you here and, this way, I've made him ready to trade with you. Now, Mister Bristoll."

The handsome fop, elegant in a broadcloth suit and the thigh-length boots he had pulled on before boarding the longboat, stepped forward to repeat the performance, this time with a coat of canvas. That done, Werowance spoke to Captain Martiau and gestured toward the semi-circle of rude huts. In the center of the cleared space between the huts flickered a log fire that sent up a long column of smoke.

"We're in for it now, Morley," Bristoll muttered. "We have to dine with his Pascataway lordship and I'll be bound your stomach never has been so insulted before this."

Despite Bristoll's warning, Dale found the meal enjoyable. There was roasted fish that was tasty, once he managed to scrape the scales from his big portion, and pone that had been baked in a clay oven and which rivaled the best he had had in Virginia. There was a stew, the ingredients of which Dale did not dare inquire about but which Captain Martiau told him later had muskrat as its principal part. There was a pot of wild honey, too fermented for Dale's taste, and there were tender broiled doves that Morley found as delicious as anything he had ever tasted at Captain Claiborne's board.

112

There were no plates or eating utensils. The Indians, Martiau, Bristoll and Dale squatted in a circle about the fire and, as they ate, dipped their hands into the communal pot of stew, picked up the hot and juicy doves, used their fingers to break off pieces of the pone and licked the honey from their hands and wrists. Dale had a momentary memory of that first supper party he had attended at Captain Claiborne's, and he grinned inwardly at the thought that the eating manners of these savages were not far different from those of the ladies and gentlemen who had grabbed and gorged at the tables tended by Benji and Toss.

The meal stretched on interminably and the sun sank deeper in the west. The shadows were long and purple before Werowance threw aside the picked-clean carcass of a dove, got to his feet, grunted once and stalked off to a nearby hut. The feast, apparently, was over.

"We'll trade in the morning," Captain Martiau explained as he left the fire with Dale and Bristoll. "Of course we could have done the whole deal today but that's not the way the Indians do things. They might be hot and eager for the trade goods we've brought them but they'd still have to go through all this folderol to pretend the trading is of no importance, really. A curious people, certainly."

"Ever been to Court, Martiau?" Bristoll asked. "It's not much different there." He looked down at his greasy hands and wrinkled his nose. "I'm for a swim to wash this filth off me," he said. "God's tears, I thought I'd puke at that stew! You gentlemen will join me?"

"I—I never learned to swim," Dale confessed, "but a wash sounds good. Mayhap there's a beach that's shielded from view where I can have a bath."

Bristoll's laughter was joined by Martiau's.

"And why not right here?" the Captain asked. " 'Tis the best beach hereabouts and if you're worried about offending *those* red maidens, rest at ease. They might gather to watch us but it'll give 'em pleasure, not shame, Mister Morley. You have to remember, sir, that these are *Indians*."

The Captain and Bristoll were peeled to the buff before Dale had more than removed his shirt and were splashing in the river, whooping at the water's chill, as he dallied with the removal of a stocking, glancing now and then at the women of the Indian village who began moving toward the shore at Bristoll's first breathless yell. By the time he had removed his breeches, there were twenty or more squaws perched on the low ledge that marked the high tide line, watching the white men at their bathing with unsmiling interest, never knowing the portent of the bawdy shouts that Bristoll called their way.

Dale slipped off his breeches and made a dash for the water, gasping as he plunged into waist's depth to hide himself from the concentrated gaze of the squaws. Bristoll and Martiau roared at his confusion, Talbot's high voice pelting Dale's ears with ribald observations.

"Ye cheated them out of a decent look, Morley," Bristoll cried. "They see a white man but two or three times a year and now ye give 'em no more than a passing peek. They'll wait, though, to catch you coming out."

"The lad will probably back out," chortled Captain Martiau. "God's truth, Mister Morley, ye'll be uncomfortable in this trade till ye learn they're but Indians, after all!"

Dale steeled himself to walk up to his clothes unhurriedly when he finished his bath and he noticed that the squaws' eyes were impersonal as they carefully regarded him. To them, he realized, he was as much a curiosity as they were to him, with their oil-slicked pelts and their utter lack of self-consciousness in their semi-nudity. He was able to towel himself leisurely, using his shirt, and, at length, to stand their stare as calmly as though he were being looked at by a herd of cows that might have wandered up to his swimming hole in the branch that ran into the James River.

Returned to the wherry, Dale sought out Martiau, a flood of questions slipping from his tongue, while Talbot Bristoll, after busying himself in his cabin for a while, had himself rowed ashore again.

114

"He's gone to do some wenching amongst the squaws," Captain Martiau said casually, as the squeak of the oars faded in the distance. "I find surprise in your not going with him, Mister Morley. Or are your personal differences still too great for you to accompany him, even in a quest for women?"

"I'm along to learn the trade," Dale said almost primly. "I'd think, besides, the Indians would resent a trader's lying with their women, treating them like sluts. Haven't I heard the Indians are jealous of their women's chastity?"

"Don't worry your mind about that, whilst ye're with the Pascataways or the Wicomesses," Captain Martiau said. "They have an odd set of morals here, and one would make a priest turn pale, right enough. For one Pascataway to play loosely with another's squaw would bring a killing before the deed was fully done, but they seem to think a white man's hand on their women is a totally different thing, an honor of some sort. Except the Chief's wives—they're not to be touched.

"Now, the Susquehannocks, they're different. From what I've seen of them, I'd rather bed with a rattlesnake than with a Susquehannock squaw. 'Tis a pity, too, because the Susquehannock women are far fairer than these women of the fishin' tribes when they're young. Aye, I've known men to see the risk and still take it, to taste one of those morsels, and pay the price. And a steep price it was they paid, too, and more than any woman or a hundred could be worth."

He clapped a hand to Dale's shoulder and said:

"So, Mister Morley, if you would have yourself an Indian maid, make sure she's of the fishin' tribes. Never force an Indian wench, Mister Morley, and never give one rum because the braves believe a woman drunk with rum has been possessed by devils and, not bein' responsible, has been forced. And that means trouble in any tribe."

Ashore, the light of the Indians' fire flickered low and then blazed up as its attendant threw on fresh fuel. Some night bird, a heron or a loon, squawked discordantly in the darkness. There was the

115

whine of a mosquito, the lap-lapping of the water along the sides of the wherry, the splash of some large fish that broached nearby. There was the muffled sound of voices in the forecastle, where the crew was gathered. At the bow, the watch stood, an unmoving silhouette.

Dale was asleep in his bunk when Talbot Bristoll returned, smelling of rum and unsteady on his feet, his face flushed and his fine clothes rumpled. He stood beside Dale, looking down at him in the uncertain light of the cabin's sconce, and grinned at Dale's sleepy response to his hail.

"Y'should've come along," he said. "I had my fill of sport this night. Tender as a partridge, she was, and as wild as a mink when the rum touched her. Mayhap you heard her snortin' out here on the ship, did you?"

"I'm tired," Dale said brusquely, "and Captain Martiau's called for an early rising. Best get some sleep, Bristoll, while you can."

"Sleep!" Talbot scoffed. "Time enough to sleep when I get old and my juices dry up. But if you need your rest so sorely, I'll put out the lamp and lie here in my bunk, thinkin' over the sweet happenings of the past hours."

The next day was given over to business. There were only the briefest ceremonies before the Pascataways began bringing out the furs they had cached against the traders' coming. Dale was astonished at the number of pelts the Indians brought out to trade and even Captain Martiau was impressed by the show of skins.

Keen bargaining it required and keen bargaining Captain Martiau did, while Dale sat on one side of him and Bristoll on the other, yawning and red-eyed from the previous night's adventure.

Dale listened and watched carefully as Martiau haggled, coaxed, flattered and praised the Pascataways who came forward with their furs, avidly eyeing the pile of trade goods behind the Captain. Useless fripperies comprised half the goods Martiau had to trade and the other half consisted of utilitarian articles such as hoes and hatchets, flint and steel, knives, bolts of cloth, articles of clothing.

116

"These fishin' Indians," he told Dale and Talbot, "will trade almost anything for white man's clothing, though they wear their shirts and breeches only once or twice a year at their *match-comaco,* their councils. The hunting tribes, the Susquehannocks and the others, wouldn't give you a rat skin for a duke's wardrobe. *They* want muskets, powder and ball above all else but Claiborne won't give 'em arms, save for a few exceptions. All of them want rum but again Claiborne won't trade with rum, though that damned Yonge will, and with muskets, too, if he can get 'em."

"I'd think that would be dangerous," Dale commented.

"It is," Martiau agreed, "but Yonge don't care. So long as his scalp's safe, he'd trade 'em cannon, if he could. There's many a whitened bone in the northern forests that was put there by Yonge's reckless greed at tradin'."

The day wore on, the maneuvering between the traders tireless. Dale Morley found his attention wandering, his mind dulled by the ceaseless grunting and hand-waving, but Captain Martiau never seemed to relax his alertness nor let down his guard. In the afternoon, hours after the bargaining had begun, the bluff captain was as quick to seize an advantage and as alert to a piece of Indian trickery as when he had first begun trading.

Talbot Bristoll, after a losing effort to keep his eyes open, left the trading circle and wandered off to find a shady place where he could stretch out. The Captain's eyes followed him disapprovingly as Bristoll, one hand held to his throbbing head, walked down the beach.

"He'll make no trader by wenching all night and sleeping the day away," he growled into his beard, "and I intend to tell Captain Claiborne as much, when we get back to Jamestown."

Dale forced himself to keep a closer eye on what was going on. As the day wore away, he was able to distinguish the intonation of one grunt from another and link the Indian word to the article at which Captain Martiau pointed. From time to time, Martiau made an aside that explained a phrase or a hand motion and near the end

117

of the trading Dale found himself possessed of a rudimentary knowledge of the Pascataway dialect. It was, he found, a very elementary language, with one word serving a dozen meanings, depending on the move of the hand that accompanied it. Finally the last fur changed hands and the trading was over.

"And not a bad day's work," the Captain said, raising his arms to stretch. He got to his feet and moved toward the shore, to direct the transfer of the furs to the wherry.

"We'll sail at dawn," he called back to Dale. "I've no stomach for running that channel in the dark. Whilst we're here, why not look over the village, Mister Morley? They have no long house at this place, where you'd not be welcome, so go wherever you will and fill your eyes with sights to tell your friends back home."

Dale seized on the suggestion and walked toward the cluster of huts beyond the tide line. The Indians seemed to pay him no heed, except for the smaller children who scattered at his approach like wild animals and scurried out of sight. The women, he saw, were pounding dried corn into a coarse meal for pone, using a rude mortar and pestle of stone for the task. Others were sewing deerskin garments with bone needles and sinews for thread, cleaning fish with a minimum of waste motion, mixing fish oil with a red pigment to make the paint with which the braves decorated their faces. At the shore a group of young squaws stood knee deep in water, bathing the parts of their bodies not covered by the brief skirt and assisting each other in plucking the hair from under the arms. Dale wondered at the Indians' fastidiousness concerning their body hair —and not one of the men showed the faintest shadow of a beard or a sign of chest hair—when their huts, as his nose plainly told him, were as slovenly as they were.

The huts themselves were rough hovels fashioned of clay reinforced by sticks and rushes. Their doors were so small that to enter them a person must crawl on his hands and knees. They were windowless except for an opening in the slightly domed roof, placed there to admit what sunlight could come through and to let at least some of the smoke from the individual hut fires escape.

Soon he reached the outer perimeter of the little village and prepared to return to the beach and the longboat. It was then that a young woman, deep-breasted and with a fine, narrow face, spoke to him with the suggestion of a smile on her lips.

"Rom?" she asked, in a voice that was little more than a whisper. "Got rom?"

The words, the un-Indian smile, offered proof that this girl had been taught by some white man who had concerned himself with more than furs. Nor could Dale blame that man, whoever he had been, for his interest in this woman. Of all the squaws he had seen in the village, this woman was outstandingly beautiful, without the swarthiness, the thick features that the others bore. Her nose was high-bridged, her lips were not as pendulous as were the others, and her breasts were full and proud, their dark nipples tinged red either by paint or by nature.

Hadn't Captain Martiau said—but no, by God, he'd have none of that! He had sworn no oath at Susan's deathbed but there was some strange unspoken word within him that told him he owed her memory this much, that he would tousle no wench while the overturned earth was still raw on her grave.

"No," he said, roughly. "No rum."

"Bead?" the girl asked. "Bells?"

She came closer to him and moved her body against his, a redskinned temptress in a scrap of deerhide skirt, the warmth of her heady in Dale's nostrils. She took his arm and gently, yet urgently, began pulling him toward the alders that fringed the camp, that white woman's smile still on her mouth.

There was no reason why Dale should have resisted. It was, he knew, the accustomed thing, a passage that would give him pleasure, an experience that might eclipse all his other jousts with women, and he would be less than a man if he shook his head again. Yet he did shake his head and pull his arm free of the girl's grasp.

"No," he said stupidly. "I'm sorry, but no."

He turned his back on the girl and plunged into the woods she had been drawing him toward, going ahead blindly, stretching the distance between himself and the squaw lest his senseless resolve crumble under the nearness of that warm, pulsating, half-naked body. He had gone perhaps a hundred yards into the copse when he stumbled across Talbot Bristoll. And Bristoll's companion.

She was a young girl, barely half-developed, and as lithe as a golden-skinned otter. She sat in Bristoll's lap while the young rake buried his face in the curve of her neck, his long-fingered hands hungrily seeking as they roamed the child's body. The girl swung her face toward Dale as he burst into the clearing and her eyes stared at him vacantly; her mouth hung half open and wet.

Not from passion, he thought instantly—great God, not that infant! Then he saw the demijohn beside Bristoll, the bleared eyes of Talbot as he raised his head, and he knew the child was drunk. A nauseating wave of disgust swept him as his lips tightened and the dimple showed deep in one cheek.

Christ, he thought, what manner of man was this who'd violate a girl that age—even an Indian girl—after he'd robbed her senses with drink? With an abundance of grown women in this place, all seemingly willing to be partners to a tumble, how could Bristoll choose this—this baby?

"Before God," he burst out, "but you're a pretty figure, Bristoll!"

"Go away," Talbot Bristoll said, his voice thick. "I'm engaged, Morley, as any fool could see. If you'd have this girl you'll have to wait till I'm finished with her, and I've scarce begun!"

Dale took a long stride forward, grasped the Indian girl by the wrist and pulled her to her feet in a movement so swift that Bristoll's grasping clutch missed the slim body.

"Go home," Dale told the tottering child roughly. "Go home to your people!"

The girl's head lolled on her neck. She took a stumbling step and then collapsed, rolled over on her back and lay there, chirruping weakly in a sound that was half laugh and half sob.

"God damn you!" Bristoll cried furiously. "Keep your hands off my wench, Morley, or I'll spike your liver!"

120

He scrambled to his feet, lurched at Dale. Dale's hand, fingers outspread, caught him in the chest and sent him staggering back. Bristoll's hand went to the hilt of his cutlass and Dale leaped in.

His left hand caught Bristoll's right wrist in a crushing grip, his right hand, balled into a fist, came up and over and crashed into Talbot's face. He grunted with satisfaction as he felt his knuckles bite deeply, pulled back his fist and clubbed again at Bristoll's head.

All the long pent-up loathing for this man erupted within Dale in a surge of black fury that sent his fist driving again and again at Bristoll's face. He laughed aloud when he saw a trickle of blood start from Talbot's nose and swung again at that battered feature. He loosed his left hand's grip and flailed with that fist to follow up his right-handed blows.

Bristoll went back, slipped and fell to one knee. When he straightened, the cutlass was out and gleaming in the sunlight that filtered down through the trees.

"Now, by God," Talbot panted, "we'll see who's cock of this walk! Draw, God damn you, and fight like the gentleman you're not! I'm no cutpurse bully to tussle with a gutter scum like you. Draw your blade whilst you can, you whore's spawn!"

Dale wrenched his own cutlass from his belt. Rage made him reckless, oblivious of the fact that any kind of swordplay against Talbot Bristoll could have but one ending. At the moment he would have run against a dozen Talbot Bristolls and never felt himself overmatched.

The cutlass was light in his hands when he made his first slashing stroke. There was a jar and the blade was turned aside, hurled off into the air while Bristoll's own stroke sliced the air dangerously close to him. Dale tried again, and again the blow went wide of its target. Again Talbot's furious counter barely escaped biting into his flesh.

Now Bristoll was on the attack, pressing Dale back and back as he fought to beat off the rain of blows that came at him. Talbot's face had lost its drunken bloat; now it was drawn and pale except

121

for the crimson rivulet of blood, the eyes half-closed, the mouth set in a curving, mirthless smile. This was Bristoll the killer, the man who had fought a score of duels and had won them all. This was the man who Captain Claiborne had said never showed a breath of mercy to any opponent, once his blade had crossed the other's. This was the Talbot Bristoll whose classmate at Oxford had slipped on a lawn made slick by dew one morning, and who had speared his fallen enemy through the ribs before the seconds could intervene.

Dale's reckless anger deserted him as abruptly as it had risen. Suddenly, where there had been hot fury there came the cold realization that he had no chance against this master swordsman, that he was facing death. Claiborne had given him a smattering of instruction in handling the light sword; he knew nothing about manipulating the cutlass beyond sweeping it as he would a scythe and that was not good enough. Bristoll was making his broad blade twinkle like a rapier in the afternoon sun, stabbing, slashing, cutting, parrying Dale's wild swipes.

There was a sudden wrench and Dale's blade went spinning out of his hand, turning over and over, to land in a clump of budding laurel ten feet away. He looked after it, then back at the pale-faced Bristoll. Talbot's lips were drawn back in a snarl that bared his long, yellow teeth and his eyes glinted insanely from under the half-closed lids.

"Now, you nameless bastard, you die!"

The name, the base truth of the epithet, wiped all fear and caution from Dale's mind. With an answering snarl he leaped forward, his big hands grasping, full into the orbit of that flashing cutlass. One arm went up to parry Bristoll's slice, made clumsy by surprise, and he felt the searing bite of the blade on his shoulder before he reached Talbot's throat. There he clung, his fingers biting deep, shaking the other man as a terrier would shake a rat in the pits, watching Bristoll's face purple, his eyes bulge, hearing the breath rattle in the other man's squeezed gullet.

Talbot's cutlass thudded to the ground as Bristoll clawed at Dale's hands with his own, trying to break the grasp that starved his lungs of air. His nails scratched at Dale's wrists, his boots thudded into Dale's shins, his eyes rolled upward and his struggle grew more feeble.

Dale clenched more tightly. He never had killed a man but he meant to now. There was a great burning joy within him as he watched Talbot Bristoll dying in his hands. So they would all die, every one of them that threw the name bastard at him!

There was something hindering him at his work, something that was trying to pull him away from this foul thing he would dispose of. There were hands on him, wrestling him backward, and beyond Bristoll, coming through the haze of hate that had misted everything about him, was a stranger's face, and another's. There was a voice in his ear, telling him to stop, ordering him to let go, beating at him with sledgehammer blows. He gripped Bristoll's throat with a stronger grasp—and then something struck the back of his head, there was an explosion of brightly-colored stars and then blackness.

When he came to, Dale found himself lying on a pallet of folded sailcloth aboard the wherry. The lift and drop of the deck told him the vessel was under way again, even before he looked aloft to see the mast swaying from side to side against the stars.

He struggled into a sitting position and was rewarded by the hot lance of a pain that threatened to cleave his skull, where Bristoll had failed. Another stab of pain spiked his shoulder and he put a hand to that ache to find his upper arm firmly bandaged. He had been hurt, then, but how? He had been ashore with Captain Martiau, trading with the Pascataways, and later he had visited the village, there had been an Indian girl who had asked him for rum or beads and then—he remembered it all, then.

He rested his elbows on his knees and dropped his head into his hands with a groan. This, his first trip for Captain Claiborne, had turned out to be a pretty mess. He had killed one of Claiborne's

123

lieutenants, Bristoll—or had he? Had the others managed to tear him away from Talbot in time or was he now on his way back to Jamestown to face the charge of murder? If so, it would be a strange thing that he be made to dance a jig on empty air for the sake of a naked Indian child.

He looked down at his ankles and saw they were unfettered. Did that mean he was no murderous prisoner or only that Captain Martiau had figured him safe enough without chains while the *Cockatrice* was at sea? He turned his head toward the stern and saw only the silhouette of the helmsman there. He looked forward and made out the thick bulk of the captain, identified by the roaring voice Martiau directed at the seamen who worked on a sheet line in the bow.

He pushed himself up out of his sitting position and clung to the mizzenmast until his brain stopped whirling and his knees firmed. Then, his head jarring with each step he took, he made his uncertain way toward where the captain stood.

Martiau turned at his approach, put his hands on his hips and ceased his bellowing. He waited as Dale made his way up to him, trying to hold himself erect, blinking his eyes against the ache in his skull.

"Bristoll," he managed, finally. "Did I—did—"

"Did you kill him; is that what you're trying to say?" the Captain asked. "Not quite, though it'll be some time before he'll be able to swallow proper and God knows when he'll get his voice back."

Dale looked down at the deck, trying to find words to say.

"I did not mean. I—"

He fell silent. He could not say he hadn't meant to kill Bristoll because he had, as fiercely as he ever had meant to do a thing. He'd not deny that, though it might mean his dismissal from Captain Claiborne's service, a return to the hoe and the manure fork.

"Ye didn't mean to strangle him, eh?" Martiau growled. "No more than he meant to snip your head from your shoulders, I'll warrant. God's blood, I took a fine pair of cockerels with me on this voyage! Get them to be friendly, Captain Claiborne tells me, and

124

the next I know I'm tearin' one's hands from the other's throat, and him bleedin' from a cruel cut on the arm."

"The man was—"

"Don't tell me what happened, Mister Morley, because the story was there for anybody with eyes to see! Mister Bristoll got an Indian girl drunk, against orders, and you interfered, for whatever reasons I don't know. You fought with cutlasses until yours went flyin' into a bush and then you used your hands. 'Tis lucky we looked for you after you disappeared from the village. I thought you'd wandered into the forest and might have lost your way. If we hadn't set out a search, you'd have the blood of a senseless murder on your hands now, Mister Morley."

"The girl was a child—"

"Child or beldame, she was an Indian and not important enough to draw blood between two white men!" Captain Martiau cried. "Oh, I don't say Mister Bristoll was in the right. That tiffety-taffety buck near cost us our friendship with the Pascataways, not to speak of his own neck. The girl was some relation of Werowance's, but not too close, thank Heav'n. I've talked my way out of some tight places in my time but never one that was quite that edgy. As it was, I had to give him—Werowance, I mean—presents I'd planned on giving the Wicomesses at the Isle of Kent to quiet him. And that means I'll have to strip my own chest to keep the Wicomesses happy. Well, by the saints, that young man will pay me for what I have to give away of my own!"

Dale put a hand to the back of his head and tenderly explored a lump on the back of his skull. Martiau grunted as Dale winced.

"Hurts, does it?" he asked without sympathy. "I had to deal you a buffet with the hilt of my blade to break you loose from Bristoll. You were a wild man, Mister Morley, and we had to use strong means to prevent a killin'. You were as limp as a mackerel when we brought you aboard and I thought I'd cracked your pate for sure but Wales, the bos'n, has picked up some doctor's learnin' somewhere and he said you'd come 'round, and you did.

"And I"—his voice soared to a higher register—"had to run that

God damned channel in the dark, to get away from the village before Werowance changed his mind about lettin' us go with our heads not bashed in. Never a landmark to help me and we touched a bar once and I thought we were aground to stay, before we pushed over it. You and Mister Bristoll have made plenty of unwelcome work for all of us this night, Mister Morley."

"Bristoll," Dale said uncertainly, "where is he?"

"He's below," Martiau said curtly. "He has my orders to keep to his cabin till we return to Jamestown, after lookin' in at Kent Island. Jesus, you must have used a club on his nose, from the looks of it! Between his flattened nose and his grackle's voice, you've spoiled the best beau in the Province, Mister Morley, and he'll not thank you for that."

His voice softened as he added:

"I'm not envious of your position, Mister Morley. Bristoll will call you out, as soon as you get back to Jamestown, and he'll kill you I think, if you engage him in a duel, with all the polite rules of fashion observed."

"I'm not afraid of him," Dale said.

"You should be," Captain Martiau returned drily. "I intend to give Captain Claiborne the whole story and it may be he can check Mister Bristoll's plans for revenge. The Captain seems to be able to handle that young cock as nobody else can. And Bristoll was in the wrong, givin' rum to a girl too young to wear a skirt, after he'd been warned against that. Claiborne might be angry enough over that to keep Bristoll from challengin' you and thereby save your life. For he would kill you, sir, as my name's Nicholas Martiau."

"He could kill me now, perhaps," Dale admitted, "but I plan to learn how to handle a sword."

"You'd best leave off all thought of eatin' or sleepin' or workin' for the Captain, then, whilst you practice," Martiau grunted. "I've seen Bristoll use a light blade and he's fair wondrous. But that's your affair, Mister Morley, and I have work to do, gettin' this ship to Kent Island against a devilish head wind."

126

He turned away and then hesitated, to look back over his shoulder at Dale.

"It might interest ye to know," he said quietly, "that I'm givin' you a good recommendation to the Captain, and not so good a word about Mister Bristoll. I think ye'll make a trader, Mister Morley— if Mister Bristoll don't carve up your guts before you have a chance to learn. Now get below to the galley and find yourself some food for there'll be work for you to do, helping me, when we land and if you feel up to it."

Dawn was creasing the eastern skies with ledges of rose-tinted clouds when the *Cockatrice* edged into the harbor of Kent Island. Even Dale's unpracticed eye and his aching head let him see that this anchorage was far superior to the Potomac River village they had stopped at the day before. The wherry passed through a narrow gut into a small bay of calm, almost glassy, water. The bay was rimmed by a sandy shore and beyond the sand stretched level fields that, in the distance, rose to meet a forest so neat it might have been an English nobleman's park.

Great flocks of wild fowl rose, with the whistling rustle of their wings, as the *Cockatrice* headed toward the shore. Ducks, geese and brent geese circled the wherry in clouds before settling to the water again with a series of tumultuous splashings. Ashore, the tall grass bent in rippling waves under the light wind, as though imitating the swells of the Chesapeake, and from those green depths rose darting songbirds, tanagers, red-birds, vireos, finches, canaries and orioles in colorful profusion.

If the Potomac River landing of the Pascataways had been a peaceful place, this island was a restful heaven. Dale Morley was struck by the thought that this place seemed to be waiting for someone who could appreciate its virtues enough to live there, drink in its beauty and batten on its bounty. There, Dale thought, on that rise to the southeast, a man could build a home that would have surroundings that would make a king envious, and these sprawling fields would certainly nourish any crop that might be planted, once the grass was cleared and the soil plowed.

He never had been one to rhapsodize over an unusual piece of
scenery, a particularly striking sunset, a picture of the forests clad
in their autumn finery, but now he found himself deeply affected by
the quiet, timeless beauty of Kent Island. It was as though the
wherry, moving into this bay, had brought him to the place he had
been journeying toward all his life, through the muck and filth of
the London alleys, the dreary marshes of Jamestown and the steaming lowlands of the James River Valley. But it was impossible, he
thought, that this wild, untenanted island could be his goal. There
was no place in his plans for settling down again, picking up the
hoe and bending his back to the humdrum life of a planter. This
island might be a seductive place but it never could tempt him to
leave off this life he had just embarked upon.

"Let 'er go!" bawled Captain Martiau, astern, and the anchor
splashed overside, the *Cockatrice* slowly turned into the wind and
came to rest in the harbor of Kent Island. Dale shook his head,
despite the ache. He was a fool, he told himself, to imagine that the
dancing waves along the shore, the rippling grass, the nodding
trees further inland and the hastening birds were all bidding him
welcome.

Chapter Four, 1630

KING CHARLES HAD AT LEAST ONE QUALITY IN common with his father: his liking for money. Old Jaimie had been wiser in most ways than Charles, irresponsible as he might have become in his last days; he'd kept his peace with Parliament, yielded a prerogative here and another there, so long as Commons granted him the gold he wanted.

The son, though, had let himself be blinded by Buckingham's spurious dazzle, seduced by Buckingham's giddy promises. He had drained his coffers to finance Buckingham's wasteful, senseless wars and had smiled forgivingly when Bucks had deserted his army to let it be massacred by the French artillery. And when the Parliament had balked at giving more moneys for more futile expeditions, Charles had prorogued the House, banished all semblance of popular government, tried to bring Commons to heel by royal will rather than by temporizing.

Well, Buckingham had met his last adventure in the form of a dagger driven deep by an assassin (one of the few survivors of the grim battlefield on the Isle of Ré, the field Bucks had fled) but his passing from the scene had not helped Charles. The King was still deadlocked with his suspended Parliament and the money was not coming in.

Sir George Calvert, first Lord Baltimore and a Catholic, could offer Charles money, prospects of a great revenue, in return for the King's grant of a colony in Virginia. Charles cared not a whit whether a man was a Catholic or an Anglican; he was too devout a worshiper of the golden calf and royal power to pay much heed to ecclesiastic differences, though he made the proper noises about his love for the episcopacy. Charles would always listen to a man who could talk and make his words echo the clink of coins.

Sir George Calvert could talk. He had talked his way into James's Privy Council; he could talk his way into Virginia, certainly. And when his voice grew weary, there was always Cecilius, his son, to take up the argument. Cecilius was as handy a man with words as his father; possibly a more clever one with a phrase than the sire who'd taught him.

Against Baltimore were Virginia's representatives among the Commissioners of Plantation and the men who acted in the interests of William Cloberry. Baltimore was confident he could deal with them, when the time came. Some could be bought and those who could not be, could have their protests beaten down by argument, with God's help—and the Virginians' own brashness. Charles, ever jealous of his prerogatives, had flared with rage more than once over the Virginia Assembly's insistence that it could *pass* laws, not merely *suggest* them to the throne. The King had slashed his "nay" across the faces of a score of bills which the Virginia Assembly, playing at ruler, had adopted. Yes, it should not be too hard to convince His Majesty that these Virginians needed reining in, that they should be reminded that Charles the First still had the say over whether the Province could flourish, or even survive.

Baltimore began his fight to get to Jamestown, well-armored with the King's writ and outfitted with a shield of royal favor off which Claiborne's barbs would bounce like hail off a helmet. But he never got any kind of a patent from Charles because, in 1632, the torments of the flesh that he had beaten back for so many years marshaled themselves for a final assault that sacked all the redoubts of the Baron's indomitable resistance and laid him, still calm-visaged, in his grave.

Thus it was Calvert's eldest son, Cecilius, second Lord Baltimore, who received the patent from Charles. It was not the grant old George had asked for, but it still was the most generous patent ever signed by Charles and, possibly, any other English king. And it was
130

Cecilius who was the first Proprietary of Mary's Land, a place he never saw, and it was Cecilius who took up the sword against Captain William Claiborne and Dale Morley and came close to ruining them both.

But many things happened before then.

Dale Morley was Captain Claiborne's first lieutenant, secretary and sometimes spokesman when he sailed for England in the Spring of 1630 with the Captain aboard the vessel *Gryphon,* Captain Thomas Smith, master, one of Cloberry and Company's high-sided, square-rigged ships in the American trade.

Talbot Bristoll sailed on that voyage, too, a fact that irritated Dale more than he showed. True, Dale knew he was closer to Claiborne than Bristoll and had improved his position ever since the first trading journey to the Pascataways, but ahead lay London and the sleek-gestured fop would certainly be more at ease in the salons of the great city and at Charles's court at Windsor—if they succeeded in getting that far—than he. His manners had improved, but Jamestown was not London and Bristoll would have an advantage in England that gave Dale uneasy moments in his speculations about the trip.

If Bristoll had despised Dale as an upstart peasant once, he hated him as a rival now; a rival for Captain Claiborne's regard and a rival for the favors of Genevieve Loman. Claiborne had told Dale recently that Jenny Loman was Bristoll's intended wife. That might have been one of the Captain's gallantries (for certainly neither Bristoll nor Jenny ever had behaved like a pair bound by honorable marriage intentions) but when Genevieve had begun showing her preference for Dale's company over Talbot's, the broken-nosed man apparently had convinced himself, at least, that Jenny had been pledged to him and that this clod whom it pleased Captain Claiborne to shape into a gentleman was trying to wreck his, Bristoll's, great love.

Dale would have been dead by Bristoll's sword long since had not Claiborne interfered.

"You'll not offend a lady's good name by brawling over her," he had growled. "One rash move and both of you'll be out of my company."

A less self-assured man, perhaps a wiser man, than William Claiborne would have dismissed either Dale or Talbot, or both, from his entourage, to let them hack at each other with their blades. But Claiborne had always prided himself on his ability to handle men, no matter how difficult; to expel Bristoll or Morley would be, to him, an admission that he could not cope with them, and he would make no such acknowledgment. It must have filled some need in him, given him some strange pleasure, to have as his lieutenants two young men who were kept from each other's throats only by the grip he held on each.

Claiborne sailed without Governor Harvey's blessing, even against the Governor's will, but he was supported by nearly every other man in the Province and though he carried no official warrants he knew he could speak for Virginia when—and if—he ever got within speaking distance of the King.

His departure from Jamestown was hurried. It followed the receipt of a letter from Cloberry, a letter that bordered on the frantic. Dale knew the contents of that letter; he had copied it, with certain omissions directed by the Captain, for circulation throughout Virginia.

"Calvert," Cloberry had written, "seems bound to rob your Province of great pieces of her territory. His scheming, and his son's scheming, the son being no less an evil danger to you than the father, spell disaster to your Province in a way that cannot be ignored by any of you, if you would save yourselves and Virginia. . . ."

"I'll go myself to England," the Captain had exclaimed, "and gain an audience with the King if I have to—"

He broke off sharply. Did he give Dale Morley a searching glance as his lips clamped down over the words that had nearly spilled out?

"I'll get an audience with the King," he continued more calmly, after a second's hesitation. "My family has friends at court who'll
132

equal Calvert's. There's Lord Cartney, one of Cloberry's investors, who'll get me to Charles, I'll warrant, and there are others who have a money interest in this affair. I'll raise a force that'll meet Calvert's on any throne room field."

He was excited now, his eyes alight with his anticipation of the fight, his hands moving in darting gestures that could have been passes made with a rapier, his teeth showing beneath his mustaches in an expectant smile. Already he was routing Lord Baltimore and the Papists, the war to keep Virginia free from Catholic encroachment was fought and won by Claiborne, single-handed. He saw Harvey gone, hooted out of the Province by the people who hailed his own triumphant return from England. He saw himself in the Governor's Mansion, knighted by an admiring King.

One of the Governor's blacks was waiting in the Mansion courtyard, holding the reins of the Captain's black stallion, Bristoll's dappled mare and Bella. Dale cast a proud glance at his horse, watching her toss her head and switch her rear like a wench just pinched, greeting his return. Bella was the prettiest animal of the three, not so fast as the black stallion but easier of pace and possessed of a hundred little mannerisms that had long since won Morley's heart. That horse dealer Jack Bagshaw had sold him a good mount whether he had intended to or not and now Bella had a rider who didn't shame her with his lack of skill in the saddle.

Bristoll, though, misused his horses as he misused his sword and his women. He broke the animals' legs and foundered them and cut their throats when he had ruined them. Even Captain Claiborne grunted his disgust at the way Bristoll treated his horses.

"The animals are mine, aren't they?" Bristoll would ask when anybody dared protest. "I paid for 'em; I'll use 'em as I please."

There was none who could deny him that right, but there was not a man in the Province of Virginia who would ever let Talbot Bristoll buy or borrow any horse of his.

133

"Keep your spavined nag, then," Talbot had snarled at Dale when he had brusquely refused Bristoll's offer for Bella. "She's not a fit brute for a gentleman to ride. I intended her to pull a cart; at least she's some faster than an ox."

"The cart that'll carry your begutted body home some day, you mean?" Dale asked. "I'll lend Bella for that task, and happily, dear friend."

So let him draw, he thought at the time. He could handle a light sword now, and a cutlass, too. Claiborne had tutored him in the use of the rapier; Nicholas Martiau had showed him how to swing the heavier blade. Both the captains might say he still was years away from Bristoll as a swordsman, but Dale held secretly that what he lacked in his wrist he'd make up in his fury. So let Bristoll draw.

But Talbot had not reached for his weapon that day, nor in the days that followed, when biting words flew between the two men and Dale matched Bristoll's venom with a new-found knack of wielding insults. Bristoll was still held back by Claiborne's threat to dismiss him from his service if more than curses were exchanged between his two lieutenants. Curiously, perhaps, Talbot held his position as Claiborne's aide in high regard, higher than his hate for Dale Morley.

Dale smarted at the thought that his enemy's blade was stayed only by Claiborne's order; he fretted over the fact that any billings-gate score he might make against Bristoll was left unchallenged only by reason of the Captain's checkrein over Talbot. He had asked Claiborne to slip the leash from Bristoll and the Captain's reply had been definite.

"Here's my sword!" Claiborne had roared, starting up from his chair and reaching for the blade, drawing the weapon from its ring. "Here, take it! Hold the hilt with both your hands, the point against your belly, and fall forward on it! 'Twill save us time and keep you from making yourself more a fool than you were born! By the living Christ, if you're bound to kill yourself, I'll send you west to throw hot ashes in Opechancanough's eyes. Get to your letters, *clerk,* and
134

leave the dueling to those who'd not slice their own crupper whilst trying to parry a thrust!"

Clerk! Hah. Some day. . .

"We'll sail on the *Gryphon,*" Claiborne was saying, as they reached their horses in the Mansion yard. The Captain swung into his saddle with a supple grace that others might imitate but seldom equal. "The three of us will go to England and I'll plead Virginia's case myself. Talbot, your man Villiers is dead now, so you'll be safe enough in London. Dale, 'twill give you an opportunity to renew your acquaintance with Old Bess."

He burst into high laughter at Dale's scowl and Bristoll's puzzled glance.

"Not Queen Bess, Talbot," he chuckled, "though a queen in her own right—of a sort, eh, Dale? Dale's Bess rules her own kingdom and her subjects with a dainty hand, or did. She might be dead now, Dale, and you could lay some pretty posies on her grave and offer up a prayer for the repose of her sweet soul."

Dale busied himself with mounting to Bella's saddle, his face dark, the tell-tale muscle twitching at his jaw. It was always this way; whenever he came close to thinking he had made something of himself, the Captain was ready with a scrap of speech to remind him that he had sprung from a harridan's hutch of abandoned bastards, that the silver-buckled shoes he wore now encased feet that once had trod the dung and gutter filth of London's stinking riverside alleys.

"But get to the accounts now, Dale," Claiborne said, his voice now the clipped order of the commander. "Copy that letter from Cloberry as I told you it must go. We'll show that message to every man in the Province who matters and let his pork-rumped Excellency, Harvey, see what happens when a man of action takes a hand. Talbot, attend me. We're riding to Henrico, first, and we'll spend the night there. Next—"

Claiborne swung his horse and went out of the courtyard at a gallop. Talbot Bristoll spurred his gray to follow. Dale Morley was left alone, except for the slave who rolled his eyes as Bella's rider glanced his way. Morley's anger at being left behind, his humiliation over the Captain's taunts, sent Dale's spurs deep into Bella's flanks and the horse leaped forward with a protesting upswing of her fine head. She danced awhile, until Dale soothed her, and then went out of the courtyard at a trot. There was no need for a canter, Dale told himself caustically; the Captain's office was no more than a long stone's throw from the Governor's Mansion and he was going no further than there.

He lost some of his gloom as he worked on Claiborne's letters and ledgers. He was going back to England and his return would be as a man whom no one could recognize as the boy who had sailed on O'Halley's *Solace*. He had always been big for his age; now he was full-grown, a young giant of a fellow, but well-proportioned everywhere.

More than that, he was at least as close to being a gentleman as any base-born freedman could possibly be. He could read and write, he could ride and use a sword, he could make a leg without an effort and kiss a soft hand without slobbering. He could carry his share of idle conversation with the ladies. He had grunted his way through a conference with Alliquint, chief of the Susquehannocks, and never erred once in a nicety of Indian custom. He had spoken for William Claiborne before a group of wealthy planters at Henrico on an occasion when it had been impossible for the Captain to be present and he had acquitted himself well. He could dance a *pavane* and take part in the rites of a Yaocomicoe *match-comaco* without blundering in either; he could delight a fashionable lady with a titillating word or touch and still know exactly where lay the boundary line between permissible daring and offensive boldness.

Yes, he could go back to England knowing he was the best-favored visitor from the Colonies that Charles's court had seen in many a day, as far as looks went, at any rate. He had no doubts about his personable bearing and if he ever had, it required only a glance into the Captain's glass to banish them. The calculating gleam that
136

leaped to Genevieve Loman's eyes at times served still better to re-assure him on that score.

Genevieve Loman. He put down the quill and leaned back in his chair to stretch his long arms above his head. Now, there was a pretty piece—to look at, anyway. He no longer needed to speculate on the difference between upturned cotton petticoats and satin skirts; the red-haired Chrissy Gauer had furnished him with that knowledge sometime before and there had been another lady of quality who had assisted in further explorations of the subject, a quieter, softer, more white-skinned woman than the oestrous Chrissy and less satisfying in some ways.

But Jenny Loman; what would she be like? The light in her eyes, the queer, slanted smile she gave him, her warm, intimate voice, her hand on his arm and his knee, all promised him delights that made him hot and flushed, just thinking of them.

If she ever had been Talbot Bristoll's, she seemed to be treating him more coldly now, whenever he, Dale, was near her. He had been given more of the sidelong glances, more of the queer, quirked smiles, than Talbot lately. But there was something else; that nagging doubt in his own mind that Genevieve Loman really meant what her expressions, her actions implied. Perhaps, he thought, she was amusing herself with him, watching him flame and flush with his desire for her and then withdrawing into the haven of cool impersonality that she seemed forever keeping open as an avenue of retreat. Perhaps she found her pleasure in laughing at the men she had aroused, gelding her snorting stallions with her abrupt changes from hot to cold, from reckless to proper, from daring to reproving.

He twisted in his chair at the thought of her, picked up the quill, nibbled at it, dropped it again. There was the way she had of deliberately bending over in front of a man—in front of him, at least —so that her gown fell away from her bosom to let him see what he might possess if he found the answer to the puzzle she posed. There was her habit of looking up at him, her eyes carrying that familiar gleam, and wetting her full lips with the tip of her red, sharp

137

tongue. There was her manner of pressing her haunch against his, softly yet urgently, and then moving away quickly to make the touch seem accidental.

He threw himself out of his chair and began pacing the office. Damn the woman! What she needed was a man's hand in her hair, twisting it to bring her to her knees or to fling her on a bed, a man's broad palm to slap her out of the cold disdain she affected, a man's knee to hold her down if she would writhe and try to escape. She must be weary of all these pretty manners, this advancing and retreating love talk, as regular as a dance step, this mincing trot when the time called for a headlong gallop and to hell with the height of a hedge.

If he had her here now, he'd show her what it was like to be made love to by a man! He'd not be put off by any tap of a fan, nor any rebuke or protest; not even by a scream or her clawing nails, if she should struggle. She was human, even if she was a woman, and she must want an end to this teasing, empty shadow-love as much as he did, even though she might not really know her own wants. There was a wondrous good in making love that was meant to be shared and she, of all the women he had ever known, looked as though she had been fashioned to enjoy it.

Inflamed, his square face close to distortion as his imagination flayed him, he flung himself out of the office, out of the house, bawling for Yago to ready Bella for a ride. He paced the yard impatiently as the black slipped the bridle over the mare's head and tightened the saddle girth, then swung up onto the roan and jerked Bella's head toward the gate. The mare squealed her indignation once, then hurtled out of the yard, fighting the bit, and pounded up the muddy road toward the Loman plantation, a good eight miles distant.

Twilight was deepening and the horse was covered with foam, her sides heaving, when Dale hauled on the reins to bring Bella down on her haunches in the Loman yard. A doltish, tow-headed indentured servant caught the reins Dale threw at him and gaped.

"Mistress Genevieve," Morley jerked out. "Where is she?"

138

"In the garden," the man said. "I'll tell her—"

"I'll find her," Dale grunted. His boots scuffed on the oyster shell path that led to the garden, set beyond the high, screening bushes. He broke through the narrow opening in the hedge and cast his eyes here, there, looking for her. She was at the far end of the rectangular plot, seated on a bench, her gown a white blur in the gathering dusk of the spring evening. It was as though she might have been waiting for him. He strode toward her, silently, purposefully.

She stood up as he came across the grass border and her voice was soft, pulsing, full of invitation.

"Friend Dale," she said. "A surprise and a welcome one, your visit. I was just—"

She stopped talking as his fingers bit into her arms. Her eyes met his, shining in the closing darkness.

"Yes?" she asked after a moment of Dale's rough breathing and no other sound. "Yes, Friend Dale?"

"It's this," Dale said hoarsely. "I've been kept waiting too long! I'll have no more of it! I'm sailing to England soon and this must be settled before I go. I have no time for fancy talk or pretty manners now. We've had our fill of that. We needs must bite into a meatier dish, and I mean to taste it now. Now!"

Her voice was even as she spoke.

"And if I say nay," she said throatily, "I suppose you mean to violate me, Friend Dale?"

"Aye, even that, for the good of both of us!"

She looked past him at the high hedges that shielded them from the house, at the deepening gloom, and then up at him again. Her lips curved in a new smile and now her voice was made ragged by her quickened breathing.

"Why, then," she said, "why then I will say yea. I'm sick of fancy talk and pretty manners, too. Ah, Dale—I would be beaten—and hurt—and ripped—and torn—"

She was still talking when he seized her. She kept on talking for

139

some time, though her words would have made sense to nobody but Dale, and they ended, finally, in a gasping, choking, hysterical sobbing.

So Dale discovered Genevieve Loman, and when he rode back to Jamestown the next day he wondered at the woman he had discovered. He had met raw passion before, but never in such quantity or intensity that it came near to frightening him, as Jenny had. She had been insatiable in her demands but he had been equal to her wants, though it had taken some doing toward the last. Neither could rightfully claim the victory when the clash was ended by a call from the Loman house, summoning the girl to the evening meal.

That call had had the sobering effect of a bucket of spring water on Dale Morley. Great God, he thought, they both must be mad to wrestle and pant in a garden only a few feet away from the place where her mother and father sat! One of them must have seen him race up to the house on Bella, and if they hadn't, that fool of a servant must have told them he was there. Ordinary parents did not let their daughters tarry long in a dark garden with a young buck; Frederick Loman or his wife could have come through the hedge to make certain that all was right and proper, and could have stumbled on the two of them, rolling in the grass in damning disarray.

But neither Frederick Loman nor his dame had come. And Genevieve, gently thrusting him from her, answered in a quiet, unflurried voice that she might have used in breaking off a dull conversation about the latest shipment of cloth goods received in Jamestown from England.

Even as she pulled her gown up to cover her perfect breasts again, she kept her voice cool and amused, raising it so it could be overheard from the house, and while Dale fumbled desperately at his own clothes she bent to retrieve her fan to use it as a brush to whisk away the twigs and stems that clung to her skirt.

She took Dale's arm then, as calmly as though she were accepting
140

him as a partner for a dance measure, and moved with him toward the opening that showed dimly in the hedge.

"You'll sup with us, of course, Friend Dale," she said lightly, "and spend the night. There's no moon and that road back to Jamestown was made for breaking necks in the darkness."

"Dare I?" Dale asked in a low voice. "Your father—I've done an unpardonable thing—I'd best go."

"I think not," she said, and there was a steely quality in her voice. "Would you run now, and leave me to face what might come, alone?"

"No—no, I'd not do that, Jenny."

"Then straighten your face and play your part. There must be some of the actor in you, as I remember how you played the gentleman when first the Captain set you up as such."

"Now, by God—"

"Oh, hush," she said, and gripped his arm in a sudden pressure. "Just think, my love, the worst that could happen, if your face shows everybody what took place back there, would be that you would marry me. And is that so blood-curdling a thought?"

"No—no, Jenny," he said with only the barest hesitation. "No, I mean to do that, in any case."

"By whose leave?" she asked lightly. "But come now, and play your role well, Friend Dale."

He never knew whether he played his part expertly (certainly Genevieve did) or whether turnip-faced Frederick Loman and his browbeaten dame would not hear his stumblings as he spoke his lines or see the defects in his characterization of a good friend who had dropped by for a casual visit. Loman, he knew by the Captain's observations, was no clever man; he was a successful planter because he spent his life watching hoes in the hands of his servants. As for Dame Loman, it was evident that between her overbearing husband and her high-spirited daughter, there was little she could do or say about anything she might see or hear; so it was possible that she had given up looking and listening.

141

The meal seemed endless to Dale and he relied heavily on the wine to carry him through Frederick Loman's colorless chant about the weather and the crops, the price of last year's tobacco and the price this year's leaf might bring. He made monosyllabic answers when it became apparent some word was expected of him, and wondered, between his twitchy responses, how in God's name this pair had produced a girl like Genevieve.

Once, he looked across the board at the girl and caught her eyes, saw her sharp tongue run the length of her wide upper lip, and looked down at his plate again. Her foot touched his under the table, one time, and pressed against his ankle before it was withdrawn. He wondered if his face was as scarlet as it felt and fairly touched his nose to his plate before he dared look up again.

On and on his host droned, while Dale Morley shifted his butt on the hard bench and tried not to look at Genevieve across the table from him; while Dame Loman ate dutifully and spoke not at all, until finally the meal was over.

They retired soon after that, because Frederick Loman was in the fields at dawn, whipping on his workers with his dry voice. Dale's pallet was spread on the table they had used for the meal, but they learned the thing creaked, after she slipped downstairs to him, and, besides, there was always the danger of rolling over the edge.

The floor was much safer and quieter, though perhaps it still was a good thing that Frederick Loman worked so hard during the day that he might have been deaf or dead, once he fell asleep. And that Dame Loman, if she heard anything, apparently convinced herself the noises were made by peculiarly heavy-footed mice.

In all the things that were whispered that night, there was no further mention of marriage.

His legs felt hollow and his eyes were gritty with weariness when he walked into Claiborne's office, at noon the next day. The Captain was at his desk, writing furiously, his pointed beard wagging with the intensity of his thought, his fingers gripping the quill as though it were a rapier and the foolscap an enemy's hide. Dale made his greeting and waited for the lightning to flash, the thunder to roll.

Claiborne's eyes rose slowly to meet his as the jerking quill stopped its fierce assault. Quietly, the Captain laid the pen down beside the inkpot, unhurriedly he turned in his chair, one arm draped over its back, to face Morley.

"He's back," he said conversationally. "Our lusty adventurer's back, by God's grace, and generously willing to take up his duties where he deserted them."

His eyes roamed over Dale in a slow sweep.

"Where've you been?" he blared out of that ominous calm.

Dale's underlip thrust forward. Clerk, eh? He'd been where Bristoll and the Captain had never been and done what they but wished they could, so let them say clerk to that!

"Where've you been, I said!" Claiborne stormed. "I told you to get to your accounting, whilst Bristoll and I rode to Henrico. We rode all night, with scarce an hour out of the saddle, and I come back to find the work half done, the office a litter of papers, my accounts spread open for all to see, even my cash box unlocked and yawning there, inviting robbery. God damn your condemned soul, *where've you been?*"

Dale held his fists behind him, stood with feet widespread, as he glared back at Claiborne.

"I've been to the moon," he snarled, "to find out who lit its light."

There was the crash of Claiborne's chair as it toppled. There was the whickering screep of the Captain's blade flashing from his sash to his hand. There was the sound of Dale's own sword leaving its ring and the two men, captain and lieutenant, faced each other over the gleaming lengths of their steel.

He will kill me, Dale thought, but maybe not if I can thrust him back over that upturned chair behind him. If he should stumble over that, I could be on him before he could recover, for all his skill, and then I'd ram my blade to my knuckles through his liver and twist it as he screamed.

143

He lunged forward and the Captain back-stepped instinctively. Rage had made him incautious and the chair's legs tripped him at the ankles. He staggered, reaching for balance, and then fell, with Dale's blade at his throat.

One thrust and it would be over, all the plaguing torment wrought by Claiborne's wicked tongue, his venomous contempt. He could kill the doughtiest swordsman in the Province and he could prove to Genevieve Loman, to all Virginia, that he was a man to be reckoned with and no mere clerk, not just a lieutenant, an underling. One thrust and Susan Willison would be avenged for all the Captain had done to her—or she had thought he was to blame for.

He did not think of London, or of the finery he wore, the mode of living that Claiborne had made possible for him, the things he would sacrifice by that one stabbing blow. His brain had no room for consideration of what would follow his triumph—flight, capture, prison, the gibbet—and if he had thought of those things at all, he would have laughed at them.

But still he stayed his hand; still he held death an inch away from William Claiborne. The Captain lay still, his sword flat along the floor, his eyes unwinking as they stared up at Dale's face, gone animal from the start of this exchange. William Claiborne lay still and waited, neither hopeful nor flinching, asking nothing, not even reproachful for what he expected to come.

The clock above Claiborne's desk ticked off a minute made up of all the centuries of time and still the two men gripped the other's eyes without moving. A mouse poked its head out of a hole in one corner's baseboard, twitched its sharp nose, squeaked and disappeared again. A wasp hummed in through the window, careened around the room and soared out. From some yard, a distance away, came the crow of a cock.

Faint as it was, that sound seemed to break the black spell that had clamped its hold on the room. Dale let out his breath in a long, rasping sigh; the sword's point moved from its poised position at the Captain's gullet. The younger man turned away, and it seemed his
144

shoulders drooped oddly as he turned his back on Claiborne and walked slowly to his own desk, in the far corner from the Captain's. He stood beside his chair long enough to replace his sword; then, he dropped to the chair and reached for the nearest stack of papers, flipped up the lid of his inkpot.

He did not look up as the Captain slowly got to his feet, nor did he raise his eyes from his work as he heard the chair righted, to creak under Claiborne's weight. There was no sound in the room except the noise of the clock, now flat, now hollow, and the rasp of his quill.

He should have felt an exultation but it was not there; he should have reveled in the fact that he had had Captain Claiborne helpless under his sword, but the picture brought back no sense of mastery, no reason for pride. He had come too close to slicing that lean throat, to ending a full, adventurous life, to get any pleasure from the remembrance.

Did all this, he asked himself, mean that when it came time to kill he would balk at the final thrust? If it had been Talbot Bristoll lying there, instead of Captain Claiborne, would he have hesitated, would he always hold back the carte and tierce that would slay?

"Dale," said the Captain at last, from his chair, "I'll not forget you dropped your blade or that I was the first to draw." His voice was strangely low, and lacking spirit. "This, I'll make up to you, some way."

"You owe me nothing," Dale said gruffly. "This letter from Massachusetts Bay, do you want one copy or another one to send to Cloberry?"

"One," said Claiborne tonelessly. "And now the rest's forgot, where *have* you been?"

Dale's ears tingled like a sheepish boy's as he muttered:

"I spent the night at Frederick Loman's. I took it on myself to tell him what you planned in England and to ask his support. He gave it."

"Ah," said the Captain, and nothing more, for quite a time. Dale

145

held himself at his work, forcing himself to keep from looking across the room at Claiborne. He sensed the Captain's eyes fixed on him and he could envisage the faint, cold smile that must be playing about Claiborne's lips. The Captain had eyes to see Dale's own red-rimmed lids, his wearied face, the other tell-tale marks left by the long and sleepless night.

"Yes," Claiborne said finally, just as Dale had begun to think he never would speak. "We need every man's support, though some would say Frederick Loman's yea would be hardly worth the traveling to get. But, as I said, we never can have too many behind us in our move."

His voice grew idly conversational.

"You'll love London, Dale—the London I'll show you. I promised you once, I remember, a chance to meet and know some ladies who'd put to shame the fairest in these parts, and I'll make good my promise, once we're in England. A man without a wife can find great pleasure in London among the ladies. Unless, that is, he's bound by some rash promise to a woman at home."

Dale turned to stare directly into Claiborne's eyes.

"But suppose," he asked flatly, "that certain happenings at home called for some sort of a promise?"

Claiborne sighed exaggeratedly.

"Ah, Dale," he said, shaking his head, "not that again—not that!"

That was all that was said then, but it was enough to tell Dale that though he might have been the first to use Genevieve Loman's garden for a couch, he had not been the first to listen to her tearless sobbing.

Ah, she was a shameless, abandoned creature, smoother than the tosspot Chrissy Gauer, perhaps, but just as ravenous. He'd not see her again, or if he did he'd somehow let her know he recognized her for what she was, not as the great lady she tried to masquerade as!

That was his resolve on the day after his night spent with Jenny. Before the *Gryphon* sailed from Jamestown, though, he saw her three more times. And if he meant to show her his changed opinion of her, he put it off each time in favor of the unarguable delights at hand.

Oh, London was a beautiful, smiling dowsabel to come back to! She might have been a blowsy, bad-breathed crone to Dale when she had sent him forth to Virginia six years before, but now she was a friendly, winsome wench with a great heart and a vast, sprawling body made for pleasure.

He never had thought he would welcome the sight of the city again, when he had sailed with O'Halley, but Dale Morley found himself thrilling to the spectacle of London's surge and bustle. He should have known well that the sound of a grim struggle for survival lay beneath that tumult, but now his ears picked up some gay note in the interminable clatter that he had missed before.

The Bridge, would there ever be a sight to equal that great span, burdened with its houses, three, four, five stories high, and the carts, the cattle, the people, streaming along the wide passageway that ran beneath the rooms where hundreds lived? There was Saint Paul's, with its square tower looming more than five hundred feet above the city, certainly the greatest church in the world. There were other steeples reaching up to the heavens: Bow Church, Saint Dunton's, Saint Michael's, Saint Lawrence's—enough churches to shrive the souls of every Englishman alive. And across the Thames, on the Surrey side of the river, was the Globe, and close by it the Bear Garden, to provide all kinds of sports. And always in sight, to remind a man there might be payment required for some pleasures, stood the Tower.

He had been a barefooted bastard when he had slipped away from Aunt Bess to board Captain O'Halley's *Solace;* now his boots were as high and of as fine doeskin as Captain Claiborne's. He'd used bricks and clubs in his alley battles; now his sword was of whippy, tempered steel, with an engraved hilt. He'd draped his big frame in rags; now he wore silk and velvet. He'd knifed another boy over a

147

muddy shilling; now his purse weighted his pocket. He'd been wordless except for curses; now he could make speech with any man who used the King's English or the Pascataway dialect, and he even knew a few words of French. He'd panted over the scum-slippery skin of child drabs; since, he'd learned the feel of pampered, perfumed flesh.

He had changed. Oh yes, the man who came back to London was a far different Dale Morley from the lout who had gone to Virginia, and all because a black-bearded adventurer named William Claiborne had taken a strange interest in him. What a pity that Aunt Bess could not see him now! He had rushed off to Little Loaf Lane at the first opportunity—only to learn that the old harridan was dead, her foul den broken up, her pitiful charges scattered. But even the failure to solve the mystery of his parentage could not, at least for the moment, dampen his spirits.

William Cloberry, head of the octopus-armed trading company for which Claiborne acted as Virginia factor, had had apartments ready for the Captain and his two-man entourage. The rooms were on the Strand, that fashionable new part of the town that was stretching toward Charing Cross, lining itself with brick houses, and they were the finest Dale Morley had ever seen. Still, he was able to credit himself with acting as though the paneled rooms with their graceful furniture, their rich accoutrements, were nothing more than he had expected or deserved, and even the Captain, smiling sardonically, had to admit Dale behaved well. Even the fact that Dale had two servants to care for his three rooms and himself failed to wring from him any indication that he was impressed, if not astonished. He had become accustomed to having Yago, Benji and Toss do his bidding at the Captain's house in Jamestown; the fact that these servants were white and had served nobility in their time, he told himself, should make no difference.

So he kept his mouth shut, not gaping or blabbing out his delight, when anyone might witness his delicious astonishment, but after the others had left to settle themselves in their new quarters and make ready for dinner at Cloberry's place, he flung himself into a chair, all soft with brocaded goods, his legs sprawled out in front of him, and ran his eyes about the room with the open grin of a boy looking at his first dancing bear.

Now, by God, this was something like living! The Captain's house at Jamestown, the Governor's Mansion, had seemed pretty fine when he had first seen them, but they were crude places, at best, compared with this. A man was a fool to hide himself in Virginia when luxury like this was to be had. No mud underfoot in that broad street beyond the windows, but cobblestones, instead, and a sedan chair with two Irishmen to carry it to be had for a lifted finger. No devilish mosquitoes here, nor any stink of low tide flats, this far from the Thames. The furniture was all as graceful as the curve of a woman's flank and the clock on the mantel over the fireplace was of ormolu that could have been gold.

A man owed it to himself to live like this, instead of following a way of life that had him squatting at a Yaocomicoe council fire, grunting flattery at some bedaubed savage, hoping to win his best skins at the smallest cost.

He left the chair and looked for a bell rope.

"I'd have some wine," he said in his best imitation of William Claiborne. "Or make it brandy, instead. And when I am unpacked, I'll wear the gray suit with the—"

Now wait a minute. William Cloberry, rich as he was, had worn plain clothes with almost no adornments when they had met him earlier. Beside the Captain and Bristoll, even beside Dale Morley, he had been a dull and unimpressive gentleman. But there had been something in his eyes, a half-twinkle, as he had looked at Claiborne's handsome splendor and at Bristoll's tailored radiance. It had been almost as though William Cloberry had been amused by the deep lace cuffs Claiborne wore, and by the wide, pleated ruff out of which Bristoll's long head had been thrust at him.

That was something to think about. Claiborne had been Dale's guide in all matters of dress and deportment but now he wondered

149

if the Captain might not be wrong in trying to outshine all London with a wardrobe that, for all its cut and quality, still had to be behind the changing modes of Charles's reign. Dale was proud of that gray suit but Cloberry had worn plain black and Cloberry was richer than Claiborne and Bristoll put together; Cloberry was at Windsor Castle almost as often as Claiborne was at the Governor's Mansion. He'd take his cue from Cloberry.

"Not the gray," he told the waiting servant. "I'll wear the black broadcloth with a plain falling band and the narrow cuffs, the black stockings and the shoes with the plain buckles."

His face made ruddy by the brandy he had sipped generously while he dressed, he surveyed himself in the pier glass and nodded approvingly. He'd be the least gaudy man in any assemblage but he'd be noticed. The black cloth brought out the breadth of his shoulders and the power of his frame, the black stockings showed up the nice turn of his leg. He had the complexion to go with black (most men looked pasty in such somber dress) and the dark clothes were suited to his black hair, that needed only the touch of a comb to fall in place as neatly as the best-made wig.

Claiborne and Bristoll were waiting in the Captain's apartment, below Dale's, when he walked into the room. Claiborne was in blue silk and Bristoll was in plum-colored velvet and they both stared frankly at the man in black as he sauntered toward the table where a decanter rested, trying to look at ease. There was a brief silence, broken by Claiborne's:

"Christ on the Cross! We have a Puritan here, Talbot, missing only his prayer book!"

"Did they lose your chests, Morley?" Bristoll asked. "Or are you in mourning for the meals you spilled overboard on the voyage across from Virginia?"

Dale poured a drink carefully, replaced the decanter's stopper. He turned and made a slight, sarcastic bow in Bristoll's direction.

"I knew I'd have no chance to meet your splendor, dear friend," he said, "so I didn't try. Black's the color for backgrounds and that's where I knew I'd be, once the others set their eyes on you."

Bristoll responded with a bow as ironic as Dale's and the Captain laughed.

"I think 'twas for another purpose," he said, "and perhaps our Mister Morley is wiser than the two of us, Talbot. But I'll not don a monk's habit, even for Cloberry. And, speaking of him, we'd best be off for his place. He hates a late dinner guest as he hates an ill-spent shilling."

If William Cloberry kept a close watch on his accounts, he showed no niggardliness in his entertaining. His house was a huge affair, surrounded by an expansive park, on the Oxford Road to Westminster, and when the three Virginians arrived at the place it seemed crowded, despite the size and number of the high-ceilinged rooms. Dale gulped inwardly at first sight of the throng; the place was a shifting mass of color and beauty such as he'd never thought could be assembled outside a king's ballroom; the women were goddesses, the men were staggeringly rich and handsome.

It needed everything the Captain had taught him to make his entrance and go through the endless introductions creditably, but he did it. He made his bows as effortlessly as Lord So-and-So and Sir Such-and-Such; Lady This and Lady That could not have asked for a more admiring obeisance.

"From Virginia," William Cloberry always added as he presented Dale and Bristoll. "A brace of our bravest Indian fighters, direct from the wilderness with their captain."

Well, the man didn't have to make it sound as though he were still greasy from a pot of muskrat stew, did he? The way Cloberry put it, these ladies might expect him to break into a *yah-ho* at any moment. But he smiled and murmured modest words, in tune with Bristoll, as he made his bows.

And he was glad he had decided to wear the black. Had he worn the gray, he'd have been lost in this gathering's display. As it was, he suspected he looked like something the Londoners wanted to see, an explorer, an adventurer who eschewed the gaudy, the flashy, and presented himself without trappings, to be judged as the man, not the products of a tailor's handiwork.

151

Explorer, adventurer—hah! These folks would feel sadly cheated if they could see old Werowance clad in a canvas coat that was too small for him, or Tayrack of the Yaocomicoes, peering out from beneath the peak of an ancient, rusty burgonet helmet that Martiau had sold him for a small fortune in beavers. But he'd not change their opinions if they wished to picture him hip-deep in redskinned bodies, swinging his blade against a charge of howling Indians.

He had a small, nicely-rounded, brown-haired girl on his left at dinner and a tall, cold-faced blonde on his right. The ashen-haired woman was a Lady Augusta Cartney, whose thick, stolid husband sat beyond her, down the board. The brunette was named Alfreda Bottomley, daughter of a gray-haired man, untitled, who sat across from Dale. Bristoll sat between two women he must have known when he was at Oxford, by his familiar manner with them. Captain Claiborne sat close to Cloberry, at the head of the long table.

His dinner partner, Mistress Bottomley, and the glacial Lady Cartney both were anxious to listen to Dale's stories about Virginia. Dale guessed that Lady Cartney's ears, at least, had become jaded with warmed-over tales of court intrigue, the stale stories of fashionable adulteries that changed only in the names of their principals. Lord Cartney seemed a gross lump of a man, hardly able to quicken the interest of a stranger, much less his own wife, and she must be bored a great deal of the time, he thought. Little Alfreda Bottomley had the eager curiosity of her teen-sized handful of years. Dale obliged both women with a whole mass of information about the Province and the Indians, the forests and the wild animals. More than half of what he said, be it to his credit, was true.

"You'll find us dull, after all that," Lady Cartney said in her peculiarly frigid voice. "We've naught here in the way of excitement to match a shadow of what you've been through."

The wine had been heady and plentiful. He dared a direct, bold look into her gelid blue eyes and lowered his voice beneath the general babble.

"There are many kinds of excitement, m'lady," he said, "and

some are better suited to a drawing room—or other places—than a wilderness. I have no doubt that I could find my fill of excitement here in England, were I to have the proper guide."

Her chiseled features did not change nor was there any difference in the expression of the eyes that held his.

"My husband might be persuaded to act as your guide, Mister Morley," she murmured. "He's more often abroad—on business, he says—than he's at home, these days and nights."

He almost held his breath before he made his next move. Suppose he should go too far and have this lady denounce him before all these others? Was it worth the risk? Yes, it was, because she bore a title.

"But your husband must be a busy man, Your Ladyship," he said directly. 'I did not have him in mind as a guide when I spoke."

"I see." Was that the beginning of a smile? "You Virginians have an impetuous approach; I will say that."

So she would not flare up in cold anger, eh? So she was as ready to play this dangerous game as he, with her husband squatted at her other elbow?

"In my work, m'lady," he explained, "we have so little time that we can count on as surely coming to us that we get into the habit of going to the point at once."

"A risky habit, surely," she said. Now she *was* smiling. He shrugged.

"What risks won't a man take, for a precious prize?" he responded.

"Perhaps we should discuss this further, at another time and in another place," she suggested. "Or will your colonial affairs keep you chained to your duties?"

"Chained, m'lady?" he asked. "No man or duty could chain me long. A lovely woman might."

Ah, bravo, Dale Morley! Bravo, thou well-tutored protégé of William Claiborne! The Captain would be proud of you if he could hear you play the cavalier to icy Lady Cartney, the woman who

153

had been deemed so unapproachable heretofore, on this, your first night among England's quality. Yes, the Captain would be delighted —or on second thought, would he?

Oh, he'd not boggle at the idea of your making a conquest of a married lady, certainly, but was not Cartney related to the Earl of Rutland, father of Buckingham's widow, the Lady Katherine Manners? And had not Cartney moved close to the King's side in Charles's struggle with the Parliament since Buck's assassination? And wouldn't it be ill-timed, if nothing more, for Claiborne's lieutenant to try to cuckold a member of Charles's inner circle, now that Claiborne and Virginia needed every friend they could muster at court?

But the talk between Dale Morley and Lady Augusta Cartney was low-voiced and Claiborne, at the far end of the table, had no way of knowing what his black-clad ward was saying that brought the rare smiles to milady's lips. Perhaps if Claiborne had known, a great many things would have been different in the end.

Dale had reached a perfect understanding with Lady Cartney by the time the lengthy dinner was over. That understanding had been earned even at the cost of shamelessly abandoning his dinner partner, brown-haired Alfreda Bottomley, deserting her to have her sit and stare miserably at her plate, wondering why she had failed to attract this handsome Virginian's interest. Dale regretted the necessity for his rudeness—Alfreda was a luscious-looking child—but his regrets were brief-lived, at best. The woman at his right was a Lady, nobility. There was a flavor to that thought that one couldn't find in the conquest of a hundred pretty children who were daughters of unknighted gentlemen.

"Now that the ladies have left us," William Cloberry said, "let us to the business at hand. Captain Claiborne is here to explain to you gentlemen just how grave is the danger of the Catholic, Calvert, injuring our investments, should he gain a foothold in Virginia."

Claiborne was terse, forceful, in his remarks. The gentlemen

154

around the table, he pointed out, all had a financial interest in Cloberry and Company. A sizeable part of Cloberry's income, in recent years, had been realized through the company's fur trade. Till now, the company had held a monopoly in the fur trade of the Chesapeake region, the richest in all America. If Lord Baltimore won a grant from Charles, that monopoly would be endangered, probably broken.

More than that, if Charles gave Baltimore the patent he asked for, it would establish a precedent that could be ruinous to Virginia; the King could parcel out more sections of Virginia's territory, until the Province would be squeezed into a tiny area around Jamestown, the land that was already settled.

"The precedent's been set already," said a man at the other end of the table, a buck-toothed individual with a pair of eyes set closely together. "His Majesty's grant to Heath set the tune."

Claiborne waved a hand to brush away that argument.

"Heath was given lands Virginia would not have," he said. "That territory never will be settled, mark what I say. What fever and pestilence won't do, the savages will, to any who would try to set up a colony in those wastes. Raleigh tried and failed, and Raleigh was a good colonizer, say what else you will about him.

"But further north from Heath's grant, there's where Baltimore would extend his grasp, and that would be dangerous. And if he should persuade His Majesty to give him lands in the Chesapeake country—that could be ruinous to all of us."

Lord Cartney shifted his bulk in his chair and reached for the goblet in front of him.

"The fur revenues from your Chesapeake," he grumbled, "were far below what they should be, last year. Perhaps the animals have all been killed there. It might be best that Cloberry pulled out of the Chesapeake and set up trading stations where there is no lack of beavers."

And leave the Chesapeake? Dale found himself climbing to his feet, steadying himself with one hand on the table.

"Your Lordship," he said, "I beg leave to speak. This season's

155

fur trade was held back by a heavy winter. There still are plenty of skins in the Chesapeake country, gentlemen, and Captain Claiborne is the man to get them out for you."

It was a schoolboy's speech, he knew, as soon as he had finished. His blurted words had no place in this discussion, participated in by men of affairs, with thousands of pounds in the balance. He was conscious of Lord Cartney's small eyes turning toward him, reflecting something like grim amusement.

"Your loyalty to your captain does you credit, young sir," the thick man said, "but loyalty pays not a sovereign to these gentlemen who've invested in Cloberry's. You could hardly know, Mister—er —Morley, that we've realized far less than a pound per pound invested in this past year, and that was the figure we were promised when we sank our gold in this venture."

"I'm sorry, m'lord," he faltered, with a bow to Cartney. "I have little knowledge of money affairs."

He reached for the brandy and splashed liquor into his goblet with an unsteady hand as Captain Claiborne smoothly took up the talk.

"My lieutenant, gentleman," he said, "has his heart wholly in this venture of ours, as I have. But while he's unversed in things financial, I may lay modest claim to more knowledge on that score, and I say there's still a great fortune to be made in the Chesapeake, if we can hold to our advantage. But let the Jesuits into Virginia and they'll corrupt the Indian with rum and idol worship till we'd be lucky to get a beaver in a year's trading. Let me give that warning."

"If rum will win the Indians," somebody said, "why not give them all their bellies can hold? Surely rum's cheaper than the trade goods we deal with now."

"Certainly," Claiborne said with a wry smile, "but rum inflames the savage, sir, past all understanding. And when an Indian's drunk, he wants to kill."

"A few killings, then," Lord Cartney muttered, "would not be too grave a thing, if they'd pave the way to bigger returns from Cloberry and Company."

Claiborne's eyes flashed and his mouth set itself in a hard line.

"I cannot believe you mean that, m'lord," he said stiffly.

Cartney made a gesture of apology with one stubby-fingered hand.

"I meant no offense, Captain," he mumbled. "Of course we want no Indian massacres, but—"

"But could there be a question of mismanagement?" inquired a smooth voice.

Heads turned in the direction of the speaker. He sat three places down the table from Talbot Bristoll and he was a thin-faced individual with a beaked nose and a long chin. His eyes were so thick-fringed with lashes that they were almost girlish in appearance, but there was nothing feminine in that thin-lipped wide mouth, set beneath the sharp-tipped nose. He wore a suit of yellow stuff that ill became his sallow complexion and the wig he wore was of straight black hair, drawn back tightly into a queue.

As the others stared at him, the man who had made his smooth interruption gazed directly at William Claiborne, his smile neither insulting nor friendly. Dale saw the dark blood rush to the Captain's face, saw one of Claiborne's hands clench as he half-started from his chair, only to sink back again, as William Cloberry spoke sharply.

"What do you mean, mismanagement, Mister Evelin?" he asked, his voice more steely than Dale had ever heard it. "Are you making the charge that—"

"I make no charges, Mister Cloberry," the man called Evelin interposed. "I'm certain that Captain Claiborne has our best interests at heart in all he does at our Chesapeake stations. My only thought was that, if the skins are there in Virginia, as the Captain says they are, and Captain Claiborne is the best fitted to get those skins, as his own lieutenant says he is, there must be mismanagement somewhere, gentlemen, if we don't get the return we expected from our investment there."

He spread his long, slender hands and gazed about the table, oblivious of the scowl Claiborne was directing his way.

"Perhaps," he said mildly, "the fault lies in our London offices, or in the transport of the furs from Virginia to England. It might

157

be a worthwhile idea for Mister Cloberry to delegate some commission from amongst us to survey the whole situation, that some defects which are not apparent to us now may be discovered and remedied. I'd gladly give my time to serve on such a commission, as I know others of our number would."

Lord Cartney, sitting next to Dale now that Lady Augusta had left her seat with the other women, made an impatient movement with one hand.

"That c'n all be dealt with later," he rumbled, "after we've decided what must be done about the Catholic, Calvert, Baron Baltimore."

"A moment, m'lord," Claiborne interjected. "I want it clear in my own mind whether Mister Evelin—Mister George Evelin it is, isn't it—thinks another better suited to our needs in the Chesapeake than me. Perhaps Mister Evelin has his eye set on the post it's my honor to hold now."

Evelin kept his enigmatic smile as he looked down the table at the Captain. Claiborne was still flushed, visibly angry, but the man named Evelin seemed neither apprehensive nor regretful over the anger his oily words had aroused.

"I've often wanted to see Virginia," was his only answer, and Captain William Claiborne was left to make of that brief statement what he might.

"We digress, gentlemen," William Cloberry put in, hastily. "We're met here tonight to determine our course in fighting the Calverts at Court. And in this fight, I can think of no better a leader than Lord Cartney."

The thickset man hunched his shoulders and looked down the board at Cloberry.

"What would you have me do?" he asked.

"Just this, m'lord," Claiborne said. "Get me and my lieutenants an audience with the King. I'll show His Majesty that it's to his advantage to reject the Papists' demands. Charles knows what we have done and what we can do—can he be so sure of Calvert? Baltimore made a stinking mess of his Newfoundland colony. Can he do better in Virginia?"

"His Majesty," said Cartney heavily, "has his father's faith in Baltimore."

"And that, Your Lordship," put in Cloberry, "we depend on you to alter."

Cartney sank back in his chair, his melon belly pushing up from the waistband of his breeches. He swigged at his brandy before he spoke.

"There are no secrets here," he said. "You all know I have the King's ear, as fully as Laud and Rupert and Glamorgan. That, to you gentlemen, should be worth something in pence and shillings. I'll not mince matters; there are some members of the King's Privy Council who are feeling the bite of debt. They must have a farthing to fondle before they'll listen to me. How deep into your purses will you go, gentlemen, to persuade m'lords to advise the King in your favor?"

There was a moment's silence, during which the men at the table could hear the chatter of the ladies in the drawing room, across the wide hallway.

"Five hundred pounds for me," said William Cloberry soberly.

"I'll meet Mister Cloberry's amount," Captain Claiborne said as quietly.

"And fifty . . . and a hundred . . . and thirty . . ."

When they were all done, Lord Cartney looked around the table and smiled. His broad, flat mouth seemed to dislike the need of moving out of its accustomed groove.

"With that much gold, gentlemen," he said, "I can almost give my word right here that His Majesty will never sign a grant in favor of the upstart, Baltimore. Laud and the others will see to that."

The round towers of Windsor Castle shimmered in the haze as Dale ascended toward the King's residence, abreast of Captain

Claiborne, Talbot Bristoll and William Cloberry. It was unseason-
ably warm and the flat fields about the castle sent up waves of heat
that would have better suited September than May.

Dale had to use all his will to keep from gaping at the splendor
of Windsor Castle, with its army of soldiers, its throng of courtiers
and attendants, the orderly bustle of the big place. King Charles, he
knew, was supposed to be a bankrupt but there was no evidence of
his insolvency here.

"This way, m'lords," a page said. "M'Lord Cartney awaits you."

The four men walked through the cool, stone-flagged halls, lined
with pike-bearing men-at-arms. They passed the doorways of great
chambers where men and women sat, drinking and eating, chatting,
singing, flirting, gaming, and at last they came to an anteroom where
Lord Cartney waited. His greeting was simple, made with an outthrust hand.

"You have the purse, Mister Cloberry?" he asked from his carp's
mouth. "I've found it best to be direct in such matters."

Cloberry sank into a chair and pointed at the large leather pouch
he had dropped beside him as he collapsed.

"There it is," he replied, "to the last groat."

Lord Cartney's eyes were bright as he picked up the pouch; his
avarice was as plain on his face as his swollen nose, his rubbery lips.
The Privy Councilors, Dale thought, *will not see all of that money.*

"Fine, fine!" Cartney muttered. "Rest yourselves, gentlemen,
while I go to make certain necessary arrangements. I'll return soon
and take you to the King."

He hurried away, the bag of gold swinging at his side as Claiborne and his lieutenants took chairs. There was a smattering of
desultory conversation but not much of that; the moment was too
tense for idle chatter.

They had to wait more than half an hour before Lord Cartney
returned to the anteroom to take them to the King. With dry throats
and thudding hearts they followed Cartney.

Charles Rex was listening to an Italian stroking a harp when they
160

entered his presence. He was a heavy man but his bulk did not spell power in any great degree. There was a sort of haughtiness written on his face, featured by a high-bridged nose, and still his features were not what could be called forbidding. There was always the faint shadow of a frown over his eyes and the eyes themselves were sunken and tired. He was thirty years old, that day, and he looked twice thirty; there would come a time when he would be a hundred, in looks, and thrice that, in trouble.

There was the rap of the Court Chamberlain's staff and the shout:

"My Lord Cartney, with petitioners to His Majesty, Charles the First, from the Province of Virginia in America. My lords and ladies, you will attend the King."

The bustle smoothed into silence as the Italian laid off his playing. Charles peered up at Cartney, the frown deepening. Following Claiborne's lead, Dale went to a knee in deep obeisance to the old young man who, by the grace of God, was ruler of all England and the Colonies.

So Dale Morley met a king.

Charles's voice was as high-pitched as Talbot Bristoll's and burdened by a stutter.

"You may rise, m'lord and gentlemen," he said. "Yuh-yuh-you have sus-some request yuh-you'd have us grant? Luh-let's have it—this Italian has a wuh-wuh-wondrous hand on a harp."

Captain Claiborne stepped forward to hand the Chamberlain a parchment scroll, stepped back and bowed. Charles toyed with a long-handled eyeglass, a white sapphire that had been chiseled until it made writing twice as large as inscribed, tapping it against his mouth as he listened.

"To the King's Most Excellent Majesty: The humble petition of his subjects in Virginia, one of His Majesty's provinces beyond the sea, is that His Majesty in his generosity preserve the boundaries of the Province which his sainted father, King James the First, established in the patent issued by him in the Year of Our Lord, one thousand six hundred and nine, and the sixth year of his reign.

161

Against all petitions and requests, your subjects in Virginia ask that Your Majesty consider that they have fought the Indians in your behalf, that they have spread the boundaries of your province to their ultimate and have made converts unto God Almighty of many of the savages there. Your Majesty's subjects have humbly striven to provide your treasuries with all the monies that were required of them and pledge their new efforts to raise more to give to the glorious causes with which His Majesty has identified himself. We, your subjects of the Province of Virginia, humbly beseech Your Majesty's favor in this matter, as Your Majesty has seen fit in your great wisdom to bestow upon us in the past."

The Chamberlain finished speaking, cleared his throat and looked at the King. Charles tapped the lens against his lips and scowled more deeply.

"Whuh-whuh-who signs thuh-thuh-this thuh-thing?" he asked. "Hawley—Harvey—whuh-who's Governor of that Province, m'Lord Cartney?"

"Sir John Harvey, sire," Lord Cartney said, "but it's not signed by him. It's signed by the Secretary of the Province, Captain William Claiborne."

The King's sunken eyes switched to the Captain as Claiborne made his bow.

"Cluh-cluh-cluh-Claiborne? We know you, d-d-don't we? Of course. Guh-guh-good family; luh-loyal family."

"Thank you, sire," the Captain murmured. There was another silence as Charles played with his lens. Then:

"Thuh-this is a puh-puh-petition against m'Lord Baltimore?" he asked.

Lord Cartney came a step closer to the King.

"Your Majesty," he said easily, "I make venture to say this is a subject that can better be handled by Your Majesty's Privy Council, in session with Your Majesty, than at this time."

Charles shook his head impatiently.

"Luh-let's finish it here," he said. "We've all buh-but given our word that Baltimore may huh-have his patent."

162

Dale's heart sank at the King's brief word. If Charles had already promised Baltimore his grant, they could do nothing here. They were too late and all because of that fat Harvey's hemming and hawing.

"Your Majesty," Claiborne said, "have I your leave to speak?"

"You have," said Charles indifferently.

"Your Majesty," the Captain said, "I'm here to plead for Virginia. I am the least fitted to plead, surely, because I am no learned courtier, no man well-versed in words. I am a captain in His Majesty's service, fighting the Indians, and my lieutenants and my men have held no commissions, have borne no titles. I beg your leave to present my lieutenants, sire."

Charles nodded without interest.

"Mister Morley, Your Majesty. Mister Bristoll."

Dale's bow was as low as Talbot's. When he straightened, he saw the King's eyes were roaming toward the Italian harpist.

"Sire," Claiborne continued, and there was a hint of desperation in his voice, "we have helped make your name the most glorious in all the world through our humble work in Virginia. We have made a garden out of a wilderness there, we have peopled a dense forest with towns and plantations and mills and roads and all for the glory of Charles the First.

"It has been no easy task, sire. We have had our enemies; the savages—and other white men who have been jealous of Your Majesty's great name and noble purpose. I know naught of treaties between thrones, of friendships which bind nations to each other's causes, of affairs of state which Your Majesty in your great wisdom tends with, so I'll not name the enemies, except savages, whom we have had to meet. I will but say that they have been fierce but we have always conquered them, with the cry of Charles and England on our lips."

Dale saw the King was not impressed. His fingers tapped the arm of his throne with growing impatience, his eyes roamed the high-vaulted room. William Claiborne, Dale realized, was scoring no success with all his flamboyant speeches about fierce savages.

163

"Huh-have you finished, Captain Claiborne?" His Majesty asked, in a bored tone.

The whispered words slurred out of the corner of Dale's mouth before he quite realized it.

"My cutlass scar," he muttered. "Wounds for the King."

Claiborne did not turn in his direction but the muscles above the Captain's pointed beard jerked and he blinked once. He gave a suggestion of a nod and took a half-step toward the throne.

"A moment more, sire," he said, "by your graciousness. You have a wondrous colony in Virginia. Your subjects there all love you against your adversaries and are ready to die for you. My lieutenant, Mister Morley, came close to dying in your service and I would have you see the wound he took."

Dale ranged himself up beside Claiborne, bowed low again. Was there ever such a reckless gamble made for such a stake? And yet, the game was lost without this throw, and where had he found the wit to propose it?

And why did the King stare so closely at him now? Why did Charles lean forward in his chair, his eyes pinned on Dale's face, an odd expression that could have been bewilderment crossing his regal features? Christ's blood, it was as though the King recognized him; had found in him some other man than Dale Morley, nameless bastard, cutpurse, ragged-shanked planter and now lieutenant to the Captain!

"Whuh-what did you say his name was?" the King demanded, his voice sharp. "Whuh-whence came he?"

"My lieutenant, sire," Claiborne repeated with another bow. "Dale Morley's his name and he has served with me in Virginia for some time."

"Morley? Morley? We duh-do not know the nuh-name."

And still that stare. Dale felt a spot between his shoulder blades begin to itch, the perspiration pop forth again upon his forehead. He would have surrendered his chances for Heaven to be out of

164

this place, standing before his King, facing the glare that spiked him from the throne. He was grateful for Claiborne's hand on his arm, steadying him, reassuring him.

"Your subjects in Virginia know the name, Your Majesty," the Captain said. "They have reason to know it and to be grateful that there is a man named Morley to defend His Majesty's possessions there against the invader."

The King kept his eyes fixed on Dale.

"This man, sire, took up his weapon in your cause not long ago," the Captain went on, his words hurrying now. "This man, this Mister Morley, heard an Indian say that His Majesty, King Charles, was not the true ruler of Virginia, that the Spaniards—aye, the ignorant savages call them *Waspaines*—would come to Virginia to set up a new King, called a Pope, to rule over all the colonies!"

There was a rustling, a murmuring, among the crowd that watched and listened. Dale saw Charles's frown grow black and he remembered, with a chill, that the King had a Catholic wife.

"I know not where these Indians got their story," Claiborne said, quickly. "I know not what spies and trouble-spawners the *Waspaines* or anyone else may have sent to Virginia to ready their way. I do know that Mister Morley took up his blade for you, sire. He cut down the man who threw that taunt and then fought off an army of Indians before help reached him. He took this wound, Your Majesty, in the fighting!"

Claiborne's hand gripped Morley's coat at the collar and yanked. The cloth ripped with a soft purr and Dale found himself stripped from the waist up on his left side. The scar that Talbot Bristoll's cutlass had left in the fight over the drunken Pascataway girl still showed plainly.

"There's the wound he took!" Claiborne cried. "Would Your Majesty take his plantation from him now?"

There was a deep, shocked silence, broken by a roar from the courtiers lining the walls. Many of the men attending the audience

165

were soldiers who bore their own wounds, suffered in fighting for Charles; they could risk even the King's displeasure in the loyalty of one veteran to another.

Charles stared at the livid scar, looked starkly up at Dale's face again and then down at his feet. He kicked petulantly at a tiny spaniel that made the mistake of wandering too close to the throne; then he gestured with his eyeglass.

"We fuh-fuh-forgive your hasty action, Captain Claiborne," he said, "knowing in our graciousness that you were carried away by yuh-our luh-luh-loyal fuh-fervor."

Claiborne, Morley and Bristoll all went into deep bows.

"This is a muh-mater for the Puh-puh-privy Council," Charles said. "Thuh-thuh-this audience is fuh-fuh-finished."

The Italian swept his hands over the harp strings. The babble took up where it had left off. Charles turned his head to speak with his Chamberlain. Dale backed out of the King's presence beside Captain Claiborne and Talbot, holding his shredded coat together with one hand.

Outside, Claiborne turned to clasp Dale tightly in both arms.

"By the gods, Dale," he said, his voice choked, "I owe you much for this day's work. We were lost but for your quick thought. Ah, Dale, I knew you'd show his wit, in time."

"Whose wit?" asked Dale Morley, but Lord Cartney was at his shoulder, interrupting.

"Your wound, young sir," he said, "has won this day for us. Now, with the Privy Council readied, Lord Baltimore will get no patent from Charles, I promise you."

Dale murmured something, then looked past Cartney's thick shoulder at Talbot Bristoll's sour sneer. And grinned.

"No! No! I *will* say no, sir. I tell you—ahh—have you no regard for a frail woman at all?"

"Not for one who has a face like yours, m'lady."

166

"That's not a face, sir!"

"But such a pretty thing, m'lady. Would you have it dealt with differently?"

"This is impossible—my laces—sir, you'll have us both ruined! If you must play the suckling child, let's to the nursery upstairs. Look, hold my hand and follow—*I say stop!*"

"Let's hurry."

"This way and around here and here's the stairs and—was there ever such an impatient boy?"

"Was there ever a woman who looked so like a beautiful frozen lake and who thawed so quickly?"

"You have the quality to heat a woman, Mister Morley."

"Like this, Lady Augusta?"

"Aye, like that—and that—and that! Ah, I'd forgotten how good —oh, I'm all undone! You treat me like a tavern wench."

"And you find great pleasure in that, too, m'lady."

"I should not. No, I'm a lady and you're a—don't frown down at me! If you say I should love it, I do! Ah, I do, Dale."

And later:

"The door!" she gasped. "I'll swear I saw it move!"

He sprang from the bed and got to his sword, hefted its unfamiliar balance. It was a weapon William Claiborne had given to him only a few hours before, its hilt surmounted by a gryphon's head wrought in silver, a costly blade that Claiborne had presented him from his own sash as a reward for Dale's quick thinking at Windsor Castle.

He walked to the door, his rapier at the ready, and opened it a crack to peer out into the gloomy hall. He saw no one but there was the sound of footsteps receding in the distance, around a bend in the corridor. From somewhere in the rear of the great house, a door boomed shut.

He turned back to Lady Augusta Cartney, all rosy white on the bed. There was a thoughtful frown on his face as he looked down at his blade.

"You're certain there was someone there?" he asked. She nodded

167

speechlessly. "Could your husband have returned from Windsor before you expected him?"

She sat up to stare at him with steady eyes, going cold again. There was no fear reflected there, but neither was there any of the exciting, humid lovelight that had glittered from beneath her half-closed lids a moment before.

"He may have returned," she said in a cool voice, "or it may have been one of the servants, playing at Peeping Tom."

"And if it was m'Lord Cartney?" he asked.

She shrugged her slender shoulders. One arm came across her perfect breasts and her long fingers clasped the other arm.

"You'll know it if it was, soon enough," she said almost casually. "And so will I."

"You mean he'll call me out?" There was a cold prickle of fear in his spine. That Cartney was a bull of a man, a favorite of the King. What chance would he have on any field against such as he, or even if he won his duel wouldn't he still be ruined? He let his breath whistle between his teeth in a long exhalation as the woman on the bed shook her head.

"Not Cartney," she told Morley. "Do you think he'd make himself the butt of every jest told at Court by letting it be known he'd been cuckolded by a colonial, a shirt-tailed boy without a shred of a title to his name?"

Dale scowled, his anger rising at the cool derision that cloaked her words.

"Now wait —" he began.

"Oh, hush!" she commanded. "You asked me a question and I'm answering it. No, he'll not call you out. He'll find another way to make you pay for this bit of play, Mister Morley. I gather that you and our captain are basing your hopes for some royal grant or other on my husband. It's hard for me to think he'd be well dispositioned in your favor after this, dear Dale."

Morley grunted at the almost physical impact of the verbal blow. He walked to the edge of the bed and sat down heavily, staring stup-
168

idly at the gryphon's head on the hilt of the sword. He had done it now! He had won the struggle for Claiborne and Cloberry and then, a handful of hours later, he had ruined everything he had done and all the work the others had done. He had made that pouch of gold sovereigns that had gone to the Privy Council worth no more than a bag of pebbles. He had given Sir George Calvert the charter that would clutch the throat of Virginia.

And when Captain Claiborne found out what had happened he would be a raging madman, certainly. There was no way even to imagine just what he would do to Dale Morley when he learned that an hour's dalliance by his lieutenant on a broad bed with a golden lady had cost him all his hopes and plans.

This was a foul mess, all of it, and just after he had scored his greatest victory over Talbot Bristoll. Now, he'd be back on those fifty acres beside the James, soon enough, if the Captain didn't choose to kill him out of hand. There'd be no more debating between a gray suit with deep ruffles and a plain black outfit that was intended to set off his shoulders properly; he'd be back in canvas and frize if he was lucky enough not to wear a noose for a falling band, before he was finished.

It was as though Lady Cartney were reading his thoughts. She stretched out a hand to touch him lightly.

"Oh, Cartney will not tell the real reason for his change of heart," she said. "He'll find some other way of explaining that, as I know him."

His breast was filled with a new hope as he turned to look down at her.

"He'll not tell?" he asked. She shook her head with a faint smile.

"By God, then," he burst out, "mayhap all's not lost! There could be a thousand reasons why your husband might remove his support —the court is crawling with intrigue. Mayhap Claiborne never will know—"

He broke off suddenly.

"But what of you?" he asked. "What will he do to you?"

She shrugged again.

"No pleasant thing, perhaps," she said negligently, "but then, he has so seldom done a pleasant thing to me. Sometimes I've thought I'd welcome his rage rather than his doltish indifference or, worse yet, his swineherd's ways at making love. Well, I'll soon find out whether Cartney's better in anger than when he is his stupid self."

She smiled up at him again, calmly, evenly. A raveled curl had broken loose from her disordered headdress and now caressed her cheek. She was a fair bundle, with skin as white as milk, prettily marked, there and there with a crimson rosebud and there with a creased dimple and there with a tawny triangle of shadow. He swallowed to ease a throat suddenly gone dry.

"You think he'll be back?" he asked hoarsely.

Her eyes lost some of their coolness.

"You're quite mad," she said throatily. "You'd pile offense on offense till he'd be forced to use his sword, against all his better judgment?"

"But will he return?"

"Who knows?" she asked almost dreamily. "But I'd say not. There's still a risk, though, certainly."

Dale's sword clattered to the floor.

"They say a risk adds flavor, Lady Augusta," he said, "and if that's so, this bit should be the most flavorful of all."

"We may as well face it," William Cloberry said, simply. "We have lost. Cartney has betrayed us. With all the gold we gave him, he's backing Calvert now. We made a misstep somewhere, gentlemen."

Captain Claiborne paced up and down the long room, his hands folded behind his back, his long face pale and twitching.

"I find it hard to understand," he said almost petulantly. "Lord Cartney was our strongest friend till a day or so ago. What changed him? Did Calvert pay him more than we could muster? What's the reason for this turn-about?"

Talbot Bristoll was reclining in a chair, his booted feet thrust out in front of him. He drew a kerchief from his wrist and waved it languidly at a hovering fly.

"*Honi soit* — and all the rest of it," he said idly, "but I've the idea he found something to dislike in our Mister Morley's interest in the fair Augusta. Friend Dale was all but fumbling for her garter during that dinner you gave us, Mister Cloberry."

Dale wet his lips, remembered to scowl.

"You seem bent on a duel, Bristoll," he managed. "Perhaps this is the insult to a lady that will give us excuse for one."

"You'll be quiet, you two!" Claiborne blared. "Haven't we enough trouble without the pair of you yapping at each other like a couple of feisty curs? Bristoll, you see a tumble in every polite word spoken by a gentleman to a lady, and it ill becomes you."

Bristoll bowed his head in mock humility.

"Your pardon, Captain," he murmured. "I'll watch my naughty thoughts more closely."

Claiborne snorted and strode to the table where the others were sitting. He pulled at his sharp beard, the deep crease of a frown on his forehead. His knuckles rapped the table to emphasize his words.

"Well, tell us, Mister Cloberry," he said. "What's been decided at Windsor? Is Calvert to get the southern hundreds of Virginia, as he planned? If so, it certainly means war, and I'd better get back to Jamestown to raise some kind of army."

Cloberry lifted his bandaged foot to a pillowed stool before he answered.

"Not the southern hundreds," he said, "but worse than that, Captain Claiborne, as I understand it. Charles won't give Baltimore land south of Jamestown 'cause Heath still claims that grant. Instead, as I get the word, His Majesty will sign a patent giving Baltimore land to the north of Jamestown — along the Chesapeake."

Claiborne turned his back to the table and raised his fisted hands toward the ceiling.

"Christ on the Cross!" he yelled. "Know you that to have a rabble

171

of Catholics and their Papish ways in the Chesapeake will cut our trade with the Indians by half?"

He turned back toward Cloberry, his dark face clouded by anger. He thrust a long forefinger at the man with the bandaged foot.

"By half, did I say?" he asked. "By three halves, better! I tell you, sir, that now we have every Indian on the Chesapeake, every Yaocomicoe, every Wicomesse, every Susquehannock, every Pascataway, believing that only Captain Claiborne and his company have any use for their furs. There was a Captain Yonge who had trade with the Indians when we came to the Chesapeake but we drove him off, turned the Indians against him, at the risk of our own skins. Now, if the Catholics get into the Bay north of Jamestown they'll give a better price than we can, they'll cut us off from all that trade. Cloberry, I beg of you to stop this thing!"

Cloberry stirred uneasily in his chair, his red face showing his chagrin. He stared at the bandaged foot on the stool before him and grunted:

"What can I do that I haven't done? Can I go to the King and tell Charles that he must do my bidding?"

Claiborne shot one glance at Dale, then turned back to Cloberry.

"Get me another audience with the King," he begged. "I have one argument left—an argument I had hoped I would not have to use. Let me tell the King what I have to say and I'll warrant he'll think twice before he signs any patent for Baltimore!"

Cloberry stared at him wonderingly.

"What argument is it," he asked, "that can cry down the voice of the Queen and the Privy Council?"

"I cannot explain it," Claiborne said, "but if anything can change our fortunes, this word to Charles will do the trick."

Cloberry puffed out his lips in an exasperated sigh.

"You'd better have given the King your mysterious evidence when you were at Windsor then," he said with finality. "I can get you no further audience with His Majesty now. Even when I tried to get a letter to Charles it was blocked by Cartney and Laud. The

Ministers of Plantation, paid by me to make a protest, got no closer to the King than Cartney would let them. No, Captain, they've plugged Charles's ears against all our arguments. We must admit we've lost this joust, I say, and make our plans to mend our fortunes at another time and on another field."

Claiborne stood there, looking at Cloberry from under his heavy brows, his face taut and grim.

"You mean we have no chance to present another plea?" he asked after a long pause.

"No chance at all, Captain Claiborne," William Cloberry said heavily. "Believe me when I say that."

"But — but they'll take the Chesapeake," Claiborne said, dully. "They'll take my trading posts, the one at the mouth of the Potomac, the one at the Susquehannock's island, the one — they'll take Kent Island."

"Kent Island?" Cloberry asked. "Where's that?"

Claiborne turned to face the west. He looked over the breadth and span of England, over the heaving deep of the Atlantic, to the place where the cat-tails bent under the breath of the evening breeze, where the ducks and geese wheeled in circular profusion, where the rockfish churned the clear water into white foam, where the partridge whirred up in bumbling clouds, where the rabbits ran their rudderless courses, where the turkey stretched his neck in his burbling call and the raccoon whickered from the oak.

"Kent Island, sir," Claiborne said distinctly, "is a place I mean to keep, should Charles even send all his armies against me and Calvert call on his Pope to take it from me."

Chapter Five, 1634

"SAIL HO!" CRIED THE LOOKOUT IN THE WIND-
shaken watchtower of Fort Comfort. "A sail—two sails—to the east,
standing in!"

And there they were, two small craft edging through the wet
snowstorm that had sifted down from the February skies since early
afternoon. Dale Morley, squinting through the snow-blurred glass,
could make them out, beating their way up through the shifting
white curtain. There were two vessels, aye, but were they the vessels
the fort had been waiting for — were they Calvert's ships?

He had been on the narrow rampart of Fort Comfort since mid-
afternoon, in command of the guard — although he was no regular
officer either of the King's Army or the makeshift Provincial force.
Strict military protocol held little place in the procedure at Fort Comfort and the post's commander, Colonel Merriweather, had been
happy to agree with Captain Claiborne's suggestion that his lieutenants, Mister Morley and Mister Bristoll, relieve the fort's regular
officers in command of the guard, especially in view of the weather.

"With pleasure, my dear Captain," the commandant had said,
grinning. "To you and your staff will go the honor of first sighting
our distinguished visitors. I only pray that no guns be fired to cele-
brate the occasion; or if they are that they are not aimed directly at
our guests — if they stop here at all."

"You think they'll not come here, sir?" Dale had asked after
Merriweather's light speech. The commandant had shrugged negligently.

"Maybe, though I doubt it," he said. "Calvert knows the temper
here and he may fear we'll sink him, in spite of all the warnings
174

we've been given that he comes here under the King's protection. We'll see."

And now there they were, for a certainty. The closer approach of the two small ships gave Dale a chance to glimpse the flutter of a black and gold pennant that must be Baltimore's, whipped by the storm's gusts. Dale lowered his glass and turned his head briefly to the soldier who stood beside him.

"Have the drummer summon the men," he ordered. "All hands to their posts, or whatever the fancy name of the order is."

He waited, his hands on his hips, as the drum in the small parade below began its roll, muffled by the falling snow. Despite himself, he felt a certain disappointment. What he had expected with the arrival of the Catholics he did not know himself but surely, he had thought, it would be more than these tiny ships. These were no great galleons from Spain or men-o'-war from Portugal. These were mere chips, even in a day when a bark of four hundred tons was considered big enough to risk the dangers of the ill-charted seas.

William Claiborne was the first man up the ladder to the rampart, after the drum began its summoning beat. Wordlessly, Dale handed him the glass and pointed in the direction of the approaching vessels. Claiborne took only a brief look and then handed back the brass tube.

"Yes, there he is," he said grimly. He pulled his cloak closer about him and brushed at a thick snowflake that had drifted down to settle on his cheek. "There he is, the damned Calvert, come to rob us of our lands and our trade."

He turned and bawled an order, taking command of the fort as though it was his right. There was no waiting in Claiborne for the arrival of Merriweather. Dale knew Claiborne regarded the Colonel as a fool who would not consider the Papists' coming anything to worry about; he had seen Merriweather smile superciliously during some of Claiborne's hot tirades. But the Colonel had no stake in Virginia or the Chesapeake; to him all Colonials were exiles like himself, but with no hope of return to England.

175

"Stand ready by the guns!" Claiborne shouted. "Maybe we'll have occasion to use them yet, pray God!"

The gunners jumped to the brazier of live coals and dipped their long pincers into the glowing mass to lift out embers that, if placed on the touch-holes, would set the cannon roaring, the sakers barking, the culverins and falcons thudding out their iron-throated messages of warning and death. The layers sighted on the two ships as they followed their straight course to the fort's anchorage. It would be a simple thing to blow those cockleshells out of the water if the command to fire came.

"A salute, Captain?" one of the fort's young subalterns asked. "It's a customary courtesy."

"No salute," Claiborne rapped out.

"But, sir—"

"No salute to those damned swine!" the Captain barked. "I'll be responsible."

Dale, huddled in his cloak and cursing the trickle of melted snow that drew an icy finger down his neck, stood beside Captain Claiborne on the parapet, watching the ships' approach.

"They sail like they they were being handled by witless children," Claiborne muttered beside him. "The word I got from the Fortunate Islands said to expect something like this. The *Dove*, one vessel's called, and the other, the *Ark*. The *Ark*—now, by God, there's a proper name. Instead of honorable beasts and fowl such as Noah carried, though, this Ark's laden down with vermin."

Talbot Bristoll lounged against the parapet, studying the two Calvert vessels with his glass. Colonel Merriweather had yet to put in his appearance. Evidently Merriweather took the view that this was William Claiborne's show; let the Colonial chill his bones in that storm while he waited for the visitors in more comfortable quarters.

The three men watched the two tiny ships come up to the anchorage. There was the rattle of lines through the blocks and the clatter of anchors going over the side. The *Dove* and the *Ark* swung slowly

176

at the end of their anchor hawsers and, completing a lazy orbit, came to rest, their long crossing of the Atlantic finished. Dale could see the men on the closer and larger vessel, the *Ark,* putting over a long-boat.

"Attend me," Claiborne said in a clipped voice. "They're coming ashore. Doubtless they expect Harvey to welcome them and Harvey's still at Jamestown, toasting his fat legs before his fireplace. He must be sent for, I suppose, but till he arrives we'll show Calvert that he's no honored guest here, at least in our regard."

He looked at them, then stabbed a finger at Dale.

"You'll meet him at the landing," he ordered, "and conduct him to the Colonel's quarters, where I'll be waiting. Treat him civilly, Dale—he holds the King's letters—but only civilly. And no matter what the provocation, hold that damned temper of yours. Do this second son of old Lord Baltimore, the Devil crack his bones, open harm and you'll find the Tower is deeper and blacker within than it looked from without. Follow me, Mister Bristoll."

He turned and stalked away toward the ladder that led to the courtyard from the parapet, his helmet gleaming in the light from the brazier that hissed its fury at the gentle, dampening fingers of the snow. The gunners still tended their live embers, repairing to the brazier now and then to pick a livelier coal from the crimson heap.

Dale waited until Claiborne and Bristoll had gained the parade, then ordered four of the soldiers on the parapet to follow him, carrying pine torches. When the detail reached the ground, Dale cast a glance at the figure of his captain, moving toward Merriweather's cabin with Bristoll tall and straight at his side.

Leaving the meeting with Calvert to a lieutenant—that was not like Claiborne. Did he really mean the detailing of a subordinate to the task as a slight to Calvert or was there another reason? Mayhap he feared his own temper while counseling Dale to hold his in check. To see the Papist set foot on Virginia soil surely would be a wrench to William Claiborne; it could be that the Captain was afraid he'd forget the King's protection that Calvert bore and draw his sword as he would against a Spanish invader.

Dale made himself as straight and as commanding as possible when he met the small group that stepped from the longboat, nosed in to the gray, smelly shore, now happily blanketed by snow. The man who led the Catholics was a slight person, seemingly half-swallowed by the fur-trimmed cloak he wore. In the light of the torches held by the soldiers his face seemed thin and curiously shaped, as though some sculptor had begun to fashion a long head and then, just beneath the aquiline nose, had changed his mind to finish his work in a hurry. The chin was round and bore a tiny beard, the mustaches he wore were thick, bristly and sticking out at all angles. It was a caricature of a mustache, that brush, and Dale felt pleasantly clean-faced, looking at it.

He had his father's eyes, though, deep and placid. This man, this Leonard Calvert, could not feel entirely comfortable coming ashore under the guns of people whose intentions he could not know but could rightly guess as unfriendly; yet he carried a grave, thoughtful, self-assured mien as he left a line of black tracks in the snow, walking toward Dale. He paused, just beyond arm's length from Dale, and reached for the snow-whitened fur cap he wore. His long wig fell forward, giving him a cowl, as he swept a deep bow toward Dale.

"My name is Calvert, Leonard Calvert," he said. His voice was steady, but thin. "I come from England carrying letters of authority signed by His Majesty, King Charles, addressed to His Excellency, Governor Harvey of the Province of Virginia."

Dale did not return the bow. Instead, he contented himself with a curt salute of one hand to the peak of his burgonet.

"I'm Dale Morley, aide to Captain William Claiborne," he said. "Governor Harvey will be summoned from Jamestown to receive your letters, sir. Captain Claiborne is waiting for you in the commandant's quarters, Your Lordship, and I'll escort you there."

Calvert raised a hand and waggled it backward and forward.

"Not 'My Lordship,' Mister Morley," he corrected. "Plain 'Sir Leonard' will have to do, I fear. My brother, Cecilius, Baron Baltimore, seems still to be in far too good health for me to take his title from him at this time."

"Sir Leonard," said Dale stiffly, with the barest suggestion of a nod. And, gesturing toward the stockade: "The gate's in that direction, sir. If you and your party would care to follow me. . ."

Leonard Calvert brushed at a patch of snow lodged in the crease of a sleeve. He kept his eyes fixed on his arm as he murmured:

"I thought 'twas usual for the bearer of a King's letter to be welcomed properly at the place he's voyaged to reach. Or perhaps your customs are different in Virginia, sir."

Dale stiffened. The guards holding the torches waited, shifting their spluttering flares from one hand to the other as they eased the ache in their arms, stretched up into the snow-slashed night. A wind born on the southwestern shore of the James came across the river to spit huge, damp flakes insultingly into their faces.

Welcomed properly; did he mean he recognized Dale Morley for a nobody not fit to bid him greeting to Virginia? Hold his temper, Captain Claiborne had told him, and that must mean he had known Calvert would resent being met by an under-officer, a subaltern. Well, be damned to the niceties, this yammering court talk! If Leonard Calvert felt he was too good to be met by a man who could break his back over his knee, who could crack his skull with one blow of his fist, who was where he was by more than accident of birth, he could find his welcome in the squawking of the gulls, the hiss of snowflakes as they struck the water.

He started to turn away brusquely and then he thought of Claiborne's anger, should he take it upon himself to give offense to this man on his own. He turned back and forced himself to make a low, unsoldierly bow.

"Sir Leonard," he said, "it's my honor to have been detailed to meet you here and convey you to my captain. Captain Claiborne asks your pardon for not being here himself but—but he is suffering from

179

a croup that cannot stand the damp." *Damn you, does that lie comfort your high-nosed arrogance?* "He bade me tell you that he has sent for His Excellency, Governor Harvey, and asks you to await His Excellency in the commandant's quarters where I'll guide you, by your leave."

He bowed again, cursing himself for a buttocks-bussing flunkey. Leonard Calvert left off brushing his sleeve to return Dale's bow with a slight nod, far different from the full sweeping bow he had offered before learning who Dale was.

"I have two butts of sack for His Excellency," he said idly. "A gift from my brother. It would be most appreciated if you would send a party to unload them from my vessel, the *Ark*. My own men have had a cruel voyage and they are distressingly weary."

"It will be attended to, Sir Leonard," Dale said.

"And my people would welcome a fire and a firm floor, after all these weeks at sea," Calvert continued. "I ask the hospitality of the fort for them while we are here."

"It is theirs," Dale said, and added: "There'll be no weapons brought ashore, Sir Leonard?"

The Catholic shot him a keen glance and his lip curled slightly.

"We come as friends, Mister Morley," he said. "Certainly Virginia has no reason to fear our handful."

"I have only my orders, sir," Dale said stiltedly. "The gentlemen, of course, may wear their swords."

The man in the fur-trimmed cloak tipped another nod and turned to walk back to the men who had landed with him, standing close to the water's edge. There was a brief conference and all but one of the small group re-entered the longboat and headed out toward the anchored vessels. The man who remained ashore kept close to Leonard Calvert's side.

"My brother, Sir George Calvert," the Catholic leader said briefly. Dale and Lord Baltimore's youngest brother exchanged bows. "Now, if you will lead us to this place where your Captain Claiborne waits. . ."

180

It was a silent journey across the snowy shore, through the gate of the stockade, over the whitened parade and to the hut that served as Colonel Merriweather's quarters. Leonard Calvert strode beside Dale, with his brother trailing a pace to the rear, snuffling now and then and sneezing twice during the brief journey. It was obvious that young George Calvert was suffering from a bad cold.

"Frail lily," Dale thought scornfully. "He'll not last a fortnight in this country."

Dale reached the door of the hut, rapped sharply and opened the door to stand aside and let the unwanted guests precede him into the low-ceilinged room.

"Sir Leonard Calvert," he announced, "and Sir George Calvert, Captain Claiborne."

And all he needed, he told himself, was a pair of crimson breeches and white stockings to be a footman.

Claiborne was sitting beside Colonel Merriweather, behind a table opposite the door. Over Calvert's shoulder, Dale saw the Captain rise and incline his head in a stiff bow.

"Sir John Harvey has been notified," he told Calvert. "Please make yourselves as comfortable as this rude place allows."

They faced each other, trader, Indian fighter, Provincial politician and the titled Englishman who had come to Virginia to carve out a new empire. Anglican and Catholic, they held each other's eyes in a level stare; veteran frontiersman and polished courtier, they looked at each other and saw their enemy. From their first meeting, they knew there could be no compromise, no agreement, between them, though treaties might be offered; from the start, each knew that one must conquer and one must fall, by diplomacy or by trade warfare or by the sword, before this thing was finished.

The silence snapped as Colonel Merriweather spoke.

"Every convenience of this place is offered to you and your people, Sir Leonard," he said, "though you'll not find many of them. And if your vessels would take on water—"

"My thanks," Calvert interrupted. "I fear we'll crowd you, but

181

my friends aboard ship would be deeply grateful for a chance to feel solid ground beneath their feet again—especially the ladies. We had rough passage from the Fortunate Islands here and there are many who still turn green at the sight of thin broth."

"Mister Morley," Claiborne barked, as though determined to balk Merriweather's move toward the center of this stage, "will you and Mister Bristoll attend the work of seeing that these people are given shelter—food if they need it?"

"They'll need no food," Leonard Calvert said with a hint of loftiness. "Just warmth and a chance to dry their clothes. We've had water over our rails for the past three days."

The fort was crowded with Catholics after the longboats brought them ashore, the men and women who had become so weary of tossing bulkheads and heaving decks that they must have thought they would go mad before they would set their feet on honest dirt again. They jammed into the fort's barracks, the crude mess hall, babbling, laughing, most of them high-smelling, spreading their hands to the fireplaces and (a few of the younger women) backing up to the crackling logs and edging toward the shadows where they could lift their sodden skirts and warm their backsides with some degree of privacy.

They besieged the privies. The men stripped off damp coats and shirts, kicked off soaked shoes and peeled wet stockings from their shanks to dry them. The women looked on enviously and wished that modesty was not a thing reserved for them. They were forced to content themselves with standing as close to the fire as possible, so that wisps of steam ascended from their damp clothes to add to the acrid smell of the place.

Dale looked at them, his lip twisting. They were a rabble that could never survive in Virginia; and that was a good thing, too. They'd freeze in the winter because they'd not know how to keep themselves warm in the wilderness; the summer heat would fry their crops because they'd be too weak or too lazy to carry water.

He glowered across the jammed room where he stood beside

Bristoll, waiting for a summons from Claiborne, now closeted with this proud Leonard Calvert and Leonard's brother. Now there was a tender babe to send out to help colonize a Virginia wilderness! If Leonard Calvert was a dauncey one, his younger brother, George, was worse. The lad should be in some schoolroom, from the looks of him, learning his sums instead of trying to imitate his brother's manner, trying to bear himself as though he'd not been frightened empty-bladdered by the crossing from England and was not still trembling in his fear of the dangers of this place.

His eyes roamed the crowded room again. Some of the Catholic women were fairly comely. There was one over there who was actually pretty, though she waggled her fleshy butt like a duck. And there was one—

She was not tall nor was she small. Her body was slight, her hair a nondescript brown and not neatly fixed now. Dale had known a hundred women who could lay more claim to beauty than this wench but when she turned her eyes toward him and he looked into their dark depths he felt his groin tighten and his throat grow suddenly thick.

Beneath her short cape she wore a white gown dotted with a small blue figure. The dress was high at the neck and the skirt brushed the floor. Her shoes showed their blunt tips, first one and then the other, as she walked across the room toward the wall against which he stood beside Talbot Bristoll. For a moment he thought she intended speaking to him but she turned aside some distance away and then he saw she was carrying a cup of water to a child held in the arms of a woman who sat on a bench near the door. She held the cup to the child's lips, supporting the baby's fuzz-naped head with her free hand. The water spilled from the child's mouth and the baby choked with a strangled cough. The brat looked ill—by God, he hoped these Papists had brought no plague to Virginia with them!

The girl frowned her concern as she wiped the splattered water

183

away from the baby's dress with her kerchief. She spoke a few words to the lumpish woman holding the brat and was answered by a desolate shake of the mother's head.

The brown-haired girl straightened and looked at Dale again. And again he felt a warm surge of excitement within him that he could not understand. Why, this girl was only a Catholic wench in a cotton gown that showed the stains and wrinkles of long wearing aboard one of these slivers of ships offshore. She—

She was the most desirable woman he had ever seen!

Susan, Jenny Loman, Lady Augusta, all the others—this woman possessed something more to be wanted than any of them or all of them. And how could a woman as plain as she have that when the others, even Susan, had been more beautiful?

Now she was walking directly toward him and he felt a sudden gripe beneath his ribs. She came straight to him and he could smell her fragrance—or did he imagine that?—as she drew close.

"Sirs," she said, in a high, clear voice, "my sister's child is ill. Is there a doctor in this place who can attend him?"

Her manner was almost lofty, for all her wrinkled clothes and disordered hair. She begged no favors, this one; her question was close to an order directing Dale or Bristoll to fetch a physician. Now, Dale thought, she was a high-nosed wench to use a tone like that to Virginians by whose sufferance she was sheltered from the storm, by whose forbearance she was not struggling in the wreckage of a cannon-shattered ship!

Before Dale could find tongue to give answer, Bristoll spoke through a mocking sneer.

"Didn't you bring doctors with you to this land of milk and honey?" he asked.

The girl switched her gaze to Bristoll and her chin rose at the tone of Talbot's voice.

"We had a doctor, yes," she explained, "but he was taken ill at the Fortunate Islands and we left him there to recover. There must be some physician at this fort—"

"Well, there is," Bristoll cut in harshly, "if you can call him a
184

physician. He's a sot named Wing and he's such a feeble specimen that even the soldiers choose to let themselves burn with the French pox than have him treat them. He's no Thomas Sydenham, this Wing, but no doubt he would suit your needs."

He turned away abruptly and walked a few paces apart to lean against the wall again, his arms folded across his chest, his opaque eyes contemptuous as he surveyed the crowd. The girl looked after him, her lips tightening, and then turned back to Dale.

"God knows," she said, "I expected little courtesy at this place but the child seems very sick and certainly even a Virginian can be civil enough to help save a baby's life. Before you stalk away, sir, tell me where I can find this Doctor Wing."

Not "please" or "by your graciousness," mind. No, the wench in the blue-figured white gown still gave the orders, despite Bristoll's rude rebuff.

"He's about the fort somewhere," he said in a clipped voice. "I have no time to go searching for him."

He turned away but the girl's hand on his arm swung him back to face her. Her eyes were blazing now with a contemptuous fury and her face was taut with anger.

"You'll take the time," she told him. "That child needs help, and now. Ah, do not snarl at me, sir; you'll assist me or I'll go to Sir Leonard and make complaint."

He shook her hand off his sleeve and brushed at his cuff, aware of Talbot Bristoll's amused stare.

"I care nothing for your Leonard Calvert or your complaints," he snapped. "I'm not under his command or any other Papist's. Find Wing yourself, Mistress Sharp-Tongue, and leave off bothering a soldier who's on duty."

The girl looked up at him, speechless with anger, and then the baby in the arms of the woman on the bench burst into a fit of feeble crying. Her eyes darted in the direction of the wailing baby and when she turned back to Dale the anger in the girl's face dissolved suddenly into an expression of desperate pleading.

"Sir," she said, "you cannot be so cruel as to let that child suffer

185

rather than direct me to this doctor. In God's name, tell me where to find this physician."

The baby's squalling grew louder as Dale watched the fear grow in the girl's eyes. The cloak she wore had parted as she had grasped him and he could see the gently molded bosom rising and falling beneath the thin stuff of the dress. The small twin mounds affected him as even Genevieve Loman's frankly flaunted breasts had not.

"Wing has a hut beyond the parade," he told the girl, "but you'd not be likely to find it or dare walk into the place if you did."

"Then, sir," the girl said, recapturing the bite to her voice, "you'll guide me to the place, perhaps."

"Perhaps," said Dale sourly. "It seems you've picked me for your servant. This way, Mistress—"

"Furness," she said, "not Sharp-Tongue, sir. My name is Anne Furness and I thank you for your help, no matter how unwillingly given."

"Furness?" he asked acidly. "Then ye're not all Calverts in this crew?"

She shook her head, her smile as unfriendly as his.

"No," she said, "there's not a Calvert among us, except Sir Leonard and his brother. My father's Jonathan Furness, the gentleman over there near the table, speaking to the man in the black cloak."

Jonathan Furness was a tall, angular person with a long, bony face creased by deep lines. His clothes, like his daughter's, showed the effects of the long voyage from England. The stockings he wore sagged about the heels of his shoes and there were steel buckles, not silver, on those damp, muddy boots. Christ's thorns, this Papist who gave orders was a pauper's daughter!

"I'm Dale Morley," he said ungraciously. "Lieutenant to Captain William Claiborne."

He turned away before she could speak and hauled open a door. A snow-laden gust of wind whirled into the crowded, smelly room and there was a chorus of protest from those nearest the door. He
186

paused to scowl at these ungrateful beggars and jerked his head toward the darkness outside.

"Through here," he growled, "and I'm sorry there's no sedan chair to carry you across the parade."

The doorway led out into the snow-covered parade and she paused a moment, just over the door sill, to huddle her cloak more closely about her. As she moved forward again, her foot slipped on a patch of ice and Dale automatically caught her elbow in a quick grasp. The warmth of her flesh came to his fingers from beneath the cloth of her sleeve. It was firm flesh, too; firm yet pliant, made for stroking.

He banged the door shut behind him, asked himself where he could take this wench for a round of dalliance before they hunted for Wing. Ordinarily, there would have been a dozen places where he could lead her, but with the invasion of this horde of Papists the whole fort was a beehive with torches flaring everywhere and the entire garrison up and about. There was even a soldier barring the entrance to the powder magazine where the soldiers were wont to fashion a bed of powder sacks to accommodate the doxies who made the fort their market place.

If Wing was stupified by rum, as he usually was, there might be a chance to use his squalid hut for the taking of this wench. No doubt the girl would find even Wing's pallet a luxury after the hard decks of the vessel she had just quitted.

"This is the place here," he told Anne Furness. "There's a lantern burning so he must be in."

He held open the door and the girl moved into the hut, barely wincing at the noisome stench that greeted her nostrils. Dale followed her and closed the door behind him. His eyes moved to the tangle of ragged coverlets in the corner of the room and he permitted himself a tight smile. Wing was drunk and snoring with the jug beside his pallet and he could take his fill of this peculiarly toothsome wench without a thought of the huddled wreck in the corner. He moved toward Anne Furness purposefully.

187

She read his eyes and backed away, one hand thrust starkly in front of her, her face stiff with fright.

"No!" she said softly, in almost a whisper. "No, Mister Morley!"

She made for the door but his hands found her and held her before she had taken three steps. Dale felt the blood pound at his temples; his tongue was thick and there was the salty taste of brutish eagerness in his mouth. He was an animal; this girl had made him so, and the coupling would be short and savage, fitted to this kind of pigsty scene.

There was no reason for his flaming lust but there did not have to be any reason. It was enough that he was hot for this woman and must have her now. Let her shrink and twist in his grip; she wanted what was coming as much as he did; her writhings were intended only to inflame him and herself.

The blue-figured white dress ripped at the neck under the tug of his ruthless fingers and his hand touched her flesh. She would melt now, have done with this coy struggling, and—and—

"O God!" she gasped. "Oh God help me! Oh, sir, you cannot be so evil that you'd rape a helpless woman!"

He gave a smothered snort of laughter as his mouth clamped down on hers. Rape? Hah!

And then her struggling ceased and she was a limp bundle in his arms, as he had expected she would be when she had finished with the foolishness that she thought was required. Her lips moved as he buried his face in the curve of her neck and the words came faintly to him, as though from a long distance.

". . . I commend into Thy mercy, o Lord, this humble servant who requires Thy aid and succor against this shame. I beg Thee, o Lord, to. . ."

His blood chilled, the fire that roared through his veins winked out, quenched by a flood of returned sanity. He dropped his hands, reeled back from the girl who stood there unmoving, her head bowed, her shoulder and breast translucent in the light from the lantern. Horror took the place of delirium and he raised an uncertain hand, dragged it down over his face.

188

Lord, was he a Talbot Bristoll who would violate a woman who had placed a trust in him? Was he no more than a bully who had to force an unwilling maid to enjoy his manhood? Did frail girls have to resort to prayer to escape his unwelcome attentions? This Anne Furness had put herself in his care and had come trustingly with him to this place, only to face a drooling madman who pawed at her breast and fumbled with her skirts, who had taken her for a whore even though she had said not one word or given one look to lend him that impression. Enemy to Virginia she might be, but she was a woman and there was nothing in any decent code that could excuse him.

Prayed, she had, like a woman caught in the claws of some monster demon, knowing that her only hope lay in prayer!

She edged toward the door again, holding her torn gown with one hand, her eyes sliding first toward him and then toward the rough wooden door that barred her escape. He put out a hand and winced at the way she drew back from it, like a person flinching from the touch of an adder.

"I—I'll not harm you," he said in a low voice. "Believe me, Mistress Furness, I will not harm you further. It was a mistake—I thought—give me the chance, I beg, to make amends."

"You think I'd listen to you?" the girl asked frostily. "You think I'd stay here, if you did not block my way, any longer than I'd stay in a bear pit?"

"But—but the baby, your sister's child," Dale pleaded. "It needs the physician, you said, and I can wake him—I will. Don't run away; I may have been mad but I'm not now."

She hesitated, remembering the sick child, and Dale took advantage of the moment to walk across the room to where Doctor Andrew Wing lay snoring, his mouth hanging loosely, his face puffed by an unhealthy bloat.

Andrew Wing, Doctor of Medicine, Civilian Surgeon to His Majesty's garrison at Fort Comfort in the Province of Virginia, drunkard, lost creature.

There was some mystery about the man, but the contempt in

189

which he was held by everyone who knew him made any thought of digging into his past a worthless project. It had been rumored about at one time that he had killed some nobleman in England by mixing a poisonous draught while befuddled by drink, mistaking one powder for another, and had been protected by other physicians enough to be permitted to sign for this unenviable post, but that was no more than a rumor, as likely to be wrong as true. It was enough that he was a tosspot now, and so little thought of that even the soldiers at the fort, doubled over with a bellyache that came from moldy meat or griped by dysentery caused by foul water, usually preferred to suffer unattended rather than let Doctor Wing mix a medicine with shaking fingers—and possibly make a second mistake to match that first rumored error.

Dale shook Wing's shoulder as one would prod a sack of meal. The doctor, apparently, had made some effort either to dress or undress before the rum he had drunk had overcome him. He still wore his soiled shirt and his wrinkled stockings but his breeches were an unwholesome lump on the floor beside the fouled pallet and his coat sagged from the back of a chair beside the table where the lantern rested.

The fire in the fireplace was nothing more than a few dying embers and the room was cold. Morley turned aside to feed some faggots to the coals, poked the embers up with the toe of his boot and saw the pine catch and blaze up. Then he went back to the sleeping man, using the same boot toe to nudge the doctor's ribs ungently.

Wing grunted and stirred. He turned over on his side and flung up an arm to shield his eyes.

"Go 'way," he muttered thickly. "I tell you . . . can take off the arm as neatly as you, Sir Stanley . . . guh phuff . . . there's mortification there, you fool, and the arm must come off!"

He threw his hand away from his face in a furious sweep.

"My instruments!" he yelled. "I can't wait another clock-tick if you'd have me save this man's life!"

190

Dale looked down at the hulk on the pallet of rags with something approaching sympathy in his eyes. What dream had that worthless wreck captured, he wondered. Did Andrew Wing think, perhaps, that he was performing some miraculous operation? He reached down to shake Wing again.

The surgeon raised his lids and blinked against the light from the lantern. Out of the red, swollen lumps that served him as eyes, he looked up at Dale, struggling to return to the awful actuality of the moment, trying to bring his drink-dulled mind out of the dreams where he physicked none but the nobility and had gold and honors showered upon him.

"Guh," he said. He coughed with a spasm of jerking throat muscles. "You want me?"

"There's a child that needs attention," Dale said briefly. "Can you rouse yourself to tend to it?"

"Child?" The doctor peered up at Morley warily, suspiciously. "Child, you said?"

"One of the Catholics," Dale explained. "They're here at the fort. The babe's condition made me interrupt your sleep."

The man with the ravaged face fought his way into a sitting position and his feet scrabbled as he tried to rise. He rubbed his grimy hands over his face and looked about the disordered room.

"I had a jug somewhere," he said vaguely, "and if you'd get me to my feet and allow me to find it, mayhap I can attend this child of yours."

"Not my child, sir!" Morley rapped out. *No, his child had never lived to suck in a breath.* "This woman's sister's child."

Yes, and he had humbled himself too much before this wench, even though he had behaved badly, so he added:

"A Catholic child, Wing."

There was the clack of heels on the floor behind him and Dale turned to look into Anne Furness's anger-tinted eyes again.

"The child's no Catholic," she flared, "if that could make a difference in his treatment! We're Anglicans, sir."

"Anglican?" Dale asked. "I thought all of you—"

"Nearly half the party's Anglican," the girl said stiffly, "though when I recall the kindnesses m'Lord Baltimore and Sir Leonard Calvert have shown us and match it against my reception here, I think I wish I could say I was a Papist! No man, no matter how rough a sailor, tore my clothes and wet my face with his spittle on the journey to this place, Catholic though he might be."

"I thought—"

She cut off his words with a gesture and moved past him to the side of the hideous, trembling figure on the pallet, making herself ignore the fact that Andrew Wing wore no breeches. The quivering wretch huddled over his middle, trying to drag the dirty, tattered shirt he wore down over his crotch.

"And you, sir," Anne Furness asked, "are you a true physician or another man who fears and hates all but his own kind? Do you measure your cures and philters according to differences in faith, real or fancied?"

Wing raised his head and Dale saw the distorted, unshaven face jerk and shudder as he tried to make reply. He drew the back of one hand across his cracked lips, wiped away the gummed traces of old vomit from the corners of his mouth. When he spoke, it was in a surprisingly firm voice.

"I'll attend the child, Madam," he said, with ridiculous dignity, "but I must warn you that I've had a sup too much to drink and my hand's unsteady at the moment. If there's surgery needed in this, I fear I cannot do my patient justice."

"There's no need for the knife," said Anne. "My sister's child has the flux. You must have a powder here to cure him of that."

"I have every powder known to medicine," Andrew Wing said grandly. Perversely, he changed from a shuddering, quaking ruin to a lordly pontiff as a quirk of alcohol presented him with a mirage of long-past honor and authority. "Some—the best—I have discovered myself. My father studied under Jerome Fabricius of Aquapendente and I myself have been well tutored; by—"

"Sure," Dale broke in, his voice grating. "So well tutored, my lords and ladies, that he must mistake a poison for a potion and run to Virginia to escape the Tyburn Necklace."

The surgeon stared up at him dully, that laughable touch of dignity gone now, his swollen eyes cast in their usual shadows of hopelessness. God, the man looked like a wounded animal, sitting there! He looked like a wolf Dale had seen on one winter trading voyage, the beast caught beneath a deadfall trap, so close to death that it could snarl no longer, its eyes only awaiting the swing of the club and an end to its pain.

"Ah, you've no right," Anne Furness fumed. "Doctor, pay no attention to his slurs, whatever they mean! Come, here's your jug and I'll help you wash and dress. I'll help you, if you need it, in mixing your powders."

Her torn dress fell apart as she reached down to help Andrew Wing get to his feet and for a moment Dale saw her small breasts, and then he looked away.

"We'll not keep you longer, Mister Morley," Anne said. "And— thank you for guiding me to this place."

"I ask your pardon for the rest of it," Dale muttered. "I—I cannot explain what caused me to act like that. I'm not that way—I would never harm a woman—I—I try to be a gentleman, a cavalier."

"A cavalier," she echoed heavily. "A cavalier!"

He turned on his heel and clumped to the door, his boots thudding on the planked flooring. He had spent too much time on this drunken fool of a doctor and this Catholic girl—or not a Catholic, and what difference could that make? He should be attending Captain Claiborne instead of trying to help this woman cajole a sodden, bare-arsed wreck up off a stinking heap of rags to physick a puking babe. He was a soldier, no nursemaid, and his place was beside his Captain, not here.

But if she could forgive him! If those few minutes of infamy could be called back! If she would not remember him as the beast he had been! He turned back to speak again, but Anne Furness was

193

bending over Wing, helping him get the jug to his mouth, and there were no words that he could summon that would change her thoughts or memories now.

He slammed the door behind him and stumped back across the yard, his brain a caldron. That must have been false, her claim to being an Anglican! Why would any but a pack of Papists be aboard a Catholic ship that carried monks? She was not half so beautiful as Genevieve Loman. She was—

"Ho, Dale!" William Claiborne said. He gripped Dale's arm, halting Morley's headlong charge across the parade. "Where have you been, and why are you scowling so blackly? Talbot told me you took some little Catholic maid into the dark. Did she turn you down that you're such a gloomy bear?"

"I left her with Wing," Dale said roughly. "I've no doubt she's given that drunken gut-cutter his fill by now."

"Wing?" Claiborne asked, and laughed. "You think he'd have anything to give a woman after he'd wooed his bottle? Not Wing."

"In any case," Dale said, shrugging, "she's stayed behind with him."

"And you're needed with me," the Captain said, "so forget your little Papist. The Governor's just arrived from Jamestown. He and Calvert are together right now, exchanging pledges of friendship with great gestures. Oh, Sir John Harvey is strutting tonight. The King's letters that Calvert carries are all addressed to Harvey and not a scrap addressed to me, the Secretary of the Province. Ah, I suppose I could expect no more, really, after Cartney's treachery that undid us all at Windsor Castle. Lord God-Damn-Him Cartney —may he find it a sorry day when he changed his allegiance to the Catholics at our cost!"

He was off again on a soliloquy that Dale had heard before.

"If I could but find out what made him change," Claiborne muttered, "I'd get more sleep o' nights. Cloberry's agents at Court have poked and pried, trying to find the answer to the puzzle, and have learned nothing. Oh, one idiot said there was a rumor that the whole

194

thing was Lady Cartney's doing but even Cloberry, with all those guineas thrown away, couldn't bring himself to believe that."

The old chill struck at Dale, the same chill that had stabbed him on each occasion within the past four years when Claiborne had dealt with the riddle of Cartney's perfidy. Lady Augusta might have assured him that her husband would never talk but there was always the chance that His Cuckolded Lordship might be deep in his cups one time and drop an incautious word. Or Lady Cartney—would she hold her tongue forever? A woman was a woman, tavern wench or great lady, and they all loved talk more than they loved men. Some women drugged themselves with words, they even babbled things to their own discredit, just so they could hold the floor. Lady Augusta had not seemed that kind of person, but who really knew what a woman was like when she was with other women, seeking to hold attention?

But, he assured himself again, months had stretched into years and the true story had not come out; surely it never would come out. Cartney would have talked before this if he was given to blabbing his secrets when full of drink. Cloberry's agents would have discovered what had really happened, if they ever could. No, he could forget the whole affair—and yet the Captain seemed to hang onto the memory of that black surprise he had received in London with a devilish tight grip. When would he forget Cartney's turncoat move, or would he ever?

"You're not attending this parley between Harvey and Calvert?" he forced himself to ask.

Claiborne smiled mirthlessly and shook his head.

"Oh no," he said. "Calvert and Harvey must exchange their confidences alone, it seems, before they'll summon me, prepare the rack they hope to stretch me on. They said they'd send a courier to call me when they'd finished with their private affairs. *Private affairs*—I'd like to know how much Harvey is asking for selling out Virginia!"

From across the parade came a hail.

"Captain Claiborne?" Talbot Bristoll called. "The messenger has brought your summons from Governor Harvey."

The Captain's teeth gleamed briefly as he turned to Dale.

"It comes now," he said. "Here is the summons to the august presence. Now Harvey and Calvert have finished their bargaining and have supped their wine and I'm to be allowed to hear what they've decided. But if they think that by keeping me out of their conference they've blinded me and deafened me to their intentions, they'll find out different."

The two men walked toward the barracks doorway where Bristoll waited, then headed for the dim window glow that marked Merriweather's quarters. The snow was thinning but the wind was still sharp and the clouds still blotted out the stars. Dale sniffed the breeze and thought there might be more snow, another storm, before the night was out. It had been a strange winter, with one day warm enough to belong to spring and the next bitter and raw, as though there'd never be another summer.

They reached the doorway of the small building that was their destination and went inside, after pausing at the threshold to stamp the wet snow from their boots. Calvert had doffed his fur-trimmed cloak and took his ease now on a bench at the far side of the room's long council table. Beside him sat his brother.

Sir John Harvey was at one end of the table, his pudgy face making no attempt to mask the triumph he was experiencing. He had a right to crow, Dale thought. Harvey had hoped for revenge over William Claiborne ever since the time, in 1630, when Claiborne had sailed to England, unbidden and unauthorized, to protest a royal grant of lands to Calvert. Well, the grant had been given and here was a Calvert armed with the King's letters and Calvert was dealing with him, Sir John Harvey, and not with Claiborne. Yes, he had a right to crow, if he ever could.

Now Harvey waved a fat, be-ringed hand at Leonard Calvert and his brother.

"You've met Captain Claiborne, I know," he said, his voice

bustling with importance, "and these are his lieutenants, Mister Bristoll and Mister Morley; Sir Leonard Calvert and Sir George Calvert."

Bristoll and Morley made their bows, correct but no more than that. Leonard and George Calvert barely nodded their responses. Leonard Calvert was silent for a time and then he raised his eyes to meet Claiborne's in a direct stare.

"I know," he began, "you will be pleased to hear, Captain Claiborne"—his voice lashed out suddenly—"that all our company took the usual required oaths of allegiance to His Majesty before we sailed from London last fall."

William Claiborne held himself stiffly and coldly as he faced the man across the table. By the saints, Dale told himself, the Captain had the steel to meet the other, holder of a King's grant though his enemy might be! There was a new quality in Leonard Calvert, too. Before, he'd seemed a calm man, though vain, certainly strangely suited to this business, but now there was a flash in his deep eyes that matched the fire in Claiborne's, a set to his jaw that had not been evident before. And his hands, Dale saw now, were square and strong. A man's hands ofttimes gave the true story better than his face.

"Another thing, Captain Claiborne," Calvert's new steely tongue went on. "When I left England, my brother, Lord Baltimore, advised me that I keep my course as far as possible from the guns of Fort Comfort, here. He knew you were our enemy, though he knew also that His Excellency, Governor Harvey, was our friend. I think he feared you might command this place and make some reckless disposal of your force that would bring catastrophe to our expedition—and disaster to Virginia!"

Claiborne's face was stiffly expressionless. He still kept his eyes locked with Calvert's. Harvey's glance shifted between the two men. Young George Calvert seemed embarrassed by this direct talk; he appeared to be unable to keep his eyes focused on any one place for long and he was continually shifting his gaze to the ceiling, to his

197

hands, to the windows. In all that conference, if it could be called that, he seldom looked directly at anybody else in the room.

"I generally heed my brother's advice, Captain Claiborne," Calvert said after the pause, "but this time I took it on my own self to come here, squarely under the guns of your fort. I could not make myself believe that a man with your reputation as a brave soldier and a Virginia cavalier would murder a band of helpless, peaceful people. And I was right, I see, and my brother was wrong."

Claiborne inhaled a deep breath and expelled it before he spoke.

"Because we did not fire on you," he said rigidly, "does not mean I'm any less your enemy, Sir Leonard, nor any more your friend. I could do far worse than sink two shiploads of people if I knew it would help Virginia to do it. But you come here bearing letters from His Majesty, King Charles, and the King can find no more loyal subject in all the world than William Claiborne, sir. My own thoughts, my own inclinations, had nothing to do with the safe conduct we've given you here. As for me, personally, I'll never change my ill-regard for you, for your family, for your idol worship or for your purpose in coming here—never!"

Governor Harvey made protesting noises in his throat, his face purpling with anger. George Calvert seemed as though he was like to burst through the door of the place to the outside, away from this frank talk, but Leonard Calvert put a cold, serene smile on his lips, beneath the brushy mustache. He leaned back a bit, both hands spread out on the tabletop, and looked up at William Claiborne.

"Now here, by God," he said, "we have a man who's blunt, and I've always had great admiration for bluntness as a virtue, even though it might hurt at times. All right, Captain Claiborne, we'll have it thus. You'll be no friend to me nor me to you, except one or the other changes more than I can fancy now.

"Yes, you can hate me till your face is as black as my heart's supposed to be, but remember, sir—I *do* have His Majesty's grant, entitling us to settle north of here, above the Potomac River. Try to injure any man or ox, any woman or ewe, any child or chick living
198

there by that patent and you try to harm His Majesty's authority, it-self, and, as loyal subjects, we would feel called upon to resist you with every means at our command! You have warned me, Captain Claiborne, and so now I warn you!"

Another pause, while the two men held each other's eyes, and then both Calvert and Claiborne relaxed. The two titans had grappled and strained and had tested each other's strength without a clear decision. Now they respected each other, though they might hate each other; it showed in their eyes and in every line of their faces as they stared across the table. One might destroy the other before all this was finished but each knew, from that moment on, that his adversary was a worthy one.

Sir John Harvey felt called upon at that time to remind the others that he was still in the room and, officially, the man to speak for Virginia. He cleared his throat and tried to put a timbre into his voice that was not there.

"The patent's in order, Captain," he said in his thin, reedy whine. "I've examined it and it's quite in order."

Claiborne turned toward the Governor as though wondering when he had entered the place, and then looked back at Leonard Calvert.

"Could I examine it?" he asked. "Not that I question it in any particle, understand, but these are things not to be looked at every day."

"Of course," Leonard Calvert said, smiling. He reached for the largest scroll of the small pile in front of him and slipped off its tape deftly. Courteously, he reversed the parchment and extended it across the table toward Claiborne.

"Er—it's writ in Latin," Harvey grunted, his tone insulting. Claiborne merely glanced his way, in as insulting a silence, and then looked down again at the scroll. His eyes roamed over the parchment until, at length, he stabbed a lean forefinger at the grant.

"Now here's a point," he said, his voice smooth, "my rusty Latin will need help on. *Hacentus inculta*—now, what's that mean, Sir Leonard?"

Calvert's eyes grew sharp again, and wary.

"The patent, if I may explain it, Captain," he said after the briefest hesitation, "gives my family all the usual rights of settlement from a point on the southerly shore of the Potomac River to the fortieth parallel, where New England ends. The patent gives my brother Cecilius the right to make all laws governing the new colony, choose officials, levy taxes, etcetera, etcetera, etcetera."

Claiborne's eyes had not looked up from the parchment scroll. Dale saw now that the Captain was shocked by what he was reading, rather than by what Calvert was telling him. Claiborne's face began to show its first signs of an awful strain. When Leonard Calvert had finished speaking, the helmeted captain took up the thread of the talk in a low voice:

"And at all times," he said as though murmuring to himself, "His Majesty's courts, in ruling on any interpretation of this patent, shall judge in a manner most advantageous and favorable to the now Lord Baltimore and his heirs and assigns."

There was a pregnant silence before Leonard Calvert showed his smile again and leaned back on his bench.

"Exactly," said the younger brother of Cecilius Calvert, second Lord Baltimore.

Dale knew little about patents and grants, charters or petitions; he knew less about courts and attorneys. But he knew by the look on Claiborne's sharp face, the drained expression that came into the Captain's eyes, the deepening lines that slanted from nostril to mouth-corner, that this last clause, as recited by Claiborne, was the cruelest blow the Captain had yet taken in this battle.

The Secretary of Virginia stood for what seemed a long time, staring down at the scroll, and then his bleak eyes came up to meet Calvert's, across the table.

"Of a certainty, m'lord," he said with a bow, "you have a strange and powerful patent here. Not only does it suit His Majesty to give you great stretches of our land, but he enjoins his courts to rule in your favor, should we try to debate our own rights."

For the first time, Leonard Calvert seemed to be uncomfortable. He stirred on the hard bench, looked down at the paper Claiborne had been scanning, and then back up at the Captain.

"There need be no wrangling in the courts," he said. "Captain Claiborne, in spite of what you may think of us, we come here with only peace in our hearts, wanting only to be good neighbors to Virginia and all the other colonies. Our strength and our arms shall be Virginia's, if need be, against the Indians, the Spaniards, the Swedes and the Dutch—against all who might wage war against us. We seek to deprive no Virginian of his lands or his goods; we ask Virginia's friendship as we offer ours."

Claiborne moved a hand, as though to wave away these fine words. His nostrils flared again and his eyes lost their beaten look as he pointed a finger once more at the phrase he had picked out of the mass of wordage on the scroll.

"Then, Sir Leonard," he said, "Virginia asks that you respect His Majesty's own prescription here, where he mentions *hacentus inculta*. I take that to signify, and so must you, that the King prescribes that no lands, discovered, explored, planted and maintained by Virginia *before* the granting of this patent are to be taken from Virginia's sovereignty. Am I right?"

It was Calvert's turn to wave a hand.

"There are no such lands, Captain Claiborne," he said, "according to the word I have from our agent, Henry Fleete, who surveyed the situation here when this patent was issued in '32. The trading posts which Cloberry has set up for dealing with the Indians cannot be termed plantations, permanent establishments. These posts must be yielded up, under the terms set forth here."

Claiborne drew himself up into the erect figure he had been when first he had faced his unwelcome visitor from the other side of the Atlantic.

"But, sir," he returned, "there is one such place that claims Virginia sovereignty under the phrase, *hacentus inculta*. That place has sent a Burgess to the Assembly at Jamestown. That place is well planted, well fortified, well populated. And that place was settled, Sir Leonard, *before* this patent was issued. This grant was signed by the King in June of 1632. I have proof that the portion of Virginia of which I speak, though it lies within the boundaries of your grant, was settled and a Burgess chosen from there at least a year earlier than this patent was signed, in 1631!"

Leonard Calvert reached for a long lace kerchief and applied it thoughtfully to the tip of his aquiline nose, his eyes steady on William Claiborne.

"And what may this land be called, Captain," he asked cautiously, "if it has a name?"

"The Island of Kent," Claiborne replied. "Or Kent Island, or Claiborne's Island, if you will."

The man with the bristly mustache dabbed at his nose again with the kerchief and smiled.

"An island?" he asked. "Surely, Captain, we'll have no difficulties over any small island in the Chesapeake." He turned to Governor Harvey. "There *is* a Burgess to your Assembly who was named from this—this Island of Kent before June of 1632?"

Claiborne flushed with anger at the implication in Calvert's question but he made no exclamation. Instead, he turned toward the fat Governor who sat at the end of the long table, squirming uncomfortably.

"Yes," Harvey grumbled. "It's a small place, of little account, Sir Leonard. The Assembly chose to name a Burgess from there in 1631, after Captain Claiborne returned from England—after his ruinous attempt to block your esteemed father's appeal for a grant. I thought so little of it, and still do, that I missed mentioning it to you in our conversations and letters."

"I see," said Leonard Calvert briefly. He turned back to Claiborne and showed his smile fleetingly. "In that event, Captain, we must work together to settle this small affair."

202

"The affair, Sir Leonard, is settled in my accounts," Claiborne retorted steadily. "Kent Island is part of Virginia and subject to Virginia's sovereignty, and always will be."

"Ah, yes," Leonard Calvert said idly. "Well, we'll see." He reached for the parchment and rolled it carefully, slipping its tape back into place. Then he looked up at Claiborne, his eyes amused. "And you, I suppose, are the Burgess to the Assembly from this Island of Kent, Captain Claiborne?"

The Captain bowed.

"I have that honor, sir," he said proudly.

He waited for no reply from Calvert or Harvey, tilted a rigid nod in the Catholic's direction, ignored the Governor, turned and strode to the door. Dale and Bristoll followed him out of the warm place, into the windswept night of the yard.

Neither lieutenant spoke as they accompanied Claiborne across the parade ground, past the barracks, through the gates of the stockade and down the snow-slippery steps that led to the place where the longboat of the *Cockatrice* had been beached when they landed at Fort Comfort. Both younger men knew Claiborne well enough to hold their tongues when he was in this kind of mood, wrapped in his own thoughts and plans more securely than he was in the cloak that was flapped by the wind off the Chesapeake. They held their silence while the longboat's crew floated the skiff and pulled out to the waiting *Cockatrice,* and they still said nothing, to the Captain or to each other, as Claiborne descended to his cabin and lit the lantern that hung by the head of the neat soldier's bunk. They waited until Claiborne had doffed his cloak and helmet, had eased the cuirass he was wearing and slipped off the sash that held his sword.

It was then, and only then, that Claiborne seemed to recognize their presence. He looked at the pair, his beard jutting, his hands on his hips, and his voice was grave.

"Make no mistake, gentlemen," he said slowly, "that Catholic's no fool, though I'd hoped for one. He's a clever man and a brave one, and that damned patent granted Baltimore is the unholiest instrument ever signed by any English King. It gives Cecilius final say in all matters—there never was a monarch with more absolute power than Baltimore in his new colony. And, beyond that, His Majesty's courts needs must decide in favor of Baltimore, by the King's direction, should we protest. Great God, what fiend of Hell had Charles's ear the day he signed that grant?"

Above them, on the deck, there was the thud of running feet, the noise of the wherry's crew, getting the ship under way at the harsh-voiced orders of Captain Thomas Smith, the new master of the *Cockatrice*. Captain Martiau had relinquished command of the wherry to a younger man, one not afflicted with his aches and pains, and had settled down to a more or less nominal position as overseer at Kent Island. The new man, Smith, knew how to handle a ship well. The timbers of the wherry creaked and the lantern tilted to show that the *Cockatrice* was under way and heeling as the wind filled the canvas.

Claiborne lowered himself to the edge of his bunk and shook his head.

"We've suffered another defeat, my cocks," he said. "We must face that. Aye, and mayhap we'll suffer others before we finally beat this Calvert to his knees. It'll take a bit of doing."

William Claiborne stayed only a few days in Jamestown after his meeting with Leonard Calvert. Most of that time he spent in trying to recruit new soldier-tenants for Kent Island, offering wages that would be bound to make William Cloberry howl when the accounting was made. In spite of the Captain's generous offers, however, he met with only mediocre success.

"The useless loafers," he cursed. "They demand a house already built and fields already planted and they want me to pledge my word they'll never have to use their muskets on anything but game. By God, they want the world in a neat parcel before they'll leave their taverns and ordinaries here!"

"You'd do better with farming folk," Dale said. "There must be plenty of men who know their land's worn out here and who'd jump at the chance to get unspoiled dirt under their hoes."

"I want soldiers, not farmers!" Claiborne rapped out. "Kent Island's a fort, a trading post, not a plantation. I need fighters, not graziers!"

Dale argued his point with a vigor he never had used before to contest Claiborne's stand.

"Farmers," he said, "will fight for their homes and their lands harder and more stubbornly than soldiers such as you'll be able to hire here at Jamestown. And your island, Captain, will support farms and homes long after its days as a fort and a trading post are finished."

"Ho!" scoffed Claiborne. "You'd have me invest in cows, instead of cannon, then; in corn instead of culverins? I thought you'd left all your passion for planting on those scabby acres beside the James."

"Your chance for real success at Kent Island lies in plantation more than cannon," Dale said, stubbornly. "You told Calvert the island's Virginia's because it was planted before his patent was granted by the King; to settle and plant it fully now would give more weight to your arguments."

"Well, well," William Claiborn laughed, "I've reared me a farmer for a lieutenant! Perhaps you're better suited to the hoe than the sword, after all." His laugh died and his mouth set itself in a thin line. "No, I won the island with muskets and cutlasses; I'll keep it by the same means. I'll get soldiers if I have to press men from the King's own guards."

But he was wrong in this, Dale knew. Dale had seen Kent Island from first glance as a place made for peace and quiet, fruitful living, rather than for guns and war. The fields that had beckoned to him that first day he had stood on the deck of the *Cockatrice* were meant to bear crops, not to soak up spilled blood. Let muskets bang and swords ring in other parts of Virginia—in the dark forests of the Susquehannocks, along the rivers still held by the Rappahannocks, over the sandy stretches around Cape Charles where the Nanticokes

205

raided now and then—but not at Kent Island unless there was no other way to hold the place for those who loved it.

Claiborne might scoff at Dale's arguments but Dale noticed, nevertheless, that the Captain approached more and more farmers, the little planters whose acres were burnt out from the over-planting of tobacco, in his search for new settlers at the island. He might say that this one had served in James's army and that that one had a smattering of experience as an armorer but Dale was gratified to see that primarily these men were planters whose earlier mistakes in the fields around Jamestown should teach them to treat their Kent Island acres more gently.

Claiborne was still in Jamestown when Talbot Bristoll brought word from Fort Comfort that the *Ark* and the *Dove* had cleared for some point up the Chesapeake.

"And it'll likely be where we've always traded with the Pascataways," Claiborne said bitterly. "It's the best spot in that region for a settlement."

Dale recalled the place well. It had been there that he had squatted beside Martiau and watched his first trading council. It had been there that he had enjoyed his near-murder of Talbot Bristoll. Martiau had told him then that some day would see that spot settled and Martiau had been right if these Catholics settled there, as the Captain seemed to think they would. He wondered if Anne Furness would find the spot as lovely as he had, the first time he had glimpsed it. Well, it was not so beautiful as Kent Island, and she would never see that place.

It was as though Talbot Bristoll could see into his mind. The fop turned soldier gave a light laugh as he spoke to Dale.

"I've news for you too, Morley," he sneered. "Your little Catholic wench must have captivated the odorous Doctor Wing. Leastwise, Wing sailed aboard one of Calvert's ships after resigning his position at the fort."

"So they've made a convert, eh?" Claiborne said. "If they're all like Wing, these converts, Virginia will not be out one worthwhile
206

man. But he must have enjoyed your little Catholic maid, eh, Dale?"

"She's not—yes, he must have and he's welcome to her," Dale growled. Oh, why did he have to feel as though he were betraying somebody or something each time he spoke of her like this? What was she to him—what would she ever be? "They'll make a good pair."

And that night, cushioning his head on Genevieve Loman's full breasts and listening to her impatient groaning as he went through the preludes to love-making, he thought:

She'd not be so good as this. She'd not be good at all. A plain, uncomely wench without a quality to speak in her favor. He was well rid of her, though he'd never had her.

207

Chapter Six, 1634

THE *ARK* AND THE *DOVE,* CALVERT'S TWO SMALL ships, sailed north from Fort Comfort, past the mouth of the York and the Rappahannock Rivers, until they reached the broad confluence of the Potomac with the Bay. There, the two vessels turned westward. They hugged the northern shore of the wide river, idling along, exploring bays and inlets, sounding depths and circling shoals, until they reached a point some thirty miles from where the broad stream spilled its great sweeping charge into the Chesapeake.

There, the *Ark* and the *Dove* anchored and Calvert called a council of his Commissioners, the gentlemen who were to govern the Colony—always subject to Lord Baltimore's final say in all matters—and it was decided that the two ships would put back toward the mouth of the river, to a spot that seemed best suited as a site for the new Colony. As Claiborne had guessed, the place they chose was the ground where the Captain had traded with the Pascataways.

Returning to that spot, the Calvert colonists disembarked. The fighting men came first, under the brothers Calvert and Captain Thomas Cornwallis; then the working men who threw up a rough stockade, and then the women and the few children, along with the Jesuits.

There is no doubt that Leonard Calvert ordered that time be taken from the work at hand for two services (the Mass and the Protestant service led by a layman that followed the Catholic service) but, for the first few days, he allowed the settlers few other free moments. Nearly every minute of those first days was used in putting up defense works. Young and old, men and women, the newcomers labored at their appointed tasks until, in a surprisingly short space of time, a strong palisade was erected, a hundred and twenty yards square, with one big cannon and six smaller guns, called "murderers," strategically located.

During the building operations, Captain Cornwallis sent out scouts, headed by Henry Fleete, a trader of sorts, interpreter, self-proclaimed explorer and guide, to see what the Indians might be up to. These parties soon scurried back to the little fort, reporting a body of savages not far distant, armed and ready for battle. It could have been that the Pascataways actually were planning to raid the fort and, on seeing the breastworks, changed their facile minds. Or it could have been that the untutored scouts under Fleete, who was held in poor regard by Virginia as an Indian fighter, mistook the Indians' hunting gear for weapons of war. At any rate, when old Werowance put in his appearance at the head of his tribe, he was in no belligerent frame of mind.

He made that quite clear in conversations with the interpreter, Fleete, and by laying arrows with their heads pointed at himself, by many grunts and hand-motions and, finally, by bringing out into the open the squaws and children of his tribe.

A less peaceful and more typical brand of settlers would have taken advantage of this opportunity to show the bestial red man just who ruled this land now. A few blasts of the cannon would have provided the argument. By firing on Werowance, Calvert's little band probably would have wiped out the tribe completely and certainly would have scattered it past any ability ever to wage a first-class war. Leonard Calvert, though, had strange ideas about how to deal with the ignorant savages. Somewhere, he had picked up the queer conviction that the land he was to settle on belonged originally to these Indians and, if he meant to have it and use it, must be bought and paid for.

So, Lord Baltimore's brother handed over to Werowance and his tribe a great heap of axes, hoes, hatchets, rakes, bolts of cloth,

209

beads, bells, knives and similar goods. It is doubtful that the old Pascataway knew exactly why this windfall was his—certainly he had offered no furs in return—but he must have decided that these white men, whoever they were, were people whose friendship was to be cultivated. Consequently, to make this bond more solid, he ordered his braves to give the whites a certain amount of smoked fish, some corn and a few mangy furs that would not be worth much in trade to any dealer. When Calvert paid for *these* goods and gave word through Fleete that he would pay for more supplies, Werowance knew he had something. He stripped his tribe of most of its immediate food supply, was paid in full for each ounce, and took his band off to get more goods.

Before he left, Fleete, at Calvert's direction, made one thing clear.

"We are not *Waspaines*," Calvert said through his interpreter. "We come in peace to be your friends."

And—was it Calvert or Fleete who added it?—there was a final word:

"Trade with us and no others and your tribe will never be without what it needs. The other white men have cheated you. We will deal honestly with our Indian brothers."

By Fleete or Calvert, the thing was said, and Werowance was wise enough to see that henceforth there would be competition between the whites, Captain Claiborne and these newcomers, for his furs and fish. He bore no malice toward Claiborne—the white chief had always treated him fairly—but until now he had had few opportunities to bargain; there might have been a great deal of haggling and argument in those trading sessions with Martiau and Morley and Bristoll but Werowance had known, as had the whites, that in the end the Indians would have to take what Claiborne's sub-chiefs offered. Now—well, his tribe could not help but benefit from this new situation and Werowance nodded his grave approval of the suggestion that he deal only with Calvert's settlement. The pledge meant nothing more, of course, than that Werowance would deal with the highest bidder, Claiborne or Calvert, but the parley did at least insure Calvert and his company against any immediate attack by the Pascataways.

They named their town Saint Mary's and their colony *Terra Mariae,* or Mary's Land. It was something new in the way of settlements, on more counts than one. The other colonies set up on the wilderness shores had been haphazard affairs, at best. But Leonard Calvert was a planner, perhaps above all else. He had the streets of Saint Mary's laid out in a definite pattern and the farm lands were surveyed to get the most good from each inch of tillable soil. He had learned a lesson from Virginia's early history, too. There, back when the Province was first settled, the colonists had refused to raise food because those crops would take land that could be used for the precious tobacco. As a result, famine had swept Virginia. In Maryland, each settler was required under threat of harsh penalties to plant corn and other food crops in a stated amount before he could set down his first tobacco seedling.

Anne Furness had not been lying when she had told Dale Morley that about half Calvert's first party of colonists were Anglicans. They were, although none of them were among the leaders. The head men were the rich Catholics who had financed Baltimore in this new venture, willing to risk their gold in a search for a place where a king's whim, a twist of politics, would not put their fortunes, their estates, their lives, in jeopardy. All the big landowners in Maryland were Catholics, but Calvert handed out land on the same system that was used in Virginia—so many acres to each adult, whether he be a member of the family or a servant—and the Catholics' advantage in acreage was a matter of financial, not religious, differences.

Injustices have been charged to the Calverts, and many rightfully so, but never from the day in 1633 when the *Ark* and the *Dove* sailed from London was there ever an incident of discrimination by the Maryland Catholics against the Maryland Protestants. Each went his own way in the affairs of his church; each aided the other in the affairs of the new colony.

The Spaniards in Florida hated all Protestants. Virginia hated

211

the Catholics. To the north, in New England, the Separatists hated Catholics, Anglicans and, in time, each other. In Maryland alone was there any semblance of religious tolerance, in fact as well as in principle. There would come a time, and not far distant from that first year, 1634, when Cecilius Calvert would name a Protestant, one William Stone, to be the Governor of Maryland as a successor to Cecil's own brother, Leonard. Some might cry political expediency at that, but the fact remains that a non-Catholic followed Leonard Calvert into the Governor's Palace at Saint Mary's.

The Maryland colony thrived from its first day of existence. It was not long before the new settlement was able to send out trading vessels to exchange corn for codfish in New England, corn for tobacco, lumber and cloth in neighboring Virginia.

At the start, Lord Baltimore maintained absolute sovereignty over his colony. He made its laws, he levied its quitrents and taxes, he appointed its officers, he set up its courts, he pocketed its revenues—those of them he did not turn back into his enterprise. His position was, and still remains, unique in history. Here was a Catholic, one of England's precariously positioned minority, and he was answerable to no one but the King himself, and then only as guarantor of his colony's loyalty to the throne in temporal affairs. Calvert could and did bypass the august Ministers of Plantation, he could side-step the King's Bench on legal questions, he had nothing to do with Parliament nor would he have had if conditions had been different and Parliament had not been prorogued, ordered out of session by the petulant Charles at the time. He was his own master as regards Maryland.

"Sail ho!"

The guard on the watch tower at Kent Island sent the cry quavering over the fields and marshes of William Claiborne's island plantations just before noon on a blustery March day that had whipped up regiments of whitecaps to advance across the Chesa-
212

peake and fling themselves at the shores of Kent Island. The yell came whirling across the yard within the small stockade, pried at the windows of the little log hut in the far corner of the enclosure and managed to make itself heard in the crowded room.

Captain Claiborne looked toward the window at the sound, then whipped his face toward Nicholas Martiau, his eyes questioning.

"A sail?" he asked. "Is one of our ships expected?"

The heavy-featured Martiau shook his head.

"The *Long Tail's* out," he said, "but she's not due back for a week or more. Unless it's the *Gryphon,* up from Jamestown with some special news—"

Nerves had been twanging, tempers short, at Kent Island ever since Claiborne's return to the post from Fort Comfort and his defeat at the hands of Leonard Calvert. The Captain's black moods were more frequent these days and quicker to descend than ever before. Dale Morley, Talbot Bristoll, Martiau, all the men around the lean-faced Captain had walked on tiptoe since that snowy night at the fort when Claiborne stared down at a scroll that bore the name of Charles Rex.

"Get your men to their guns," Claiborne barked now at Martiau. "Morley, get down to the wherry and tell Captain Smith to be ready for an attack! Bristoll, you know your place—it's not here!"

Dale ran across the yard, his boots thudding against the frozen ground, dodged through the rear gate and headed for the wharf beside which the *Cockatrice* lay. Halfway to the wherry, he saw that Smith had already gone into action. The vessel's crew was casting off the lines, the jib was going up and the *Cockatrice* was beginning to edge out from the pier toward deeper water where she could maneuver, if she had to. As the wherry turned, the small brass cannon in her sternsheets caught the sun with a twinkling flash. There was an answering wink from the gun in the bow as the wherry's nose came up into the wind.

"Run her back," came the cry of the gunner's mate, in the bow. "Load. Step lively! Run her out. Stand by."

The wherry was an armed vessel now, at Captain Claiborne's order, with men who had been in the King's navy tending her guns. The *Long Tail,* when she came in from her voyage up into Delaware Bay, would have a gun mounted and the *Gryphon* would have several put aboard when next she touched at Kent Island. If there was to be a war, Captain Claiborne meant to have a navy to help him fight it.

Dale turned and retraced his steps to the stockade, trotting now. He felt a quickening excitement tightening his lungs, stepping up the tempo of his heart. That unexpected sail might mean that there would be fighting and Dale Morley still had to find out whether he was a brave man or a coward in any other kind of fight than a brawl. A gun, now—how would his kidneys serve him when he heard a ball go whistling past his head? Would the lump in his throat dissolve or swell up to strangle him when a cannon belched its smoke in his direction?

Oh, he had told himself enough times that he would give as good an account of himself as Talbot Bristoll, at least, but was that really so? He had heard from Martiau and the soldiers at Fort Comfort that many a man was a killer in a fight with fists and feet, only to find his strength deserting him, his only thought the one to run, when the rattle of musketry sent lead shrilling past his ears or the boom of guns threw great balls that smashed into the palisade he was shrinking behind.

"I've wanted to run myself," Nicholas Martiau had confessed, "and held myself to my position only with the sternest kind of effort. And then, when the fight was joined, I found myself wondering why I'd feared any of this in the first place, though men were dropping all about me by that time. There's a sort of fever, a madness, that takes a man in charge when the first fear finally lets go its grip."

Dale hoped that if there was a fight, and he fell victim to that fear, it would not be too clinging with its hold. It would be better to take a ball in the forehead than to let Talbot Bristoll catch one

214

glimpse that might tell him that he was afraid. But Bristoll, too, was human—or nearly so—and it might be that he could watch the other tremble and quake. That would be sweet, but he had little honest hope of that happening.

Captain Claiborne had the glass to his eye as Morley rejoined the group on the parapet of the stockade, between the two sakers that held their muzzles on the ship that was beating in toward Kent Island. The gun crews were waiting, their pieces laid on the visitor, the gunners keeping their eyes fixed on Martiau, beside Claiborne. Bristoll stood beyond the Captain, shading his eyes against the sun that sent spiked reflections up from the choppy waves.

Claiborne grunted, the spyglass still leveled at the white patch of sail to the west.

"It's Calvert, right enough," he said, to Martiau, "or one of his ships, at any rate. She's the smaller of the two, the *Dove* by the looks of her, and she's carrying no guns that I can see."

He lowered the telescope and glowered out over the water.

"She's headed here, that's plain," he said. "I wonder what's his reason."

Dale followed Captain Claiborne down the ladder and through the front gate of the stockade, Bristoll close to him. Despite the Captain's sneers and harsh manner of late, Dale was sorry for him. Through the years, a sense of *kinship* had grown undetected into Dale Morley's regard for Captain William Claiborne. If he had admitted it, studied it, dissected it, he might have realized that he was casting Claiborne in the role of the father who never had loved him and disciplined him, the older brother who never had cuffed him and shared with him, the fond uncle who never had counseled him when he had been in need of advice.

There were rare occasions when a strangely soft-voiced William Claiborne had talked with Dale, in confidences he never shared with any other man. These were the times when the two were closest, when Claiborne dropped his dramatic swashbuckling, cooled his hot ambitions, forgot his bitter hates, his persistent plans

215

for revenge, his schemes for political coups. These interims never lasted long, but while they did Dale had the chance to look past the Captain's hard exterior, as cold and gleaming as a polished breastplate, and see the man few others knew existed.

On one such occasion, he had said a strange thing, for William Claiborne.

"I wonder," he ruminated, "if that cow-mouthed Frederick Loman could be right, this once. He's said that the day when Virginia needed soldiers and Indian fighters is past; that now the planters and the graziers, the merchants and the carpenters, are more important than the cavaliers."

His fist crashed down on the arm of his chair as his mood wrenched itself away from him.

"Christ's thorns," he blared, "I surely must have a touch of the vapors to give a thought to Loman's mooing! No, Virginia still needs a soldier's hand and more than ever now, with the Papists reaching for her lands."

It was William Claiborne, the soldier, whom Dale Morley and Talbot Bristoll followed through the main gate of the stockade and down to the shore where the *Dove's* longboat would beach. The captain of the pinnace obviously had no intention of running the unfamiliar channel to the sheltered narrows where Smith was moving his armed wherry into position. Instead, the *Dove's* anchor went over with a splash offshore, her sails came down in an untidy lump that bespoke indifferent seamanship and the little craft swung into the wind. From the small vessel's gaff there showed the black and gold pennant of the House of Baltimore.

There was some delay aboard the pinnace and Claiborne's breath whistled with impatience as he waited for the longboat to be swung over the side of the *Dove*. It was easy for those on shore to see that the vessel was handled by a crew that would have felt the cat in Smith's hands for one of the dozen blunders these Marylanders fumbled through. The boat was launched, finally, with a splash that all but foundered the thing and there was a spell of bailing before the landing party was able to board.

216

"If that's the way they handle a ship," Talbot Bristol laughed hoarsely, "I wonder that they ever got to Virginia from England."

"They got here with the Devil's help," said Claiborne sourly. "Beelzebub looks after his own."

The longboat made its way toward shore, the oars splashing raggedly, and finally touched the beach. A seaman leaped over the side, wincing at the icy water's sting, and hauled the boat's nose up onto the sand. Then Leonard Calvert stepped ashore at Kent Island.

He wore a cloak of heavy, rough material gathered closely about him. His face was reddened by the wind and patchily chapped and there was an angry sore at one corner of his mouth; but still the Catholic carried his dignity with as much assurance as he had at the conference table back at Fort Comfort.

Behind Leonard was George Calvert, looking cold, wet and miserable as he stepped from the longboat. The others were all common sailors and stayed at their places at the oars.

William Claiborne stepped forward to meet the visitors, lifting a hand to his helmet in brief salute.

"I bid you welcome to Kent Island, Sir Leonard," he said correctly, coldly, and waited.

"Our thanks for your welcome, sir," Calvert responded automatically. His eyes turned from Claiborne to rove over the scene inshore: the stockade with its ready guns, the houses, the barns, the mill which Dale had persuaded Claiborne to have built a short month before, the long, low barracks where the slaves were quartered, the huts that housed the unmarried indentured servants, the larger cottages occupied by the married servants.

"You have a pleasant place here, Captain Claiborne," Calvert said, when he was finished with his scanning.

"We find it so," Claiborne replied stiffly. "This is a part of Virginia I hold dear above all the others—selfishly, I confess. But will you come to my quarters where you and your brother may warm yourselves? Your men can find shelter, too, within the stockade."

Leonard Calvert shook his head. He was wearing a plumed hat, all out of keeping for a water trip in this weather, and the wind tore at the feather, shredding it.

"They'll stay where they are," Calvert said indifferently. "But your words of hospitality are welcome to these numbed ears of mine."

"If you'll follow me, sir?" Claiborne said, with a slight bow. "It's in this direction."

Claiborne led the Catholic to his own house, set apart from the other buildings and furnished with the fine pieces he had moved from his place at Jamestown. This Kent Island home was larger than the Jamestown establishment, with wider rooms and higher ceilings, more windows and more generous hallways. The main house was of wood but the two wings, stretching to the north and south, were of brick; and the Captain intended some day to replace the main structure with a brick building to match the wings. That was to be done when the trouble with Calvert's people was finally settled and all Virginia belonged to Virginians again.

Leonard Calvert's searching eyes were not idle as he walked into the sunlit, paneled drawing room off the main hall. He kept his expression under a tight rein but Dale could tell the Catholic leader had not expected either the richness of Kent Island that was apparent even in this drab month of March, or the graciousness of Claiborne's home.

The visitor, trailed by his innocuous brother, walked across the room and took the chair toward which Claiborne gestured. The Captain bawled an order to Toss and the slave appeared with a bottle-burdened tray, goblets clinking. Claiborne poured the brandy and Toss handed the drinks around. Dale savored the mellow, warming draught, started to pour a second one and then held off. Let Bristoll swill his liquor; he'd stay with Claiborne on one sup and a clear head.

"I must compliment you, sir, on your establishment," Leonard Calvert said. " 'Tis far more comfortable a place than my own rude quarters at Saint Mary's, though I hope to have better accommodations built soon."

The Maryland leader relaxed in his chair a bit, made a tent of his spatulate fingers.

"You've made your little island a pleasant place—" he resumed mildly.

"Little? It's big enough to stand up against your grabbing, sir!"

Leonard Calvert shook his head so that the long curls of his wig brushed his cheeks.

"You misunderstand me, Captain," he said gently, "whether by design or accident. I meant no slight to your trading post, believe me. It is a pretty place and there should be no odds between us over how it shall be governed. You, Captain Claiborne, should have a free hand in administering the affairs of the island."

Claiborne drew up, checked by Calvert's unexpected announcement. He had been ready for almost anything but this from the man across the Bay, and for a floundering moment he was at a disadvantage. He recovered quickly, but not before Leonard Calvert's smile had deepened.

"I intend to keep on having a free hand in this island's affairs," Claiborne managed, ungraciously. "Did you come here to tell me that?"

Calvert used his kerchief at the reddened tip of his nose with deliberate languor.

"By my leave, you'll keep on with your rule of this place," he said calmly, "and only by my leave, Captain."

William Claiborne's hand went to the hilt of his sword, as did Dale's and Bristoll's. All three men dropped their hands in the realization that Calvert did not even carry a dagger. His cloak lay open and there was no sash or belt about his coat; he was no Italian to carry a stiletto in his sleeve. Leonard Calvert saw their hesitation and held up both hands, palms upward.

"No, I'm not armed," he said, "and neither is my brother. We did not think we would need weapons to accept your hospitality, Captain Claiborne."

"If that's your say, then," said Claiborne heavily, "there's no more need to waste time here. If you think it's by your leave that I can stay on this island, then we'll argue this thing in louder voices that speak with powder and shot."

Calvert nodded, as though agreeing that the sun was shining.

"We can do that," he said idly, "but gentlemen may settle differences with thoughtful speech while common men have need of force. I know you for a gentleman, Captain Claiborne, no matter what your opinion of me, and I'd tell you this:

"You make certain claims to this island; I say the place is Maryland's under the King's patent. Then should we put it to His Majesty to decide our differences?"

He shook his head again in answer to his own question.

"Not," he said, "unless all other means fail. His Majesty is beset by his troubles with Parliament and the Army these times, as you well know. Neither I nor any other loyal subject would add to the burden of cares he's carrying if it could be helped."

He hesitated and dabbed at his nose again with the square of fine lace.

"Get on with it, man!" Claiborne said hoarsely. "This shilly-shallying would sound better coming from a woman!"

"Here's my proposal, then," Calvert said smoothly. "I say that you'll continue on at Kent Island as you have. I can pledge you my word that your trade will not be interrupted by any man of Maryland. William Cloberry would approve of that."

Claiborne's eyes were cautious as they waited.

"And in return," Calvert said easily, "I'd ask only your oath of fealty to Maryland. Your sovereignty here at Kent Island would stay intact, I swear it."

"And my overlord," said Claiborne slowly, "would be your brother, Baltimore. That's the bone under the meat, Sir Leonard."

Calvert nodded silently, his eyes on Claiborne's face.

"Peace and success under Baltimore," he said. "War and ruin under Virginia—that you owe nothing."

Dale shifted his weight from one foot to the other. There was an offer he would hate to have to accept or reject.

220

Take the offer, Dale's mind breathed. Then he saw Talbot Bristoll's eager face and wondered whether his own thoughts really were dictated by a love of Kent Island or by a fear of war, the dread that he might prove craven when the musket balls moaned overhead and the smoke blossoms of the cannon spilled their deadly seed.

It was the man who knew he wanted peace and a fruitful Kent Island against the man who did not know what war was like or how he would meet the awful impersonal menace of battle. He wet his lips and spoke without remembering he was a lieutenant, a subaltern, and without noticing that his Captain was still hesitating.

"A bear," he said, his voice strong, "may raid a honey tree and never feel the sting of the bees but a man can be stung to death doing the same thing. I see no great thick pelt on you, Sir Leonard."

There was a moment's silence and then William Claiborne's laughter sounded crashingly, on a note of relief.

"Now, by God, there's your answer!" the Captain cried. "Mister Morley has put it well—you've no pelt to save you from the stings we'll spike you with, Sir Leonard, and this honey tree will stay unviolated!"

His boot heels clacked on the floor as he strode to a place directly in front of the Catholic. He placed his hands on his hips and bent forward slightly to jut his beard at Calvert's impassive face.

"Before you war on us," he thundered, "think twice or a dozen times twice! We have a navy now, and it will be stronger. We have an army that has been blooded in Indian battles, and that will be stronger, too, when your first musket misfires. We have all the strength of Virginia against your puny forces, Sir Leonard, because, mark you, Virginia will give us her men, her ships, her guns, to hold this place!"

Calvert's eyes told Claiborne of the Catholic's disbelief on that point.

"You think not?" the Captain asked. "You think because Harvey made you pledges that Virginia will stand by and watch you steal this island? I could tell you how lowly Harvey's real position is, if I'd take the time. Ask Captain Mathews, Colonel Utie, how Virginia will stand in any war against one of her islands! Why, sir, we'll seal off the mouth of the Chesapeake against your vessels, blockade you, till you'll be happy to call surrender! Not one of your shallops will venture a foot off shore without risking our attack. And you come to me, making threats!"

Leonard Calvert arose slowly, drew his cloak about him. His younger brother moved to his side, as though seeking the protection of his shadow.

"Have done, Captain Claiborne," Calvert said, his fingers busy with the clasp of his cloak. "I did not come here to match boasts or hurl prophesies. I came to reason with a thoughtful man."

"We've reasoned, then," Claiborne said savagely. "My lieutenants will see you to your boat."

Calvert stalked toward the doorway and then turned.

"One thing you will grant me, maybe," he said with that carefully preserved calm.

"What is it?"

"Take what I've said to Jamestown," Leonard Calvert suggested. "Let the Burgesses there consider my proposal. You owe that to Virginia and to your King. Offer them peace instead of slaughter, prosperous times at Kent Island instead of war. See how they take my offer."

"I'll do that," Claiborne agreed, his lip curling, "and I'll present my arguments against your pretty scheme. I could give you Virginia's answer now, sir!"

"But as Secretary of Virginia," said Calvert in his unruffled voice, "I ask you to advise the Burgesses of what I've said."

Claiborne gave the visitor a curt bow.

"I said I'd do it, Sir Leonard," he promised, "though it'll never benefit your hopes."

Calvert bowed in return and moved through the doorway. Just past the threshold he paused and turned back again.

"Captain Claiborne," he said, "I envy you your confidence in your position here. I confess I thought to find you worried over what's occurred in London."

"What's this? What's this?"

"Surely," said Calvert as he spread his hands, "you've heard that you're not in William Cloberry's complete favor. My brother writes me Cloberry has spoken ill of you publicly and is thinking of sending another man to take charge here."

Dale watched the surge of dark blood to the Captain's lean face.

"Now that," he growled, "is nonsense! Why would Mister Cloberry hold any ill will against me?"

Calvert flicked at the tip of his nose once more before he turned and answered.

"I am not sure," he admitted idly, almost insultingly, "but from what I've heard, Cloberry and his creature, George Evelin, have lately learned something about your dealings with m'Lord Cartney —or shall we say with some person close to Cartney? And Cloberry, they say, is very displeased."

Dale stiffened, his blood chilling. Great God, then the pot was spilled, at last! How much did Cloberry know? How much did Calvert know?

William Claiborne's puzzled frown was genuine.

"You charged me with speaking in riddles," he said after a pause. "Now I charge you with the same. What are you trying to say?"

Calvert shrugged, his eyes amused.

"No doubt Mister Cloberry will inform you," he said coolly, "at his leisure." He bowed sweepingly. "My brother and I thank you for your hospitality, sir. I hope we meet again in a more pleasant circumstance."

Before Claiborne could make answer, Leonard Calvert hauled his cloak over one shoulder and strode out into the hallway, stumped to the front door and pulled it open. George trailed him, for all the world like a scuttling page boy. Dale and Bristoll, at

223

Claiborne's head-jerk, followed the two Marylanders out into the windy cold.

Later, when he was alone in his chamber at the Captain's house, Dale paced the floor, thudding one fisted hand into the palm of the other. If William Cloberry knew of the affair of Lady Augusta Cartney, why had he not told Captain Claiborne before this? It was obvious that Claiborne had not been advised that his defeat at Windsor Castle was of Dale's making. But why didn't the Captain know? What purpose did Cloberry have in keeping it a secret?

Calvert had all but accused William Claiborne of denting Lady Augusta's pillow—Claiborne, who had no more than touched her hand in a dance measure. Leonard Calvert did not seem to be the kind of man, somehow, who would twist a story to goad an enemy. Yes, it could be taken as the truth that Calvert had relayed the accepted word from London: that Cloberry and Evelin thought it was Claiborne, not Dale Morley, whom Lord Cartney had seen in Lady Augusta's bed.

Was such a thing possible? He thought back to that evening in London. The door had opened but a crack and his back—his back had been toward the peeper. His hair was the same shade as Claiborne's, his skin as dark. And beside the bed had been the sword that Captain Claiborne had just given him, the same blade that the Captain had worn at Cloberry's dinner and at Windsor Castle, made distinctive by the gryphon's head on its hilt.

He threw back his head and chuckled. Now, here was a laugh! All his fears had been for naught; Cartney believed it was William Claiborne, not Dale, who had shared his wife's couch that day!

But if that were so, why had Cartney balked at calling Claiborne out? Lady Augusta had told him her husband could not challenge a yokel, but William Claiborne was no nameless oaf—ah, but Claiborne bore no title beyond his Provincial ones; a proud man like Cartney would be as reluctant to cross swords with the Captain as he would with the lieutenant.

Everything fitted and he was freed at last of all those nightmare fears.

He laughed again in his new freedom—and did not think at all of what William Claiborne's misplaced guilt might mean to Kent Island.

On March 14th, 1634, six days after Leonard Calvert visited Kent Island, the Burgesses at Jamestown used high-sounding words to reject unanimously Leonard Calvert's proposal that the island bow to Maryland sovereignty.

So, the gauntlet was flung down to Maryland and the Island of Kent was the prize for which the struggle would be joined.

A LETTER FROM CECILIUS CALVERT, SECOND LORD BALTIMORE, TO SIR LEONARD CALVERT, GOVERNOR OF MARYLAND, DATED MAY 16TH, 1634:

"... and I am well pleased with the progress and prosperity of the Colony which you detail in your reports and letters. I know our father would be content with your excellent administration of the affairs of our venture.

"As concerns the questions you asked about the man, Claiborne, and his island, it is my wish that you let matters rest as they do for the present. It is my thought that our Colony, so new and beset by so many problems, can ill afford a war at this time with Claiborne or Virginia. C., as you well know, is an uncertain person and there are signs that his favor is fastened on Virginia at the moment so that it would be better to keep our affairs with Claiborne on a peaceful ground for at least a year if we can.

"This does not mean that we give up our claim to the

225

island. As it is, the place is a sword aimed at our gullet and it must be put under our flag. Count on me, my dear brother, and on all the personages at Court who have an interest in our venture to gain our rightful possession of the island when the time is ripe. But I counsel no immediate steps against the interloper, Claiborne.

"I count on your good judgment in this affair as in other things which concern the peace and prosperity of our Colony. I pray each day for your health, dear brother, and your safety and . . ."

* * * *

A LETTER FROM WILLIAM CLOBERRY OF LONDON TO CAPTAIN WILLIAM CLAIBORNE OF KENT ISLAND, PROVINCE OF VIRGINIA, DATED MAY 24TH, 1634:

". . . and I have reason to believe our fortunes at Court are mending for the better. His Majesty has expressed himself to Heath in all sincerity that he is bound that Virginia's settled and planted lands, including the Island of Kent, shall not be included in the Catholic patent. The King, however, still holds Harvey in high regard and all our efforts to have him returned to England and a man more favorably disposed to us put in his place have gone for naught.

"Your query about your position in my regard has given me much surprise. I'd answer your questions more fully save it might lend weight in your mind to a false rumor. It is enough to say you still hold every trust I could place in a friend.

"As to Mister Evelin, about whom you inquired, he is your friend and has always spoken highly of you. He has a large amount of money invested in our enterprise, as you know, and so has the right to inquire into our affairs. He has lately spoken of a wish to visit the Company's properties in Virginia and as a shareholder he has this right, certainly.

"But if the man, Calvert, spoke of or hinted at Mister Evelin taking your place he lied most ignobly and I would so charge him to his face if it were possible.

"Our false friend, Cartney, is in mourning for his wife. Lady Augusta was found one day at the bottom of a set of steps with a broken neck she must have suffered in a fall during the night. I pass this information on, knowing it would interest you.

"The fashion in furs here in London is for minks and I would have you forward as many of those skins as you can gather up, and otters as well. The call for beavers is not so great as it was and there is hardly any liking for lion skins at all. Further, I would advise you . . ."

A few days after Claiborne's receipt of William Cloberry's letter of reassurance, the *Long Tail* put in to Kent Island from Jamestown with a cargo of powder, a dozen new muskets, salt, nails and one passenger. Dale was at the landing when the smallest craft in Claiborne's little fleet slipped up to its mooring and it was Dale who headed the gang detailed to unload the vessel.

George Holmes, who had captained the *Long Tail* on its brief voyage, called Morley to the vessel's tiny cabin as soon as Dale set foot on the pinnace's deck. Inside, Holmes closed the door and gestured to a bench.

"I've taken something upon myself," the captain said, "that could mean a devil of a row with Captain Claiborne, Dale. I need your help."

Holmes was a taciturn, hard-working seaman. He had been in Claiborne's service for years but his self-effacement, his lack of assertive push, his willingness to let others step past him in the climb to authority, had kept him limited to command of such rou-

227

tine missions as the *Long Tail's* just-finished voyage to Jamestown.

"What happened, George?" Dale asked now. "You know you'll have my help, if I can give it."

The *Long Tail's* captain frowned, stroking his bristled chin.

"I am a careful man," he said, as though his words needed that introduction, "but this time I've acted foolishly. I discharged my cargo at Jamestown all right, and took on my new cargo as I was ordered. And then I was approached by this man."

He sighed at the recollection and almost grinned.

"Approached is hardly the word," he amended. "I was on my way back to my vessel after a drink at an ordinary—it was quite dark—when this man stepped out of a shadow and plucked at the sleeve of my coat. He spoke in whispers—I thought it was some beggar or pimp at first—and he asked me to hide him."

He looked across the cabin at Dale, apologetically, and then down at the floor again.

"I brushed him away, at first, but he clung like a leech. Said he'd heard the talk in the ordinary and knew I was sailing within the hour and he had to get out of Jamestown. I asked him his trouble and he told me."

He sighed again, as though perplexed.

"At least," he went on, "he gave me a tale about learning of some plot against the King, in England, and being threatened by those who were involved—all noblemen, he said. He told me he'd come to Virginia to escape being murdered and had just found spies of the plotters in that very town. Now, he said, he had to run again and would I stow him aboard the *Long Tail?*"

He shook his head sadly.

"When the spell of his talk wore off," he said, "I knew I'd been diddled but by that time we were halfway home, with him aboard. And now he's here and I must make some accounting to Captain Claiborne. I know what he'll say—that this man's one of Calvert's spies, as well he may be."

"What does he call himself?" Dale asked.

"He says his name's Carter," Holmes replied, "but I think he really has another name."

"Fetch the man," Dale said, "and we'll try to find out if he really is a Calvert agent. If he is and we can prove it, Captain Claiborne will have a purse for you for trapping him."

The man Holmes brought to the *Long Tail's* cabin proved to be short, bandy-legged and shrinking. He rumpled a shabby cap between his hands and bobbed his head persistently as he was half-led, half-shoved into the cubicle by the pinnace's captain.

"Your mercy, sir," he said without preliminaries. "To send me back to England means I'd be stabbed to death before I'd walked the wharf to dry land. I'll work till my fingers bleed and ask no wages, not a groat. I'll do whatever task you set and not complain. And I'm a hand with horses, sir, like you've never seen before. Aye, I can gentle the wildest stallion and doctor the sickest colt. I promise you, sir—"

"Less talk," Dale Morley growled. "You rattle on like a woman. I'll ask the questions and you answer them and—you say you know horses?"

The head nodded vociferously.

"That I do. Ask anybody how Jack Ba—how James Carter—handles horses, sir, and they'll all swear I'm fair amazin' with 'em."

Dale leaned back on the bench, his eyes narrowed. The voice, the bow-legged figure, were familiar. And horses—his memory suddenly came to life.

"For God's sake," he said in a low voice. "Jack Bagshaw! You brought me Bella."

The little man peered at him, half-curiously, half-fearfully.

"Bella?" he asked. "I know no woman named Bella."

"She's a mare, you fool," Dale explained. "You sold her to me at Jamestown five—no, nearly six years ago. Your name was Bagshaw then."

The squat man began to edge toward the door.

"Now, sir," he said in a rising whine, " 'Tis often a fine judge of horses like m'self is misled by an animal's lines. I truly thought the mare—Bella, you said?—was all I told you she was, but if she wasn't, then I'm not to be held to account, sir, by your mercy. I never lied about a horse I handled, though I've made mistakes, bein' no more than human, so if the mare—"

"Now, wait!" Dale said roughly, "Stop your yammering! The mare was all you said, and more."

"She—was?"

"Yes, and still is," Dale said. "If you made a mistake, it was in my favor, Bagshaw."

The little man straightened, lost his cringing manner abruptly. He threw back his head so that the light from the companionway showed his red hair and a broad, triumphant grin spread over his wizened features.

"So, you see?" he crowed. "There's none like Jack Bagshaw to deal honestly in horses with a gentleman!"

"I thought you said your name was Carter," George Holmes said.

Bagshaw's eyes switched to Holmes and then away.

"A name's a handy thing," he said evasively, "to change when it could bring trouble."

"And what's your real trouble now?" Dale asked. "This story you've told Captain Holmes is stable dung from the start."

"Oh no, sir," Jack Bagshaw protested. "It's all as I told the captain. I overheard some noblemen plotting the King's death and—"

"Where did you overhear these fine gentlemen?" Dale rapped out. "Since when have noblemen mingled with horse traders? You think I'd believe a baron or a knight involved in so desperate a thing as a plot against the throne would spill words into the ears of a Jack Bagshaw? More likely, you're one of Leonard Calvert's spies, sent here to learn our secrets."

"Calvert?" asked the horse trader in a puzzled voice. "Who is Leonard Calvert?"

230

Dale Morley arose from the bench and hooked his thumbs in the broad leather belt he wore.

"We'll soon find out whether you know the Papist," he said harshly. "We'll go to Captain Claiborne now and have him use his ways of finding out your secrets. You'll find him expert at that, though not too gentle."

Sweat popping from his forehead, Bagshaw pawed at Dale's sleeve as he made to move past the bandy-legged hostler.

"Now, sir," he pleaded, "ye'll not desert me in my distress! Remember the mare, sir! I made a sacrifice—a great sacrifice—in that sale because I admired you so completely, sir! In God's name, show me a bit o' mercy now!"

Dale kept his scowl pulled down over his eyes.

"Tell the true story then," he commanded, "and I'll know it, the first lying word you offer. What are you trying to escape from?"

Bagshaw's brief cockiness had vanished entirely by now. His hands went back to twisting the disreputable cap and he jiggled from one foot to the other.

"I'll tell ye then," he said humbly, "and every word's God's truth, I swear it. Some time ago, I came to Virginia with some horses and I met a countryman of yours who put the Devil's word in my ear. I could get rich, he said, if I bought tobacco with the money I collected for the horses, make a quick profit and pocket the difference between what the tobacco cost and what I sold it for, with none of my employers in England the wiser."

That's true, Dale thought, *it was I who mentioned that!*

"I fought the temptation," Bagshaw went on, "till this last voyage. That time, curse my own greed, I used my employer's money to buy tobacco up to the last piece of gold in my purse. Ah, I'd be the proud one when I went back to England! There'd not be enough rum for me to buy or enough girls to dandle; I'd show them all that Jack Bagshaw was the clever one!"

He stopped talking and his wide shoulders drooped.

"Well?" Dale asked as the pause lengthened.

231

Bagshaw hunched his shoulders and spread his hands.

"Only this," he said in a doleful voice. "The price of tobacco went down. It was as though they were waiting for me to buy before they began giving the nasty stuff away, almost. Before I could get rid of what I'd bought, I'd lost enough pounds to make you shudder, sir."

"I warned you there was no pledge that it would go up," Dale said, and could have bitten his tongue as the last word slipped past it. Bagshaw peered at him again, his eyes narrowed speculatively.

"Ahhh," he said slowly, "'twas *you* who told me to buy tobacco! 'Twas *you* that led me into this predicament!"

"Now, wait a minute," Dale said roughly. "I told you—"

"Ah, I do not hold it against you, sir," Bagshaw interrupted, his voice docile again. "They can't say Jack Bagshaw ever held a grudge against a man who offered him a chance to profit, no matter how unfortunate the chance proved."

"I offered you nothing," Dale said in exasperation. "I only said—"

"I know, I know," the little horse trader broke in, "and I still thank you for it, though it's brought me to my ruin. These things happen and all we can do to cross out bad advice is try to make amends. Just give me shelter, sir, and Jack Bagshaw will forget the rest."

Dale turned away from the bandy-legged man, pulling at his lip, uncertain whether to laugh or curse. This little thief had wasted no time in seizing his advantage; an incautious word had been dropped and now he was making it seem that he, Dale, *owed* the runty red-head sanctuary. Actually, he owed this embezzler nothing—well only, perhaps, in a manner of speaking. He turned back to Bagshaw, keeping his frown intact.

"You lost your employer's money," he said. "What did you do then?"

Bagshaw had regained some of his arrogance and was beginning to strut with head and shoulders again.

232

"I thought I'd fixed the damage," he said, "when I went back to England and settled my accounts. I told my employer that four of his best animals died of the fever on the voyage to Virginia and that made up my tobacco losses."

His monkey's face donned an aggrieved expression.

"The suspicious whoreson," he said mournfully, "mistrusted me, Jack Bagshaw! He talked with the ship's captain and that hound's whelp betrayed me. Only one horse died, he said, and that one a sorry nag."

He sighed again at the recollection.

"Then there was a hue and cry," he said. "Up and down all England they chased me till my tongue hung to my knees and I began to wear the very smell of the fox. At last I hid away aboard a vessel bound for the Indies, I thought, and after I'd worked under the whip till I wished I'd been caught in England I found m'self back in Jamestown again. God's truth, I never saw a more stinking sight than that place, when they dumped me there with a kick and a curse!"

He ran a splayed hand over his unruly hair.

"I nearly starved," he went on, "till I found work for my keep at a plantation near Henrico. Then, not two days ago, I came to Jamestown and chanced to see a man I knew in England, a lick-spittle creature of the nobleman whose horses—er—died at sea. A word here and there and I knew he was hunting me, so I hid. I heard this gracious captain speak of sailing with the tide and begged his mercy—and here I am, sir."

There was silence in the cabin of the pinnace as Jack Bagshaw waited. Dale considered the little man's predicament. If he were returned to Jamestown and capture, Bagshaw could expect the gibbet or, at the very least, a slow death in some dungeon keep; that much was certain. Claiborne wanted no transported convicts at Kent Island. The Captain had repeatedly refused to buy up convict contracts, no matter how desperately he might need men for his army or his ships.

"Scum," Claiborne called them, "and always treacherous. It's enough to have an enemy facing one's sword without having to wonder about a dagger in the back."

Captain Claiborne would be almost sure to ship Jack Bagshaw back to Jamestown if he knew the little horse-trader's true history, as he would have returned a runaway slave, without a qualm. And that probably was the wisest course, to avoid all trouble with the King's law by sending this bowlegged man back to face his bitter punishment.

Still—Dale *had* suggested that Bagshaw gamble in tobacco. True, that had been six years before, almost, and he had been a fifty-acre farmer in a canvas shirt, but he had planted the idea in Bagshaw's low-browed head. And this man had sold him Bella and the mare had turned out to be one of the finest animals in the Province, Dale's proudest possession even now. He owed Bagshaw something for that.

"This is what we'll do," he said suddenly. "We need a farrier on this island and you can fill that place, so long as you do your work and keep out of trouble here. One slip, and it'll be back to Jamestown and England for you, so watch your tongue and your strut. I'll tell a story to the Captain that'll pinch the truth, in places, but will fit the occasion. Yes, I think you'll be safe here, Jack Bagshaw."

"I thank you," Bagshaw said fervently. "And ye'll never have reason to regret this day."

Chapter Seven, 1634

THE *HUNTER* WAS BEATING DOWN THE CHESA-
peake under a wind that had become stronger and increasingly
erratic since an hour out of Kent Island; and the little ship, loaded
past her safe capacity with trade goods, was making heavy weather
of it, when the storm came howling out of the southeast, borne on
slate-gray, twisting clouds. The whitecaps that had been reaching
higher and higher by the minute now transformed themselves into
curling combers that crashed over the windward rail, sending great
sheets of green water sluicing over the decks. The overloaded
Hunter, taking water through her hatches, grew sluggish; she began wallowing.

Dale would barely admit it to himself, but he was afraid. This
was his first command and all the things he had been taught by
Martiau and Smith seemed to desert him now. He had a ship and
a crew of eleven men, he had a cargo valued at hundreds of pounds,
and all these things were his responsibility. To lose ship, crew and
cargo on his first voyage would mean going back to Claiborne in
disgrace (for some reason he had no thought that he might be lost,
himself) and facing Talbot Bristoll's sneering laugh.

He had, long since, ordered the *Hunter's* sticks stripped of everything except a tops'l, and now that parted with a crackling report
that could be heard even over the whining scream of the storm.
The *Hunter* staggered, dipped her nose into a thunderous sea and
swung her prow over, toward the west.

The helmsman fought the wheel but he could not hold her, even
though Dale leaped to his side to help strain at the spokes. The
rain came out of the leaden sky in a torrent, and for a moment

235

Dale's heart lurched with the thought that the *Hunter* was awash. His pulse steadied when he saw the little vessel raise her prow valiantly and, as he cast a half-glance over the side, glimpsed the freeboard the cutter still retained.

The helmsman's eyes were wide and staring as he looked at Dale, begging speechlessly for some command that would get the *Hunter* and him out of the howling tumult that closed in on them. The rain shut out the horizon like a curtain, and now only the savage course of the waves showed Dale his directions. The cutter turned, went over on beam's end for an agonizing moment and then began lifting and surging as it fled before the vicious following sea. Without a shred of canvas aloft, the heavily laden *Hunter* could not outrace the waves that pursued her. One after another, the combers smashed in over the stern, striking at Dale and jamming the helmsman against the wheel. And with the pounding blow of each crashing sea, the *Hunter* seemed to settle a bit lower in the water.

He had to get some canvas up; he knew that. He had to get up enough sail to give the cutter speed with which to keep ahead of the down-swinging strokes of the following seas.

"As she is," he screamed into the helmsman's ear. The man might have heard him, though that was doubtful, considering the ripping force of the wind. In any case, he wrestled at the wheel, trying to keep the cutter from switching her stern broadside. The cords stood out on his neck and the muscles of his bare arms were ropes that knotted and twisted as he fought for control of the vessel.

Dale battled his way forward to the companionway that led below. He pounded on the hatch cover until a face showed in the gloom below; a white, broad face transfixed by terror.

"All hands!" Dale roared. He gestured with one hand, calling the men up on deck. The white face disappeared and was replaced by another.

"All hands, God damn ye!" Dale howled. "Do you want to drown like muskrats in a snare? All hands!"

236

They came up, although grudgingly. They were sailors, after a fashion, but they were not the best men Martiau and Smith could muster. The most able men served on the *Cockatrice* and the next best on the *Long Tail*. Most of the men under Dale were indentured men, capable enough for the ordinary voyage but bewildered, appalled now by the fury of the storm.

But they came up on deck and somehow Dale managed to get them to stretch a fores'l, though how it was done was something that he could never rightly explain later. It was sloppily rigged, it would have brought curses from Smith; but it was finally raised and it gave the *Hunter* the drive she needed to keep just ahead of those punishing seas abaft. Dale clung to the lines as he made his way back to the helmsman. The man at the wheel was drooping now, worn out by his heartbreaking struggle to keep the cutter from broaching to, and Dale pushed him aside roughly as he took over the wheel. The helmsman made one faltering step and then slid forward on his face, to roll with the list of the deck into the scuppers where he lay motionless. Another sailor came out through the curtain of rain to put his hands under the fallen man's arms and drag him toward the companionway and down into the cabin.

Then another man appeared through the rain curtain, a bowlegged, sturdy little figure in a pair of cotton breeches that were plastered to him by the wet, a man whose red hair was soaked black by the downpour.

Jack Bagshaw might be scared but his grin did not show he was. He came up to the wheel, his curled toes gripping at the slippery deck, and moved to Dale's side.

"What—you—doing here?" Dale gasped.

"That old bitch's whelp Smith pressed me," the little farrier said, cheerfully. "He learned I'd done a bit o' work on water and he grabbed me, at the last minute before ye sailed, sayin' he was short-handed. I been hidin' to escape the work but now I guess ye need me. Always handy to help a friend—that's Jack Bagshaw."

He laid his hand beside Dale's until he got the feel of the rudder and could judge the power of its surging; then he nodded to Dale, who released his grip to clutch at the lashed boom overhead and steady himself.

"As she goes!" he yelled, and Bagshaw nodded.

A minute's watching told Dale that the diminutive farrier knew this work, no matter how strange it might seem for him. His labors at the smithy had given Bagshaw tremendous strength in his arms and shoulders and the little man held the wheel in a more authoritative grip than either Dale or the original helmsman. Bagshaw handled the *Hunter* like a man with the reins of a vicious horse, and the bucking, plunging cutter seemed to react like a mount that recognized its master's touch on the lines.

Now there was the question of just how far the *Hunter* could run before the storm without ripping her bottom out on one of the rocky reefs that stretched out from the western shore of the Bay. Dale dared not try to bring the cutter about, sodden as she was.

There was nothing to do, then, but to go with the wind and hope that when the *Hunter* struck she'd hit mud and that the seas would not break her up before the storm subsided. He stood beside Bagshaw, trying to peer through the rain screen, his teeth edged by the expectancy of the jarring, grinding shock of the ship's keel crunching on rock at the next moment.

The rain slackened, poured down again, lessened and then stopped. As suddenly as though a hand working a bellows had quit its work, the wind left off hammering at the little vessel. The churned waters still heaved and swirled about the cutter, but now a man could see.

"By my mother's good name," said Jack Bagshaw, softly. "Look there, sir!"

Dale followed the direction of the farrier's pointed finger and saw a harbor to starboard. It was a sheltered port that held six small vessels, and beyond them lay a log stockade and beyond the fort were houses and outbuildings, all laid out in a neat pattern. He turned to look over the port side and saw that the *Hunter* was in a

238

small bay or, perhaps, a river, or a deep cove. He cast his eyes here and there—yes, this place was familiar, though the fort and the houses were new. This was the place where he had come with Martiau to deal with the Pascataways on his first trading journey! There was the beach where he had swum and Bristoll had laughed at his reluctance to expose himself, all naked, to the Indian squaws who watched. This was—this was Saint Mary's, then! This was the stronghold of the Catholics!

He had to go about, and quickly, raise his mains'l and get out of there before the Papists used their guns on him.

"All hands!" he shouted. "Mains'l and set a new tops'l! And lively! That's Saint Mary's off the starboard bow!"

The men scampered to their places and the mainsail began to rise, slowly, as the wet lines went through the water-swollen blocks. And then the *Hunter* struck.

She did not hit hard. She put her nose onto a mudbank with the gentle nudge of a tired woman nuzzling her face into a welcome pillow. But when she went aground, quietly as it was, she went firmly aground.

Cursing, Dale sent his men forward with long oars and poles, to try to push the cutter free. But the poles and oars only sank into the mud, a seaman fell overboard and had to be fished out, spluttering and gasping, and the *Hunter* did not stir before the small boats began moving out from the shore.

The first boat to reach the *Hunter* was a four-oared craft with a tall, stringy man in helmet and breastplate standing in the bow. The man's armor was a replica of Martiau's, bespeaking long service, and he carried a cutlass. In his wide leather belt was thrust a "small musket," one of the Italian weapons of which Dale had heard, a "dagg" or *pistoia,* a weapon that could be held in one hand and fired like a musket, though it was effective only at close range. Well, this distance was close enough, he thought grimly. He had wanted to see a dagg and now, it seemed, he would see one by looking down its throat.

The man in the weatherbeaten burgonet kept his eyes on Dale as the dory moved closer to the *Hunter*. The other boats encircled the cutter like hounds moving around a crippled stag.

When the boats were within speaking distance, Dale moistened his lips, hoping the action would not betray his anxiety to the men about him.

"This is the cutter, *Hunter,* out of Kent Island, Virginia," he said formally, "and bound for Lord Delaware's Bay on a peaceful trading voyage. There can be no reason why we should not be peaceably received at this place."

The thin man bowed ironically.

"And I am Captain Cornwallis," he told Dale, "in command of Lord Baltimore's army in the Colony of Mary's Land. And it is for Sir Leonard Calvert to say how you shall be received here."

"Then let him be called," Dale retorted hotly, "to give his orders! I must put my men to the pumps and mend what breaks must be repaired, but I'll not have that done if you'd seize my vessel. We'll do no work for you, if that's your plan!"

Cornwallis' deep eyes glimmered murkily as his craggy face tautened. His voice crashed out across the water with a volume surprising in one so thin.

"Sir Leonard does not come running at a Kent Islander's bidding," he roared. "And as for doing our work, I'll wager you'll bend your backs enough in our service if Sir Leonard orders you made prisoners. Now get over your longboat and we'll escort you to the Governor. And till you find what he wants done with you, keep a civil tongue in your head."

Dale hesitated, but he knew there was no alternative but to follow Cornwallis' blunt orders. He turned and spoke briefly to Jack Bagshaw, who stood a pace forward from the other sailors, huddled in the sternsheets.

"Get the longboat overside, Jack," he said. "I'll go ashore and see how Calvert means to deal with us."

"And I'll row ye in," Bagshaw said instantly. "It'd not be fitting for ye to handle the oars yourself."

240

"All right, and my thanks," Dale nodded. He raised his voice. "All hands to pumping and moving cargo so it'll not be spoiled by water while I'm ashore. Find those leaks and patch them lively. I'll not be gone long."

Dale thought of Claiborne and how the Captain would rage when word reached him that one of his ships had wallowed onto a mudbank to be captured at the Catholics' leisure. He half heard the curses Claiborne would hurl at him, Dale Morley, whose first chance to captain a vessel had ended so ignominiously. If there had been a chance to fight—at least to go down under the Maryland guns—

His face must have reflected his anguish because Jack Bagshaw spoke softly from his place at the oars.

"Steady on, Cap'n," the little red-head said quietly. "Ye'll not show these people a frown they might mistake for fear, I know."

The farrier's low-voiced words brought Dale's head up again and he forced a cold, contemptuous smile to his lips for Cornwallis and the other Catholics to see. No, by God, these Marylanders would never see a look of fear on his face; not these people who had to depend on a storm's whim to lay hands on a Kent Island vessel.

Saint Mary's, he discovered, had a sturdy wharf and bulkhead. Nor did the harbor carry any of the stench that hung over Jamestown. Of course the settlement was young, he told himself, but reluctantly he had to admit that these Marylanders seemed better managers in sanitary matters than the people of Virginia. Jamestown could do with a little of the cleanliness and order that he could see here.

He helped draw the longboat ashore and then straightened, waiting for Cornwallis' next move. A squad of soldiers, all carrying muskets, responded to the stringy captain's curt order and fell into line on each side of Dale and Bagshaw.

"This way," said Cornwallis, and turned toward the street that led up from the wharf. Dale followed, with Bagshaw at his heels, the Maryland soldiers pacing beside him.

He felt like some criminal being led to the scaffold, some highwayman caught and tried and sentenced to dance on the wind, some pirate brought to justice. He kept his eyes straight to the front, trying to ignore the curious glances, the baleful glares, of the men and women who left their houses and the waterfront sheds to stare at him. As he passed down the ragged-edged aisle, he heard a swell of murmuring, a bitter word spoken here and there.

"*Silence!*" roared Captain Cornwallis, and the muttering stopped abruptly. This man, Morley thought with a fleck of grudging admiration, maintained a tight-reined discipline even over the townspeople who were not his soldiers.

The brief journey led up a gentle rise to a building which, when it was completed, would eclipse the Governor's Mansion at Jamestown in size and splendor. Now, only one section of the building was habitable but by the number of men about the place, holding hammers and adzes and axes as they stopped work to stare at Dale, it would not be long before this grand house was finished. Leonard Calvert had told Claiborne that he hoped to have a home as comfortable as the Captain's, in time. He had wasted few hours in starting the building.

Captain Cornwallis pushed open a rough, temporary door set in the wall of the completed side of the mansion and stepped aside, gesturing to Dale and Bagshaw to enter. They traversed a short hallway that led to a room where Leonard Calvert waited.

He sat in a carved, high-backed chair and he was wearing a robe of rich, crimson velvet with fur at the throat and cuffs, despite the warmth of the day. His dark hair was carefully arranged, though his mustaches still bristled, untended, and his beard was still the sparse projection he affected. His hands, one marked by a ring with a huge stone, lay along the arms of his chair and his ankles were crossed beneath the furred hem of the robe. He might have been a King's judge, a priest of the Inquisition, a monarch in his own right, by the dignity he displayed.

His dark eyes, as they surveyed Dale, showed no hint of the triumph he might have felt at this easy, bloodless capture of Willam

242

Claiborne's lieutenant. Neither was there any sign of compassion on his face with its curiously high brow and rounded chin. His first glance at Morley was as impersonal as though some stranger had been brought before him.

For a time, the two men stared at each other in silence.

The Catholic's eyes held Dale's as, quite leisurely, Dale reached up to doff the tasseled wool sailor's cap he was wearing and ran a hand over his hair to smooth it. Calvert's voice was easy, almost gentle.

"Just what are we going to do with you, Mister Morley?" he asked, slowly.

Dale glanced about the room. In a corner sat a clerk in dusty black, crouched over a quill that jerked and splattered its way across a sheet of foolscap. There sat the man Dale had been a few short years ago, barely noticeable in the shadow of his lord, this Sir Leonard; and would this Papist scribbler have the good fortune to rise out of his furrow of inkhorns and ledgers? No, this man was too old to hope for much change; he was a starvation-thin person with a bobbing Adam's apple—why, it was Anne Furness' father! And how was Anne, and was she somewhere around where he could see her, maybe talk to her? Could he tell her that the scene in Wing's stinking hut had all been a mistake? Could he make amends that she would listen to?

"I asked a question, Mister Morley." Leonard Calvert's soft voice insinuated itself into Dale's thoughts, tearing them away from the vision of Anne Furness. "Or are you thinking over your answer?"

"I was asking myself, Sir Leonard," Dale said, "when I'd be invited to sit. Or am I a prisoner, not due the simple courtesies?"

Calvert gestured negligently toward a chair across the room from his. Dale strode over to the chair and lowered himself into its embrace gratefully. Till then, he had felt no effects of his battle with the storm; now he was swamped by a bone-melting weariness. Jack Bagshaw, unbidden, stumped across the floor to take a stand at Morley's side.

243

"And now that you're comfortable," Calvert said languidly, "I'll put my question again: What are we going to do with you? Punish you as a poacher? Claim you tried to raid us and were beaten? Hang you as a pirate? Or offer you the post of aide to Captain Cornwallis?"

Dale felt his mouth drop in an astounded gape. The man was serious in his last remark! Aide to Cornwallis? Was Calvert mad to think—

"I see I've startled you, Mister Morley," the man in the crimson robe said smilingly. "Or maybe you think I'd taunt you with some crude jest."

"I do not see—I do not know—"

"Then listen, Mister Morley! I pride myself on knowing men at a single glance. I noticed you when I first met Claiborne at Fort Comfort; I got a deeper impression when I called on your captain at Kent Island, when you rescued—as you thought—your captain from agreeing to my terms and betraying his position as Secretary of Virginia. And did you do that because you loved Virginia? No, you said what you said about the bear and the bee tree because you'd set up an idol, a statue in your mind that was Will Claiborne, and you spoke up when you did rather than see your statue crumble into a powder of greed and ambition."

And that's all wrong. I spoke because I was afraid I'd turn coward in battle.

"So I told myself that here was a man whose allegiance I could use, on the right side. Here was a man who would see, if I reasoned with him, that he deserved a better position."

"I—"

"Let me finish, Mister Morley." Leonard Calvert hunched forward in his chair, his big hands gesturing as he talked. "I meant a better position in more than pence and pounds. I meant a position wherein you could know you were on the side of right, rather than wrong."

He straightened to fling an arm in a gesture toward the windows.

"Look outside, Mister Morley," he cried. "What do you see?
244

You find planters and workers and men and women who came here because they hoped to build a new life for themselves here! You'll find no men who work for Cloberry and Company out there! You'll find no man who must turn against his brother at the demand of some fat money man in England who knows nothing and cares less what this Chesapeake country is like!"

He left his carved chair and walked over to Dale, the fur trimming on his long gown brushing the floor.

"You'd like it here, Mister Morley," he said earnestly, "and we need men like you. When Kent Island is ours, you'll have the running of the place if you throw in with us. I said that Claiborne is finished and I say it again. There'll be no reproach against your name—you were captured here and you gave your parole to save your crew."

So there it was. This man could make it sound as though there were no other course to follow save accept the Catholic's bidding. And he had promised that when Kent Island belonged to the Papists—but Kent Island would never belong to them!

Right or wrong, there was a loyalty he was pledged to, and what was a man who'd go against his word to save his neck? He tried to picture William Claiborne in this same position, or even Talbot Bristoll, and he knew their responses as clearly as though they had spoken at his side.

"Sir Leonard," he said evenly, "if it's a choice between hanging and denying my allegiance to Captain Claiborne, I can only say that I hope your hangman has a skillful hand with the knot."

He heard Jack Bagshaw gasp, and added:

"My men were under my command, whatever our mission. If you hold me a pirate or a poacher, at least admit they're innocent."

He watched Leonard Calvert's head drop surprisingly, and the fire and zeal run out of the man in the crimson robe until he seemed a curiously shrunken figure. When he spoke, the Maryland Governor's voice was flat and lifeless.

"I'm no murderer, though maybe I should be to flourish here," he

245

said dully. "You'll not be held, any of you. You're free to leave here as soon as you can get your craft afloat again, and you'll not be molested unless you invite trouble yourselves."

Dale raised himself from his chair. Of all the things he had expected Leonard Calvert to do or say, none of them had included the sudden change to this merciful stand. He swallowed, hunting for words and not finding them, till Jack Bagshaw plucked at his sleeve.

"Let's be off, yer honor," the little farrier half-whispered, "before his lordship changes his mind."

The red-haired man's words carried across the room to where Calvert sat and the Maryland Governor raised his head.

"Yes," he said, "your man speaks wisely, Mister Morley. You'd best be off before I steel myself to do what I should do, what my brother, what Captain Cornwallis, and what every sensible man in Maryland would have me do—hang you to show William Claiborne he's dealing with a man who can be as ruthless as he. Now be off!"

Dale directed a stiff bow toward the crimson-robed man across the room.

"My thanks, sir," he said, "for your graciousness. Perhaps I can balance this account some day."

Calvert's only reply was a tired wave of the hand. The clerk, Furness, turned in his chair to direct a stare of loathing at Dale before he went back to his papers and ledgers. Captain Cornwallis, his face rigid with disapproval, stood aside as Dale passed him and walked through the doorway, out of the room. His heavy boot heels thumped on the planking of the hallway, drowning out the patter of Jack Bagshaw's bare feet, and to the threshold that led to the lumber-littered yard beside the half-completed mansion.

They went down the hill toward the town, walking between the two files of soldiers, and saw the carpenters drop their tools, the farmers leave their fields, the clerks abandon their accounts, the housewives desert their cookpots, again. There were more Marylanders to watch Dale's return from Calvert's mansion than there had been when he had made the trip up the hill; but now all were silent, with no murmur to mark Dale's and Bagshaw's passing between the ranks of onlookers.

Dale put on a cold, superior smile and glanced from side to side as he strode along the street in pace with his escort. He did not know why Calvert had spared him; but he had, and Dale meant to take advantage of the situation. Let these Papists see that a man of William Claiborne's troop could be hailed before the Governor of Maryland and walk out as confident as when he went in.

A little past halfway to the shore he saw her, standing beside her lumpish sister. There was a basket of woven marsh grass on her arm; her face was shaded by a wide-brimmed bonnet, a gray linsey-woolsey gown draped her slight body. And she was wonderful, by God, as she had always been!

He stopped, his heels skidding in the drying mud of the road. The soldiers of the escort detail jerked to a stop with him and Jack Bagshaw collided with one of the Maryland musketeers with an oath before he realized that Dale had come to a halt.

"Anne," Dale said. "Mistress Furness."

Her eyes were blue-gray and never faltering. It was a situation that might have been embarrassing for another woman; a hated Kent Island man, a pirate who had called her "Anne" before he had remembered to call her "Mistress Furness"; but Anne Furness used the voice she might have used in speaking to a child whose ear was caught in the clamp of a schoolmaster's fingers.

"Why, it's Mister Morley," she said.

"Yes," he said. What to say now, with all these peasants gawking? "Your—your sister's child—did Doctor Wing's powders save the baby's life?"

He moved toward her, elbowing aside one of the Maryland soldiers, until he faced her at arm's length. Her eyes were still unwary; she had no reason to fear him here.

"The child was saved, by God's mercy," she replied, "even as I was, that night at Fort Comfort."

247

He found his tongue thick as he tried to tell her all he had to say, in this brief moment and with the hungry, naked faces hanging over the elbows and shoulders of the bodies that clustered around them.

"That—that—" he stammered. "I can explain—"

"Then do!" she told him. Her voice rang out, sharp and clear. "There are gossips listening who think that because I was alone with you for an hour that night, and was all rumpled on my return from the doctor's hut, that I'm a trull. Tell them, Mister Morley; pray do!"

His eyes swept the crowd that lurched in about him. One sharp-nosed dame with pink-balled eyes was pressing eagerly toward him, her hand cupped to her ear as though she was afraid she would miss one syllable of the talk. Dale directed his remarks to her.

"Mistress Furness," he said, distinctly, "begged me to lead her to the surgeon at Fort Comfort, the first evening you all came to Virginia. I led her there and there I tried to play her for the strumpet." *God's teeth, how far did Calvert's promise of protection go?* "And she fought me off like the modest maid she is, and—and we were interrupted, so she was not harmed."

He turned away as a surly grumble arose from the men in the crowd.

"Jesus," Jack Bagshaw murmured beside Dale. "They'll be about our ears like hornets now! Did ye have to say that?"

"Yes," Dale said firmly. "I had to say that."

They had taken only a few steps, jostled now by the crowd, before Anne Furness' voice sounded above the bubbling mutter of the mob.

"My thanks, Dale Morley," she called, "for clearing my name among my neighbors."

He pressed on, forcing his way through the pack that Calvert's soldiers now found hard to keep back. Jack Bagshaw panted at his elbow, not from exertion but from the urge to strike out at the clamor that surged in ever closer about them.

"Gi' me one poke," he begged Dale, "and one of these bastards 'll wish he'd stayed at home with his idols. Gi' me—"

"Steady on," Dale said. "There's the boat."

They got into the dory with the soldiers forming a protective ring about them and shoved off. A stone splashed beside the boat when it was a length offshore, another thudded on the gunwale. Dale stood in the stern, looking back at Saint Mary's, resolved that no man of William Claiborne's troop would turn his back on this rabble. A clod of muck hit the afterthwart and splattered to coat his chin in black slime. There was a shout of hard laughter from the beach.

"That reached 'm . . . should've been a musket ball, the pirate scoundrel . . . let's to the boats and sink 'em—sink 'em all!"

Dale watched the rush to the small boats drawn up along the shore under the bulkhead. Cornwallis' soldiers were floundering aimlessly, unable to control the crowd without their commander. They used their weapons as staves in an attempt to push back the mob but their fellow townsmen swarmed around them and through them and past them.

"Dig deep with your oars," he told Jack Bagshaw, over his shoulder. "We must make the cutter or we're done for."

"They'll never catch me," Bagshaw gasped as he strained at the sweeps. "I can outrow, outride, outfight and outdrink any Maryland louse that was ever born."

The race, however, was uneven from the start and Dale saw that he and Bagshaw could never make the comparative safety of the *Hunter's* deck before his boat would be overtaken by the Marylanders. The other boats were lightly built, whereas the *Hunter's* longboat was stoutly fashioned of solid oak, built for seaworthiness, not for speed. Bagshaw might boast of his oarsmanship but the Maryland dories speedily closed the distance between them and the Kent Islander who had confessed publicly that he had tried to violate a Maryland girl.

They drew alongside now, howling curses and threats. Aboard the *Hunter,* Dale could see the sailors tending the bow falconet. He saw, too, that the list of the stranded cutter would prevent the gun crew from bringing the small brass piece to bear, even if the men aboard the *Hunter* would risk firing into the fleet of Maryland long-boats and take the chance of hitting their commander.

"It appears," said Dale grimly, "that we're due for a ducking. I hope you can swim, Jack."

"I never learned the trick," said Bagshaw, shaking his head. "Though, maybe, it'll come to me, once I'm in the water."

"I doubt that, even of you," Dale said. "Try to cling to the boat, should they overturn us."

Whether the Marylanders meant to drown Dale or merely give him a ducking was a question that was never answered. For as the pursuit closed in on Dale and Jack Bagshaw and the runty farrier stood up to use an oar as a flail, there was a barking report from the shore and a cloud of smoke drifted up from the belled muzzle of one of the soldiers' muskets. Dale turned with the others to see the tall, lean figure of Thomas Cornwallis standing on the end of the wharf, his long arms gesticulating wildly in motions calling the Marylanders back to shore.

The men in the boats surrounding Dale obeyed instantly, albeit with many a curse at being robbed of their sport. They flung taunts and jeers at Dale and Bagshaw, but they backed water with their oars, and reluctantly, with many a black glance at the two Kent Islanders, they headed back to the beach.

"And that," said Jack, softly, "was the closest I hope I ever come to bein' laid out amongst the fishes. Thank heaven Calvert is as good as his word in promisin' we wouldn't be harmed."

It required four hours of top speed work to get the *Hunter* free of the mudbank and to pump and patch the cutter enough to stand out from Saint Mary's. Once out of the Potomac, the *Hunter* anchored and Dale set the crew to work repairing the damaged stern and shifting the cargo. Fortunately for Cloberry and Company, the goods that had been water-soaked were not among the perishables that Dale carried; some metal tools that were in the hold would very likely be rusty by the time they reached Delaware Bay and some of the cloth goods would be spotted by brine; but there was no competition for trade in the Delaware country and he knew he would be able to get as many furs with damaged goods there as he would get for perfect merchandise in the Chesapeake.

He should have been more than satisfied in this and surely he had reason to count himself lucky in having delivered himself and his ship into the hands of the Marylanders, and escaping without hurt to either and without a single gesture of surrender. Still, he wore no smile as the cutter beat down the Chesapeake, rounded Cape Charles and started northward toward the wide mouth of Lord Delaware's Bay.

He had acquitted himself well with Calvert, he told himself, and he had shown Cornwallis that he had his share of courage; he had not exhibited the slightest flicker of fear in the face of the hooting Maryland colonists; he had dared speak openly to clear Anne Furness' name.

And yet the thing was incomplete—in all the time he had faced Anne and had spoken with her, there had been no smile on the girl's face, nothing but a cold contempt had been reflected in her eyes. He might love her with unreasoning passion, but he knew she despised him, as much as it was in her nature to loathe anyone.

CHAPTER EIGHT, 1634-1636

PEACE BETWEEN THE MARYLAND COLONY AND Kent Island, never more than a tenuous armed truce at best, could not endure for long. Neither William Claiborne nor Leonard Calvert expected anything but an eventual clash of arms, and the only question in the late days of 1634 was which side would provoke the first battle and so accept the charge of being the aggressor.

Claiborne's vessels, with Dale and Bristoll and Thomas Smith commanding them, made deeper and deeper inroads into Calvert's newly-founded trading domain. The Captain built two new pinnaces, the *Bittern* and the *Gamecock,* and with these additions to the fleet Kent Islanders ranged from the Susquehannock River at the top of the Chesapeake to Cape Charles at the bottom, venturing up the Potomac and Patuxent Rivers as freely as they sailed the tidewaters about their own island.

Then too, Cloberry and Company in London were grudgingly shipping better trade goods to Claiborne than they had in some time, to match the quality of the stuff Leonard Calvert was offering. Dale had thought the Captain would be openly gratified by this reluctant generosity on Cloberry's part, but the Captain viewed the matter without too much enthusiasm.

"There could be more to this than we know," he told his lieutenant when Dale had finished reading a letter from Cloberry. "I do not like it overmuch. True, we'll get more furs and the balances might prove the same, but the fishy eyes of those investors in England look only to the expenses and they'll blame me when they go higher, by Cloberry's order. You'll see."

He pulled at his beard and scowled out the window.

252

"Besides," he continued, "I've had advices from my brother which you didn't see, letters I showed to nobody before I burned them. The hints Calvert laid that day he came to visit us may have had some truth in them. My brother tells me that George Evelin has been boasting that the day is not far off when he'll handle all Cloberry's properties in Virginia."

Dale grunted disdainfully.

"Evelin!" he said. "He'd not last an hour in this country. I tell you, Captain, your people here on the island—yes, in all Virginia—would never follow another leader but you."

Claiborne seemed preoccupied with some view through the window at which he was standing.

"You're young, Dale Morley," he said slowly, "but some day you'll learn that most men will follow the captain who's headed for a triumph and most men will desert a captain who's headed for a defeat, no matter how long they may have served him or how their services have been rewarded over the good years."

"You're in a black mood, for fair," Dale laughed. "It's time you went to Jamestown and joined your friends in a riot for an evening. That would take your mind off your worries."

Claiborne shook his head.

"And nay to that, too," he said with a sigh. "I'm too old and too busy with my troubles to enjoy even a wild night such as we used to have. But you go, Dale. You've worked hard without a rest for months and you're due a vacation. Let a week in Jamestown repay you for your excellent services."

He cast a curious glance at his lieutenant before he continued.

"You have a great admiration for Mistress Loman, I take it?" he asked.

Dale busied himself with the inspection of one lace cuff.

"Jenny is a splendid friend," he said.

"And no more than that?" Claiborne asked.

Dale's head jerked up.

"What do you mean by that, Captain?"

It was Claiborne's turn to look down at his cuffs.

"I do not mean to pry," he said, "or give advice that'd not be welcomed. But I have thought for some time, now, you should take another wife, Dale."

"*Jenny Loman?*" Dale cried. "Christ on the Cross, you practically warned against marrying her! You said—"

The Captain raised a hand and moved it from side to side to cut off Dale's spurt of words.

"We'll not go back to that," he ordered. "I remember what I said then and I remember why I said it. The—the situation has changed, Dale. I had certain plans at that time and the man who would not change his plans to meet the moment is a fool. So I—so I have changed my mind on that score."

"But Jenny Loman! You must know that I—that we—"

He stopped and spread his hands in a gesture that finished his sentence.

"Make Jenny my wife?" he asked. "How could I even consider it?"

Claiborne began pacing back and forth in front of the window, his hands hooked into his belt, his eyes on the floor.

"And why not?" he asked. "The lady is well-born, she will inherit wealth some day and she certainly is one of the most beautiful women in the Province. She would make a fine hostess for any man's home."

"Captain," Dale said, "you don't understand. I'll speak no ill of her, but—"

"I understand enough," Claiborne broke in. "I am not blind, you know. But—times change, Dale. And certain rules, certain conventions, change with them. What was sinful, unforgivable, ten years ago—yes, five or four or two—seem paltry things now, at least among the Cavaliers."

He swung his head back toward Dale and held his eyes steadily.

"We can be frank with each other here," he said, "because no word spoken here will go any further. I think I know your thoughts.

254

You think that Genevieve Loman is a light woman, not worthy to be your wife. And I say that if you'd marry her she'd make you a good and faithful partner."

He shrugged eloquently.

"Oh, yes—a virgin is a wonderful thing but many a virgin has proved a snarling, ill-favored, dishonest wife with nothing to recommend her once her veil was pierced. And there have been many women who came to the marriage bed no virgins and proved themselves more chaste and dutiful by a thousandfold than their more careful or more timid sisters. And that, I say, is the woman Genevieve Loman would be."

Dale moved to a chair and lowered himself heavily, his brain aswirl. Yet through the shock of surprise there filtered the thought that he should at least think about what the Captain had said. He was twenty-four years old, as well as anybody knew, and he was a lusty man who needed a woman to keep his blood running free, if not to love. It was time he built his home and his family. The brief encounters with Indian girls and slave wenches were wild enough, and brutally satisfying, but a man needed more than them, lest in time he lose the sense of degradation that followed each such bout, and became a thing like Talbot Bristoll.

What Captain Claiborne had said might be true. Genevieve Loman was honest, in her own strange way. She had made no demands on him except the demands she had made on his male strength when she was with him; she had exacted no promises, no protestations of love; she had wanted nothing more from him than she had given him, in turn. Married to him—great God, those words seemed strange!—she would fill her part of the bargain as fully as he would fill his, no more, no less. And as for love—love was a dream for fools like him, who thought of Anne Furness smiling up at him.

"You forget the lady," he said at length. "Maybe she'll have her own ideas about marrying a man like me."

"She'll have you," Claiborne said from the window. "She's liked
255

you, Dale, since the first night she met you at my Jamestown place, when you came riding up to my door with your sore buttocks bouncing on your new horse."

"And that was a few hours, no more, after you'd held your sword at my gullet and invited me to dine with you," Dale laughed. "Was there ever a stranger invitation?"

"And was there ever a more hot-blooded cockerel in all the Province than Dale Morley was then?" Claiborne asked in turn. He ran his eyes up and down his lieutenant and he nodded. "Time has changed you, Dale, and for the better."

"Time and your teaching have helped me," Dale said, "if there's any betterment in me. But there's been many a time lately that I've wondered if you'd not have done as well to leave me on the stinking farm where you found me, after all."

Claiborne's eyes narrowed. He walked away from the window toward Dale and leaned on the back of a chair that was in his path. His hands, gripping the chair, were white at the knuckles and he bent forward in his earnestness.

"You're not happy here, Dale?" he asked. "You'd rather be back where I found you?"

"How can I tell you or anyone who'd ask me?" he demanded. "You've given me everything I thought I'd ever want and still I'm—I'm not content. Ask me what it is I need to make me happy and I can't tell you, Captain. Maybe a name, a real name, even though it made me kin to the greatest scoundrel in the world, would satisfy me. If you had left me on my little farm I'd not have given a curse whether I was a bastard or not, but now when you've brought me to this sort of life and I see what store men put in their families and their forebears, maybe—"

He broke off. He knew that what he'd said was only a hollow mouthing of words to try to hide his real torment.

"I—I love a Maryland maid," he confessed.

"Love," Captain Claiborne grunted, "is a puzzling word."

Dale jerked up his head to look sharply at Claiborne. His an-
256

nouncement that he loved Anne Furness, a Marylander, had brought no exclamation of surprise from Claiborne, though Dale had expected an explosion to follow his confession. He kept his eyes on Claiborne as the Captain paced to the window, his hands clasped behind him.

"You speak of love for this Catholic maid—Furness is her name?" he asked. His lips spread in a thin smile at Dale's astonishment. "Oh, I have my spies at Saint Mary's and I knew of what took place there, when you confessed publicly to pawing at her petticoats and being beaten off, before you'd got the *Hunter* under way again for Delaware's Bay, almost."

"I—she hates me," Dale muttered.

"From what I hear," Claiborne nodded, "she must. The word that comes to me says you tried to have her at your first meeting and you must have been a clumsy dolt about it, certainly, to have her refuse."

"Mind you, she's not a Catholic," Dale said. "It'd make no difference if she were, but as it happens she's an Anglican, like you and me."

"And a woman of Maryland," Claiborne said sharply. "An enemy, Mister Morley!"

He jabbed a finger at Dale's chest.

"You have your duty to Kent Island, Dale Morley, and to me! You can't share your allegiance between this place and a Papist woman who despises you! What is this love—a product of your having been too long without a wench? You need white flesh instead of black or red? My God, I thought I had a real lieutenant in you, not a man who'd sigh and simper for a doxy who'd beat any Papist buck to a bed yet still played the great lady with you!"

He turned abruptly and stamped his way toward Dale.

"Love!" he spat. "You'd eat out your own heart for a wench who hates you while you have a full, warm woman waiting to make you the proudest wife Kent Island will ever shelter? Yes, I'll speak the truth; Jenny Loman will grace the finest board and the finest bed

257

you'll ever see, Dale Morley, as your wife! So she has been reckless in her time and you'd not be the first to cover her! And still she has name and family and money, and more than that, she loves you, Dale! Not like the stupid love you hold for the Catholic girl but a real love, a love that will put her whole being in your trust."

He rested his hands on his hips, his dark eyes boring deep into Morley's.

"I know what I say, Dale," he said earnestly. "You have some kind of hopeless infatuation for this Furness girl that'd disappear with one feel of the flesh. With Genevieve, you'd be happy because she is your kind and I and everyone in my service would work to see that the two of you were content. A house? You'd have one as fine as this. Servants—I'll give you Yago, for one. Land—you'll have the finest acres on this island, and with clear title. I could not befriend another human more than I'd befriend you, Dale Morley—if you were married to Jenny Loman, with your madness for this Anne Furness forgotten."

Anne's blue-gray eyes had been contemptuous. The voice in which she'd thanked him for risking his life to clear her name had been cold, beneath the words. She'd never see him as anything but a hot-handed brute who had pawed at her bodice. It would be better to admit, right now, that the strange love which afflicted him was impossible, from the start.

And, on the other hand, there were the things that Claiborne offered, a home, a plantation, a closer tie to Kent Island. A man would be a fool to spurn those things for a love that Claiborne called madness and which probably was. He was no youth to lose the world for love and count the loss worthwhile; he was a man, now, with a man's practical eye to the future.

And if he did not love Jenny Loman—well, she would be all the things Claiborne had said she would be, and that would be enough, without love. Love was a thing for poets. A soldier could be satisfied with its fleshly counterpart and Jenny had an abundance of that quality.

258

The answer had to be given now, while William Claiborne was in this mood. To give the nod now would bind the Captain to his impulsive promises; tomorrow might be a different day. He cast the thought of Anne's rare smile from him and his voice was steady.

"By your leave," he said, "I'll take the *Bittern* on the morrow for a visit to Jamestown."

Claiborne nodded, waiting for the next words.

"And I'll return soon," Dale added, "with the lady who, I trust, will be Dame Morley."

"And you'd have me for a wife?" Genevieve Loman asked. Her voice was uncertain, wondering. "You—you are quite sure, Dale?"

"Quite sure," he replied, nodding, "and I'll be the most fortunate man in Virginia if you say yes to me."

He wondered vaguely whether it would be expected that he drop to his knees in making his proposal and decided against it.

"I've not much to offer, Jenny," he said, "but Captain Claiborne has promised me a house and land if—"

She waved his words away.

"What do those things matter?" she asked. "And as for having nothing to offer me, this—this thing you've asked me to do, to be, is the finest—"

She broke off, biting her lip and keeping her eyes on her hands, twisting in her lap.

"I must be honest with you, Dale," she said, in a small voice. "You were not the first—"

"Hush, Jenny!" Dale broke in roughly. Christ's thorns, he wanted to hear none of that!

"—and even since you—since we—when you've been away there have been—"

"And do you think I've been reading church tracts and saying prayers while I've been away from you?" Dale interrupted again. "Let's speak no more of that."

"But a Cavalier, a soldier, may do things and laugh at them and a woman may find only shame in doing the same things," she protested insistently.

He hesitated and then went to his knees, after all. He had an admiration for the honesty that would make her strip her shame for him to see, but if she were to be his wife she must be reassured, she must come into this arrangement with her head high and her eyes clear. He wanted no wife who'd be burdened by a shamed humility; he wanted the Jenny Loman he had always known, to be Dame Morley, the laughing, nimble-witted, audacious girl who would attract all men's eyes and reserve her own eyes for him alone. And so he had to work with words more cleverly convincing than he ever had been called upon to use before.

He rested his folded arms on her knees and looked up into her eyes.

"Have you felt shame, Jenny?" he asked quietly.

"S-sometimes," she stammered. Where was Jamestown's self-sufficient belle now? "But never with you, dear Dale."

"And I've felt shame, too," he said, "and never with you. So if we were together always as man and wife we'd rid ourselves of both our shame. I need you, Jenny, and I believe you need me, so that our lives can be complete."

"Ah, Dale!" she cried, and gathered his head in her arms to strain him to her. "God grant you'll not regret this!"

"And I," said Dale, his voice muffled by the pjessure of his mouth to the girl's bosom, "make the same prayer for you."

His friends in Jamestown, Tindall, Peregrine and the others, took his announcement that he was to marry Genevieve Loman with no expression other than delighted surprise. Dale tried to keep himself from thinking of them as possible—probable—former lovers of Jenny but when the thought crept into his mind, he found himself surprisingly lacking in jealousy. After all, he told himself, he was not being hoodwinked into this thing. He knew what he knew because Jenny had told him, if he had needed the telling, and it did not matter much. Jealousy belonged to a man in love and this marriage was a marriage of convenience, no matter what Genevieve might think.

Captain Claiborne did not come to Jamestown for the wedding. Events at Kent Island, he wrote Dale, seemed directed toward an early crisis. Dale was needed at the Island but he was not to hurry the wedding plans, for all that. If Genevieve wanted the banns published and the formalities observed, it was Dale's duty to stay by her till all the rigmarole so dear to womenfolk was finished.

So Dale fretted in Jamestown for three weeks instead of the few days he had planned to spend there. He sweated through a dozen receptions where he met Genevieve's relatives, who flocked into the town by the hundreds, it seemed.

The wedding day came, finally, and Genevieve Loman and Dale Morley were united in the holy bonds of matrimony at Saint Luke's Brick Church in the Isle of Wight Hundred. That church, Dale recalled, was the one Captain Claiborne had chosen for Dale's marriage to Susan Willison and had been beaten down by little Thomas Willison in the only argument Willison ever won from the Captain. He was glad now that he was not to marry Genevieve in the church behind which Susan's grave lay.

It was, by general agreement, the most fashionable wedding yet held in the Province. The ladies who attended might have smiled at each other with arched eyebrows and even whispered behind their fans at Genevieve's virginal expression as, dressed in white, she knelt to receive the sacrament with Dale; but there were few women in the church who did not envy the bride, even while they were grimacing. And later, at the supper party Tindall gave for the couple they clustered around Jenny with a babble of chirruping which if she had believed a word of it, would have made Genevieve's head swim with pride.

The *Bittern* had returned to Kent Island during the weeks of wedding preparations, but she was back at Jamestown that night, outfitted as no trading pinnace ever had been intended to be. Pennants of colored cloth fluttered from her halyards and her decks shone with the results of long, curse-studded days of sanding. The bridal cabin had been equipped with furnishings that must have made Smith snort. Sheets of the finest linen were on the bunk, a table had been built into one bulkhead and was laden with such trifles as combs, a hand glass, a perfume vial, a wine decanter and goblets, all heavy with silver. Aboard the *Bittern,* too, were Yago and a young slave girl named Rellie who curtseyed deeply to Genevieve as she came aboard and announced herself as Captain Claiborne's gift to the bride.

Genevieve turned to the red-faced Dale, her eyes dancing like a young maiden's.

"Truly, Dale," she cried, "no queen ever had so fine a wedding barge!"

And later, much later, as the *Bittern* turned the point and headed up the Chesapeake, no queen, no tender, frightened maid, was ever treated more gently than Dale Morley treated Genevieve. The fire, the raw passion, would come back later on—there would be plenty of time for that—but now, Dale knew, was the time for soft kisses and quiet caresses. He might not love her, but he owed her this: the tenderness a man would show his bride if the two of them had never been the man and woman in the garden behind Genevieve's house, four years before.

LETTER FROM CECILIUS, SECOND LORD BALTIMORE, TO HIS BROTHER, LEONARD CALVERT, GOVERNOR OF MARYLAND:

"... and the time for action has thus arrived, my dear brother. You inform me that the scoundrel, Claiborne, and his hirelings are disturbing our rightful commerce with the Indians and challenging our authority as vested in us by His Majesty's patent.

"I direct you, then, to straightway warn this Captain Claiborne that unless he acknowledges Maryland's sovereignty over the Island of Kent and subjects himself and his people to the orders and directions of the authority of Maryland, he will be seized and jailed at Saint Mary's and his plantations and all his effects will be taken in possession by you and your forces.

"I pray for you, dear brother, each day and hope your health is. . ."

* * * *

LETTER FROM HIS MAJESTY, CHARLES THE FIRST, KING OF GREAT BRITAIN AND IRELAND, TO GOVERNOR SIR JOHN HARVEY AND THE COUNCIL OF THE PROVINCE OF VIRGINIA:

". . . We, therefore, on this day have ordered the Governor of the Colony of Mary's Land to cease and put an end to all acts of assault and hurt against Our loyal subjects in Virginia who are inhabiting the Island of Kent in the Bay called the Chesapeake.

"And We have called the Lord Cecilius Calvert, Baron Baltimore, to Our presence and have told him that his colonists of Mary's Land will be held disloyal and disobedient to Our commands if they do any violence to Our subjects on the Island of Kent or do disturb or hinder them in their trade. A copy of this letter goes to Mary's Land for the instruction of the colonists there."

On October 22nd, 1634, the Kent Island pinnace *Long Tail*, bound down the Patuxent River for home after a successful trading voyage that had carried her deep into Calvert's territory, rounded a point and found herself staring into the guns of the Maryland schooner, *Saint Helen and Saint Margaret*.

Thomas Smith was master of the *Long Tail* and he admitted later that he had acted like a featherbrained cabin boy from the start of the whole affair. In the first place, Smith had allowed himself to be lulled into a false sense of security. He had been furnished with a copy of the King's letter to the Virginia Council, as had all William Claiborne's top men, and he had taken it for granted that the Marylanders would not dare to dispute the King's order. Smith had taken it upon himself to consider the feud between Kent Island and Saint Mary's over, finished by the directive from Charles, with the Island the winner.

Acting on this assurance, Smith had left his stern and bow guns unloaded and untended. Even with the lookout's warning of a sail, the *Long Tail's* captain had not called his men to quarters. Hence, he found himself helpless under the schooner's guns, without a chance to fight or run, if he would.

Still, even when the *Long Tail* hove to under the orders from the Maryland schooner, Captain Smith was not too much disturbed. As the pinnace dropped her sails and her anchor went over the side, the Kent Islander went below to his strongbox to get his copy of the King's proclamation, his guarantee of safety. When the Maryland boarding party clambered over the rail of the pinnace, Smith was ready for them—or so he thought.

He was barely civil to the Maryland commander because he hated Papists as much as any Virginian, and the man from Saint Mary's was less civil than Smith.

"This vessel," said the Marylander, "is seized by the authority of Sir Leonard Calvert, Governor of Maryland, on the complaint of conducting illegal trade in the waters of the Colony."

"Now just one moment," Smith said coldly. "Read this proclamation of His Majesty, King Charles, before you make any rash move."

He proffered the parchment on which Dale had copied the King's order. The man from Saint Mary's, a pock-marked individual with a scraggly beard, took the paper and scanned it. Then, with a contemptuous grunt, he balled the parchment into a wad and flung it over the side, into the Patuxent.

Smith, with a howl of rage, sprang at the Maryland commander, his hands reaching for the other man's throat. Smith was a squat,

264

powerful man and it required four of the Maryland boarders to hold him off from their chief.

"God damn ye!" the Kent Islander screeched. "They'll put you to the torture in London when they hear what ye've done to a King's order!"

"And you'll swing from a gibbet for piracy," the other man jerked out, "as I know the laws! That paper was a crude forgery and you know it, and the King will have your ears for flaunting false papers carrying his name. Put this man in irons! If anybody aboard this stinking craft makes one wrong move, shoot him down or run him through!"

Smith was borne struggling below decks and shackled with the irons the boarding party had brought with them. The other members of the *Long Tail's* crew had no chance to resist. The boarders took over command of the pinnace and the *Long Tail* followed the *Saint Helen and Saint Margaret* to Saint Mary's where all the Kent Islanders were thrown into Calvert's new jail.

Thomas Smith kept up his roaring imprecations for two days and two nights before he was taken before Leonard Calvert. The brother of Baltimore wore a grave expression as he sat in his great carved oak chair and his hand constantly pulled at his bristly mustaches. He knew that this seizure was bound to bring open warfare between Kent Island and Saint Mary's; he knew it would not be long before guns would bellow and steel ring against steel, and it may have been that he regretted this opening clash, coming at a time when his preparations were not yet quite complete.

It never was exactly determined whether or not Leonard Calvert had ever seen a copy of the King's letter, although Charles had told the Virginia Council that he was sending a copy to Saint Mary's. Charles was already well embarked on that course of double-dealing that led ultimately to his ruin and death, in the end. Already he was trying to keep friends with all factions, promising each side everything, and it might have been that he never advised Maryland or Lord Baltimore that they must not molest the Kent Islanders. A

265

second possibility is that the copy of the proclamation was dispatched to Calvert but had not reached Saint Mary's at the time the *Long Tail* was seized. Or it might have been that Calvert received the letter and had been advised by his brother in London that the King's position at home was so confused, so muddled, that the order could be safely ignored.

"Hold your tongue!" Calvert said sharply as Smith launched into another tirade when he was brought before the Governor. "You're not dealing with a Kent Island savage now! You face serious charges, sir, and you'd best show whatever manners you own."

"But—but the King's letter!" Smith spluttered. "You cannot do this thing to me, when I was carrying a King's letter!"

"I know of no letter," Calvert said abruptly. "What would the master of a floating flea warren be doing with a King's letter?"

Thomas Smith inhaled a deep breath, struggling for control of himself against the insult. Floating flea warren, eh, when the least of William Claiborne's vessels was more trim, more shipshape, than the best of Leonard Calvert's ill-manned craft!

"Sir," he said in a voice he forced to stay level, "that letter was sent to the Governor of Virginia and was forwarded to Captain Claiborne at Kent Island. The Captain had copies made for every commander of Kent Island vessels. And that—that damned pirate who boarded my ship had the impudence to destroy the King's letter!"

Leonard Calvert leaned forward in his chair, his face dark.

"Now listen to what I say, man," he told Smith. "I know of no letter from the King and I don't believe there ever was any such letter. I do know your vessel was found in waters belonging to the Colony of Maryland, her hold filled with furs stolen from us, maybe taken from one of our storage places, and—"

"Why, you—"

"Quiet! And because the furs are ours, by right of patent if not by right of recovery, we are seizing the cargo. And as a penalty for poaching in our waters, we are seizing the pinnace, too. But I am

266

a merciful man. You and your crew will be allowed to go free. You can return to your Kent Island and tell your precious Captain Claiborne that another day we will deal less kindly with any of his men we find stealing our furs within our boundaries. As for you, if you run afoul of us in one more instance, I'll have you hanged!''

Smith, white-faced with rage and trembling, kept his eyes fixed on Calvert. He was not wanting in courage, this doughty little captain, but he had his crew to protect and he knew that Calvert, having gone this far, could go further if he were angered further. The main thing, Smith realized, was to get back to Kent Island and Claiborne to join the war that was coming, that had been started by this seizure.

"My thanks, merciful sir," he said, his voice rigid with irony. "And how am I and my men expected to return to Kent Island, may I be so bold as to ask?"

Calvert leaned back in his chair again and smiled blandly.

"Why, Captain," he said easily, "Claiborne was once heard to say he'd drive us from the Chesapeake if every Kent Islander had to wield a paddle in an Indian war canoe to sweep us from the Bay. To give you practice for that event, we'll give you a long canoe and you can take yourselves back to your devil's den in that."

And that was how Captain Thomas Smith and his men returned to Kent Island, straining awkwardly at the cumbersome paddles of an unwieldy, leaking Pascataway long canoe. It took them close to four days, fighting adverse winds, and when they stumbled ashore at the Island they were gaunt with hunger and thick-tongued with thirst.

The war was on.

William Claiborne lashed back at Leonard Calvert with the *Cockatrice,* ten days after Smith and his little band staggered ashore at Kent Island. He chose Talbot Bristoll to command the wherry, against Dale's protests and Nicholas Martiau's.

"Yes, it's Bristoll who'll take the *Cockatrice* out," Claiborne con-

tinued, "and here's your order, Talbot. You'll harry Calvert's shipping on the Bay, taking what prizes you can, but you'll not leave the
Chesapeake to run up a river and be trapped, no matter how juicy
the bird might seem, fluttering ahead of you."

He stabbed a finger at the chart in front of him.

"Here's where you'll take the wherry and lie to," he said. "Just
off the mouth of the Potomac. Calvert must send his vessels through
that channel and when they come out of the river, you'll nab 'em.
If you meet the schooner, the *Saint Helen and Saint Margaret*, you'll
run; the *Cockatrice* is still no match for that vessel. But you should
be able to handle the others without much trouble, so long as you
don't venture into their river where they can maneuver on their own
doorstep and you'll be in strange waters."

He turned to face the others.

"I don't care for this kind of war," he said. "It is the game that
Calvert would play, picking off one vessel at a time. If I could, I'd
sail my whole fleet up the Potomac and attack his fort, bombard his
town; but we are not ready for that. We first must nibble at the
edges of the cake before we take our gulp. Get me a prize, Talbot, or
sink one of his vessels and we'll be avenged in part for the loss of
the *Long Tail*."

"I'll get you prizes, sir," Bristoll said expansively, "and sink the
Papist ships till there's not a dory left to them. My luck is always
good when there's fighting to be done."

But Talbot Bristoll's luck did not serve him well on that voyage.
He was under Claiborne's orders to seek out Calvert's craft on the
open Bay, but after two days' patrol without sighting a Maryland
sail he took it upon himself to push up the Potomac toward Saint
Mary's. He was in the river only a little over two hours before the
Saint Helen and Saint Margaret slid out of a cove where she had
been waiting and crossed the river between the *Cockatrice* and the
Bay.

The Kent Island wherry might still have run for it and probably
gained open water before the *Saint Helen and Saint Margaret* could
268

have brought more than her bow guns into play. But Talbot Bristoll elected to stand to and fight. He ordered the wherry swung broadside to the gaunt-nosed schooner and his larboard guns, two three-and-a-half-inch sakers, boomed. The shot was short and sent twin geysers aloft a dozen yards from the swift-swinging schooner.

The *Saint Helen and Saint Margaret* replied with one shot of her bow guns as she turned, shot intended only for range. The first ball cleared the *Cockatrice* and thumped into the water beyond the wherry. The next round fired by the schooner's bow minion smashed into the sea a half-length ahead of the *Cockatrice's* prow and squarely in line.

Bristoll bawled an order that brought the hermaphrodite-rigged wherry about in a sharp tack but his move was too late. The schooner turned inside Bristoll's course and the Marylanders' broadside belched forth before Bristoll could bring his guns to bear.

The wherry's mizzen sagged as splinters flew and the *Cockatrice* heeled sharply under the impact of half a dozen hits. The wherry answered with her stern gun and was far wide of the schooner. The *Saint Helen and Saint Margaret* closed boldly and another sheet of flame swept out, from forepeak to taffrail. A hail of iron and lead crashed across the wherry's deck. There were screams from wounded men, blood-choked gurgles from the slain.

Bristoll himself manned the one gun with which the *Cockatrice* answered the murderous fire from the schooner. He managed to send one ball smashing through the other ship's side, just above the water line, before the *Saint Helen and Saint Margaret* fired her third salvo and the battle was over.

Somebody (Talbot Bristoll always swore it was not he and it was unlikely that it was) struck the wherry's colors and the schooner came up to grapple and board. The Marylanders found eight Kent Islanders dead, five wounded seriously, and two others with only minor hurts. They also found Bristoll's elegant breastplate and helmet on the deck where he had shed them just before plunging over the side, but they did not find Bristoll. He always had been an excellent swimmer and now he found his talent for swimming underwater standing him in good stead. Hampered though he was by his clothes and boots, he managed to make the shore undetected. There he hid by day and traveled by night until he reached a Pascataway village some twenty miles north of Saint Mary's. Once again, a Kent Island ship's commander returned to the Island in an Indian canoe.

For days, weeks, Claiborne kept a full guard on the ramparts of his Kent Island fort but, surprisingly, Leonard Calvert did not follow up the advantage he had earned with his capture of the shattered *Cockatrice*. With the loss of the wherry, Claiborne was left without a single vessel that could offer anything like an equal battle to the *Saint Helen and Saint Margaret,* and he was forced to pull in the remnants of his depleted fleet to the protection of the fort. A log boom was stretched across the entrance to the harbor, a rude stockade was thrown up along the shore below the fort and torches blazed all night, every night, against the possibility of a surprise attack. And still Leonard Calvert made no move.

Claiborne of course lodged a bitter protest with the King, through the Virginia Assembly and the Ministers of Plantation, but nothing came of it. Charles was too busy with his own embroilments to take any direct action in a tiny war going on halfway across the world. William Cloberry, too, seemed strangely loath to pursue Claiborne's protests in Charles's confused court. He wrote the Captain, complaining peevishly about the loss of two vessels in "rash and senseless action against the Catholics" and while he promised to send Claiborne another large vessel, the tone of his message was stiff, without a hint of sympathy.

To Dale, the one bright feature of the sad situation was that Talbot Bristoll was in disgrace. He had disobeyed Claiborne's orders by entering the Potomac when he had been told to stay in the Bay. Furthermore, he had deserted the wherry—after the battle was lost, but with wounded men of his command to be cared for and joined in whatever fate befell them.

Dale was not present at the brief and bitter session in which Tal-
270

bot Bristoll faced his Captain. Even Martiau was excluded from that scene by Claiborne's order and both Morley and Martiau were at the fort when Bristoll rejoined them, his face white and pinched, his mouth drawn down at the corners in ugly lines. He held himself unnaturally straight as he walked up to Dale and his voice was as harsh as a grackle's when he spoke.

"Mister Morley," he said, "Captain Claiborne has ordered me to place myself under your command."

"*My* command!" Dale ejaculated.

"Yes," said Bristoll stonily. "The Captain gave me the choice of serving under you or returning to Jamestown and I think I can still prove my worth with my sword, here at Kent Island."

A year before, Morley would have taken full advantage of this strange state of affairs. He would have picked the most menial, humiliating tasks he could find for Bristoll and take pleasure in every minute of the other man's debasement. Now he wondered at himself for failing to heap ignominy on Bristoll's head, giving the man he had always hated no sterner tasks than he assigned himself.

"I'm getting soft," he told Genevieve at the table, one evening. "That damned Bristoll would have me shoveling manure, if our positions were reversed, and yet I can't bring myself to treat the man as he deserves."

She smiled at him and he was struck again by his wife's beauty, a beauty that had grown more natural, less dazzling, day by day since she had come to Kent Island.

"I wouldn't want you different," she said. "True, Talbot would be a beast to you if ever you came under his command but that's because he is Talbot Bristoll and you're Dale Morley and it's one of the reasons I love you so, my husband."

My husband, she used that phrase a hundred times a day, as though she savored the words like some rich sweetmeat. Those were the words she used in the transports of their love-making now, where once she had gasped wild exclamations that would have shocked any man not caught up in the same delirium. They were the

271

words she used in quiet conversation, the phrase she used whenever she referred to Dale in speaking with someone else.

"My husband says . . . my husband thinks . . . my husband saw . . ."

She had fitted herself into the life at Kent Island with an ease that had astonished Dale. Captain Claiborne's predictions notwithstanding, he had been half-afraid that she would chafe at the absence of the social life she had made her career in Jamestown. But if she ever missed that gaudy whirl, she never showed a sign of wanting to return to it. The women of Kent Island were not from the fashionable levels where Genevieve Loman had moved but they liked her at once and she, them. They could know nothing about Dame Morley that would make them whisper behind their hands, and Dale's wife, in her new role and her new setting, made sure they would have no reason for the slightest murmur. Except when she was alone with Dale in their chamber, she was a modest, gracious, smiling, soft-spoken lady. At night, with the light of a single candle casting tantalizing shadows on her perfection, she was a sybaritic temptress, an inventive voluptuary, sometimes a demoniac bacchante, sometimes a sighing, shuddering maid. She made each embrace a new adventure for Dale Morley and always the words were on her lips: "My husband!"

Dale always wondered which of those nights was the one on which his wife conceived his son. For on Christmas Eve, 1634, Genevieve Morley informed her husband that what she had prayed for had come true. The moon had waxed and waned twice since she had first suspected that she was pregnant and now there could be no doubt.

The winter passed, a hard, cold winter that choked the Chesapeake with ice floes and made all water travel almost impossible. Had that been an open winter, Leonard Calvert might have sent his fleet against Kent Island; perhaps he intended to strike at Claiborne late in the fall on the arrival from England of a bark, the *Corpus*

Christi, but if he entertained that plan the unusually early freeze that stretched ice across the Potomac from far inland to the river's mouth ruined the idea. Claiborne's spies brought him word that the big bark was frozen in solidly at its moorings off Saint Mary's before her guns could be mounted and, with the *Saint Helen and Saint Margaret*, was out of action until the spring thaw.

Claiborne found himself in no better position. The sloop Cloberry had promised finally arrived; but ice made it impossible to bring her into the Kent Island harbor, although the Captain had gangs of slaves, servants and soldiers chopping at the floes for days before he gave up his attempt to cut through a channel. The sloop, named the *James and Anne*, was locked in three feet of ice before Christmas and was as helpless as Calvert's vessels. Moreover, Claiborne faced the danger of having his one large ship damaged when the ice broke up, whereas Calvert's two converted warships were safeguarded from ice packs by the shelter of Saint Mary's harbor.

With trade at a standstill, Claiborne kept his men busy outfitting the sloop with arms, building new fortifications, strengthening the old emplacements and endlessly drilling despite the bitter cold.

The winter broke, eventually, in a wild, warm wind from the southwest accompanied by slanting sheets of rain. The ice boomed and cracked and broke into mile-square floes; then heaved and buckled into jagged-edged chunks that piled themselves into shelves ten and twenty feet high under the prodding of the gale.

There was little sleep for the men of Kent Island that week. Day and night, gangs of hollow-eyed Islanders, slave working beside captain, labored at keeping the ice from grinding the hull of the *James and Anne* to splinters. Lashed on by a tireless Claiborne, they scrambled over precariously shifting ice to thrust rams at the bergs to shove them from a course that would threaten the sloop.

Dale commanded a gang ordered to try again to clear a channel into the harbor. He found this task hopeless at the start, impossible after the first day, insurmountable the second day, improbable on

273

the third and done on the fourth. Most of the time he worked knee-deep in icy water and during the few minutes he could get home, Genevieve massaged life back into his legs while he lay in a coma of exhaustion.

Nearly a hundred men, straining on tow lines, pulled the *James and Anne* into the harbor of Kent Island on the fifth day after the start of the equinoctial storm. By that time, the tempest had followed the clock around to the northeast and while the gale was stronger, the ice was bumbling and churning its way out into the Bay, away from Kent Island.

Dale staggered back to his house, walking like an ancient, dull-eyed, his face beard-blackened, his joints creaking. He managed to reach the chamber he shared with Genevieve before he collapsed and hit the bed like a felled pine, to lie there in sodden clothes until his wife and Rellie stripped him, toweled him, tugged and shoved at his big frame until he was under the covers, and blankets piled on him to ward off the ague.

He slept for twelve hours and then insisted on getting up and dressing, to report to Captain Claiborne. He found the Captain in his office, as alert as though he had not done as much work at freeing the *James and Anne* as Dale and Bristoll together. If he noticed Dale's drawn face and slumping shoulders, he gave no sign.

"Sit down," he ordered, "and hear my new plan. Calvert is getting all the ice that we had here, with this northeast wind. I intend to sail as soon as the storm lifts and attack him before he gets his ships out of his harbor. We'll stand just off the ice and use all our guns to blow him out of the water."

He was the old William Claiborne now, with his hands moving this way and that, his eyebrows lifting and lowering, his nose fairly twitching with his impatience to be off and against the Marylanders at Saint Mary's.

"Martiau and I will take the *James and Anne*," he continued, "and you'll have the *Hunter*. I'll give Bristoll the *Bittern*—he's done his penance by now for his foolhardiness last fall—and Smith will
274

take the *Gamecock*. With four vessels and with Calvert hampered by the ice, we'll make a pudding for the dogfish, Dale."

Dale sat slackly in his chair, his mind trying to pierce the veil of exhaustion. Any other man but William Claiborne, he thought sluggishly, would be sitting back, content with the fact that he had saved the *James and Anne;* but not Captain Claiborne. Now, with half his garrison out of action because of sheer exhaustion, he was planning his next move against Leonard Calvert.

"The scheme might work," Dale admitted finally, "but we'd better wait a few days to let our men recover."

"And lose our advantage?" Claiborne asked. "No, Dale, we must set sail tonight or dawn tomorrow, at the latest. Then we'll be able to destroy him before he knows we're not icebound as he is."

"The men," Dale objected, "can't pull on a line or lift a gun. Martiau complains of pains in his joints so bad they make him howl like a wolf, at times. I'm not myself, by far, and neither can Bristoll be. You'll be sending a bone-weary fleet against the Catholics, Captain."

"We'll sail!" Claiborne snapped. "And the men will do what has to be done. We sail at dawn."

The Kent Island fleet did sail at dawn the next day, when the howling northeaster decided to move on, to leave the region to a mild southeast wind etched by misty rain. This meant that the ice-pack would not pile down toward the Potomac in a thunderous body but, at the same time, the swift-running tides brought on by the storm would dissipate the floes, aided by the pelting, melting rain.

Nicholas Martiau was not able to leave his bed to join the expedition, although he cursed and swore and struggled with the servants who kept him in bed with his crippling rheumatism. With Martiau stricken, Claiborne took over the command of the *James and Anne* with Holmes as mate. The sloop led the flotilla out of Kent Island harbor and headed down the Chesapeake just as a lightening of the heavy skies showed that the sun was somewhere on the horizon, trying to pierce the murk.

Dale stood beside the helmsman of the *Hunter,* the third ship in the line that filed out of the harbor. Ahead of him was Smith, on the *Gamecock* and behind him was Bristoll, on the *Bittern.* The fog showed Dale only brief glimpses of the *Gamecock's* stern and, looking aft, he could make out the bowsprit and foresail of the *Bittern* only at patchy intervals.

"This is bad," Dale told himself. "If the *James and Anne* hits the ice under full sail, how can we come about in time? Most likely, we'll all ram each other and be sunk before this game's begun."

Twice within an hour out of Kent Island, the helmsman of the *Hunter* had to spin his wheel madly and come off his tack to escape ramming the *Gamecock,* ahead. The third time there was a near collision. Dale spat out his words, knowing that what he had to do might be considered a breach of orders by Captain Claiborne.

"Take her off two points by the starboard," he said. "If I have to swim, I want it to be because of Calvert's guns and not because we put our nose up another vessel's tail."

Off on a wide tack, the *Hunter* swept through the twisting, writhing fog at a speed five knots more than Dale would have preferred. He looked back over the stern, watching the gray-white foaming wake dotted by chunks of ice, and tried to judge his pace. Ahead of him, somewhere, lay the main ice shelf armed with a thousand serrated underwater spears, and there was no way of telling whether the menace lay twenty leagues or twenty feet in front of the *Hunter's* bow.

"Come about," Dale ordered curtly, "and sound the lead. We'll anchor here till the fog lifts if we can reach bottom."

The lead showed five fathoms and sand. The *Hunter's* sails came down and her anchor went over the side. A lantern went to the top of the foremast to warn off any other ships of Claiborne's fleet that might have struck off on that tack, and the *Hunter's* crew and her master settled down to a period of agonized waiting for the fog to lift.

You should have followed the Gamecock *and the* James and Anne! *They'll go into action and you'll not be with them and you'll be called a coward who took his vessel out of line rather than risk Calvert's guns. Talbot Bristoll will laugh at you and boast that while he may have been beaten, he met the enemy, at least, and made them taste his shot.*

But, Christ's thorns, when a man has others under his command he can't risk his vessel and their lives, can he, following a reckless order to stay in line? In this fog, he'd be more likely to ram the ship ahead than get through safely. And Claiborne himself has said a commander's duty is to his ship, first, and his men, next, above everything else. Besides—

"Fog clearing, sir," Jack Bagshaw said softly. "And there's the ice."

There was the ice, in a shelved and sullen mass, rising in places above the *Hunter's* mainmast, streaming rivulets of tears that were half rain and half melt, lurching clumsily under the goad of the southeast wind. The *Hunter* had come to anchor less than ten ship's lengths from destruction, and the icepack was slowly, grudgingly, moving up the Bay, whence it had come, and bearing down on his vessel.

There was the ice; but off to port, six or seven ship's lengths distant, there was no ice. There, in what must have been the very middle of the Chesapeake, the ice barrier was split by a gut, a channel, a chasm, that was as neatly carved as though man had used ax and chisel to cut it. That space marked the course of the tides; it had stayed clear throughout that bitter winter and the moon had directed the surgings of the water through that gut to keep it free, though on each side the ice mounted in a dully glittering wall.

"Up anchor!" Dale bawled. "Mains'l and fores'l! Prepare to come about!"

The cutter swung in a neat half-circle as his men heaved on the lines to bring the stained canvas up to her spars. The *Hunter* put her leeward rail under water before she made that turn and headed for the opening in the ice. Dale had two choices. He could risk the journey through the narrow opening, hoping for clear water beyond the ice barrier, or he could run before the grumbling ice to safety. Had Claiborne found the opening and led the *Bittern* and the *Gamecock* through to Saint Mary's? Or had Claiborne's fleet met the icepack and, finding no opening, turned back?

"Put her through," Dale said briefly.

"But if she loses the wind when she gets in there," Bagshaw gritted, "we'll be on the ice and—"

"Put her through!" Dale said, and by his tone it could have been William Claiborne who gave the order.

The *Hunter* went through the icepack, though she scraped her keel four times in the passage. Once past the shelf, Dale found himself in a sea of floating ice cakes tossed by the freshening wind and he and Bagshaw worked with the others to pole off the larger lumps that might endanger the cutter's hull. It was close to mid-afternoon when the *Hunter* came off the mouth of the Potomac River, and no other Kent Isand sail had been sighted.

The ice, in the southern reaches of the Chesapeake, was not too bad. The steady warm rain thrown by the southeast wind had begun eating into the floes to the northward so that now the pieces of ice that floated against the tide were small and rotted by the downpour.

Again the *Hunter* dropped her anchor while Dale debated his next step. For all he knew, the *James and Anne* and the other vessels had passed up the river. Even now, they might be using their guns on Calvert's fleet. On the other hand, it was equally possible that Claiborne had turned back at the ice jam, or he might be cruising north of the shelf, waiting for the wind to shift again to bear the great mass of hull-shredding stuff southward toward the ocean so that the Kent Island ships could follow.

It was a situation to conjure with, and Dale worked his brain

278

until it ached in trying to reach a decision on what to do. He was still far from a conclusion when his action was forced upon him by the cry of his lookout:

"Sail ho! To the westward, and she flies the Calvert black and gold!"

It was the Maryland bark, *Corpus Christi,* and she seemed tremendous as she bore down on the *Hunter* through the ice-caked waters. All Claiborne's dreams of catching the big ship icebound, then, had been wrong; the *Corpus Christi* was ready for action— she was going into action! Through his spyglass, Dale could see the Marylanders running about the bark's decks, readying their guns, preparing for the coming fight.

He yelled his own orders and the *Hunter* got under way, to run before the bark like a frightened fox. Dale saw a puff of white smoke blossom at the bow of the *Corpus Christi,* and there was a splash some twenty yards astern. Seconds later, the flat report of a small gun reached the ears of the men aboard the cutter.

"Prepare to come about!" Dale shouted. "Bow and stern chasers fire when I tell you. Lay them on well, mates! This clumsy bark's our prize if your eyes are keen at getting the range today!"

The *Hunter,* at Dale's command, swung sharply under full sail, and when the decks had leveled again he gave the order to fire. The two culverins, fore and aft, barked as one, and Dale held his breath as he waited for the balls to reach the swinging *Corpus Christi.*

His luck was with him! The shots were good, both of them! The forward gun's missile crashed into the bark's mainmast close to the deck. The stick sagged and then leaned drunkenly, kept from falling by a tangle of ratlines. The two aft guns scored direct hits just at the waterline, fair amidships, and Dale knew that while the forward gun's results were more spectacular, those waterline hits were more damaging.·

"Waist guns!" he yelled. "Fire!"

The minions mounted in the *Hunter's* middle yapped, *pr-r-r-*

rang, pr-r-r-r-rang, and again the Kent Island guns were on the target. Both charges hit the wreckage of the Maryland vessel's mainmast and shredded the ratlines that had been keeping the stick from crashing. Now it went over the side and the *Corpus Christi* listed drunkenly, her deck canting at such an angle that her guns, when they hammered out their reply, lofted their charges high over the scurrying cutter.

"Fore and aft guns!" Dale screamed, and the culverins banged in unison, as though they had a single touchhole. His men worked swiftly at their tasks, without a single wasted motion. Now all the hours of gun drill Claiborne had insisted on were showing their worth.

The captain of the *Corpus Christi* tried to swing away from the bedeviling cutter, at least long enough to clear away the wreckage of the mainmast, but it was just then that the *Hunter's* greater maneuverability came into play. Dale's orders sent his ship into a tight turn and before the wobbling bark could more than start her own sweep, the *Hunter* was closing, all her guns blaring now.

The *Corpus Christi* managed to send one ragged salvo thudding toward the cutter, but the aim was high again and the only damage was a split mizzen sail and a few nipped lines of the topsail rigging. In return, the *Hunter* sent ball after ball smashing into the bark's hull, dancing in and away from the lumbering *Corpus Christi* like a mastiff feinting a bear off balance.

"Muskets and cutlasses!" Dale cried. "We board her!"

There were only thirty-two men aboard the *Hunter,* as against close to a hundred on the Maryland bark; but it was plain for Dale and the other Kent Islanders to see that the crew of the *Corpus Christi* had suffered heavily in that one-sided exchange, and that those who had escaped wounds or worse were close to complete demoralization. Calvert's men had swooped down on the smaller cutter aboard the biggest, strongest warship in that part of the world; they had expected a quick victory and an easy one; now they slipped about on bloody decks, trying to hack away wreckage that
280

crippled their fine vessel, and always the iron and lead of the brash Kent Island vessel stormed about them.

They were in neither the condition nor the mood to make more than a half-hearted gesture toward repelling the boarders who swarmed up over the side, their muskets banging, their cutlasses slashing and cutting. Dale was the first man aboard the bark, with Bagshaw at his shoulder.

"Surrender!" Dale howled. "Surrender or die!"

"No surrender!" snarled a voice. "Better to be killed than tortured by Claiborne's pirate bastards! Fight on!"

It was the bark's master, standing at the head of the ladder that ran from the well to the foredeck, his blade sweeping backward and forward against the thrusts of the two Kent Islanders who were trying to get at him.

"Hold steady, sir," Bagshaw said. The red-haired man raised a musket he had picked up somewhere. He sighted carefully and there was a jarring explosion in Dale's ear. The Maryland captain pitched forward, full on the Kent Island swords that had been thrusting at his guard.

The death of the *Corpus Christi's* master marked the end of the fight. The bark's crew was left leaderless then and they had had no stomach for the battle since the *Hunter's* first roundshot had pounded them. Within a few minutes from the time the Maryland captain had toppled down the ladder, all the men aboard the brig threw down their arms and were herded aft, under the prodding of the muskets and swords of the Kent Island men.

Dale, his heart ballooned by elation, took an accounting of his losses. Three of his crew had been killed in the boarding action and a fourth lay on the deck, gasping what had to be acknowledged as his last breaths when one looked at the deep neck wound he had suffered. Dale estimated that at least fifteen of Leonard Calvert's men had been killed; the wounded numbered well over a score. The bark, though taking water, could be patched enough to be sailed back to Kent Island as a prize.

He had to get out of there with the *Corpus Christi* as soon as he could. The noise of the fight must certainly have reached the ears of the people at Saint Mary's, and he had no wish to meet the *Saint Helen and Saint Margaret* now.

"Put all seaworthy longboats over the side," he told Bagshaw. "We'll get these people ashore and turn back to Kent Island."

Only one longboat was found to be undamaged and it required several trips to ferry the survivors and the dead Marylanders to the beach. It was while he was supervising the loading of the boat for its third trip that Dale put out a hand to grasp the shoulder of a slight, shabby Marylander who was just about to go down the ladder.

"By God," Morley said quietly. "It's Doctor Wing."

Andrew Wing looked up at him, his eyes direct, his mouth firm. He was a different man from the one Dale had roused that snowy night at Fort Comfort. The rum bloat was gone from his face, his eyes were clear instead of red and gummy, there was no terror now on his full lips, no palsied twitching in his hands.

"Doctor Wing," Dale repeated in the same gentle voice. "Once surgeon to His Majesty's forces at Fort Comfort and now a sailor in this band of pirates."

"I'm no sailor," Wing said unflinchingly. "I'm a physician, or at least I try to be. I was aboard this bark as a passenger, going to Jamestown to buy the medicines I need. We've had the winter fever at Saint Mary's and I've long since used up the powders and philters that I had, the port being icebound and no fresh supplies being able to get through."

The winter fevers? Did that mean that Anne Furness might be stricken? She was such a slight thing and he'd wager that Calvert did not pay her father, as a clerk, enough to provide her with a warm cloak.

"Mistress Furness," he asked awkwardly. "She's well?"

Wing's face broadened into a beaming smile.

"Dame Wing is in the best of health," he said. "and as happy as a doctor's wife can be."

282

"*Dame Wing!* You mean she's married to you?"

Wing nodded delightedly.

"Yes, Mister Morley," he said, "though I'm still not reconciled to my good fortune."

"Married—to—you!"

"Indeed," Andrew Wing chirruped. He seemed anxious to talk. "You know I was a hopeless wreck at Fort Comfort, Mister Morley, unable to grasp a scalpel without the help of a steadier hand. My wife—Mistress Furness, then—took pity on the poor wretch that I was, supported me while I attended her sister's child, and saw me back to my foul hut after the ordeal, when I was taken with the trembles. She sat the night with me, cleaned up the place, she bathed and shaved me, sir, and doled out my rum with an increasingly sparse hand."

"This does not interest me," Dale made himself say coldly.

Wing's voice continued; he was wound up in his tale.

"And finally, at length, she weaned me from the stuff, Mister Morley," he said. "Oh, I had the horrors then, but she was always beside me, helping me fend off the dragons and witches that assaulted me. So, when she said she had to leave with the others, I asked if I could sail with them. I tendered my resignation—"

"I've heard of that."

"—and it was accepted, for God knows Fort Comfort was not losing much. And at Saint Mary's, Sir Leonard set me up in a complete apothecary, at Anne's suggestion, made through her father who's Sir Leonard's clerk. I dosed and even dared to do an amputation on a Negro who'd been hurt in the collapse of a scaffold, and always Anne was beside me, in thought if not in fact."

"You talk like an old woman," Dale said scornfully. "Now if you'll—"

"And then, one day, we were alone together, Mister Morley. I began to tell her how much I owed her for saving me and she turned her dear face to me and—"

"*Now, Jesus Christ!*"

The little doctor paused, breathless. He was a threadbare thing,

283

Dale told himself. His breeches were better suited to a scarecrow and his falling band was of common cotton. He was a fit mate, indeed, for the scrawny Maryland girl who was less beautiful in her entirety than Genevieve's little finger. She had found a fitting mate in this discredited doctor and this was an end to his thoughts of Anne Furness.

His swimming gaze fixed itself, finally, on the earnest eyes of Andrew Wing and he started to turn away.

"The boat's waiting," he said raspingly, "and you'd better get into it before I change my mind and hold you as a prisoner."

Wing nodded slowly and started toward the place at the rail where the rope ladder was hung. He stopped and turned back to Morley.

"I did not know," he said softly. "I did not know you loved her too, Mister Morley."

"Neither did she," Dale replied, then caught himself. "Get over the side before I shoot you down like the traitor to Virginia you are! Get over, I say!"

Wing threw a leg over the rail and then looked up again at Morley.

"I must beg one thing of you," he said. "Spare me a few blankets to cover the wounded men ashore. In this rain, most of them will chill and die unless they have them."

Dale glared at him, turned on his heel and stalked away. But with the next boatload that moved to the shore there was a pile of quilts and blankets, stored aboard on Dale's orders. And ashore, where the survivors had built a fire, Doctor Wing raised a hand in grateful salute to the Kent Island captain who watched through his spyglass. Dale grunted angrily, put down the glass and began yelling orders to his crew.

A work party from the *Hunter* used the heavy mats they found aboard the bark to plug the breaches in the hull of the *Corpus Christi*. The bark's mainmast was cut away and a jury rig raised. Not five minutes after the last of the Marylanders, the living and the dead, had been ferried ashore, the *Corpus Christi* swung awkwardly away from the *Hunter* and began heading down the river toward the Bay and Kent Island. The cutter followed, cruising in wide reaches, ready to offer fight to any Maryland vessels that might try to recapture the bark.

They found the opening in the ice shelf, wider now and with the walls slumping under the steady drumming of the rain, and they managed to maneuver the cumbersome, half-crippled bark through the channel; still no Maryland sails showed in their wake. Once past the ice barrier and with the Bay almost entirely free of floating cakes, they pointed toward Kent Island and raised the fort at dusk of the second night. Torches bloomed a welcome ashore, a cannon bellowed a salute and when Dale reached the landing, he found himself welcomed by a jubilant, shouting, jostling throng led by Claiborne and Martiau.

"No, Dale!" were Claiborne's first words. "We thought you were lost! When you dropped out of the line, I was sure you'd hit ice that had stove in your bottom. We would have put about and searched for you, but in that damned fog we couldn't. The ice stopped us and we had to come back to the Island, finally."

He raised a hand to clap his lieutenant's shoulder with a hearty blow.

"I should have you put in chains for ignoring my orders and falling out of line, I suppose," he said jovially, "but how can I punish a man who's just scored a great victory? You took the bark alone! Hawkins or Drake could not have done as much! Ah, this is a fine day for Kent Island!"

He laid an arm across Dale's shoulders as he led him up to the dock, all unaware of his lieutenant's cold stiffness.

"Tell us about it, Dale," he said. "Describe every minute of it. Did you lose many men? What's the bark's cargo? Where did you meet her and did she fire first, or you?"

Morley gave the Captain an account of the battle, his voice weary, his back giving him aching reminders that he had not been to bed in almost four days.

"—and so we boarded, Captain," he finished. "They gave us

285

some fight but they surrendered, after a few of them had died. The bark's master was killed, and I'd say about a dozen others. I put the wounded and the others ashore, thinking you'd not want to feed a crowd of prisoners."

"You did right, there," Claiborne nodded.

"And one of them," Morley went on, woodenly, mechanically, "was Andrew Wing, the surgeon at Fort Comfort who's joined Calvert's band."

"He hasn't killed himself with rum yet, then?" Claiborne asked.

Dale turned away, his legs as leaden as his heart.

"Not yet," he said. "He's married to Anne Furness, so he says."

"Anne Furness!" Talbot Bristoll said, out of a shadow. "You mean the little Catholic girl you coddled that first night Calvert came to Virginia?"

Morley flung himself around to snarl at Bristoll's dim silhouette.

"God damn you," he grated. "I did not coddle her because she couldn't bear the touch of my hand. She's pure, sir, which is something you can't understand."

"Now, Dale—" William Claiborne began.

"Oh, let him speak, Captain," Bristoll interrupted. "It's bound to come out sometime! He moons after this Catholic wench as though she were some saint."

Dale's hand grasped the hilt of his cutlass, wrenched the blade free.

"Yes," he shouted. "I love the girl and I can fight for her name! Draw, you whoreson!"

Bristoll's blade was a dancing flicker in the uncertain light of the landing stage. Dale pressed forward, hacking savagely with his heavy cutlass, trying to break Bristoll's lighter sword, and saw his enemy retreat, bobbing, weaving, making the least target of himself that he could provide.

Dale's wrist flamed as Bristoll's tierce speared through his flailing guard. Bristoll shifted his feet, feinted and tried a septime thrust at Morley's groin. Dale hacked clumsily, his wrist streaming
286

blood, and he saw Bristoll's sword point rise and level at his throat. He could not raise his guard in time; he was lost and—

Captain Claiborne threw his body between the two men, his hands upflung.

"Stop, you fools!" he cried. "I'll have you both thrown in irons unless you quit this nonsense!"

Dale slowly lowered his cutlass, still glaring at Bristoll's evil grin. He saw Talbot carefully replace his crimson-stained blade in its ring, shrugging idly, and then he turned away.

There was a silence, broken by the sound of footsteps crunching on the shell road, and Genevieve Morley came out of the shadows near the bend in the lane that led up from the landing. Her cloak was of some dark stuff but the skirt beneath it was white. The men turned to watch her approach, Bristoll sweeping his wet, limp-feathered hat from his head in a deep bow, Martiau saluting, Claiborne making a brief bow from the hips.

She ignored all of them as she walked, half-ran, up to Dale and threw herself into his arms, her face buried in his shoulder.

"Oh, my husband," she cried, "they told me they were afraid you'd been lost! I never knew a woman could keep on living without a heart at all, till then! Oh, my husband!"

She clutched him closer, her face crushed against the soaked front of his oiled rain cape. He stood there for a moment, feeling her faintly swollen body against his and then he put his hands on his wife's shoulders and pushed her far enough away so that he could bend and kiss her. And his wounded wrist flamed in a sudden spurt of pain as though to remind him that he had just taken up his sword to defend the name of the woman he loved instead of this girl, his wife.

Yes, she was his wife and she was carrying the fruit of his seed and she had been better to him than he deserved, treating him at home like a nobleman, living only for his comfort and happiness, and he had been bellowing like a mad bull, screaming for all Kent Island to hear that he loved another woman. And if he did not

287

love Jenny as he loved Anne Furness—Anne Wing—it was not because she was not worthy to be loved.

He was engulfed by a wave of shame and remorse and he lowered his mouth to kiss Genevieve a second time.

"You should not be out in all this rain," he said softly.

"Do you think I could stay home?" she asked. "Do you think I could sit by the fire when the word came that you were back and safe, after all, when I had feared you dead, drowned?"

He released her long enough to fling a side of his rain cape about his wife's shoulders and then he led her up the road toward their house, away from the crowd that had been silenced, first by Dale's wild confession of love for a Maryland maid and then by the brief swordplay.

His wrist ached but he knew the wound was little more than a scratch. He could tend that cut when he got home and blame it on the action aboard the *Corpus Christi* when Jenny asked him about it. She need not know the real story and—

But how much had she heard? Had Jenny been there in the shadows for some time, listening to her husband yell that he loved another woman? He tried half a dozen times to get the question out of his mouth, but the words would not come. They talked of the sea battle, of the capture of the *Corpus Christi*, of the spring that was coming and how good it would be to see blue water instead of gray ice on the Bay, but they kept away from all mention of Dale's reception at the landing.

They talked again of the name they'd give the boy—William, Tobias, George, Anthony, Nicholas—never Dale, because that was a name Aunt Bess might have heard in her wine dreams, nor Frederick, because neither of them had any love for the parsimonious slave-whipper who had sired Genevieve. And Jenny again brought up the names of Helen and Deborah and Jane and Catherine.

"Great God," Dale exclaimed, "you insist on thinking up girls' names when you know it will be a boy! But Deborah—if all my calculations are wrong and it *is* a girl, let's make it something simple, like Mary or Ruth or—"

"Or Anne," Genevieve said.

Dale's feet crunched four times on the road before he spoke. Ahead of him, on the rise where the house lay, the windows showed their blurred yellow blobs of light through the rain and fog. Over to his right, the fort's flambeaux sent up a brighter glow.

"So—you heard," he said in a low voice.

Her reply was couched in a brisk, sprightly tone he never had heard her use before.

"Heard what, my husband?" she asked. "We were only choosing names and I mentioned the name of Anne for the child, if it's a girl. What could I have heard?"

He looked down at her, marking the trace of tears on her cheeks, channeled through the rice powder she had donned for the occasion, to hide the signs of other tears, shed when she had thought him lost.

"Believe me, Jenny," he said. He groped for his words like a man reaching into a bucket of claw-snapping channel crabs, "what you heard was—was what a man will say when he's tired and angry and—and foolish, as I was. I—I—I—have a great respect for you, Jenny, and whatever you may think, from what you overheard, there's no one in this life who can match you in my regard."

She held her silence for the space of three steps and when she spoke her voice was hampered by the sobs that kept fighting their way up into her throat. Her head was bent and beneath the arm he had thrown over her shoulders, Dale could feel her trembling.

"I don't understand you, my husband," she said, at length. "I overheard nothing I placed any importance in, at all. What's important is that you're back, alive and safe."

Nor did Genevieve Morley mention the name of Anne again. In time, Dale was almost able to convince himself that his wife actually did not hear his exchange with Captain Claiborne that dripping night. Almost convince himself, that is, because beneath his half-conviction always lay the bitter realization that she must have overheard and that he had hurt her past any wound she could deserve.

The battle between Claiborne's *Hunter* and the big *Corpus Christi* had an immediate result that even William Claiborne could not have foreseen. Leonard Calvert lodged a damning protest against the Kent Islanders with Governor Harvey, demanding the return of the captured bark and the hangman's rope for the pirates who had killed his men and seized his ship.

Harvey was always ready to bend a knee to Calvert's outbursts and this occasion proved no exception. The Governor called a special session of the Virginia Assembly, read Leonard Calvert's complaint and called on the Assembly to throw Claiborne out of his office as Secretary of the Province and ship him to England in chains, to face charges of piracy.

Harvey's action backfired like an overloaded culverin. The *Hunter's* victory had aroused such enthusiasm in Virginia that the Assembly unceremoniously tossed Harvey out of office, replacing him with Captain Francis West. At Windsor Castle, King Charles was furious, but he was too deeply involved in his struggle with Parliament to assert his authority across the Atlantic.

As the wife of Dale Morley, Genevieve followed these turns of political fortune with avid interest, for they would affect the life of the child she was about to bear. Her labor was brief and easy; but while she was in travail Dale Morley paced the yard outside the house, white-faced and taut, remembering Susan, fearing that this girl who loved him so much would be visited by the same rending death. When he heard the first squalling cries of the baby, he put both hands to his face in shuddering relief and found his brow wet with sweat.

290

Genevieve lay smiling in the wide tester bed, an astonishingly slender figure beneath the covers after all those weeks of swollen pregnancy. The women who had attended her frowned at Dale as women will scowl at a husband after attending another woman in childbirth, but they stood aside and let him tiptoe to the side of the bed.

"You're—you're all right?" he asked, timidly.

"Certainly" she said, "and the child's well-formed. See, my husband, how happy a baby we have."

She nodded to the crook of her arm where the baby lay and Dale stared at this strange, miraculous thing that rested there, all black-haired and red-faced, its eyes closed tight, its mouth slack and wet, its nose a mere dollop of flesh, its tiny, perfect hands reaching and clutching at the ripened breast it lay beside.

Now here was something Dale could love completely! This thing was his, without a single dark memory attached to it. In all his life there had been nothing he could love so completely, nothing so entirely free of impediment to his devotion.

"It's—what is it?" Dale asked.

"A boy, certainly," Thomas Smith's sister said, "and a perfect giant of a boy, at that."

"A perfect wonder of a boy," Genevieve said.

Dale's thoughts went back to the first night he ever had seen Genevieve. Then she had been the sensually flaunting belle of Captain Claiborne's supper party; the same breast that would give food to this child now had been something to be peered at lasciviously then; the same lips that smiled with such contentment now had been exciting, wine-wetted arcs then; the same body that lay there so quietly, tired after its brief agony, had been a thing that every man had stripped and clutched in his mind's eye when Genevieve Loman had been the Cavalier's companion.

They named the child William Nicholas Morley and both Claiborne and Martiau were struck with pride over the boy's size and lustiness. Claiborne was voluble in his admiration of the boy, and

291

in those first weeks he seldom let a day pass without visiting Genevieve with some gift for the baby or the mother. Martiau was less articulate and less demonstrative, but he was constantly slipping away from his duties at the fort to visit the brick house that Claiborne had built for Genevieve and Dale.

With Calvert owning a new respect for Claiborne's guns; with Harvey gone, with the whole Chesapeake opened up again to the Kent Islanders, times were good for William Claiborne and his colonists that summer of 1635. Lord Baltimore might grumble threats in London, but on the Chesapeake a Maryland vessel that sighted a Kent Island sail scurried like a scared doe from the "pirates and their bloody cutlasses."

Leonard Calvert's loss was William Claiborne's gain and the Kent Island vessels kept control of the Chesapeake Bay all that summer.

Up the Bay, William Claiborne was building steadily. At Dale's suggestion, he planted one large section of his island in fruit trees and watched them flourish until the most humble household had its supply of apples and peaches. The milch and beef cattle herds which Dale had started grew larger and fatter. With the increase in the island's population and the corresponding drain on the wild fowl that nested in the Kent Island marshes, Claiborne yielded to Dale's urging that he import the finest strains of domesticated geese from England; it was not long before Kent Island geese were known from Cape Fear to Salem as the plumpest, juiciest birds to be had anywhere in the world.

Yes, that was a good summer for Kent Island in 1635, and so was the next year. Little Will Morley, his back as straight as his father's, his shoulders as square and his temper as uncertain as Dale's once had been, learned to crawl and then to walk, and then
292

to swagger in a way that made William Claiborne howl with laughter, seeing Dale in miniature. The child fought the skirts his mother would have kept him in but delighted in the breeches and tiny doeskin boots that Dale had made for him.

The following summer, in 1636, Dale sailed to Delaware's Bay in command of the *Bittern,* accompanied by Holmes, aboard the *Gamecock,* and found the Dutch under Wouter van Twiller unprepared to protest their poaching in New Netherlands trading territory. Dale and Holmes filled their pinnaces with furs and then, more as a lark than anything else, sailed further up the Delaware River to Fort Nassau. The place was ungarrisoned and sliding into ruin, its cannon fouled past usefulness.

When he left the Dutch fort to return to the Island, Dale burned with the plan of convincing Captain Claiborne that he must send an expedition against the rundown post. He knew from what he had seen of Van Twiller's administration and from what the Indians of the area had told him that the Dutch Director-general could be depended upon to let the outpost remain in its idle, unattended state. Even if the Dutch did repair the station and put a garrison there, Dale thought, Claiborne's fleet could take the place in a surprise attack.

He and Holmes drafted their ambitious plans for Claiborne's war against the Dutch on their return voyage, waxing more enthusiastic with every swallow of rum as they talked. Dale's enthusiasm carried him to William Claiborne's office, when the *Bittern* touched Kent Island, even before he went to his home to greet his son and wife. He brushed past Toss with a word and clumped through the doorway of the small room off the hallway.

"Ho, Captain," he called, as Claiborne turned from his desk, "I have a wonderful plan! We can—"

He stopped as a slender figure arose from a chair that was half-hidden in the shadows of one corner of the room. Claiborne's visitor was lean to the point of gauntness and as Dale's eyes accustomed themselves to the dim light he saw the man had thick-fringed eyes that were almost ridiculously feminine in such a thin and sharp-nosed face.

The eyes—Dale remembered someone with eyes like this man's, lolling at a table in—in—in London—William Cloberry's table! Then this was—

The mellifluous voice from the corner gave him his answer as Claiborne's guest advanced.

"Mister Morley," said the thin man. "I heard the story of your glorious sea victory over the Catholic, Calvert, and I was proud at the time to be able to say that I'd met you in London. Honored."

He went into a deep, exaggerated bow and Dale responded after the briefest pause.

"Uh—honored," he replied. "Honored, certainly—Mister Eve-lin."

CHAPTER NINE, 1636-1637

GEORGE EVELIN ARRIVED AT KENT ISLAND WITH the announcement that he had no other interests than to see this strange new country, maybe to explore a bit, to go with Claiborne's vessels to the wilder regions of the Chesapeake where he could see the Indians in their own habitat. Mister Evelin also liked to use a fowling piece; and he had brought with him from England a curious pole of shaved hickory to which, as the Kent Island fishermen gaped, he attached a linen line, a ball of cork and a steel hook, somewhat similar to the bone hooks the Indians sometimes used on their hand lines but smaller and thinner and with a more pronounced barb.

"It is the latest refinement," he explained to Dale in his fluid voice. "There's some—Tom Barker, to name one—who use feathers instead of worms and frogs to lure the fish, but I'm a poor beginner at this sport and so would not disgrace myself by misusing that delicate art."

Dale stared wonderingly at the man who had been put in his care by William Claiborne.

"And it's fish you'd take with—with these slight things?" he asked. "But certainly you've seen the fish our nets bring up. If it's fish you want, sir, come with me and I'll get you a hogshead in a few minutes. Why, a decent rockfish would give you a bath if you hung onto that stick with the fish at the other end of that string."

George Evelin's thick lashes brushed his sallow cheeks as he looked down at the rod he was holding.

"Do you think so, Mister Morley?" he purred. "There is a certain ironmonger in London, a man named Isaak Walton, who

hooked and brought to land a pike that a priest of his parish certi-
fied was nine pounds in weight; his rod was lighter than this one."

"Nine pounds!" Dale burst out. "But the rockfish we have here,
and the salmon, too, often weigh more than thirty pounds! A nine
pound pike would be only a swallow for most of our big fish here
in the Chesapeake."

But Evelin insisted on using his strange hickory wand, with a
small alewife on the hook. Although he lost more fish than he
caught, he did manage to boat some catches that made the scoffers
blink in disbelief. Furthermore, he seemed to get so much pleasure
out of playing the furiously struggling hooked fish that several
Kent Islanders made themselves their own fishing poles, or rods,
and had steel hooks like Evelin's fashioned at Jack Bagshaw's
forge. Talbot Bristoll was one of the early converts to "angling,"
as Evelin termed it; it was of the mode and anything considered
fashionable was bound to attract Bristoll. In fact, although Claiborne had detailed Morley as Evelin's guide during the Londoner's
visit, Bristoll was with the smooth-voiced man from England as
much as Dale, begging for the latest gossip in London, finding
mutual friends in England, ingratiating himself into Evelin's regard.

But Dale would have none of this new sport, angling.

"When I have a hunger for fish," he snorted, "I'll help pull a
seine and get a hundred pounds while Mister Evelin with his
dauncey toy is getting one. But I have to admit that he's good at
killing ducks and geese with scatter shot."

He was an extraordinary man with a fowling piece, this smooth-
voiced, maiden-eyed visitor from London. He consistently outshot
the men of Kent Island who had been hunting wild fowl since
they were old enough to level a gun and here again he used a set
of rules that were quite as strange as the laws he set for himself in
angling.

It had been the Islanders' practice to use a shallop or a canoe to
steal up on the great flocks of ducks and geese that spent the fall
and winter nights in close-packed masses on the flats stretching be-

296

tween the shore and the channel. Once the small, silent craft were in position, the hunters would fire blasts of shot into the midst of the flocks. Mornings that dawned on the scene of these raids would find the flats littered with scores, hundreds, even thousands of dead and crippled ducks and geese and swan.

Mister Evelin, however, wrinkled his beaked nose when Dale explained just how the hunting party he had dutifully arranged for the visitor would be conducted.

"I'm not starving, sir," he said disdainfully, "that I have to slaughter my fowl that way. Don't you ever hunt in the daytime when the birds have at least a chance to escape?"

The muscle at the side of Dale's mouth jumped, once. There never was, he told himself, a face that was more fitted for knuckle bruises than Evelin's, with its quiet, well-bred sneer and its wide mouth that could name a man a rough savage without saying as much. Never, that is, unless it was Talbot Bristoll's face. The two of them made a precious pair, certainly, with their lofty talk and affected manners.

"In England," Evelin was saying, "it is the mode to have a punt poled through the marshes with the gunman in the bow of the craft, the lackey poling from the stern. That way, the huntsman has only a snap shot at the ducks he raises and it needs real skill to bring down a bird. What you propose would be little more than a massacre, I'll vow."

"I have seen the Wicomicoes," Dale said bitingly, "use the method you say is the mode in England and bring down ducks and geese with an arrow through the head each time. I know nothing of the wild fowl in England but I'd say you'd be lucky to bring down one duck out of ten sent up that way with that pretty weapon of yours."

"Done and done for twenty pounds," George Evelin said promptly. "And another twenty that no Indian can put an arrow through the head of a flying duck with more than a chance shot."

"And done," Dale said.

He lost his first wager but he won his second. He got word to

297

Tayrack of the Wicomicoes, bidding him send his best hunter to Kent Island, promising fine presents for both the bowman and the chief. Tayrack sent an old brave, one Boggisske, who killed eight ducks in a narrow marsh waterway with eight arrows. Each feathered shaft spiked the mallard through its sheened green head.

"By heaven!" George Evelin said softly. "I did not think it was possible!"

Dale was still puffed over his winning a wager from Evelin when the other man evened the score with his fowling piece. He had bet that Evelin would not bring down more than one duck in ten flushed with his light fowling piece; but he watched the beak-nosed Londoner send six ducks splashing down in succession before he missed the seventh.

Yes, George Evelin was clever with a fowling piece and with his light, pliant fishing rod. His excellence in the saddle came close to matching William Claiborne's. He handled a sailing skiff as though he had been born on the water and he had a smooth and easy manner with the women of Kent Island as well as a rough and ready wit that he used with the men, so that it was not long before he was a favorite in any company, excepting Claiborne's, Morley's and Martiau's.

Evelin had been at Kent Island some eight months when William Claiborne summoned Dale to his house from the wharf where he was supervising the unloading of a vessel just arrived from England. She was the old *Gryphon,* battered and salt-stained now but still the queen of William Cloberry and Company's fleet by right of her long record.

She had brought a supply of trade goods to Kent Island on this voyage and Dale was agreeably surprised by the quantity and value of the things London had sent this time. Most of the recent shipments made by Cloberry, after his brief spurt of generosity had ended, had been comprised chiefly of second-rate stuff, damaged and used goods that even the Indians were beginning to reject; but this cargo was all of the finest quality and there was more of it than the men in England had ever sent before.

"By the gods," Dale swore, soon after the unloading had begun, "old William Cloberry must have drunk more rum than usual when he consigned this shipment to Captain Claiborne!"

The master of the *Gryphon* was a gnarled Irishman named Burke. When Dale made his explosive statement the bark's skipper cast him a glance from the corner of his eye, spat over the rail and then studied the shrouds of his vessel carefully.

"Maybe," he said, "old Cloberry thought this cargo was intended for other hands."

The remark made no sense to Dale, and Burke stubbed away along the deck after making it and went below. For a moment, Dale was tempted to follow the man and get an explanation; but just at that time a bale of goods being lowered to the wharf parted the line to which it was attached, hit the dock and split its wrappings to spill bolts of bright-colored gingham and calico over the wharf's planking. By the time the litter was cleared away and the unloading operations started again, Dale had forgotten Burke's cryptic words.

Now, as he entered Claiborne's big house, he remembered them sharply and wished he had followed Burke below, regardless. The air of the place seemed charged with ominous portent. Toss, who answered his knock, walked on tiptoe, his ebony face cast in the lugubrious lines that usually marked one of the Captain's more spectacular rages. From the room the slave indicated with a silent gesture came the rapid, blurred voice of William Claiborne at his most vituperative.

Dale walked into the room and stopped just inside the doorway. Claiborne was pacing the floor by the windows, a straight, slender, angry figure in black velvet, wearing black hose and buckled shoes instead of the usual high boots. The Captain's long curls switched wrathfully at every turn he made, the lace at his wrists flapped and twisted as he gesticulated, the pleated ruff at his throat was brushed by the jerking of his pointed beard.

"The whoreson!" he was saying. "I'll call him out! I'll put my steel through his heart unless he turns and runs—and he will—and

299

then I'll put it through his arse! I'll cut him into fish bait and use his own twig of a fishing pole to feed him to the eels. I'll—"

And on and on, without a pause except when he needed more breath. By the desk in the corner lounged Talbot Bristoll, one long booted leg thrown over the arm of his chair, his fingers toying with the hilt of his sword, his eyes opaquely alive and his mouth twisted in his familiar half-smile.

"You sent for me, Captain?" Dale said, to break into the tirade.

"I did, eh?" Claiborne barked. "By Christ's bones and blood, there's a smart remark! Did you crawl here on hands and knees or did you stop off at your house to dally with your wife's slave girl Rellie before you answered my call? An hour has passed since—"

"Wait, Captain!" Dale said. He fought to keep his tone even. "I left the wharf the minute I got your call, even though it meant giving Holmes the job of unloading the *Gryphon* and he's almost asleep on his feet. He captained the watch at the fort last night, you know, and—"

"Know?" Claiborne screamed. "Of course I could not know! I know nothing of what happens here at Kent Island! Know? Know what? Know my name's William Claiborne, maybe, but there's times like this that I could doubt even that!"

He met an exquisitely shaped light chair in his pacing and his savage kick sent the piece sailing six feet through the air before it hit the wall and crumpled into splintered fragments. Talbot Bristoll slipped his leg back over the chair arm and moved his sword a trifle along his thigh.

Dale waited until the Captain paused for breath, then threw in his own words.

"You're doing nothing," he said, "but loosening the plaster in the walls with your roaring, sir. If you can tell us what's wrong we'll do what we can to help you, Captain. Or"—as Claiborne's deadly pale face, framed by the black hair, swung toward him— "if I've done something wrong, let me know what it was and hear my answer, if there is one. This raving gets us nowhere. For hea-
300

ven's sake, sit down, and tell us what's the cause of all this uproar."

"Well said, well said," Talbot Bristoll drawled from his chair by the desk. "By God, you'll be a lawyer yet, Friend Dale."

William Claiborne stood transfixed, paralyzed by the paternally reproving tones of the young man he had dragged out of a shabby hut, some eight or nine years before, and had molded into a sure-voiced gentleman who could bid him hush now and take his seat in the corner and speak gently.

Claiborne slowly left the windows where he had been pacing and moved to a chair across the room, keeping his eyes pinned on Dale, who walked to another chair by a small table and poured himself a glass of sack from the decanter there without waiting to be bidden. It had been some time now since Dale had kept on his feet until invited to sit down or licked dry lips while waiting for an offer of a glass. The transition from servant to lieutenant to this status had been a gradual one but now it was complete.

"Now, Captain," he said after his first sip, "what's the reason for this excitement?"

Claiborne's words were biting as they came back at him.

"Sometimes," said the man in black velvet, his voice flat, "I wonder if you're not with *them,* against me."

Dale flushed but his hand was steady as he took another sip of the wine.

"I don't know who you mean by *them,*" he said, "but you know, or you should know, that I'm not with anyone against you. If I've not proved that by now I never can."

William Claiborne passed a long hand over his eyes in a weary swipe.

"I know, I know," he admitted. His mood veered now toward self-reproach. "Don't mind me today, Dale. This thing has caught me like a tomahawk in the back of the head."

"What thing?" Dale pursued.

From one of the pockets of the black suit came a sheaf of papers at which the Captain stared for a moment and then wadded in his

301

hand, as though he would crush the meaning of the documents in his grasp.

"This thing," he said. "It's the lading bill for the *Gryphon's* cargo—and every bead and pin and scrap of cloth aboard the bark is consigned to George Evelin!"

"Evelin!" Dale cried.

"Yes, Evelin!" the Captain ground out. "That nasty, smirking traitor I've treated as a guest and friend. All the *Gryphon's* goods are consigned to George Evelin, and that could mean only that Cloberry and his damned advisors have thrown me overboard."

"But—but—that can't be possible, Captain!" Dale protested. "Your last letters from Cloberry all praised your administration here! Evelin himself has spoken highly of your work. It was only a day or so ago that Dame Morley told me—"

He stopped as Claiborne made a savage gesture.

"Never mind," the Captain said. "I've told you enough times that in this trade—yes, in all this life—what a man writes or says doesn't have to mean what he thinks. I've suspected a plot against me for some time, led by this Evelin, in spite of all the things Cloberry wrote me. The man was too generous in his praise of what I've done here at Kent Island. My brother in London and others, too, warned me that when we lost the *Cockatrice* Cloberry went into a rage and swore he'd see that I paid dearly for that blow to his purse. And now I find he means to make me pay for that defeat by taking my island from me."

Talbot Bristoll sprang to his feet and walked to the windows, his shoulders swinging.

"And so it's I who'll be blamed for all this, eh?" he demanded, in an ugly voice. "Because I had bad luck with the damned *Cockatrice* you'll take the stand that I cost you your position here? Well, this is once when I'll not be the scapegoat for your bad luck, Captain Claiborne!"

Both Claiborne and Dale stared at Bristoll in amazement. Talbot's outburst was so unexpected, so little warranted, that Clai-
302

borne's eyes narrowed in suspicion as he looked at his lieutenant.

"Who spoke of blaming you?" he asked. "The *Cockatrice* affair is over and done with and you've served your penance. Why this show of temper now?"

Bristoll swung around from the window, his mouth twisted by an ugly sneer.

"I only forestalled your plan to lay the blame on me," he jerked out. "It's been your custom, lately, Captain Claiborne, and I'm sick of it. Never a word of praise from you for all my years of service— no, all the praise that's handed out is meant for Morley, here."

He dropped his thumbs to his belt, his dark face suffused with anger.

"Now let me say my piece," he told Claiborne directly. "I've taken a lot from you for a long time but now I'll have no more of it; I'll not be stepchild of this family for another day."

"You sound mad, Bristoll!" Captain Claiborne said harshly. "You're talking like a child!"

"I am? Maybe I'm not the only fool on Kent Island, Captain! There are some who'd say you've been more foolish than I, strutting around playing king and never seeing that your control of this place was slipping out of your hands."

"And you saw it, then?" Claiborne asked slowly. "You saw it and never warned me what was going on?"

Bristoll flung out a hand in a scornful gesture.

"Since when would you listen to my warnings?" he asked. "You'll listen to your precious Dale Morley and even that old man, Martiau, but you'd pay no heed to me."

His mouth widened in an unpleasant grin.

"No, you'd not listen," he said distinctly, "but maybe I've found a man who will. Perhaps Mister Evelin will accept my advice."

Claiborne's voice grew steely as he nodded.

"Then that's it," he said. "I've noticed that you've been thick with Evelin, Talbot, and now I see I've found a traitor for an aide, a traitor fashioned by jealousy."

303

"Call me anything you want," Bristoll sneered. "You'll find soon enough that your words don't mean a thing, Will Claiborne, now that George Evelin has taken charge."

Dale's hand went to the hilt of his sword as hot, thick anger surged up within him.

"Now, by God," he roared, "it's time to put a stop to this raving! Draw, Bristoll—or maybe you'd rather knife me in the back, like you and Evelin have knifed the Captain."

Bristoll's blade leapt to his hand as his murky eyes glittered.

"I welcome this," he snarled. "Now that I've broken with Claiborne I'm not bound to let you live, Morley. On guard, you nameless bastard, and we'll settle this thing right here."

"Stop!" Claiborne cried, his voice terrible with rage. "We'll have no brawling in this house that's still mine! Morley, put down your weapon—Bristoll, sheathe your blade! God's blood, I'll—"

"Quiet, you maundering old idiot," Bristoll grated. "Who obeys your orders now?"

He came at Dale, thrusting savagely, and Morley was hard pressed at the start to turn Bristoll's onslaught aside. But parry he did, his brain cold and calculating, and made his riposte neatly. Bristoll forced his way closer, hacking recklessly, and Dale retreated slowly, balancing himself on the balls of his feet, his eyes wary, his sword flickering lightly.

William Claiborne howled his imprecations but there was no stopping the two men now. All the years of their mutual hatred had worked to set off this explosion and there was a fierce joy in Dale's heart as his blade clashed against Bristoll's. He felt invincible, tireless, as he circled about Bristoll, stabbing and parrying. There had been a day when he knew he was no match for Talbot as a swordsman but that day had long since passed; now he could prove to himself that he need ask no odds from any man when the duel was joined. All the sneers and insults that had passed between him and Bristoll could be avenged now—yes, and Talbot Bristoll would not call another man a nameless bastard.

304

He moved in on Bristoll and it was then that Talbot showed his murderous caliber. The broken-nosed man reached to one side, switched a light stool around and flung it at Morley's legs. One of Dale's spurs caught in a chair rung and he staggered, nearly lost his balance altogether.

"Treachery!" Claiborne bawled. "By God, that was a whoreson's trick!"

Bristoll laughed savagely and leaped in for the kill. The overturned chair with which he had intended to cripple Dale shot back across the floor at him as Dale kicked at it. Bristoll stumbled, his sword's point dropped, and he waved his arms wildly as he tried to regain his balance. Dale's blade moved in a blinding tierce and he felt the steel strike Bristoll's arm. Talbot gasped, his sword fell from his nerveless fingers and he staggered back, clutching at his wounded arm with a hand from between the fingers of which leaked a crimson flow.

Claiborne was upon Dale then, grappling with his lieutenant's sword arm to block the death stroke that Dale was aiming at Bristoll's throat. For a moment, the two men, Captain and aide, were locked in a struggle, and then Claiborne wrenched Dale's sword from his hand, flung it across the room.

"Quit it!" he panted hoarsely, "would you hang for murder, Dale?"

"Murder?" Dale gasped. "Who'd call it murder to cut down a man who'd use a chair as he did?"

"I wouldn't," said Claiborne, "but do you think Evelin wouldn't? You'd play right into his hands, Dale, and wind up on the gallows or a fugitive, at least. You've won your duel and satisfied your honor; this carrion's wounded and he's drawn no blood of yours. Now be content."

"A wise suggestion, Mister Morley," came a quiet purr from the doorway. Dale and Claiborne turned to see George Evelin lounging against the door frame, his eyes showing quiet amusement. He wore plum-colored satin and there was no weapon, dag-

305

ger or sword, at his belt although he was armed with an air of authority Dale had never seen him display before.

He advanced into the room now, his long-lashed eyes full on the wounded Bristoll, his voice biting when he spoke.

"Mister Bristoll," he said, "is this the way you serve my interests? You pledged yourself to follow my orders and I remember giving you no order like this."

Talbot Bristoll kept his eyes on the floor, his hand still clutching his wound, his heavy-featured face writhing in a snarling scowl.

"Better get your wound attended to," Evelin said, returning to his easy, liquid voice, "and keep yourself to your quarters, sir, till I say otherwise."

"Now, by my tripes," William Claiborne burst out, "since when do you give orders to my men, sir?"

Evelin's face showed a trace of amusement again and he directed a stilted bow toward Claiborne.

"Since this day," he replied casually. "Henceforth, I give the orders at Kent Island."

"By whose authority?" Claiborne rasped.

"Perhaps," Evelin returned in all good humor, "you'd like to see this paper I carry. It will satisfy you that I'm acting within my rights. It's signed by William Cloberry and it gives me power of attorney to deal with all matters of business here. It also orders you, my dear Captain, to return to London immediately to make an accounting of your stewardship here."

While he spoke, he brought out a folded sheet of heavy paper which he proffered to Claiborne with another brief bow. For a moment it appeared that the Captain might spurn the thing; but after a brief hesitation he took it, unfolded it, ran his eyes over its contents. As Dale looked on, he saw Claiborne's face turn gray, a dozen years attach themselves to the Captain's age; or so it seemed.

"Why, he's become an old man!" he thought instinctively.

William Claiborne, old, weary, defeated? How could Dale ever have imagined such a thing a few short years before? Who would

306

ever have thought he'd lose the fire and dash that had always marked him, in adversity as well as in triumph? And yet the Captain's shoulders were sagging now and his voice, when he spoke, was tonelessly leaden. Not the defeat so much as the duplicity that had engineered it, seemed to strip Claiborne of all his commanding boldness until he seemed almost humble before the cool stare of George Evelin.

"I compliment you, Mister Evelin," he managed after a lengthy pause. "It's evident you've had this paper since you first arrived here at Kent Island. I can't help wondering why you didn't show it when you first reached here instead of playing the grateful guest, accepting our hospitality for all these months."

Evelin's smile widened.

"Surely you'll agree, Captain," he replied, "that a careful study of the field before the battle is worth more to a commander than an extra troop of musketeers. I had Mister Cloberry's instructions to look around, dig into the situation, before I revealed myself to you as the new commander of this island."

"I see," said Claiborne heavily. "And did you have Cloberry's orders to make a traitor of my lieutenant, Bristoll, as well?"

"No, Captain Claiborne," Evelin replied, unruffled. "Better put it that Mister Bristoll kept his eyes more open than you and saw what was happening and which way to jump. I'll swear he approached me, not I him. He's been valuable to me, too, although I don't like his over-eagerness with the sword."

His eyes flicked briefly at the sullen Bristoll and his voice hardened a trifle.

"Which reminds me," he added, "that I ordered you to have your wound attended and then to keep to your quarters, sir."

Bristoll kept his eyes lowered, his hand still clutching his damaged arm, as he brushed past Dale and Claiborne on his way to the door. The Captain drew aside sharply as the flat-nosed man who had betrayed his trust walked in front of him, and Dale's face was wrinkled with disgust as Bristoll passed.

"Dale," said Claiborne, as Bristoll left the room, "open a window. This place stinks of villainy."

Dale moved to a window to fling it up and he breathed deeply of the wind that swept through the opening into the room. What Claiborne had said was true; the stench of treachery and dishonesty lay miasmatic over the scene. Dale turned back, his voice urgent as he addressed the Captain.

"You'll fight this thing, sir?" he asked. "Surely you'll not let this—this *gentleman* take your island, Captain, in spite of all his writs and warrants?"

William Claiborne nodded, but without much conviction.

"Oh, yes," he said dully, "I'll fight Mister Evelin and beat him, too, in the end."

"You think so?" Evelin purred. "You'll find me stronger, Captain, than you expect, perhaps. You'll not be dealing with a muddle-headed Colonial, you know."

"I know," Claiborne nodded. "I'll be dealing with a man who took advantage of my hospitality to spy on me, though you must still be searching for the dishonest thing you meant to find to my discredit. I know what this accounting I must make to Cloberry will really be—a mockery. I've little doubt but that you and your cutpurse friends like Bristoll have changed the ledgers to make me out a thief."

Dale tensed, expecting Evelin to make his challenge. The cheeks of the man with the thick-lashed eyes might have been a trifle more taut than usual but his voice lost none of its suavity. He made a show of examining a long fingernail as he spoke.

"I think I know what you're trying to do, Captain, and that's to goad me into challenging you. But I have you beaten there, too. I'm not going to be tricked into making any challenge, no matter what your insults. I stand on my power of attorney, attested to by the King's Bench, as my right to be here; and if I'm killed in any way but in a duel, or made to disappear, there'll be His Majesty's justices to answer to, my dear Captain."

His smile deepened, serene, utterly confident, braving the Captain's thunderous frown.

"One more thing, sir," he said. "Should you be tempted to have some *accident* take care of my obnoxious presence, be assured, Captain Claiborne, that both Mister Cloberry and Governor West in Jamestown have been advised that I fear an attempt might be made on my life and that if I were to die suddenly, the murder should be laid at your feet. And now I'll have those lading bills, sir!"

William Claiborne handed over the crumpled papers in a gesture a man might use if he had some inexplicable reason to feed a frog to a snake. George Evelin's smile faltered for a second as he watched Claiborne drag the hand that had almost touched his own, across the side of the black velvet coat he wore, as if the Captain were wiping off some bit of filth.

"Thank you," said the man from London. "And I can advise Mister Cloberry that you'll follow his orders and wait on him to make an accounting?"

"I'll be in London before any lying letter of yours," Claiborne said coldly.

"And," said Evelin, with a mocking bow, "find a merry reception waiting for you there, I don't doubt."

Morley waited for the Captain to flare into a burst of his old pungent spirits but he waited in vain. Claiborne made as if to speak and then closed his mouth without a word. And Dale was struck by the knifing realization that William Claiborne, the man who had been his leader for so many years, the captain who had always seemed so fearless before, was beset now by a *fear* that this defeat he had suffered could never be redeemed or transformed into ultimate victory.

He had to speak in Claiborne's stead, to answer this long-lashed devil with the oily voice.

"Captain Claiborne," he said abruptly, "will find a merrier reception than you'll get when you go back to England after all this

309

is finished. Because, Mister Evelin, the Captain will win out in the end in spite of all such leg-lifting dogs as you and Cartney and Cloberry. If we have to, we'll fight the King himself to hold Kent Island for our own people."

"And there," said Evelin, smirking, "speaks the brave hero. It is too bad, Mister Morley, that you're so valiant in such a feeble cause."

"Do you think Captain Claiborne can win out in the end, my husband?" Genevieve asked Dale that evening, after he had given her an account of Evelin's coup and Bristoll's turncoat knavery.

Dale ran his fingers through his hair, wishing he could give back a confident "yes" to his wife's question. In all honesty, however, he had to admit that Claiborne was reacting badly to this crisis. Where once he would have leaped to battle Evelin eagerly, he now seemed content to curse the man from London, Bristoll and Cloberry, rather than make any definite plans for a struggle to keep control of Kent Island.

Dale was shocked by his lassitude. To let this man Evelin take precious Kent Island without a battle? Unthinkable!

"I'll go to London with you, Captain," he told Claiborne, "if you want me to. Together, we can convince Cloberry that this is a dirty reward for all the years you've spent in his service. The man must have some sense of justice in his makeup to know you deserve better than this."

"No," Claiborne said morosely. "Justice means little to Cloberry, when there's money involved. No, you'll stay in Virginia, Dale, and keep in touch with what goes on here. Maybe it would be better if you'd live in Jamestown—certainly Bristoll and Evelin would make your position here unpleasant."

"Leave Kent Island?" Dale demanded. "No, Captain, they'd have to drive me off the Island and then they couldn't keep me away long. I'll stay on here, sir, and take care of your interests as well as I can."

But now, talking to Genevieve, Dale wondered just how long
310

he could stay at Kent Island, with Evelin in charge and Bristoll his lieutenant. He could depend upon Martiau as an ally, but the old soldier was virtually bedridden now, his spirit undaunted but his body racked by aches and pains. Claiborne had not exaggerated when he predicted that Bristoll and Evelin would make his position unpleasant; they would be certain to make Dale's life miserable if he stayed on at Kent Island in the Captain's absence.

Still, he would not leave this place if it were humanly possible to stay on. His whole life and that of his little family was bound up in the Island and, by staying, he might be able to prevent Evelin and Bristoll from spoiling the place—how he did not know now.

He realized with a start that he had not answered Jenny's question and he forced his voice to be hearty as he replied. No need to worry Genevieve with his fears.

"Oh yes," he told her, "William Claiborne can't be beaten long by men like Evelin and Bristoll. You'll see; he'll return to Kent Island stronger than ever, once he uses his magic words, as only he knows how."

"But while he's gone—" She left the sentence hanging.

"While he's away," Dale said firmly, "we'll have to put on a bold front and give neither Evelin nor Bristoll a chance to laugh at us."

She crossed the room to lean over him, her arms cradling his head against her soft bosom, straining him to her in a sudden frenzy of apprehension.

"He's an evil man, my husband," she said, her voice taut, "and if he hurt you, I believe I'd die. Let's take Captain Claiborne's advice and go to Jamestown till this thing is over."

"I'll not run from Talbot Bristoll or George Evelin or any man," Dale said stubbornly. "Not run away and leave Kent Island to their pick-bone fingers."

Nor could she persuade him to change his mind, although she pleaded with him to take Little Will and her to Jamestown; pleaded until, at length, he exploded in roaring anger.

"Christ's thorns, Madam!" he yelled. "Would you make a coward of your husband? I said I'd stay here and I intend to do just that!"

"Then do just this," Genevieve begged. "Come to Jamestown with the boy and me for a short visit with my people, while this place cools off a bit. You know my mother's been ill and I want her to see the boy before—before it is too late."

Dale gnawed his lip before he nodded grudgingly. It was true, from the sound of letters from Jamestown, that Genevieve's mother had not long to live.

"All right, all right," he said eventually. "I'll go to Jamestown with you and the boy when Captain Claiborne sails. But I'll come back here as soon as I can, and here I'll stay, Bristoll or no Bristoll, Evelin or no Evelin."

Actually, Dale was grateful for an excuse to get Little Will and Genevieve away from the Island for a spell. There was always the underlying dread that Bristoll, brooding over the fact that Dale had beaten him in swordplay, in spite of his low trickery with the stool, might try to harm the child or Genevieve, goaded by his twisted thinking. And Evelin, in his new capacity as factor of Kent Island, would be certain to humiliate Dale as much as he could and likely cause pain to Genevieve in the doing.

Before he left the Island, Captain William Claiborne summoned all the people on the place for a farewell speech. But his words were uninspired, lacking the old fire. It was a disappointing performance.

"I've lost my island and my people," Dale heard him mutter at the end.

Tears were trembling on his lids as Claiborne stalked away.

Dale and Genevieve and Little Will sailed with Captain Claiborne when he left Kent Island aboard the *Gryphon,* slipping out of the channel and past a silent fort that fired no salute as had been customary. Once William Claiborne had refused to fire a salute for

Leonard Calvert and now George Evelin was dealing the man he had supplanted a similar slight.

Dale watched his captain from a position near the mainmast, wondering at the change that had come over the man. It was understandable that the passing years might rob a man of his fire and fervor, but Claiborne was more changed than the years could be blamed for. As he was, he was no man to face William Cloberry and the others in London who had plotted to ruin him. As he was, he was not suited to defend his rightful place on a tavern bench.

And Dale knew, deep down, the reason for the Captain's change: bewilderment. As though Claiborne had asked the question aloud, he knew the Captain was wondering *why* Cloberry had deserted him, *why* Cloberry had changed from being his staunchest supporter to being his hidden enemy?

And Claiborne, Dale knew, was wondering how he was to defend himself against charges of which he would have no warning until they were hurled at him at his trial. His failure before Charles at Windsor Castle—but that had all been Cartney's doing, and Lord Cartney was still close to Cloberry. As though Claiborne had cried aloud, Dale heard the Captain plead for someone, something, to tell him *why* he had been dishonored this way.

And so there was something Dale had to do; something he had shrunk from doing for years. If Claiborne was to have any chance to make any defense in his own behalf, he must be told the secret of Cloberry's turning against him. He must be told even if it meant earning the Captain's undying hatred for the man who was truly to blame for all of Claiborne's reverses.

That man was Dale Morley and it had been Dale's dalliance with Lady Augusta Cartney that had been mistaken for William Claiborne's rutting. Cloberry still believed that it had been Claiborne, not Morley, whom Cartney had seen in his wife's bed on the day before His Lordship went to Windsor Castle to rip up all plans for Calvert's defeat before the King.

So now Dale must face the risk of telling Claiborne the truth,

313

come what might. If he knew the truth, the Captain might storm into London with all his old-time fire and prove to the men who would throw him out that all their case was built on a mistake, that he was being accused of something a mere lieutenant—discredited, dismissed, cast out now—had actually done.

If he could do that, Claiborne would return to Kent Island. If he dragged himself to London to appear, apologetic, fearful, bewildered, before his inquisitors, there was little chance that he could win out to come back to the Chesapeake.

And Kent Island needed William Claiborne if it was to survive. Under the administration of Evelin and Bristoll, the Island would never flourish; most probably it would decline to a state where it would be an easy prey for the Catholics down the Bay. Yes, Will Claiborne had to come back to the Island, even if Dale had to confess his secret to revive Claiborne's old, commanding self.

And if the Captain drew his sword in his rage—well, that was a possibility that had to be faced for Kent Island. The jewel of the Chesapeake had given him much; it deserved a great deal from Dale, even his life. For if Claiborne drew and thrust, Dale knew he would not be able to make a pretense of a parry; the day that he could aim his sword's point at Claiborne's throat had dawned and died a long time back.

He waited until Claiborne had dragged himself to his cabin and then followed, rapped once on the door and slipped inside the room at the Captain's bidding. Claiborne sat on his bunk, still wearing his mist-drenched cape and helmet, the sword resting slackly between his spread knees, his palms up along his thighs, the picture of helpless misery. Dale glanced at him and felt a twinge of pain for the man who had been brought to this estate.

Unbidden, he took a bench across the cabin from Claiborne and leaned forward, his forearms resting on his knees.

"Captain Claiborne," he said quietly, "there's something you must know before you go to London—something that will help you when you face Cloberry."

Claiborne raised haggard eyes slowly and waited.

314

"You may remember," Dale said, "that when Leonard Calvert came to Kent Island that day, he said something about Cloberry being angry over your dealings with Lord Cartney, or with someone close to Cartney."

Claiborne reached up to tilt his helmet back on his head.

"That was some time ago," he complained. "So much has happened—"

"I remember it well," Dale said grimly, "because I knew what Calvert spoke about, while you were all at sea. It's this, Captain Claiborne—Cloberry believed that you bedded Lady Cartney while we were in London."

The silence in the little cabin was broken by the grunt and squeak of straining timbers as the *Gryphon* caught a morning wind and picked up speed. Claiborne's eyes were wide, held on Dale's, and his mouth hung open.

"I—bedded—Lady—Cartney!" Claiborne said slowly. "Why, I barely knew the lady enough to bow to her, Dale! How could a lie like that be spread?"

Dale looked down at his hands, unable to meet Claiborne's stare.

"Lady Cartney was bedded," he said, "and she and her partner were seen by Lord Cartney. She's dead now, poor woman, and I think by Cartney's hand, in one way or another. But Lord Cartney did have reason to be outraged and that's why he turned against us in the matter of the Calvert patent, when you and Mister Cloberry were on the brink of success."

Claiborne's hoarse breathing rasped through the room for several seconds. When he spoke, the Captain's voice was harsh, direct, and not the flaccid thing it had been.

"Who was it?" he demanded, his intonation ugly. "That scoundrel Bristoll? It sounds like something he would do."

Morley kept his eyes lowered as he shook his head.

"No, Captain Claiborne," he said quietly. "Not Bristoll. It was me who ruined everything in London by climbing into a bed where I did not belong."

"*You!*"

"Yes." Morley raised his eyes to meet the Captain's burning glare at last and forced himself to keep them steady. "It was me in Lady Cartney's arms that time and Cartney thought it was you. We're about the same size, and my back was to him and that sword you'd given me an hour or so before was beside the bed. He must have recognized it and thought—"

"Enough!" Claiborne rapped out. "In the name of Jesus, stop your mouthings, Dale Morley!"

He sprang from his bunk and began pacing up and down the narrow confines of the cabin, his voice racketing about the room.

"So this is my reward," he grated, "for taking you out of a swamp and making you a cavalier! This is the return you give me for my sponsorship, my direction—aye, even my love! Before God, I thought Bristoll was the smelliest skunk alive, but you—"

He whirled and his narrow face was twisted with rage. Morley half-expected him to go for his sword and wondered almost idly if he would be permitted to gain his feet before the Captain's blade spiked him.

"Why didn't you tell me?" the Captain was demanding. "Why did you keep your rotten secret so long and tell me now?"

Dale spread his fingers in a helpless gesture.

"I was afraid you'd kill me, sir," he admitted honestly, "and I believe you would have, at the time."

"And you think I won't now?" Claiborne growled.

"Maybe," Dale said simply. "I took that risk because I knew you'd need the truth when you faced Cloberry. Run me through now and you can tell Cloberry that I confessed the Lady Cartney thing at last and got what I deserved—I think it'd satisfy your people in London as nothing else would."

Claiborne stared at him, his eyes narrowing.

"And you invite death?" he asked suspiciously. "You'd sit there and let me spike your gizzard—and for what purpose?"

Now Dale Morley found the telling hard, immeasurably more difficult than it had been to confess his guilt in the case of Lady
316

Augusta Cartney. His eyes dropped again and his speech was labored as he struggled to sift his words until he found those that would come close, at least, to explaining his intent.

"It is—the Island, sir," he said in a low voice. "With my confession, you might win before Cloberry and come back to Kent Island soon, to throw out Evelin and Bristoll; and that's what matters."

"But—but—you have your own position, Dale. Do you think I could keep you on as my lieutenant after telling Cloberry the true story? It would be impossible, man!"

"Then it is impossible," Dale managed, "but you'd have the Island back and keep it from the Papists."

"Your home, your family—do you think you could go back to digging in the dirt again? Do you think Dame Morley would be content to take your son and share your exile with you?"

"Yes," Dale said in a subdued voice. "I think my wife would share a piece of Hell with me and the boy, if she had to. You see, sir, she loves me, even though she knows my love for her is not so complete and even though I'm not worthy of her love."

Claiborne returned slowly to his bunk and lowered himself to the blanketed top. His face had lost some of its initial fury but it was still alive, still lit by the anger that had returned hope to the features that had been slack and beaten too long.

"Yes," he said, and his voice came close to matching Dale's. "I believe you're right there. And you, I see, still have your senseless love for the Catholic maid, Anne Furness, or Wing, or whatever her name might be now."

Dale could not answer. It had been some time since he had brought Anne Wing's name to mind but the same inexplicable love for the girl was there within him and, he guessed, would always be. He could admit the worth of Genevieve's love and curse himself for a fool in not returning it wholly, he could realize the hopelessness of his infatuation for Anne Furness, but he could not change himself, no matter how he might try. He was kind to Gene-

317

vieve, he could credit himself with that, and she must be happy, beyond her knowledge that her husband loved another woman more than he did her; there were times when his passion for her perfect body came close to something finer than passion, but if this was a scene of confession he could not honestly say he had rid himself of his love for the girl of Maryland.

Claiborne moved on the bunk and his sword clinked against the frame of the low berth.

"God's truth," he gritted, "we men are strange things. Dame Morley is worth a thousand—but what does it matter what I say? The thing is what I'm to do with what you've told me."

"Do?" Dale asked. "There's only one thing to do, isn't there? Tell Cloberry you were innocent in the Cartney affair, convince him of that, and you can, and win out over Evelin in your London trial."

"And lose my lieutenant, whoremonger though he be—or was, at least?"

Dale looked up, startled and glimpsed an expression in Claiborne's eyes that he had never seen there before. For that brief instant, the Captain's face reflected an enveloping love, nakedly exposed, such as it was given few men ever to bestow on one another. Then the curtain closed down again and Claiborne looked away, leaving Dale Morley shaken in his realization that whatever the Captain's original intent in binding a ragged freedman to him, the years had molded an affection that could even forgive a hurt as disastrous as Dale had dealt Claiborne in Lady Augusta's bedchamber.

"I—" Dale began, and stopped. There was nothing he could say to this.

"No, Dale," the Captain went on after a pause. He shook his head so that the long hair danced under the rim of his burgonet. "No, I'll not tell Cloberry the story. It's all long past; maybe his thinking I was to blame for making an enemy of Cartney started Cloberry against me, but there's more to it than that now."

318

He pounded a booted thigh with a broad hand.

"But there's one big puzzle solved," he cried, "and I find myself on solid ground there, at last. And knowing what you've told me, I'll find the answers to the other puzzles, once I'm in front of Cloberry!"

He snorted, his hand still slapping his thigh.

"Why, I've acted like a sniveling weakling," he said. "Who bewitched me, to make me think all was lost, because Evelin and Bristoll betrayed me?"

Dale's heart surged as he listened to the old William Claiborne; his dangerous confession was not to be used by the Captain as Dale had planned, but his admission had brought the hoped for result. Now Claiborne was alive again, now his eyes were bright, his face eager, as though he were thinking ahead to the clash that was coming in London. Again he held himself invincible, no matter how strong the enemy; again his confidence was strengthening to provide him with his keenest weapon.

He left the bunk again and walked across to Dale, his boot heels hammering. His hand gripped Dale's shoulder.

"You were a bigger man than even I had thought," he said earnestly, "to admit your wrong and face my sword to help me and Kent Island! I'll not forget this, Dale, and if I'm ever tempted to surrender, over there in England, I'll remember this loyalty such as no man, not even a king, can claim. I'll beat Cloberry in London and Evelin at Kent Island. I'll give Bristoll what's coming to him wherever I run him down to earth, and the two of us will hold Kent Island till the day they put pennies on our eyes to keep them closed!"

The *Gryphon* reached Jamestown just before dusk and nosed her way into the cluttered, unkempt harbor of Virginia's capital, aided by an incoming tide that swirled the rubbish and filth about in wide, sluggish circles. A new quay had been put up since Dale's

319

last visit and this embankment was a busy scene, with men and carts moving back and forth between the warehouses and the vessels that were loading and unloading.

Ashore, Little Will was kept agog by the bustle that surrounded him, his wide eyes moving from one unfamiliar sight to another, his mouth frankly gaping.

The little group, with Captain Claiborne at its head, threaded its way through the crowd to a square beyond the quay where Claiborne paused to give his orders.

"Dale," he said, "I'll need you with me when I go to see Governor West at once. You can spare him for the evening, Dame Morley? You'll want to go directly to Loman Plantation, I take it?"

"I think it best, Captain," Genevieve said.

"In that event," Claiborne said, "I'll assign a dependable man to escort you there. Jamestown is no London but there are still some people in this place who might annoy a lady without an escort."

He looked about him and his mouth twisted into a smile.

"Now where did he come from?" he asked, half under his breath. "He holds the job of farrier at the Island, but still I've noticed he's more squire to you, Dale, than smith. There he is, dressed as a sailor. Ho, you there—come here!"

Jack Bagshaw stumped toward the Captain, an uneasy grin on his wrinkled face.

"Aye, sir," he said, bobbing. "Ye beckoned me?"

"Why aren't you at your forge," Claiborne demanded, "'stead of strutting the streets of Jamestown like an admiral?"

Bagshaw had doffed his stocking cap at Claiborne's first hail. Now he tugged at his foreknot uncomfortably.

"By your leave, Cap'n," he said, "I needed to come to Jamestown for certain supplies. Also, I did not like the Island with Mister Morley away and Mister Bristoll in charge, so to speak. So I begged leave of the *Gryphon's* master, Cap'n Burke, to come here with Mister Morley."

320

Dale covered his mouth with his hand to hide a smile as the Captain turned toward him.

"You see?" Claiborne asked. "You have a loyal follower, Dale."

"He's a good man, Captain," Dale replied, "and he served me well at Saint Mary's, that time we went aground. I'd have him escort Dame Morley to her father's house, if it's agreeable to you."

Claiborne nodded. Since the scene in the cabin, he had been in high spirits.

"Very well," he said, "but if you let the lady come to harm, Bagshaw, I'll have your ears. You can get a conveyance of some kind at the stable near the tavern."

"I've sold 'em many a nag in my former calling," Bagshaw replied, "and I'll get the best they have for the journey."

"Then be off," Claiborne smiled, "so you may get to Loman Plantation before night."

The Captain bent over Genevieve's hand with his old courtliness.

"I'll bid you farewell, then, Dame Morley," he said, "for the time being. Never fear but I'll come back to Kent Island and all our fortunes will be mended."

"God speed you back, Captain Claiborne," Dale's wife said earnestly. "We'll all be waiting for you, down to the tiniest child."

Claiborne straightened and shot a keen glance at Dale.

"And maybe," he said, "the tiniest child of all will be a brother or a sister for Little Will, eh? I've heard it said—"

"Old wives' tales, Captain," Genevieve broke in, blushing faintly. "And now we'd better be off and leave my husband and you to your affairs."

She placed both hands on Dale's arms and raised her face to touch her cheek briefly against his in a fleeting embrace that made passersby gape.

Dale caught up Little Will and smacked him heartily, then set him down again with a pat on the seat of his breeches. He looked up to see Jack Bagshaw grinning at the child affectionately and knew that the boy would be as safe with the farrier as he would be with his own father.   321

"Come on, Dale," Claiborne said. "Maybe we can get to West before his dinner and coax out of him an invitation to his table. Every man is easier to talk with over a full plate and there's much I'd talk about with the Governor this night."

Genevieve and Bagshaw turned away and began walking toward the stable, Little Will between them. As Dale's eyes followed them through the gloom, he saw among the crowd through which they filed a diminutive figure that looked familiar for one instant and then, in the next moment, could not possibly have been anyone Dale could know. There had been something about the man—but this person obviously was a derelict, shabby, stumbling, far past his capacity for wine or rum or whatever his tipple might be. Still . . .

"Are you asleep, man?" Captain Claiborne was asking irritably. "You've been staring after your wife and Bagshaw since long after they've disappeared in the crowd. We have work to do."

Dale shook his mind loose from its insistent attempt to identify the shabby sot he had glimpsed and turned to follow the Captain toward the Governor's Mansion, shouldering his way through the crowd that swarmed and jostled about them. He was separated from Claiborne by a passing cart, drawn by four yoke of oxen, and when the creaking vehicle had finally crawled past, he found the Captain deep in conversation with a tall man who bent his head close to Claiborne's and moved his hands jerkily in emphasizing whatever it was he had to say.

As Dale walked up, the tall man straightened and Morley saw it was John Peregrine, his companion on many a wild night of roistering in the old days.

"Well, John," Dale said, extending his hand. "It's good to see you, sir."

Peregrine took his hand in a warm clasp but there was no answering smile to replace the worried look he wore.

"Friend Dale," he said, "I've just been telling Captain Claiborne—"

"It's nothing," the Captain broke in impatiently. "There's nothing to worry you in this, Dale."

"But a warning can do no harm, certainly," Peregrine returned, "and it would put him on his guard if there was a danger."

"What is all this?" Dale demanded. "Why do I have to be on guard here in Jamestown?"

Claiborne made a restless gesture. He was hot to be away to the Governor's Mansion and he resented this interruption.

"John has heard some gossip he thinks has to do with you," he said ungraciously. "As for me, I call it nothing."

"But I do, Captain," said Peregrine firmly. He turned to face Dale squarely. "I told the Captain that you have a bitter enemy here in Jamestown, Dale. Thomas Willison, and he has gone quite mad."

"Willison!" Dale barked. "That was the man I saw in the crowd! But—but could that really have been Thomas Willison?"

Peregrine reached out a hand to clutch Dale's shoulder.

"You saw him here tonight?" he asked.

"A minute ago, or less," Dale said. "Leastwise it could have been him, although this man was in rags and staggering with drink, and Willison—"

"—is quite mad, as I said," Peregrine broke in. "His brain deserted him some time ago. You know how he grieved over his daughter's death, Dale, and in the end it drove him mad. He's a changed man, drunk day and night. He's lost all his properties and his seat in the Assembly and on the Council. His friends have tried to help but he would have none of them, insulted them at every turn and attacked more than one of them. I've tried to have him put in chains, poor madman, but the church where he was warden once, maintains he's possessed of devils and that prayer will cure him. So he's allowed to wander abroad where he will."

Dale shook his head, numbed with shock. Thomas Willison had been more than good to him when he had been Willison's indentured servant; he had encouraged Dale's education at Susan's hands;

323

he had given Dale his only daughter in marriage. And now the poor man was mad, his mind lost in his grief for the girl who had died giving birth to Dale's dead child.

"I must find him," Dale said slowly. "Maybe I can help him as he once helped me."

"On your life, avoid him!" Peregrine said sharply. "Lately, he's taken to staggering about Jamestown with two daggs thrust in his belt, telling everybody that he means to kill you on sight. Oh, I know the Captain believes it's only a sot's raving, but I tell you, Friend Dale, it's more than that. Ever since Bristoll's last visit here, and his talk with Willison, the old man has hung around the quay, hoping some vessel would bring you here. When—"

"Bristoll!" Dale interrupted. "What's this about Bristoll?"

"Why, Talbot came to Jamestown two weeks or so ago," Peregrine said. "He met Willison and must have tried to reason with him, for the two of them hung over a table at the tavern for a long time. I wondered then that such a hoity-toity one as Talbot would try to aid a besotted madman, but—"

"And since then Willison has been waiting for me with daggs in his belt?" Dale asked. "Ah, Friend Talbot was not trying to help any madman but himself, John. No doubt he set the poor old man against me with his lies."

"Bristoll?" Peregrine asked, his eyebrows rising. "Could that be possible?"

"It could," Claiborne broke in roughly. "The man's a treacherous dog, John, as I'll explain later. But if what you say is so, perhaps Dale would best be on his guard, after all. Though I don't think a man who's fought the Papists in a war should be scared of an oldster's drunken threats."

"My God, Captain!" John Peregrine snapped angrily. "Do you think I'm a man who faints at every idle rumor? I tell you Thomas Willison is a danger to Dale and to anyone who's dear to him. I—"

He broke off sharply and whirled on Dale.

324

"I thought I saw a lady with you, Dale," he said. "Was it Jenny?"

Dale nodded.

"Yes," he said. "She made the trip to see—"

"*Where is she, man?*"

"Why—why she's with my son and Jack Bagshaw," Dale replied. "Why?"

"Because Willison's been making threats against her, too," Peregrine explained excitedly. "Someone—Bristoll if you say so—has given him the idea that she's to blame in some way for his daughter's death! I've heard it said—"

But Dale had spun about and was running through the crowd, heedless of the people he roughly shoved aside, heading for the stable toward which Genevieve and Little Will and Jack Bagshaw had been going. Behind him, he left a wake of curses but he did not hear them. Oxcarts seemed to move deliberately into his path to bar his headlong charge and he scrambled around them, stooping to run under the dripping muzzles of the great beasts. And still the stables where Genevieve and Little Will must be, seemed as far away as when he had started his wild race.

He was still a hundred yards from his goal when he heard the shot.

It had a thunderous impact and the explosion was followed by a dead silence that covered the square like a heavy coverlet, to be ripped and shredded by the cacophony of screams and yells that followed.

Dale's blood congealed in an icy lump that had been his heart, but he kept on running, sobbing now beneath his whistling breath.

There was a second shot. More clamor.

He burst through a ring of men who stood rigidly staring at something at their feet. He slithered to a stop in the greasy mud and looked down at the two bodies that lay there.

Genevieve was lying with her face half-turned toward him, her arms outstretched as though she were grasping for something she

325

could not reach. Her eyes were open but there was no sight in them. The mouth he had kissed so often was slack, the lips losing their color. In her side there was a spreading stain, black in the dimming light but sure to be bright crimson in reality.

Close to Genevieve lay the sprawled, ragged bundle that had been Thomas Willison. He lay face up and he was not a pleasant sight. His throat gaped widely and Dale Morley thought automatically that another saber stroke would have severed his head from his shoulders. The madman's two *pistoias* were still clutched in his hands. Their work was done.

To one side stood Jack Bagshaw, his eyes wide and staring in horror as he looked down at the two bodies, his reddened cutlass still gripped tightly. The boy, Little Will, clung to the blacksmith's leg, wailing. Bagshaw looked at the boy and tenderly put a roughened hand on Little Will's curls. Then he looked up, still wonderingly, and saw Dale.

"Oh God!" he said. "To have this happen—there was no warning, Mister Morley! Just the shot and Dame Morley falling and—I cut him down with my first stroke but he fired a second time—at Little Will! I saved him! I swear to God, Mister Morley—but the boy's safe!"

Dale's paralysis broke and he leaped to the side of Genevieve's body to drop to his knees. He had to get her face out of the mud. She was dirtying her pretty gown and she was always so neat. She could not lie there for all these gawkers to gape at; it was not right that she should be there.

He turned her over as gently as he could and wiped the dirt from her cheek with the sleeve of his coat.

"Jenny," he said softly, urgently. "Jenny, you must get up. You can't stay here, Jenny. My wife, my treasure. Come, Little Will wants you and—"

There was a hand at his shoulder and Captain Claiborne's voice, as hard as flint, came down at him.

"Let me, Dale," he said. "I've had some practice in these things.

326

Ah, Jesus Christ, why do these things happen? Look after the boy, Dale! He needs you now more than Dame Morley does."

Dale looked up from Genevieve's white face and stared into the dazed, black eyes of his son, who had stopped his wailing now and clung speechlessly to Bagshaw. The boy's face was stiff with fright and when he looked at Dale there was no recognition in his eyes. Dale got to his feet, reached for his son, wincing as the boy shrank away from him. Then he caught Little Will up in his arms and held him close.

"What—what—" the boy stammered.

"It's nothing," Dale found the strength to say. "They were all playing games, you see, and—and—" What could he say next?

"Before God," Bagshaw was mumbling dazedly, "I did not see the madman! First the shot and then—"

"Shut up!" Claiborne said roughly. "There's no one who can blame you for this!"

A woman stepped forward and raised fat arms toward Little Will.

"I was your neighbor once, Mister Morley," she said quietly. "I'll take the lad, sir. He needs a comfortin' no man can give him. Come here, my duck."

Dale vaguely recognized the woman as a friend of Susan's, a neighbor when he and Susan had lived in the Jamestown house— how many years ago? Her name was—Loftstone?

Little Will held out his hands to the woman and Dale relinquished his hold on the child, watching his son bury his head in the woman's comfortable bosom and hearing the boy burst out again into more hiccoughing sobs. Well, that was better for the child, he had the sense to know, than the blankness that had stiffened him before.

He turned back to Genevieve and Captain Claiborne.

"She's still alive," Claiborne said crisply, "and the wound's not too bad. Here, help me carry her into that tavern. They'll have a bed for her there. Peregrine, send for a physician and—"

327

"Already sent for," John Peregrine said. "He should be here soon. Ah God, if I'd been able to warn you sooner, Dale—"

"It will do no good to blame ourselves," Claiborne broke in. "What's needed now is to work to save Dame Morley's life. Here, Dale, lift her, so. Don't flinch, man; she can feel no pain now. But easy, easy. Now, there. Make way, you scum, or I'll—that way, Dale, toward the door that's open for us."

They carried Genevieve Morley through the door of the tavern and across the main eating room, with the innkeeper clearing a way for them through the tables and benches. They bore her up the narrow stairway and down a hall to a room where a wide bed waited. Gently they lowered her onto a fresh white coverlet that never would be white again. Barely had they finished their grim task before a spare man in a black suit, carrying a small leather bag, entered the room.

"Doctor Sackett, sirs," he said in introduction. "At your service. Terrible thing, this—terrible! I'll need a woman to aid me."

"My wife will be happy to help," the tavern keeper said from the doorway. "Dame Morley did her a kindness once, and my wife's done some midwifing and she has a nimble hand."

Captain Claiborne put a hand to Dale's elbow to half-prod, half-pull him out of the room and down the hall. Below, in the main room, Claiborne strode to the street door, slammed it shut against the wall of peering faces, and dropped the heavy night bar into place. That done, he walked to a cupboard where bottles were stored, took down a demijohn of rum, picked up two battered mugs and came back to the table beside which Dale had slumped on a bench.

"Drink this," he ordered and, as Dale shook his head: "Drink this, I say! I don't want to raise false hopes, but Dame Morley still lives and they say the physician is a good one. You'll need something to keep up your own strength, Dale, for you'll need your strength now as you never have before. Where's Little Will?"

Dale sipped the rum and felt it trace a fiery path down his throat, giving back life to his numbed heart and belly.

328

"A—a woman took him," he said in a low voice. "I know her, though I'm not sure of her name. A Dame Loftstone, I think. The boy—he seemed to need a woman's care."

"Good," the Captain said. He splashed more rum into Dale's pewter mug.

"Bagshaw?" Morley asked. "Willison?"

"Bagshaw must be with the boy," Captain Claiborne said, "and Peregrine will attend to what needs to be done about Willison."

The Captain raised his own mug to his lips and then set it down with a jar that splashed some of the rum over the cup's rim.

"I'll never forgive myself for not paying more attention to Peregrine's warning," he said, shaking his head. "I'd heard that Thomas Willison was mad, but I never thought—"

He fell silent again, scowling. Upstairs, footsteps sounded along a hallway and a door closed.

"She'll die," Dale Morley said in dull, flat tones. "Poor Jenny— I've brought her nothing but trouble."

"You've brought her more happiness than she ever knew there was," Claiborne said bluntly. "And you could bring her more, if you would."

He reached across the scarred, worn table and laid a hand on Morley's wrist.

"Listen," he said swiftly. "When she gains her senses again, you must be ready to help her fight her wound, Dale Morley!"

"What can I do?" Morley mumbled. "The physician—there was a hole in her side—I'm no doctor."

"No," said Claiborne harshly, "but you're her husband! She loves you as she loves no other, except maybe her child. And now you must be ready to give her what she's given you all this time— your whole love, as loudly and as truthfully as you can swear it! If she can hear you declare that, and see the truth in our eyes, it'll mean more to her than any doctor's pills or powders. You gave her your name and made her the proudest woman in Christendom— now give her your true love and make her the happiest, so happy

329

that she must survive to fondle every moment of it in her heart."

Dale looked down at his blunt hands cradling the mug. Even now, with all this anguish burdening him, would he be able to tell Jenny that he loved her wholly and make it ring true? If the lie would save her, he would have to—but could he?

He left his bench and began a restless pacing, conscious of Claiborne's eyes on his back. He spoke in disjointed sentences, more to himself than to the other man.

"When I asked her if she'd have me for a husband, she said that she prayed God I'd never regret it, and I made the same prayer for her. And now see what has happened! First Susan and now Jenny. I tell you, Captain, I've been cursed from the day my mother gave me birth. She must have been an evil thing, my mother, who gave me her vileness to pass on to all women who would fall in love with me. She must have been a proper bitch who'd—"

"Stop your damned tongue!"

Dale turned slowly, wonderingly. The Captain was crouched over the table, his eyes afire, his mouth a straight, hard line. For a moment, the two men's eyes were locked; and then Claiborne relaxed, gestured toward the bench Dale had just quitted.

"Sit down, Dale," Claiborne said quietly. "It's time you knew who you really are."

Dale gestured toward the stairway.

"After all these years," he asked, "you'd pick a time to tell me while Jenny's up there, in pain?"

"You'll be called as soon as the physician's through," Claiborne said, "and I won't see you kept in the dark a moment longer—not when you curse your mother for this tragedy. I'll tell my secret now, by God, and you will listen!"

Dale advanced slowly, warily, to the table and seated himself on the bench. Claiborne fumbled inside his coat for a moment and then brought forth a flat package wrapped in oiled silk. He tapped the bound envelope with a forefinger.

"It's all here," he announced, "in black and white and attested to, but we won't need these papers. I can tell it better myself."

330

"Tell me what?" Dale asked.

"Just why I hunted you up, Dale Morley, when I found you'd come to Virginia with Captain O'Halley years ago."

Dale shook his head.

"It's too late for that," he said. "Once, I'd have given my right hand to learn the truth of that secret but now it doesn't mean anything. What does it matter why you took me in hand? Can that help Genevieve upstairs? That's all that matters now, that she lives."

Claiborne leaned forward over the table, his hands gripping his mug.

"No, that's not all that matters," he said. "It's important, too, that *you* be made whole, at last, by knowing what I know. Yes, I'm the criminal, maybe, for not telling you sooner, for fear your pride, if you knew the true story, would make you less the lieutenant that I'd have you be."

"Pride?" Morley asked. "You think I'd have reason to be proud for having sprung from a hellhole like Aunt Bess's place, an unwanted brat?"

He slumped on the bench, reached for the pewter mug that still held a swallow of rum.

"No," he said, "I'd not be proud of my mother though she were a Queen if she'd throw me into that kind of a place."

"But if she was not there to stop it—but listen, Dale Morley."

He looked down at his cup thoughtfully, jiggling the pewter mug between his hands.

"Some years ago," he said, "I was in love with a great lady—a beautiful lady, high-born, genteel, and as good and generous as she was beautiful. Her name was—Caroline. And her father held high position in James's court."

He made a sound that was between a laugh and a snort.

"Ah, I aimed high," he said, "for a tradesman's son, but for a time I believed she returned my love and I think she really did. And then, one day, she told me she loved another, a man so powerful in those days that he could have crushed me like a bug if he had been so minded."

He was silent for a moment, meditative, and then he raised his eyes.

"My love was hopeless from that time on," he said, "although I stood to one side and hoped the chance might come when I could save her from her own misguided passion. And the years passed and at length I came to Virginia to make my fortune here and forget my Caroline."

Another pause and Claiborne's eyes dropped.

"And then," he went on, "I got word that she was dead, and she but little more than a child at the time. So I sorrowed in my silence."

He reached for the demijohn and refilled his cup and Dale's before he continued.

"Now," he said, after a swallow, "time makes a leap to just nine years ago. I was in London, on Cloberry's business, when I happened to meet a gentleman I had known in the old days, when Caroline was alive, and found his fortunes were in bad shape. Gaming and guzzling had stripped him of all his holdings and his good name and he was close to desperation to keep from either being thrown into debtors' prison or joining the army to escape his creditors. His name was—but his name doesn't matter here.

"At one time, this gentleman had been attached to the household of the—of Caroline's father. He was later dismissed. He knew of my feeling toward Caroline; he knew of Caroline's attachment to this other man, my successful rival. And for some money, he told me his secret."

A shadow of pain crossed his face as he raised his cup to drink.

"Caroline," he said deliberately, "had died in childbirth, and her shame had been kept secret. She had died bearing the son of the nobleman who had beaten me in her affections, though he probably never knew I was even alive. And the child—Caroline's son who should have been mine—was taken to a place in London where such children were kept hidden by those who could not find the heart, or courage, to put them to death outright."

"Aunt Bess!" Dale jerked out.

Claiborne nodded slowly.

"Yes," he said. "Aunt Bess. This—this scoundrel who told me these things admitted he had carried the child there himself, at the bidding of Caroline's father to get rid of the baby, no matter how. And so I hurried to Little Loaf Lane to find Caroline's son—and discovered you'd run away to Virginia."

He drew the back of a hand across his forehead to wipe at the perspiration that glistened there.

"It was not so easy to track you as it may sound," he said. "But I found O'Halley and I threatened him until he told me he'd sold your indenture contract to Thomas Willison. And so, finally, I found you and saw in you something of Caroline and a great deal of your father and I've kept you close to me since that day."

He shrugged his shoulders and pushed the pewter mug away from him, as though the rum revolted him suddenly.

"I could not be honest with myself, at first," he said, "as to whether I loved you or hated you. Ah, I loved you for the glimpses of Caroline I could see at times, but I hated you, too, because you'd come from another's loins, not mine. And because, maybe, you really were more high-born than me, with a great and gracious lady for a mother and a proud and powerful nobleman for a father. Yes, I guess I hated you for that, at first."

Dale's hands gripped the edge of the table until the knuckles whitened.

"Who was my father?" he rasped.

William Claiborne's eyes were somber as they stared across the board at Dale.

"Your father," he said directly, "bore the name of Villiers— George Villiers. He may never have known he sired you, but your father was the Duke of Buckingham, curse the memory of his name for what he did to my Caroline!"

Dale propped his head in trembling hands, trying to assemble his whirling thoughts. All his life he had been tortured by the

333

question of who his parents had been; he had envisioned his mother as an alley trull, at times, and his father as a two-groat customer; on other occasions he had indulged in dreams of discovering that both his parents had been gentlefolk and he the victim of weird circumstances that had brought him to Aunt Bess's hovel.

And now—his mother had not cast him off! Even his father, a Duke, might not have known that he ever existed, else he might have accepted him!

He pondered on himself as a son of the Duke of Buckingham, that reckless, dashing coxcomb who had made himself one of the most powerful men in all England in his day, and had met his death under an assassin's dagger. He knew nothing about his mother, this Caroline, beyond Claiborne's word that she had been a great lady, but he knew of Buckingham, certainly. "Bucks" might be hated or he might be loved, but certainly he could never be ignored so long as he lived. He might have, and probably did, take Dale's mother as a tender flower ripe for the plucking and never thought a second time about the possible consequences of his dalliance, but still a Duke's blood flowed in his, Dale's veins.

And, he asked himself, what of that? What did it matter, now that he knew himself as the product of a high-born coupling? He was more Dale Morley than a Duke's child! What he was he'd made himself, with Claiborne's help, and had not been born to.

No, what mattered was that it had not been his mother's fault that he had been thrown to Aunt Bess! If she lived, she would have loved him—that he knew.

"The King himself," Claiborne was saying, "saw your resemblance to your father that day at Windsor Castle, if you'll recall, and it bothered him. And when you acted as you did in the matter of your wound, I came near telling you that you had Buckingham's quick wit."

He moved his cup an inch or so on the table.

"I meant," he said slowly, "to use the secret of your birth as a

334

lever to force His Majesty's favor to our side. Charles was always fond of Bucks and I thought that knowing you were Bucks' son would bring him over to our side. But you yourself made that unnecessary and when I tried to get another audience with the King and present my proof of who you were, it was too late. Besides, it would have been hard for me to bare Caroline's misfortune—though I believe I would have done it."

Dale raised himself from his bench again and squared his shoulders.

"So that's the story, eh?" he asked. "I thank you for telling me, Captain. Being Buckingham's bastard means nothing to me, but it's good to know my mother didn't give me to Aunt Bess. As for my father—you'll always seem more of a father to me than any Duke, Captain Claiborne."

Again he saw that open look of love on Claiborne's face but the sound of footsteps on the stairs jerked Dale's head about to see Doctor Sackett descending, bag in hand.

Dale came back to the present with a shock of the realization that Genevieve was lying on the stained bed upstairs, her straight, narrow-flanked side holed by a dagg's leaden slug. He half-ran across the room to meet the doctor at the bottom step.

"Is she—" he began, and could go no further.

"She's still alive," Dr. Sackett said. His lined face was sobered by something more than his professional dignity. "Aye, she's alive but—well—all our efforts are always in the hands of God."

"You mean she'll die?" Dale asked huskily.

The doctor put a hand to Dale's shoulder. His eyes were slate blue.

"I will be truthful, sir," he said. "I've had little experience with bullet wounds. The ball is lodged in the lady's side, and deeply, and to try to take it out would mean to take her life, I believe. She's bled so much I don't dare to cup her any more. And there's another thing."

He lowered his voice a trifle.

335

"You knew, no doubt, that she was carrying a child?" he asked. Dale nodded.

"Three months," he said hoarsely.

"The shock of this brought on a misbirth," Sackett said. "There's that to add to the lady's wound."

"She'll die, then?" Dale asked gravely.

"God has performed miracles before this," the physician replied. "Maybe He'll perform another in this tavern."

"Is she in pain?" Dale asked through dry lips.

"No," Sackett said, with a shake of his gray-locked head. "She feels nothing now. If she regains her senses she'll feel her hurt, surely, but her feeling it may mean she'll live. So remember that, should she make an outcry."

He dropped his hand from Dale's shoulder and started for the door.

"The goodwife of the innkeeper is with her now," he said. "There's nothing you can do for her, but I suppose you want to be with her."

Genevieve lay on her side, her face toward the door. The landlord's wife sat in a corner, a dim figure. The light from the candle on the chest at the foot of the bed showed that Genevieve's eyelids were closed and deeply shadowed, her face suddenly gaunt, her mouth still slack with the teeth glimmering dully between colorless lips. He could hear her breathing, faintly hoarse.

So there she lay, a few breaths away from death, as he kneeled at the side of the bed.

"Dear Jenny," he said in a whisper, "you must hear me! I've dealt poorly with you, holding back my complete love from you, but you come back to me now and I'll make it up to you. I love you, Jenny, with all of me—though I did not know it till now."

He bent to touch his lips to her hand, her hot, fevered hand.

"You were always so determined that I'd not see your hurt at my love's lack," he said, "that I never understood. But I know I love you entirely now and all the other was nothing but a wild dream. There's no Anne, Jenny—there's nobody but you!"

336

The landlord's wife stirred in her chair and yawned.

"She cannot hear you, sir," she ventured.

"She must hear me," Dale said fiercely. "She must hear what I have to say!"

All that night Genevieve Morley lay a hand's span from death and did not answer to Dale's fervent whisperings in anything but an occasional moan or grumbling mutter. William Claiborne stayed at the tavern until a late hour when he was peremptorily called to the Governor's Mansion by West. And still later, Genevieve's father came to the inn.

"I've taken the boy," he said. "That Bagshaw man is fair wondrous with his care of the child. But can't Jenny be moved to my place? This will all cost a fat purse, I'll warrant, with that thief of a landlord doubtless charging—"

"Get out," said Morley tonelessly. Frederick Loman left and did not come back, fearful that some of the costs of all this might fall on him if he stayed within asking distance.

Throughout the long night Dale stayed at the bedside, holding Genevieve's limp hand. From time to time he put a kerchief, dampened with water, to his wife's lips but she did not seem to relish it, or even know what had been done. Toward morning she grew fitful, moaning at close intervals, murmuring indistinguishable words under her breath, tossing her slender body on the bed and crying at the pain she brought upon herself with her movements. At such times, Dale would press her shoulders back gently to the soiled sheets, trying to keep her still.

"Quiet, Jenny," he would say huskily. "Don't toss so, my dearest, or you'll make your hurt worse. Lie still, my sweet, and the doctor will mend you in the morning. Ah, I know there's pain, but it'll pass in the morning."

But after the eastern sky had paled and the sun had raised itself over the horizon, Genevieve's pain grew worse, her cries sharper, the hurried babble of her slurred words more urgent, her tossing

337

more violent. Sweat stood out on Dale's clammy forehead as he struggled to keep her still, his heart groaned in his anguish at her suffering and his teeth were set, his lips drawn back, against the cry of protest he would send up that she must bear this agony.

"Just till the doctor comes, Jenny," he promised. "Once he's here, he'll ease your pain. He must!"

But when Dr. Sackett arrived, he could do nothing, though Dale entreated him to relieve her torment.

"She must bear the pain," the physician told him, "to stay alive. It's the pain that keeps the blood moving through the veins, sir. I do not agree with those who use opiates to dull the senses."

"Christ's thorns," Dale raged, "if they will ease my wife, I don't care what you agree with! Give these potions to her, I say!"

Sackett's long face grew frosty as he shook his head.

"I have no such potions," he told Dale. "My opinion is that God created pain to keep the human husk alive lest, lacking it, the life's spark wink out."

"To hell with your opinions!" Morley barked. "Get me another doctor, then, who'll be merciful."

Again Sackett shook his head, and this time there was a hint of a smirk on his thin lips.

"There is no other physician in Jamestown, Mister Morley," he said. "Till now I've never had my ability questioned, may I add. To be blunt, there's not another doctor in the colonies who could do more than I have done, not with that wound and with the complication of the misbirth."

"She will not die!" Dale said hoarsely. "She cannot!"

"She's in God's hands," Sackett said piously, "and you had better reconcile yourself to that, sir."

He turned and stalked out of the small, close room, leaving Dale beside the bed, his head in his hands, his body a cold shell around a void. He was still in that position, with Genevieve moaning faintly on the bed, when William Claiborne entered.

"Friend Dale," the Captain said soberly, "I must leave you. The

338

Gryphon sails within the hour on the tide and West has ordered me to be aboard her or resign my post as Secretary of the Province. I told him what had happened, but he would not—"

"She suffers so," Dale broke in dully. "She cries out constantly."

Claiborne's hand touched his shoulder.

"She will not remember the pain when she awakens," he said consolingly. "And Dr. Sackett will—"

"To hell with Sackett," Dale ripped out. "He's a charlatan who won't give her anything to lessen the pain."

"I met him on the street," Clairborne said. "He told me you were angry and bade me calm you, Dale. Jenny can't take a potion now, even if he would give one, he said, and it is true that he's the only doctor in Jamestown. You would do better to accept his services, Dale."

Morley's head hung low between his shoulders and he nodded wearily.

"I know you're right," he said dully, "but I would to God there was an abler man to attend my wife."

There was a silence during which Genevieve uttered a muffled groan and stirred restlessly. Dale's hand went up to touch her shoulder lightly.

"You'll forgive me for abandoning you like this, Dale?" Claiborne asked after a pause.

"Yes," Dale said. His sleeplessness and his heartache made him only half aware of what the Captain was saying. "Yes, I'll forgive you."

William Claiborne held out a hand. His grip was firm, his eyes sorrowful.

"I'll pray," he said simply. "Even my poor prayers may help."

Dale struggled with his fogged brain to say a word that would be fitting.

"Godspeed," he managed finally. "We'll await you at Kent Island."

He watched the Captain's straight form walk through the hallway and disappear down the stairs. Then he turned back to the bed and his vigil.

And a moment later, less than a minute after Claiborne had left, Genevieve's eyes opened and she stared directly up at him. As he watched, he saw bewilderment becloud his wife's eyes and then they came into focus and fastened on him. Genevieve's mouth twisted with the effort as she whispered:

"My husband."

"Genevieve," he said. A sob tried to escape and he swallowed it back, forced a smile to his lips. "You're feeling better, praise be to God!"

"What—what—"

"You've been hurt, Jenny," he said, "but it will all be well, after a time. You'll see, my Jenny. In a little while you'll—"

His words were cut off by the eerie scream that hissed between her teeth as the pain stabbed deep into her side. Her face was contorted by her agony and her back arched as she was torn by the paroxysm. He grasped her hands and felt the nails bite deeply into his flesh, and he wished more than he ever had wished for anything before that he could take all her pain unto himself, let her somehow transmit her suffering through her hands to his body.

"Ah, Jenny—Jenny—"

The seizure passed and she fell back, her face white, her eyes strained by the fear of the pain's return.

"I cannot bear it," she whimpered. "Oh, my husband, let me die now! It will come back and—oh Christ!"

She clung to his hands, grunting hoarsely now as the pain hammered at her with savage blows, her lids squeezed shut and tears trickling from under her lashes, her teeth caught over her lower lip until blood showed on the chin.

She fell back again, panting. He leaned over her and his voice was low and hurried, rushing to be heard before the pain came again.

"Jenny, my treasure," he said, "I love you. I know you thought I loved another more than you, but I did not, I never did—not truly!
340

I love you, Jenny, and you must live for me and Little Will. You must! You are my whole life, Jenny, and without you I cannot live. Jenny, Jenny, I've loved you always but never as you should be loved till now!"

For a moment her eyes were clear, unshadowed, free of torment. For that one second, she was released from pain, cognizant of what he had said and realizing its meaning. For the space of half a dozen breaths, Genevieve Morley was supremely happy, for this was what she had wanted to hear and had despaired of ever hearing, these were words she had never demanded but words that had forced themselves through all her husband's doubts and uncertainties to make themselves doubly blessed.

"Dale," she whispered. "Oh, my dear Dale."

Then came another spasm and her screams, despite all she tried to do to smother them, and he held her, weeping openly now, until the knifing convulsion was past. And as she fell back, eased by unconsciousness at last, there was a sound at the doorway.

He swung his tormented eyes in that direction, half expecting Sackett's return. He blinked and then he blinked again, raised a hand to his face and rubbed at his forehead to dispel this impossible vision that harried him.

The man who was standing in the doorway advanced into the room.

"Mister Morley," he said. "They told us that your wife had been—hurt. We came here to see if we could help."

"Wing," said Dale hoarsely. "It *is* you, then."

"Yes," Andrew Wing nodded. "We came to Jamestown yesterday on the *Blue Heron* to buy medicines. I met my colleague, Dr. Sackett, on the street just now and he mentioned you and your wife's condition. I—I'm here with Sackett's consent, though I'd have come without it."

He moved a step aside and then Dale saw that Anne Furness— Anne Wing—was standing beside him. His breath exploded from his lungs in an involuntary grunt.

"You!" he exclaimed.

"Yes," said the girl evenly. "I've had experience in nursing, working with my husband's patients, and Doctor Sackett said there wasn't an able nurse to be found in Jamestown. So I came here, too, hoping I might help."

Dale brushed his hand over his eyes.

"But why?" he burst out. "You—you must hate all Kent Island people and me the most of all. After what I did—"

"Why, sir," Andrew Wing broke in smoothly, "it was you who provided the means by which we met, we two, you must remember." He smiled quietly in the gloom of the noisome room. "And then you gave me blankets that day, after your victory over the *Corpus Christi*. And Anne has told me how you risked your neck to set things right one day at Saint Mary's, and quiet the gossip. What could we do but try to help?"

He moved to the bedside and looked down at Genevieve, raised an eyelid, reached down to feel her heart. When he looked up at the dazed Morley again, his voice was brisk.

"We'll need some things, Mister Morley," he said. "Clean bed-clothing, before anything else, and some air in this place. That window, Anne—thank you. She must be bathed and made as comfortable as she can be before we try for the ball."

"The ball!" Dale ejaculated. "You mean—"

Wing swung his eyes toward Dale and nodded.

"Sackett told me he'd not tried for that," he said. We must, sir, I fear."

"But—but Sackett said it would kill her," Dale croaked.

Anne Wing moved to her husband's side and her eyes were proud as she looked at the man who had tried to tumble her once and who had loved her for years, though she had never known that.

"You must have faith in Andrew, Mister Morley," she said in a high, clear voice, "because he deserves it. He's found new ways to operate and he'll go in, and successfully, too, where dodderers like Sackett would hesitate till it's too late."

342

"Hush, Anne," Wing murmured. "My colleague—"

"It's the truth," she said stoutly. "If you love your wife, Mister Morley, and would see her live, have faith in my husband."

"And in Anne," Wing added with quiet emphasis, "for she's half this combination and more."

Dale bowed his head as tears rushed to his eyes. The man he had once scorned, the girl he had once tried to rape—they were from Maryland and he was still pledged to fight Calvert and all his people to defend Kent Island—Andrew Wing and his wife Anne were here where they had no need to be, offering to use their skill to save Genevieve from the agonizing death that clutched at her.

"Yes," he choked. "Yes, I'll trust you—and thank God for sending you here. And now—now, I'm weary. I—"

He staggered back until the chair he had just quitted caught him behind the knees. He slumped down onto the solid bit of furniture and his head lolled in utter exhaustion. Sleep, born of confidence in these people who had relieved his vigil, swept over him in an overpowering wave.

He was dimly conscious, much later, of having been led from the sickroom to another place and lowered to a bed. Still later, somebody handed him a bowl of stew and he ate hungrily, albeit without tasting the food, and slumped back again. The next time he awoke, he knew where he was and hurled himself off the bed and through the doorway of the room and down the hall to where Genevieve lay.

Andrew Wing was crouched over Genevieve's white body, which was now lying on clean sheets, and the doctor's hands were flying nimbly as Anne stood at his side, handling her husband first a knife and then a length of silk thread and then a barbed thing of shining steel and then another surgical tool. She glanced at Dale briefly before she turned back, while Wing did not even do that.

Dale clung to the doorway, hearing the doctor's low-voiced instructions, Genevieve's hoarse breathing, the grate of a saw against bone, the insucked breath of Andrew Wing as he dug and dug again into the side of the wounded woman he was trying to save.

"In God's name," Dale muttered, "do not make her suffer."

Neither Wing nor Anne paid any attention and then Wing straightened, with something gory and dripping held in a pincers instrument.

"There's the thing," he said, "at last. I thought for a time—now if we can stop the leaking—"

The extracted pistol ball dropped into a crimson-stained bucket with a clack and doctor and nurse were back to work. Dale's head reeled as he watched. There was a sudden spurt of some foul yellowish stuff that bathed Anne's hand to the wrist and Morley saw that the girl never flinched at her gruesome bath. Nor did either of them hesitate in their quick movements until, after what seemed to Dale like an age, Wing forced himself erect again and pressed his hands to the small of his back with a groan.

"It's done," he said, his voice inexpressibly weary, "and I think, with God's help, we've won."

Anne nodded. There was a smile on her face as she turned to Dale, although the smile was as weary as Wing's voice.

"You see, Mister Morley," she said, "your trust was well-placed in my husband."

She spoke the word "husband" as Genevieve did, with deep affection. Would Jenny ever say the word again?

"And now," Wing went on, "it is a matter of rest and keeping the wound drained. We got the ball out in time, praise God. Another hour, perhaps, and there'd be festering there. The other—you knew about the misbirth, Mister Morley?"

He nodded speechlessly.

"Well, it's a pity, of course, but the—the organs were not damaged. There is no reason why she should not have more children."

He stretched to relieve cramped muscles and then smiled at Dale.

344

"Rest assured she'll live, with care, Mister Morley," he said. "One or the other of us will be with her all the time until she's able to be alone, so you might get some rest yourself."

"I—I must be here when she wakens," Dale faltered. "There's much that I have to tell her."

Wing nodded, moving to a basin to wash his hands.

"We'll call you the moment she opens her eyes," he promised. "Now take some rest, man, before we have another patient to deal with."

But before he could leave the room, Dale had to move to the bed and look down at Genevieve. Was it imagination or did her color seem better? Certainly her features were more relaxed than they had been. He reached down to touch her forehead timidly.

"She will recover," Anne Wing said in a low voice as she stood beside him. "I know she will."

"She must," Dale said gravely. "I have so much to tell her."

Yes, Anne, I must tell her that I love only her and tell her that so often and with such sincerity in my eyes that she cannot help but believe it. I must make my love sound so genuine that she will never doubt again that I am wholly hers. So, as I stand beside you now, so close to your loveliness, I'll tell you without speaking that you are the only woman I ever could completely love. I'll tell you that, without a word, this last once, and then turn to my new task of finding complete happiness for Genevieve.

His unspoken message finished, Dale Morley turned and walked out of the room.

Andrew Wing called him just a few minutes after dawn had cast its first light into the little tavern room next to Genevieve's where Dale was sleeping.

"She's—" Dale asked, lurching from his sleep.

"Awake," Wing smiled, "and feeling much better, though still in some pain, as could be expected. Her first words asked for you, Mister Morley."

He entered her room on tip-toe and felt a tremor shake him

345

when he saw that her lovely eyes were fully open and fixed on the doorway through which he stepped. Her lips were still pale, her face still gaunt, but her eyes were alive and her voice came to him, low and husky though it might be.

"My husband—"

He kneeled beside her bed and held a hand to his lips, unable to speak, unable to say one of the things he had tried to force through the deafnesss of her coma, that he had spoken during her brief spell of lucidity before Wing's arrival. He put his face against her hair and was not ashamed, though he knew his eyes were streaming.

"There, there," she murmured, as though she were comforting Little Will. "It will be all right."

"Ah, Jenny," he said at last, the words breaking loose from the strangling grip of relief that had clutched his throat. "Ah, Jenny, I love you so! I've never told you rightly and I must. You must get well quickly, my Jenny, so I can make it up to you. I've been a hound in this, my Jenny, but I'll be better, I'll give you my pledge."

Her hand crept up to touch his wet cheek.

"Hush," she whispered. "No woman had a better man than my husband. I'll not have you denying that."

Her eyes moved about the room, came to rest on Andrew Wing, standing at the foot of the bed.

"What happened to me?" she asked. "And how did I come here?"

"I'll tell you the whole thing, once you're stronger," Dale promised. "But why you're alive and getting better I'll tell you now. It is because this—this saint of a doctor, Andrew Wing, and his good wife saved your life, when all I could do was hold your hands and watch you die."

Wing made a deprecatory gesture but Dale got to his feet and walked to the foot of the bed to grasp the physician's arm and lead him to Genevieve's side.

"Look well at him, Jenny," he said earnestly, "for you owe

everything to him and Dame Wing. They came here, unbidden, because they'd heard you had been hurt and they worked, both of them, to keep you from dying and they won."

"Wing?" Genevieve asked with a faint frown. "Wasn't there a Doctor Wing at Saint Mary's?"

"The same man," Dale said, "and it was God's will that he and his wife were here in Jamestown when they were. The other doctor, Sackett, could do nothing save—"

"It was not an uncommon operation, though tiresome," Wing broke in modestly. "Sackett is a good doctor, make no mistake about that."

There were footsteps in the hallway outside and Anne Wing entered, come to relieve her husband of his bedside watch over Genevieve. She smiled at the woman on the bed as she undid her bonnet ties and Dale thought there never was anyone lovelier.

But as an angel, a madonna, more than a woman—yes, he would think of her as that from now on. He might never understand the fever he had had for Anne Furness but now he must look at her and find her beautiful and never want her as a woman. Genevieve was his woman, brought back to him by this girl who was more than that, but who must henceforth be set apart, even in his innermost thoughts, from any touch of earthly passion.

Anne moved to the side of the bed and put her arm through her husband's.

"I'm happy to see you so much better, Dame Morley," she said. "Your husband was quite frantic with fear for a while, and rightly so."

Genevieve's eyes dwelt on Anne's and the two women gazed at each other.

"You have my feeble thanks, Dame Wing," Genevieve said after a long pause.

"Dame Wing," the younger woman laughed. "I feel so ancient when I'm called that! You'd make me grateful if you called me Anne; please do."

347

Genevieve's eyes were deep as she managed a pale smile. Dale knew his wife recognized this girl now as the one about whom Dale had spoken that night he had returned to Kent Island from his victory over the *Corpus Christi;* he knew Genevieve realized that this was the Maryland woman he had said he loved.

Her eyes sought his and he was able to give her an unflinching look of pure love in return. And Genevieve Morley read in his gaze what he had meant to have her see and her smile widened as she turned back to Anne.

"Yes," she said with a faint laugh. "Yes, I'll call you that, and gladly, for I would be friends with you, Anne—for all time."

CHAPTER TEN, 1637-1638

THE WINGS, DOCTOR AND NURSE, SAILED BACK TO
Saint Mary's three days after Genevieve was pronounced out of
danger, aboard one of the Maryland supply ships that plied more or
less freely between the two colonies in those days. And Genevieve,
after she regained sufficient strength, was taken to the Loman
Plantation near Henrico.

Once at the plantation, it was a comparatively easy thing for
Genevieve to persuade her husband to delay his return to Kent
Island. She needed him, he knew, to keep his proclaimed love
before her and help her recover from the shock of her frightful experience. Little Will needed him, too; he had gone through too
much on that Jamestown street and it had left him nervous and uncertain, needing the reassurance and sense of security he derived
from his father's presence.

So Morley stayed on at the plantation as the days lengthened into
weeks and months. He fretted, at the start, to get back to the Island
and face Bristoll with a bared sword and the charge that he had
engineered Willison's mad attack on Genevieve, but gradually his
burning lust for revenge faded in the pleasant life on the plantation
—made more pleasant by the fact that he had little contact with his
father-in-law and none at all with the bedridden Dame Loman—
and it was not long before he found himself enjoying idleness such
as he never had lolled about in before.

He dispatched a note to Nicholas Martiau at Kent Island, in-
forming the aged Captain that he intended staying at Loman Plantation until Genevieve was fully recovered, unless his presence at the
Island was imperative. He got no reply from Martiau and while the
Captain's silence worried him for a time, he persuaded himself to

believe that it could only mean that affairs at the Island did not need his immediate return.

William Claiborne's letters from London counseled Dale's staying at the plantation for the time being and these notes influenced Dale to remain at his father-in-law's place, almost as much as did Genevieve's importuning. The Captain wrote confidently of the forthcoming successful outcome of his parleys with Cloberry and Dale was reassured, even though he could not help sensing that any definite conclusion, one way or the other, in the Captain's affairs would be delayed long past the time Claiborne had first set.

The days slipped past unheeded; the summer passed into fall while Dale Morley's sloth increased insidiously. He grew fat from rich eating and little exercise; he lay abed late, and midnight found him on his feet more often than between the sheets; he lived the full life of the Virginia Cavalier and found it good, and Genevieve approved of all this change in her husband.

She was a woman and now she was having all of Dale as she had never had before. No more was her husband up at dawn in answer to his captain's summons, no more did he spend the day apart from her to return home fairly staggering with weariness. She knew each morning that Dale would be with her in the evening and not miles away on some hastily ordered voyage that might lead him into battle and death. Now there was time for all the dalliance they had missed earlier in their married life. Now Dale had the opportunity to be the lover and he was as ardent in his demands on her as her condition permitted, while she responded with a new flush of passion that sprang from her surety that Anne Furness, or Anne Wing, was no longer a rival for her husband's love.

She saw signs of returning restlessness in Dale with misgiving, and had resigned herself to a return to Kent Island that September, when death struck twice in quick succession and left Dale Morley master of sprawling Loman Plantation.

Dame Loman succumbed in mid-September to the painful disease that had long afflicted her. She passed from the scene as she had occupied it, a background shadow, a vague creature only half-remembered by even her daughter. Frederick Loman's passing was more dramatic but equally unmourned. Apoplexy speared him without warning one day, when he had scarcely finished grumbling about the expenses of his wife's burial, and sent him toppling out of his saddle as he was watching his slaves work.

Thus Dale perforce had to delay his departure for Kent Island again while he took over the reins of management. He was astounded by the extent of Frederick Loman's wealth and the number of his acres, the discovery that he was the husband of an extremely rich woman. The days of carefree carousing grew fewer as Dale bent himself to the task of settling Loman's affairs before returning to Kent Island.

Nicholas Martiau, however, reached Loman Plantation before Dale was ready to sail for the Island. It was a chill, windy day when Genevieve looked up from her sewing and out of a drawing room window to see the old soldier turn into the driveway from the main road, his big frame hunched in his saddle against the gusts that swept in off the James.

She got to her feet, calling for a servant to attend Martiau, and was at the doorway when the aged captain stumped up onto the porch and bent over her hand, his face gray with fatigue.

"It's good to find you well, Dame Morley," Martiau rumbled. "I'd heard that you'd recovered, but—"

"Come inside, Captain," Genevieve said quickly, as she saw Martiau sway. "Warm yourself by the fire while I have something hot to drink fetched from the kitchen."

"That'd be welcome," the grizzled captain nodded. He followed Genevieve inside and huddled close to the fire as she gave directions to a Negro girl. "I thought the journey would never end. I am too old for this, but I had to come to find Dale. Where is he?"

"Away hunting, with Little Will and Jack Bagshaw," she said. "He should be back soon, and he'll be happy to see you, I know. But why this grueling journey instead of a letter, Captain? Not that we're not happy to have you here, of course."

Martiau's bushy-browed eyes turned to her and he frowned.

"A letter, madam?" he asked. "I'm here to find out why Dale's answered none of the letters I sent."

"He got no letters from you, Captain Martiau. In fact, he told me that he wrote to you and you'd not answered him. He wondered at that till he took it that you felt no need to write."

Martiau scowled more deeply and shook his massive head.

"No letters, eh? Ah, that can be Evelin's doing," he growled. "The man has bribed all those that wouldn't be cowed, I swear. I've sent Dale at least a dozen letters and I'll warrant every one of them ended in Evelin's fireplace or between Bristoll's fingers. And I got no word from your husband, either."

He took the toddy that Genevieve passed him from the tray brought by the slave and sipped it. He exhaled gustily and wiped his mustaches.

"Ah, that's better," he said. "I was chilled to the marrow and at times I'd have turned back to Jamestown and a fire, but I had to see Dale. About the letters—I should've known your husband would not desert Kent Island. But God's truth, madam, it's become so bad that no man can trust another these days and I was tempted to doubt even Dale Morley's stand."

"You need him at the Island?" Genevieve asked in a small voice.

No more snuggling play, then, in the mornings before they reluctantly dragged themselves from their bed. No more afternoons with the blinds drawn against the sun to make a warm and intimate cave of their chamber. No more exciting nights when the wine heated the blood in their veins and everything, all the world, was bound up in their welded bodies.

"Need him?" Martiau was saying. A pause and then, heavily: "No place ever needed a man like Kent Island needs Dale Morley now."

"I'll be honest," Genevieve said, "and tell you I'd hoped we could spend the winter here. I'll be more honest and confess I wished he'd never have to go back, Captain Martiau."

The bushy-bearded captain looked down at his steaming mug and nodded slowly.

"I can understand that," he said. "No wife would have her husband leave this place, with all its peace and quiet, to return to what waits at Kent Island. But Dale Morley would blame himself for the

352

rest of his life if he did not go back when he was needed—you know that, too, don't ye?"

Genevieve plucked at a fold of her gown.

"I know that, too," she said in a low voice.

The front door boomed shut and there was Little Will's high laughter in the hallway, the thud of Dale's boots. He came through the doorway into the room with his son astride his shoulders, both the man and the boy flushed with the wind and delight in the day's sport just completed.

"We have a great hunter here, Madam," Dale cried, when he was just over the threshold. "He'll shame his father one day with—"

He broke off short as he caught sight of Martiau beside the fireplace.

"Now, God's truth," he shouted, "here's Captain Martiau come to visit us at last, Will!"

He slipped the boy from his shoulders and strode across the room, his hand outstretched.

"It's good to see you, Nicholas! No, don't leave your chair, sir. And you can stay awhile and enjoy our easy life here, eh? Will you—"

He stopped and his broad smile died as he looked down at Martiau's grim face.

"Oh," he said, after a pause. "Then you're not here on any pleasure trip, Captain?"

"No," said Martiau soberly. "No pleasure trip certainly."

Then his heavy face brightened as Little Will ran to him to hurl himself on his beloved Captain Martiau. The old soldier's mug of toddy slopped over in the collision and Genevieve cried a warning as she rose to recapture her exuberant son and draw him toward the doorway.

"Later, you shall talk with the captain," she promised, "but now you'll have your meal and rest awhile. Captain Martiau, Dale, you'll excuse me for a moment?"

Martiau climbed to his feet and bowed, despite his aches, and Dale cast Genevieve an absent nod as the woman herded Little Will into the hallway, protesting. As the child's babble died away toward the rear of the great house, Dale turned back to Martiau, pinching at his lower lip.

"So there's trouble," he said quietly. "But I thought—I wrote—"

"Oh, yes, Dale. Dame Morley said you wrote and I told her I'd sent you a dozen letters, all asking you to come back, but none of them reached you, no more than yours reached me. Evelin and Bristoll saw to that."

Dale walked across the room to take a place on a settee close to Martiau.

"It's bad then, Nicholas?" he asked.

"It's worse than bad," Martiau replied somberly. "Evelin has stripped the Island as a rake would strip a woman. Already he's removed most of our goods—even the fruit trees—to the estate he's set up across the Bay in Papist territory; a place he calls Evelinton. He's shipped the better part of our herds there and God knows how many of our slaves. He's not spent a groat on keeping up the fort and Smith tells me all his ships are in need of repairs that Evelin won't give him the men to make. The servants are all grumbling over their mistreatment and underfeeding—those of them that haven't run away. The Indians deal only with Calvert now, since Evelin will pay them next to nothing for their goods. And that's not all."

He sipped at his drink and Dale, his face dark, moved to the silver pitcher on the table near the window, poured himself a mugful of toddy, returned to the settee.

"No, that's not all," Martiau repeated. "Each day, almost, Evelin urges the people left on the Island to accept Calvert's rule as a certain way to better their lot. And I have it on good word that he or Bristoll is at Saint Mary's constantly, urging the Papists to attack our Island, take it over. They're demons, Dale, and I can't hope to cope with them, in my condition. I'm barred from the fort now—I've not been able to get in there for over a month and I've been almost a prisoner in my own home. By God, I had to slip away from the Island like a thief in the night, with Yago handling a skiff, to bring you this word!"

Dale's lips made a thin, pale line. His eyes sought the crackling

354

fire and were riveted there.

"Bristoll's the complete traitor, then?" he asked. "I thought—though I should know him better—that he might find Evelin too much for even him to stomach."

Martiau made a motion with one gnarled hand.

"He's worse than Evelin, if that is possible," he grunted. "It's as though the man's really mad, Dale, the way he inflicts his evils on the Island. He takes great delight in whipping the slaves, though the poor blacks deserve no lash. And he taunts me constantly till I'm tempted to go for my blade, though I well know it's what he wants."

Dale's mouth curled into a snarl that bared his teeth.

"Maybe," he said, "I'll exercise his blade for him. I owe him a little debt I want to repay. I sail for Kent Island tomorrow. I've been away too long."

Outside the doorway, Genevieve Morley bowed her head, perhaps in prayer, more likely a gesture of acceptance of the inevitable. But when she entered the room, her chin was up and her eyes showed none of the fear that was in her heart.

Dale's first glimpse of Kent Island from the skiff that brought him and Martiau and Bagshaw from the James River up a cold and choppy Chesapeake made his heart lurch sickeningly. Even from some distance out, the miserable estate into which the place had fallen was all too evident.

The buildings along the shore looked as though they had weathered a dozen hard winters since he had seen them last. They sagged and were sway-backed and one of the wharf warehouses had collapsed at one end to show the gaunt skeleton ribs of its framework. The vessels lying at anchor in the harbor were grimy, with tangled rigging, and there was no sign of life on any of them. They seemed to have been abandoned, as did the fort from which no lookout hailed the skiff's approach. The flagpole from which the Virginia standard should be fluttering was bare, and there was no smoke curling from the braziers on the ramparts at which the soldiers on guard were accustomed to warm their chilled hands and shanks in other days.

Dale expertly brought the little sailboat up to the landing—the same landing onto which he had leaped from the deck of the *Hunter* that day he had come back from the Potomac with the *Corpus Christi* as a prize; the same place where he had carried his bride, Genevieve, ashore from the pennant-flapping *Bittern;* the landing he had run across that day he had brought William Claiborne his plan for capturing the Dutch Fort Nassau—and had found George Evelin in the Captain's office. Now the landing was weak with rotted planks, and one piling, eaten away by worms, had given way so that a part of the dock lay under water.

Yago, who had returned to Kent Island after dropping Martiau at Jamestown, met them at the landing, shivering under rags that in other times he would not have used to wipe down Bella. He had been warned of their coming by some mysterious signal that only the blacks could hear or understand. He kneeled instinctively as Dale came close to him and almost sobbed as he spoke.

"T'ank Gawd you here, Master Morley, sahr," he said. "I been hidin' from de lash and de sword since you been gone. T'ank Gawd good times comes ag'in to Kent Island, like befo'."

"Get up, Yago," Dale commanded quietly. "You need never kneel to me."

Yago told him the most recent news in a spurt of words. George Evelin and Talbot Bristoll were both away, as they frequently were these days, and there was nobody in actual command of the Island, since Thomas Smith was in chains in the island's jail, the only new building Evelin had built.

"In chains!" Dale exclaimed. "In God's name, why?"

The story, as told by Yago, was almost unbelievable. The fleet, as Dale had seen, had been permitted to fall into disrepair until the only fit vessel was the *James and Anne* and she was used exclusively to carry Evelin's loot from Kent Island to Evelinton. Still, when a Maryland sloop had boldly cruised up to the very mouth of the Kent Island channel, Captain Smith had gone to meet her in the tiny, leaking *Gamecock* and had attacked the interloper so savagely that the Calvert sloop had been forced to run. For that, Yago said, Evelin had thrown Smith into chains and had sent an apology to Maryland for the incident.

"Where is this jail?" Dale demanded grimly. "We'll free Smith before we do anything else."

Yago led the way and Dale used his dagg to blow open the lock that held the stoutly planked door. They found Smith more dead than alive from hunger and thirst and they half-led him, half-carried him to Martiau's house, babbling curses against Evelin and Bristoll. At Martiau's place, Smith was put to bed by Yago, and Nicholas Martiau himself was not long in following. Dale Morley found the old warrior shaking with chattering chills and insisted he rest to ward off the fever that his long, hard journey to Jamestown might bring on.

Martiau protested but Dale was firm.

"We want you at your best when the time comes, Nicholas," he said. "There'll be no place for a sick man when we defend the Island against the Papists, and Evelin and Bristoll."

With Martiau finally convinced his place was in bed, Dale and Bagshaw set out on a tour of the Island, leaving Yago to attend the two sick men. As he walked past the empty, dilapidated warehouses, Dale wondered silently how buildings could so deteriorate in less than a year. It seemed as though with the departure of William Claiborne, the whole Island itself had lost heart, like a woman who has lost her self-respect, allowed herself to grow slovenly and slatternly, without pride in her appearance or shame in her decline.

The few soldiers, workmen and blacks they passed seemed infected with the same virus that had sickened the landing stage and the warehouses. They all appeared spiritless, slumped in a sort of lethargic dejection, and the greetings they gave Dale, when they spoke at all, were not those that a lieutenant of Captain Claiborne should have expected after a long absence. Once Dale stopped a soldier who, blue-nosed with cold and bundled in a frayed greatcoat, shambled past him without a word or a salute.

"Who's in command of the fort?" Morley asked in a clipped voice.

The soldier wiped his sleeve across his dripping nose and spoke in a whining voice.

"In command, ye ask?" he demanded in turn. "Now there's a question I could never answer. We've had no commander, or pay, or even food for these many days. A pox on this place, I say, and on the liar that said I'd do well to sign for service on Kent Island."

Dale's hand shot out and knocked down the soldier's hand from its owner's nose.

"Don't finger your face while you talk to me!" he blared. "And stand up straight and try to look a soldier! Did they never tell you to salute an officer?"

The ragged soldier went pop-eyed with surprise.

"Officer, are you?" he asked. "Y'r pardon, sir, but it's dark—I did not rightly see you. They sent me out to gather wood, the others did, and I can't find a stick that some other dog hasn't scavenged ahead of me. They'll treat me cruel, sir, if I don't find some wood and—"

"Stop your clacking!" Dale cut in. "Who's 'they' and where can I find them?"

"They're at the fort in the barracks, sir," the drip-nosed soldier said. "Them that hasn't deserted. Two boatloads of them took off this afternoon, stealin' longboats to row down the Bay to a likelier place than this. And can ye blame them? Today, all we've had to eat—"

Dale turned and strode away, sickened by this tale of calamity recited in a whining voice. Behind him, he could hear Bagshaw muttering.

"'Twas a man called Clifford, sir," the bow-legged farrier said, "and one who never was of much account, as I remember him. But if it's true the soldiers are deserting . . ."

The barracks were as dilapidated as the warehouses and as dreary. When Dale kicked open the door of one place that showed a light, he found a miserable group huddled about a tiny fire. All the men were gaunt, all were unkempt, all stared at him with sullen eyes. These men could well have been remnants of a beaten, broken army, before a single shot had been fired.

"Get to your feet!" Morley rasped. "It may surprise you, but you have a commander now! And clean up this place! Who's the ranking man among you?"

There was a hesitant silence and then one of the shabby creatures about the fire laboriously got to his feet and essayed a salute.

"My name is Grimes, Mister Morley," he said. "I guess I'm in charge here, if anybody is."

"Then look the part," Morley grated. "By God, Captain Claiborne would have a sword flat to all of your backs, if he were here, for letting the place go to ruin like this!"

The man called Grimes stepped up to Dale and his flat face took on a belligerent scowl.

"Captain Claiborne, is it?" he asked. "And where's our Captain now? Taking his ease in London, that's where, and he's left us in our trouble. And you, Mister Morley, ye may have me lashed for sayin' it, but you deserted us, too, when we had need of you. If ye'd stayed and countered Evelin and Bristoll, ye might have found this fort in better condition."

Dale stepped back, his hand moving to his sword hilt, and then the truth of what this man said stayed his hand. While he'd waxed fat at Loman Plantation, these miserable men had been left without a friend to fight Evelin and Bristoll for them. While he'd dallied with Genevieve, he'd left Claiborne's interests in the hands of a sick old man who might try to do what was expected of him but who was beaten from the start.

His voice was low as he spoke into the shadowed gloom of the untidy barracks room.

"I'm man enough to admit you speak the truth," he said. "I have failed you but now I'm here to make up for it, if you'll follow me against Evelin and Bristoll and Calvert."

The face of the soldier confronting him slacked off its tight look of anger as he replied.

"We'll follow you, Mister Morley," he said, "but I think you've come back to Kent Island too late. Most of your men are gone, your weapons are gone, your fort is almost gone. We'll fight Evelin and Bristol and Calvert if you tell us how and what with."

"I'll find the means," Dale said. "I'll get word to Governor West at Jamestown and he'll send us supplies. West is no Harvey. Grimes, we'll have this place a hornet's nest for Papist blunderers again before long, I'll swear."

The soldier shook his head doubtfully.

"God grant you're right, sir," he said, "but is there time before they strike? We've nothing here but pikes to use against cannon, knives to use against muskets and daggs. Evelin—may God damn him—has transported all else to his place across the Chesapeake."

Dale put out a hand to touch Grimes's shoulder briefly.

"There'll be time," he said. "There has to be."

But later that night, after Dale had visited the plantation owners, those of them that had not left the Island, the farmers who had had their last year's crops boldly confiscated by Evelin, the servants and slaves who still bore the scars of Bristoll's lash, the sailors who had been ordered off their decks and put to menial tasks, he wondered if there was enough time left in all Creation to mend the harm that George Evelin and Talbot Bristoll had done Kent Island while he was away.

"Sail ho! Three sails! Four! Five sails to the sou'west and they fly the Calvert black and gold!"

Dale Morley, in the guard room of the fort, leaped from his bed and pulled on his boots, buckled on his belt, grabbed up his cutlass. They were coming and there was nothing to hinder them now. His appeal to Virginia for arms and supplies had gone out only the day before; there was no hope that Kent Island could stave off the attack of one shipload of Marylanders, much less five, with what they had.

He mounted to the wind-swept parapet, his cloak flapping about him, and saw the enemy ships as soon as he reached the top of the ladder. There was the *Saint Helen and Saint Margaret* leading the fleet and behind her a new schooner of equal size. Strung out behind the two schooners were two pinnaces, one of which was the renamed *Long Tail,* and bringing up the rear was a wherry, the old *Cockatrice,* refitted and also renamed. His spyglass showed him the glint of

360

brass cannon on all the vessels and the heads of a small army of men showed above the rails.

He looked about him and his despair mounted. The entire stretch of the parapet showed only one culverin and his previous examination of that piece had shown him that the barrel was so rusted that even if there was powder and shot available, to fire it would mean risking a burst gun. He had fourteen soldiers with him, and of this number three carried muskets of dubious fitness and the others had only cutlasses and pikes. Dale himself carried a dagg and a sword. His bullet pouch carried three balls; the powder flash contained enough for two charges.

The Island's powder magazine had been found to be entirely empty. The armory had yielded only the weapons the men on the parapet carried now. The pistol he wore belonged to Captain Martiau, the sword was his own gryphon-headed blade.

The thing was hopeless from the outset and yet the fight had to be made. Calvert and Lord Baltimore would take Kent Island, after all these years of waiting, but they must not be allowed to walk ashore and do their devil's work without a shred of resistance.

"Call up the other men," he told Bagshaw without turning, knowing the little man would be at his elbow.

"I called them," Bagshaw spat contemptuously. "They ran."

Dale jerked the spyglass from his eye and whirled on the red-haired man.

"Ran?" he asked. "You mean a Kent Islander ran?"

"They all ran," Jack said. "They said they'd not fight with clubs and rocks and be killed. They're hiding in the marsh, all except one. I cut him down with my cutlass, the coward! That was Clifford, sir."

"Coward or no," burst out a soldier who had overheard Bagshaw's message, "it's better to run than be murdered without a chance! Good God, sir, there must be a thousand of 'em and all well-armed, while we have nothing! Do you expect us to battle them with our fists?"

"Aye," yelled another. "I'm for surrender! We have no chance!"

Dale Morley's lips tightened as he freed his sword.

361

"Surrender, did you say?" he asked. "Let one man call surrender and I'll cut him in two with this blade or brain him with the butt of my dagg—I'd not waste a ball on him!"

There was a clang and Dale turned to see one of the three men who carried muskets fling down his piece.

"This is no mutiny!" he yelled. "It's not mutiny to go against a madman's orders! And it would be madness to try to fight an army without a single cannon! Let's get out o' here while we're able!"

Dale slashed at the man with his sword but the mutineer was out of reach. He made a leap for the soldier and there was a stunning blow across his shoulders. He went forward on hands and knees, still gripping his sword, and slumped under a volley of blows, rained upon him from all sides.

Above him, he heard Bagshaw roaring curses. Then there was the crash of a musket shot and the thud of a falling body, close to him. He rolled over, reached for the gun in his belt and fired from the ground at the nearest man standing over him. There was a yelp, a curse, and a pike came slicing through the air at him. He flung up an arm in time to fend off the pike, hearing it hit the stone paving of the parapet beside his head. He tried to get to his feet, lay into these dogs, and then something—the flat of a cutlass, a musket butt —smashed into the side of his head and he went down again. Dimly he heard the clatter of feet rushing away toward the ladder, and the jabber of the men as they fled. There was the creak and grate of the ladder, carrying the men to the courtyard and safety, and then all was quiet.

He lay there for what seemed a long time before his senses came back enough to tell him he must get on his feet. His head was swimming as he clambered erect and looked about him. Close by, Bagshaw was sitting with both hands pressed to his side, staring stupidly down at his fingers through which there leaked a crimson rivulet. Dale staggered over to the little man and kneeled beside him.

"They hurt you, Jack?" he asked. "The whoresons shot you?"

The farrier nodded ponderously.

"The cowards," he said distinctly. "Let 'em come back and I'll show 'em what it means to shoot Jack Bagshaw."

He fell backward before Dale could reach out a hand to support him, and his head hit the stone flooring with a thud. But Jack Bagshaw never felt the pain of that fall. He never felt another pain in all the world.

Dale looked down at the little man, his belly chilled. The hand that still pressed the bloody shirt had been the hand that had handed over Bella's bridle that day on the wharf at Jamestown. That hand had been the one that held little Will's tiny hand as Genevieve and his son and the smith had walked away from him, toward Thomas Willison's guns. Calloused, stained, it had pointed at the harbor of Saint Mary's when the *Hunter* ran aground. Now it was stiffening into a claw-like thing, but there had been a time when it had been a hand to depend upon, a hand of friendship never doubted, a hand that a curious fate had made dip into a bag of forbidden gold so that Jack Bagshaw might come to Kent Island and find a new life there and, now, die there.

There was the boom of a cannon beyond the parapet. Dale Morley stood erect again, swaying against the pain in his head, and stumbled across the flagging. The single shot apparently had been a signal, for now the Marylanders were leaving their ships and coming toward the shore in their longboats, each loaded to the gunwales with men who bristled with muskets. They had to be met, though there might be only one man to do the meeting. He swayed toward the ladder, pausing only long enough to pick up his fallen sword.

He nearly fell twice while descending the ladder, but he made the courtyard. He staggered toward the gate of the stockade, wrenched it open enough to let him through, and stumbled over the sand, his sword in hand, toward the beach.

"Wait, Morley!" cried a voice. "Wait for us!"

He turned to see Thomas Smith, his stubby legs twinkling in his run, coming after him, a blade of some sort gleaming in the morning sun. And behind Smith was Yago with a pike he had picked up somewhere.

"Yago got me out of that damned bed," the undersized captain panted when he came abreast of Dale. "He knew I'd want one last chance at these devils."

"Never had dis t'ing in my han's befo'," Yago complained, "but mebbe I cut a couple of dem befo' dey gits me."

Dale should have felt gratitude at what these men, the black man and the white, were doing, but he was past all feeling now, save the one despairing thought that Kent Island was doomed and nearly everything worthwhile was doomed with it. He pointed his blade at the prow of the first Maryland boat, grating on the beach, and cried:

"There they are! At them!"

The three men of Kent Island, the only three who would or could defend the place against four hundred men of Calvert, stumbled forward through the deep sand to the attack.

The struggle was ludicrously short-lived. Yago went down first, when he thrust his pike awkwardly, and had it jerked from his grasp. He was instantly buried under a pile of Saint Mary's men and held, struggling, on the sand like a schoolboy bested in a wrestling match.

Thomas Smith was the second one to be overpowered. He danced in and out, his cutlass flailing, for a matter of perhaps twenty seconds before a Maryland soldier, clubbing his musket, knocked the blade ten feet away and his companions rushed in.

Dale Morley found himself separated from the other two men as he instinctively sought a higher place on the beach on which to make his stand. Two Marylanders came at him, but halted at a voice that spoke behind them.

"The man is mine," said the voice. "I'll stab the first one who touches him."

The two Calvert soldiers dropped their weapons and moved aside as another man, a slender figure in black cuirass and gleaming helmet, advanced on Dale.

"Ah, Mister Morley," said Talbot Bristoll with a grin. "It seems I'm to have the pleasure of killing you after all."

Dale's astonishment overcame his rage for a moment.

"Bristoll!" he gasped. "You mean you fight with Maryland?"

The flat-nosed man made a mocking bow.

364

"I have the honor to command this expedition under Lord Baltimore's flag," he said. "I find it a better cloth than Claiborne's rag, with juicier rewards."

"I knew you for a villain," Dale ground out, "but not so complete a one as this, even you!"

"Enjoy your cursing," Bristoll drawled. "Ye'll be dead soon enough. Or perhaps you want to surrender, beg my mercy?"

"Hah!" Dale snorted. "Defend yourself!"

He thrust at Bristoll and felt his stroke parried easily. He managed to beat back Talbot's return, but just in time. Then the red mist of hate that had clouded his eyes was swept away like a fog cleared by a sudden gust of wind and he could see his enemy in every detail, from the top of that shining helmet to the toes of those immaculate boots, his opaque eyes, his broken nose, his lizard's mouth, the throat he had to reach above that cuirass to kill this man he had always hated.

This, then, would be his recompense for the loss of Kent Island and his life; he'd send this treacherous dog to Hell before the others leapt on him and killed him. There was a surge of triumph through his body, as though all the odds were now with him, instead of against him. His veins were filled with something more than the lust for battle; they bore a fiery tide which carried the hot conviction that regardless of his fate once it was done, he was going to kill Talbot Bristoll.

There was no William Claiborne to gainsay him now; there was no hindrance now to fulfillment of his old savage urge. Now Bristoll would pay for everything, from the first sneer he had dealt Dale that evening at Claiborne's supper party, to Bristoll's whispered words in mad Thomas Willison's ear, words that had nearly cost Genevieve her life. That broken-nosed devil would find no chair on this beach to fling at his legs and try to trip him. Now he would pay for all the taunts he'd dealt Martiau, the lashes he had given Yago, the treachery with which he'd answered Claiborne's trust—yes, even the forgotten kisses he'd shared with Genevieve, before he had hated her enough as Dale's wife to plot her murder.

His arm was iron, his legs were steel, his wrist was granite. He

365

pressed in, boldly but not recklessly, and grinned as he saw the other man give ground.

Bristoll's mouth writhed now in a bloodless grimace, his eyes were opalescent as they always were when the man scented blood. He moved lightly, despite the sand, and he was still the master of *tierce* and *sixte, quarte* and *prime*. His thrusts were always dangerous, his parries smoothly turned. But still he moved back before Dale's assault.

Now Bristoll's blade flashed forward and there was a gasp from the Marylanders who ringed the duelists as blood flowed from a wound on Morley's sword arm. Dale felt the sting but laughed at it. It would require a deeper thrust than that to hurt him and this day Bristoll did not have that thrust in his blade.

The men who watched the battle made up a silent audience that looked at the deadly play with a curious calm. The men of Maryland neither called encouragement to Bristoll nor reviled Morley, as they might have been expected to do. The crowd might have been a group watching an exhibition between two experts with the foils, with the loss of some petty prize in pounds and pence the forfeit due the winner instead of the other man's life, yet each man who watched that struggle on the beach knew that it would never end while one of the swordsmen still lived.

Bristoll, finding himself on the downgrade of a slope that was the high tide mark, tried to circle to Dale's right, then to his left, but Dale met each move with a renewed flurry that kept Bristoll on his original course of retreat. Talbot bore in with a sudden, savage attack, trying to break down Dale's guard through sheer power; but Dale repulsed that assault and kept boring in.

Bristoll had no chair to throw at Dale, but he had sand. Stooping with incredible swiftness, the flat-nosed traitor grabbed up a handful of the grainy stuff and flung it full in Dale's face, followed it with a lunge. For a second Dale was blinded, but his instinct saved him. He went to one knee and bent his head, heard Bristoll's sword screep over the top of his helmet. Blindly Dale swept his blade in a try for a hamstringing cut and he heard the grate of Bristoll's boots as his enemy leaped back to escape the scything blow. Dale lurched

366

to his feet, wiped a hand across his eyes and recovered his vision in time to parry Talbot's incoming lunge.

The Marylanders surrounding them growled in a low, ominous rumble.

Now Bristoll's boots were crunching on shells and pebbles that told him he must be nearing the water's edge. A new look came to his viper's eyes, a look that was strange for Bristoll in combat. He took another backward step to evade Dale's thrust and heard his left foot splash the water.

Bristoll's mouth twisted and he threw himself at Dale. Morley's sword slashed once, twice across Bristoll's face and the blood welled out of two cuts that striped the other man's cheeks, just below the rim of the helmet. Talbot Bristoll's eyes switched for a split second toward the ring of onlookers, then turned back to Dale.

"To me!" Bristoll gasped, in his crow's voice. "To me, for Calvert!"

Not a Maryland man moved. It was as though Bristoll had not called and Dale's heart leaped again. These Papists, then, had no more love for a traitor than did any other honest man. Calvert might have given Bristoll command over the force sent out to take Kent Island but that had not given the flat-nosed villain the regard of his troops. The Marylanders might—they probably would—kill him once he had disposed of Bristoll, but they'd not interfere in this duel that Bristoll had claimed for himself. He pressed in.

Bristoll was ankle deep in water, then the Chesapeake was halfway to his knees and hampering his footwork. He retreated another step, slipped on a rock and staggered for an instant before he managed to make a desperate parry of Dale's *septime* and flounder backward again.

"God's name!" he croaked. "Ye'd not fight me here! Leave off and we'll continue on dry ground!"

"You'd do the same for me?" Dale jeered. "I thought you—*hah* —preferred the going wet. That dewy grass at Cambridge—*huh*— or was it Oxford? Or maybe you can find a fish to throw at me, now that it's too deep to reach for sand."

367

He hacked at Bristoll, disregarding the finer points of swordplay now, using his blade as a cutlass as his rage welled up again at the memory of Genevieve lying, racked with agony, on the blood-stained bed in the Jamestown tavern. And Bristoll, his face pale and his mouth slack, wailed aloud.

"Oh, Jesus!" he cried. "Ye'd not kill me thus, Friend Dale! The years together—the things we did—"

He still held his sword on guard but it was a feeble thing now as Dale pressed home his final thrusts. The shoulder, and Bristoll screamed and turned to flounder out of reach. The back, and Bristoll turned again and cut futilely at his tormentor. The shoulder again and then—and then the throat!

Bristoll dropped his sword, reached up to clutch his gullet with both hands. He gave a wheezing sob and then he crumpled, falling forward with a great splash.

Dale Morley stood there, his eyes fixed on the spot where the Chesapeake's icy waters were stained by a carmine streak. It rose curling from the bottom in a twisting ribbon that spread to a crimson splotch on the surface and it kept rising long past the time Dale would have thought a man had blood left in his body. The bubbles that rose with the red, wavering ribbon stopped long before the blood ceased rising.

Behind him, Dale heard a sigh expelled by many men. He knew he should turn to meet the other Marylanders but he was suddenly too weary to raise his wounded sword arm another time. He heard the splash of feet, a hand gripping his arm. . .

He awoke grudgingly, knowing that full consciousness would intensify the pain in his head that had been nagging at him for a long time through the darkness that had enveloped him. He opened his eyes, grunted at the swift stab of agony that spiked his brain, and closed them again. There would be time enough for looking about later. Better to rest now, with closed eyes, and try to think.

368

There had been periods when he had nearly come awake, but not quite. Once, it had seemed that he was on a ship; there had been the smell of tar and the sound of creaking timbers, but he could not be certain that all that had not been part of a dream. Then, quite clearly, he remembered a jolting—Christ, that had made the pain nag brutally—as though he were being carried somewhere on a litter. And now—where was he now, and what had happened?

He risked lifting his lids again and this time the pain was not quite so bad. The third time he opened his eyes there was only a splitting headache to be borne and he could stand that, after what had gone before. He moved his eyes, not his head, from side to side.

He was in a wide, sunlit room, lying on a poster bed. The place was pine-paneled and within the restricted range of Dale's vision there was a small table, a bench, and, on the other side of the bed, a plain chair. It could have been a room in any house in Jamestown or Kent Island—or Saint Mary's.

He braved the ache the movement cost him to turn his head toward the wall from which the sunlight streamed. There were no bars at the window, he found, so this could not be Saint Mary's. He moved his head again in the opposite direction and found the door. Lounging in the doorway was a man he had never seen before and he was resting his arms on a musket. So he was under guard. So this *was* Saint Mary's and they were waiting for his head to heal enough to lead him out and crack his neck as a pirate.

He must have made a sound unconsciously, because the soldier in the doorway turned and peered at him. He met the man's eyes as squarely as he could, despite his throbbing head.

"So ye're awake, after all, eh?" the guard asked. "I'll summon the doctor for ye."

He was gone and Dale lay there, experimenting with the lifting of a hand. He was striving to get it higher when the doorway held Andrew Wing and the guard.

"You can go," Wing said in a voice of authority. "I'll call you if I need you."

369

The soldier left, looking back at Dale and grinning over some great jest of his own. The doctor went to the chair, sat down, and reached for Dale's wrist.

"We meet again, Mister Morley," he said conversationally, "though in bad times, I'm afraid. You've had a bad knock—a good many of them, I'd say. But there's no bones broken in your head that I can find. A week or two in bed should make you fit again."

"So I may hang?" Dale asked. His voice was stronger now.

Doctor Wing shook his head as his fingers went to the bandages that covered Dale's skull.

"I'm no hangman," he said. "I try to cure people, not to kill them. You should know that, Mister Morley."

"Oh, yes," Dale said in a subdued voice. "I know if it was left to you, I'd fare all right but—but we may be friends and still I'm an enemy of Calvert."

"I'd offer you no false hopes," Wing said quietly, busy with the bandages, "but I'd say that if they planned to hang you they wouldn't have waited this long. An unconscious man hangs as easily as a conscious one, I'd say."

Dale gasped with pain as Wing's fingers touched the tenderest spot of all on his head.

"That hurts, eh?" the doctor asked. "It should. You must have a skull of iron, Mister Morley, else your head would have been burst like a pumpkin at the blows you must have taken,"

Morley was silent as the doctor rewrapped the bandages. Then:

"I'm at Saint Mary's, I take it?"

"Yes," said Wing. "They brought you back aboard the *Saint Helen and Saint Margaret,* as limp as a sack of meal."

"The others, too?"

"Hmm. There was a Negro called Yago brought back with you, undamaged but for a trifling wound on one arm. He's in the jail."

"And Captain Martiau? And Captain Smith?"

"About Martiau, I've heard they found him on the road between his home and your fort, trying to join you. They returned him to his house and to his bed, unharmed."

370

"And Smith?" Dale persisted. Doctor Wing's eyes held his for a moment and then slid away.

"I was not there, remember," he said uneasily. "I do not recall any word of a Captain Smith. Now you must rest, Mister Morley. I'll have food sent to you such as you should eat—gruel, milk and such. That arm does not bother you much, does it?"

"I can hardly feel it," Dale said. "And—I thank you. It seems I must be in your debt to the very last."

"Rest," Wing said quietly, "and don't give up hope."

When he was gone, Dale tried to stay awake, to wonder why the Marylanders who must hate him were treating him with this outward kindness, bandaging his wounds, sending their doctor to care for him when they could have left him to die on the beach at Kent Island or, as Wing had pointed out, strung him up while he was still unconscious. There must be some plot in all this—but what? Could it be that . . . he was asleep.

He awoke once to be fed porridge and some milk by the grinning soldier who was his guard, and was amazed to find himself hungry. The brief meal finished, he fell back on his pillow and slept again. He was awakened the next time by a hand at his shoulder shaking him.

Standing beside the bed was a man he recognized as the soldier he had met that time he had run aground at Saint Mary's, Captain Thomas Cornwallis. Beside Cornwallis was the richly-dressed, bristle-mustached Sir Leonard Calvert, brother of Lord Baltimore.

Dale glared at the Maryland Governor and at the Captain who had employed a traitor to take Kent Island. If they had come to taunt him, they'd find a Cavalier of William Claiborne's troop would not be baited.

"Can you talk?" asked Leonard Calvert abruptly, "or is your pain too great?"

"Yes," he said, forcing his voice to match Calvert's in strength. "I can talk, if I will."

Leonard Calvert dabbed at his mustache with a knuckle.

"You can listen then, Mister Morley," he said. "When they brought you here, I ordered you hanged as a pirate. I'd have you know that."

Dale said nothing, waiting.

"But you have your supporters in my colony, Mister Morley—even admirers," Calvert's cold voice went on, "though I have little admiration for your kind myself, sir. Captain Cornwallis has pleaded your case before me, insisting that you but did your duty as a soldier and should not be hanged for that. I took the trouble to question some men who were aboard the *Corpus Christi* when you captured her, and it is their story that our vessel fired on your ship first, against my orders. So, in a lenient way of thinking, I suppose that outrage cannot be termed an act of piracy."

He frowned as though to show Dale he still was of another opinion in the matter.

"Moreover," he continued, "a gentleman and his lady to whom this colony and I owe much, Doctor Wing and his dame, have seen fit to ask for mercy in your case. Doctor Wing says you sent blankets to our wounded men taken from the *Corpus Christi* and that you mistreated none of our men. Dame Wing says she is a friend of your wife, Mister Morley, and begs my indulgence because of that."

"I owe Doctor and Dame Wing as much as you do, Sir Leonard," Dale said, his voice remarkably strong. "They saved my wife's life when nobody else could, and did it although they had no reason to love me. But as for their begging your indulgence—I'd rather they had not if it puts men in the light of pleading for your mercy. I believe I fought an honorable war and broke no laws I know of in the winning or the losing—unless my killing your creature, Talbot Bristoll, after he'd howled for another chance to live and betray others, can be called breaking some law. I do not call it that."

Calvert's hand was busy with his mustaches as he looked down at Dale, scowling. At length he said:

"I hold no brief for Mister Bristoll. He—he offered an advantage I could not refuse, no matter how much I may have wanted to. What

I'm here for is to offer you the chance to give your parole. If you won't, you'll be cast into jail. If you do, your wife and son will be brought here and you'll all return to Kent Island, in time, to rebuild the place under my direction."

"And be a traitor, sir, like Bristoll?" Dale asked furiously.

"You call it that?" Calvert asked in a steely voice. "Look, the Island is fully in our hands. The place is destitute, as you must know, because your man, Evelin, made it so. My plans, Maryland's plans, are to make the Island what it was—a beautiful spot."

He leaned over the bed, his voice tense.

"And I know you're depending on your Will Claiborne to return, Mister Morley," he continued. "You think you'd serve him falsely if you agreed to this parole. I have a letter here for you to read—or I'll read it to you, if you're not up to it. It's from my brother and it reached here on the day I sent that force to Kent Island—with orders to Mister Bristoll that the letter be read, the people be told the true state of affairs, before any attack was launched. Mister Bristoll flouted my orders and—but I'll not speak ill of him, even now."

He extracted a folded sheet of paper from one pocket of his rich velvet coat, straightened it.

"It says," he read, "that on this day, for valuable considerations, William Cloberry and Company is agreed that Kent Island shall be joined under the flag of Mary's Land, her people to be governed by the government of Mary's Land, situated at Saint Mary's, her commerce to be directed by Mary's Land, her plantations sustained and improved, and all rights hitherto claimed by William Cloberry to be vested in the government of Mary's Land."

He paused and added impressively:

"This letter is signed by William Claiborne, among others."

Dale Morley closed his eyes. Captain Claiborne had given up the long fight finally, and now Kent Island belonged to Maryland. She was a stricken Kent Island now, but Calvert had said he would make her alive and lush and beautiful again, haggard and decaying and

373

desolate though she was now. The fight was over and Claiborne had lost—surrendered—and if he'd carry on this war he'd be alone and helpless behind prison bars.

What sense was there to that? And even if he could wage war, he was sick of fighting now. Above all else, he wanted Genevieve and Little Will and the fine days they had had together and could have more of, on Kent Island.

"I accept, sir," he said without opening his eyes. "I give you my parole."

Sir Leonard said nothing. When Dale opened his eyes again, the Maryland Governor was leaving the room with a jingle of spurs. Captain Cornwallis paused long enough to drop a hand to Dale's shoulder.

"You'll not regret this, Mister Morley," he said. "I know your feelings now, but content yourself that you acted bravely, though you lost, and need feel no shame."

He was halfway to the door when Dale called after him.

"What of Thomas Smith, Captain?" he asked. "Did he come through the fight unharmed?"

Cornwallis hesitated before he replied.

"Aye," he said in a grave voice. "He came through the fight but —but he was hanged by Sir Leonard's order, I regret to tell you—as a pirate."

Dale Morley stood on a hill overlooking the Chesapeake, his eyes turned toward the northeast where lay Kent Island. In another day or so, he would be going back; Doctor Wing finally had pronounced him fit to travel and work. Now that the hour of his return was so close at hand, he found himself as impatient as a young husband mounting the stairs to his bride's chamber. There was so much to be done, so many things to undo that Evelin had done, and the work would be as blessed under one banner as under another.

Virginia had all but formally ceded possession of the Island to Maryland. Captain Claiborne was staying on in England. The time would come when he would denounce the letter Calvert had shown Dale as a forgery, but now he was keeping an inscrutable silence, without one brief note to Dale.

As for George Evelin, all his double-dealing had gone for nothing; he had been turned down frigidly when he had applied for the position of Commissioner of Kent Island. Instead of rewarding him, Calvert had ordered him to satisfy the mountainous debts he had piled up, settle his accounts within a month or be shipped back to England to face the people he had defrauded. There was no chance that Evelin could pay—his future was black enough to cause another man to send a bullet through his head. And all this made Dale Morley laugh aloud, long and humorlessly.

So now, to all intents and purposes, he was a Marylander, a member of the band he had always despised. True, he was technically a paroled prisoner, but once back on Kent Island he would always stay there and his sons would grow up there and in a few years who would know whether or not he had always been a man of Maryland?

He turned at the light whisper of footsteps on the dried grass and she was standing beside him, wearing a wine-colored gown with a white yoke, a gray cape over her shoulders, the easy wind lifting the tendrils of her brown hair from her head and gently letting them fall again. Her smile, as she looked up at him, was as warm as the wind that had come up out of some tropical place to make this February day belong to May.

She had come to Saint Mary's the day after he had given his parole to Calvert and their meeting had been a silent one, with tight-clutching arms saying more than words or tears. And she had nursed him tirelessly, over-careful of him to the point where once he had exploded in a loud voice, bidding her stop treating him as if he were Little Will. She had smiled, recognizing her husband as he had been before his defeat at Kent Island.

"You're eager to be back there?" she asked him now.

"It will be good," he said. He reached down for her hand and felt the warm pressure of her clasp. "There will be much work to do. Perhaps it would be more pleasant for you at the plantation."

"Away from you?" she asked quietly.

"No," he said. "Not that, ever again."

They both were silent, looking out over the dancing waters, and he spoke at the horizon, rather than down at her.

"I wonder," he asked, "what Captain Claiborne is feeling now—and why he's not written me a single word?"

"He has his pride, Dale," she said quietly, "that he holds above all else, even you. He felt, I think, that he failed you, as you feel you failed Kent Island."

There was another silence and then Dale said:

"He was a great man, Jenny, and maybe he will be again in time. His fortunes have always ebbed and flowed like a Chesapeake tide. This once, when he needed to be stronger than he had ever needed to be before, he fizzled like a damp charge of powder; next time he may thunder again with all his strength."

"God grant there'll be no next time, if it means more war," Genevieve said. "It's time you men saw Kent Island, the whole Chesapeake, for what it really is—a place meant for peace and happiness instead of wars and fighting to put one flag or another over it. In time the Island and the Bay—maybe all the places in the world—will be what they were intended to be, places to live in, with everybody at peace."

Dale Morley smiled down at her.

"With men like William Claiborne and Leonard Calvert and me alive?" he asked. "I would not doubt you, Jenny, but it seems a long way off."

"It is," she nodded, "but it will come. Meanwhile, we'll find our own peace, our own contentment, there on the Island, and that's waiting for us now, my husband—waiting for us now."